Tetelestai

ROBERT ALLAN YOUNG

ISBN 978-0-9685114-3-5
Revised 2025

Tetelestai

You held me up, you let me lean, but more than anything, you've opened the eyes of my tortured soul so when it all becomes too dark to see, I can still believe and I can still feel.

Chapter 1

Why is it that the essence of evil can linger, unhindered and free, in a space where its physical existence had never been present? Like the thick, suffocating stench of damp cigar smoke that refuses to fade, darkness hung in the stale air throughout the well-appointed office of James Rosin, the ten-year president of North Texas Industrial Bank. It was a heaviness that pressed against the walls, soaking into the expensive decor. Even the faint, bluish glow emanating from the LCD computer monitor situated in the center of the massive African mahogany desk was not enough to cut through the pitch black. But it was enough to highlight Rosin's cold, distorted face—or at least, what was left of it. The shadows played tricks on the ruin of his features, dancing macabrely in the low light. There was neither movement nor sound inside the executive's office—just a still, cold, deadly silence that wasn't going to depart anytime soon. It was the kind of silence that rings in the ears, heavy with the finality of violence.

Outside the sixty-eight-story office tower, the thick Texas humidity and searing heat were almost unbearable, despite the late hour. It wrapped around the city like a wet wool blanket, stifling breath and dampening skin. It felt like one was forced to breathe in warm water rather than air. Eighteen stories below Rosin's office, on a dark, deserted, downtown Dallas street, an aging homeless man—almost twenty years younger than his haggard appearance suggested—thrust his dirty arm deep inside an overfilled trash can. Black flies, disturbed from their feast, scattered in the air, buzzing angrily as his cracked, weathered fingers frantically searched through the nauseous remains of the day. He pushed past slime-covered wrappers and discarded cups, his desperation masking the rot. His find was to be his last meal before retiring to the cardboard bed he had meticulously laid out down the adjacent alley. His mind, so preoccupied with the gnawing ache in his empty stomach, was completely unaware of the blinding bright light that had flashed just moments before, high above his head inside the bank president's office.

In an instant, the atmosphere around the derelict changed. The oppressive heat vanished, replaced instantly by a vacuum of temperature. His body shook violently as a bitter, unnatural cold wave rushed from somewhere behind him, cutting through his ragged clothes to the bone. It wasn't just a breeze; it was a physical force. Without a thought, and without removing his arm from the filthy trashcan, his head frantically whipped from side to side, his eyes wide with primal fear, trying to find the origin of the chill. It lasted only for a brief, terrifying moment. The deathly cold disappeared as quickly as it had arrived, the humid heat crashing back down on him, and he returned to the undertaking of finding his last morsel before retiring for the night, shaking off the sensation as a ghost of the streets.

Eighteen stories above, inside James Rosin's office, evil still hung in the air, heavier now than before. The rancid smell of discharged gunpowder, sharp and metallic, mixed with the copper scent of blood and bodily excrement, burning through the darkness. The only light evident was still the eerie glow from the monitor in the center of the large desk. The screen emitted just enough light to act as a spotlight, emphasizing the right side of the bank president's distorted face, freezing his final expression in a pale wash of blue. The left side of his head was all but gone. His bloody remains were splayed along the bookcase behind his thick leather chair, painting a horrific abstract mural on the dark wood. His leather-bound, first-edition collection of the classics, once neatly displayed along the shelves as trophies of culture, was now covered in pieces of brain matter—the remnants of what was once a financial genius's intellectual mind. They clung in little bits to the gold-leafed spines of the journals, ruining centuries of literature in a split second. An empty Glock handgun hung a few inches above the plush carpet, suspended in the dead man's grip, Rosin's lifeless index finger still curled rigidly around the trigger.

Suddenly, without assistance or command, the glow disappeared. The monitor went black, and the entire system powered down with a dying hum. The darkness became even more intense, swallowing the room whole, and the evil remained, waiting patiently inside the room for its next command.

Chapter 2

She hated cats. They always did what they pleased, moving with an arrogance that suggested they owned the world, and never had to answer to anyone. To Danica Harris, a thirty-five-year-old Dallas Police detective who lived her life by strict codes and procedures, the most maddening of all feline characteristics was the fact that they slept whenever and wherever they desired. Nothing ever interfered with their peace of mind. They answered to no one and cared only for themselves, oblivious to the schedules of the humans who fed them. The spiteful, selfish animals could find a sense of peace and contentment at any time, despite their surroundings or the chaos of the house. That was the most infuriating attribute of all, especially at moments like this when she lay awake, her mind racing while the world slept. She had lost count of how many nights in a row it had been, but there had been too many hours spent staring at the shadows shifting on the ceiling.

It was now after two o'clock in the morning, and she could hear the satisfied, rhythmic purr of the sleeping cat coming from the foot of her bed. It was a sound of pure mockery. The irritation vibrated all the way up her uncovered legs, along her spine, and dominated the thoughts inside her head, drowning out the quiet hum of the city outside. Like almost every night for the past few weeks, she stared at the ceiling, analyzing the cracks in the plaster, then tossed and turned in frustration for what seemed like endless hours, fighting a losing battle against insomnia. And really, she thought, biting her lip, why should this night be any different from the others? The pattern was set.

Danica Harris just could not sleep again, and she decided firmly that it was the cat's fault. She even refused to name the egocentric animal. A name would have only symbolized attachment, a bond she wasn't willing to forge, and that was the last thing she wanted in her life at this point. Attachments led to loss, and she was done with loss.

Lying in bed, staring wide-eyed at the ceiling, she recalled the exact moment her mother delivered the well-intentioned pet as a house-warming gift the day after Danica had moved into her Lemmon Avenue loft.

"You need something to come home to," her mother had insisted, placing the carrier on the hardwood floor. "You shouldn't be alone so much. It's not healthy for a young woman to have an empty house."

Her voice could be grating to the point of extreme irritation at times, filled with unsolicited advice and old-fashioned expectations. But lately, Danica was starting to miss that sound. She missed the cadence of it, the certainty. She missed her mother most on these long, restless nights when the silence of the loft felt amplified. She wasn't ready to admit it, but loneliness was just one of the many voids in her life, expanding slowly like a crack in a windshield.

It had been just over a year since Eve Harris had passed away suddenly from a massive brain aneurysm. It happened with the snap of a finger. From what her father had told her—later confirmed by the family physician—her death had been quick and painless. David Harris's wife of forty-two years had been tending to her prize-winning rose bushes one minute, shears in hand, and gone the next. One minute Danica Harris had a loving mother, the next she didn't. The permanence of it was staggering. But now she had the cat.

It was similar to her relationship with Paul Andrews, her fiancé of eight months; one minute she was engaged, planning a future, and the next she wasn't. Like her mother's death, Danica had no control over the end of that relationship either. Paul had never been comfortable with her career choice, the danger and the hours grating on him. She had insisted, making it quite clear that it was her choice and she wasn't going to compromise her identity for a ring. In the end, Paul made his own choice and refused to compromise as well, walking out the door and taking the future with him. It had been, and continued to be, a hard year for Danica Harris.

The unnamed cat wasn't the only gift she had received from her parents. The loft itself had been their big one. The exclusive area of Uptown Dallas was not affordable for most, but it was definitely a desire for many, a symbol of having "made it." Prices were set high enough to attract the right kind of residents while keeping the wrong kind away. The restaurants were eclectic, the shops expensive, the clubs exclusive, and Starbucks was always crowded with people who wanted to be seen.

The condominium had been her father's idea, a way to keep her in his world. The retired oil executive just couldn't come to grips with his daughter's career choice. After all, she was their only child, and David Harris had wanted more for her all along—almost demanding better. That was the reason he had paid the full tuition at Southern Methodist University without so much as a flinch, expecting a return on his investment in the form of a high-society marriage or corporate career. In high school, Danica's grades and athletic ability had qualified her for several scholarships at some of the nation's top schools, but no daughter of David Harris was going to be educated on someone else's dollar. To make matters worse, a scholarship student at SMU was never really fully accepted and certainly could never fit in with the "right" crowd. His daughter deserved more than that, and he would use his hard-earned money and power to ensure her future was paved with gold, whether she wanted it or not.

At the end of her sophomore year, Danica quietly and privately made a decision. She had known for some time that the academic life and the social climbing weren't for her. She felt a different calling, something visceral and real: law enforcement. Her mind was set, and she enrolled in the Dallas Police Academy before anyone knew, trading textbooks for penal codes.

She was well into her sixth week at the academy before she announced her decision around the Harris dining table. Her father was speechless. He slammed his crystal wine glass against the antique wood, the sound echoing like a gunshot in the large dining room, and stormed from the room while her mother quietly cried into her napkin.

It wasn't until after the academy graduation ceremony that the Harrises even acknowledged their daughter's decision. But even the fact that she had graduated in the top five percent of her class was still not enough to impress them. It wasn't the prestige he wanted.

Danica rose through the ranks quickly, her dedication bordering on obsession. She made Detective First Grade in record time. But it still took the entire seven years of her career before she gained her father's acceptance. And even that was a quiet, grudging, "How's the job?"

She never regretted her decision, but she still felt something was missing in her life. There always seemed to be an emptiness she never could quite identify, a hollow space in her chest, but it was there. For the most part, she had been content, and when Paul came along, she felt her life would soon be complete. But still, something was…

The purring seemed to be getting louder, vibrating through the mattress. It was even more irritating now. She kicked the thin sheet off her legs again, hoping to wake the cat. She kicked even harder until the displeased animal jumped from the bed with a soft thud and disappeared down the hall in search of peace somewhere else in the loft.

Minutes later, a similar noise returned, and it wasn't long before Danica understood the sound wasn't from the cat. She turned over and looked at the nightstand beside the bed. Her Blackberry was lit up, buzzing angrily against the wood. She jolted up, rubbed her eyes to clear the fatigue, and reached for the cell phone. The message displayed an unfamiliar downtown address followed by the numbers "911."

Chapter 3

It was a confusing scene. Usually, at that time of the morning, the financial district in the heart of downtown Dallas resembled a dark and deserted ghost town, the steel and glass canyons silent and empty. But now it was alive with chaotic activity as Detective Danica Harris turned the non-descript, unmarked police car down the side alley behind the North Texas Industrial Bank's head office. The rotating red and blue lights bounced off the glass skyscrapers, creating a disorienting strobe effect.

She slammed the car's transmission into park and turned the engine off. A deep sigh filled the inside of the silent car as she reached for the second Starbucks cup inside the holder. Danica had already downed the first cup within minutes of leaving the drive-through near her loft, the caffeine barely touching her exhaustion. It took just shy of eight minutes to throw on a pair of faded jeans and her most comfortable SMU sweatshirt, and pull her shoulder-length auburn hair into a tight ponytail. At three o'clock in the morning, there was no one she needed to impress, especially at a crime scene where the only audience was the dead and the weary.

From the dark alley, she made her way around the corner of the building. She stopped and counted six patrol cars with their lights still flashing and a lone ambulance out front, its engine idling. On the far side of the ambulance, hidden at first by the bulk of the emergency vehicle, Danica saw the coroner's black SUV. She knew that was never a good sign; it was the harbinger of finality. Even with five years of experience behind her as a homicide detective, the presence of that vehicle at a scene still made her uneasy. She really didn't care for this part—the cold administrative processing of a life ended. At thirty-five years old, she had already seen and experienced enough loss in her life to last a lifetime.

Danica stopped a good forty feet away from the scene and the bright yellow police tape that cordoned off the building's front entrance. She took another mouthful of coffee, savoring the bitter warmth, while trying to analyze the entire setting. There were just as many reporters, news vehicles, and bystanders as she expected, drawn like moths to the tragedy, but still too many for a simple suicide.

Without drawing attention to herself, she eased her way through the crowd, ignoring the slim, overly made-up female reporter standing in front of the bright lights and the camera, rehearsing her somber face. Two uniformed officers stood at attention on the steps of the building's concourse, watching the crowd with crossed arms. She didn't recognize them, but they certainly knew her. Danica flashed her police ID in front of the officers even though it wasn't necessary. The younger officer had already raised the police tape high enough for her to enter the area.

"Evening, Detective," he said as her head cleared the tape, his voice respectful but tired.

"Thanks. What floor?" she turned and asked.

"Eighteen," he replied. "All the action's up there. The CSI team's been here for almost forty-five minutes."

"And the victim?" she asked.

"James Rosin, ma'am. He is—or was—the president of the bank from what we've been told."

"Who's the lead on this?" Danica asked, adjusting her sweatshirt.

"Brainerd, ma'am."

Pam Brainerd was the department's top forensic investigator, a legend in the field. Her reputation preceded her throughout the law enforcement community not only in Texas but also throughout the country. Her papers, reports, and findings were the basis of many legal appeals and decisions. Brainerd and her team usually were called in when the case was high profile, complex, or baffling. Celebrities, sports stars, and the wealthy had a way of attracting attention in their private lives, and even more so in their death.

"Brainerd?" Danica asked, a bit surprised. "I thought this was a suicide according to the message I got?"

She already didn't like the whole scenario. Brainerd didn't come out for standard jumpers or overdose cases. But she kept her thoughts to herself, turned, and walked away from the two officers. She often wondered why, whenever she tried to enter a crime scene, the male officers always lifted the police tape like gentlemen opening a car door. Their feeble attempt at chivalry was completely defeated when she heard the snickers coming from behind her. It always bothered her that a female detective never quite carried the same respect and attention as her male counterparts, no matter how competent, tough, or successful the women were.

The elevator ride up the eighteen floors was solemn. She counted the numbers as they lit up—4, 5, 6...—until the car stopped smoothly on eighteen. A lone uniformed officer stood by the glass doors to the entrance of the executive suite. The name North Texas Industrial Bank had been elegantly etched in the glass, backlit by the foyer lights. As she moved closer, the officer opened the door and directed her down a hallway lined with expensive art. She didn't need any further direction from that point; the noise and activity from down the hall were enough to guide her to the exact spot. Several more officers stood milling around the outside of the last office. A few were laughing and carrying on everyday normal conversations, a defense mechanism against the grim reality inside, until they noticed the detective approaching. Their demeanor quickly changed, straightening up, and after acknowledging them, Danica made her way inside. A quick look around and Danica was immediately impressed with the office surroundings. She knew the president's corner office would have an impressive view of the Dallas skyline day or night, but the reality of actually seeing it astounded her for a moment. The city lights twinkled beautifully, indifferent to the horror in the room.

She spotted the lead CSI, Pam Brainerd, off to the side of the office making notes on her standard clipboard, her movements sharp and precise.

"What have we got, Pam?" Danica asked as she walked closer to the crime scene investigator.

"Not much yet, we're still processing," Brainerd responded, not looking up from her notes.

"I'm surprised they called you out," Danica stated. "You don't usually handle suicides."

"You're right about the suicide part, but a couple of things don't add up. Come here."

Danica followed close behind her. They approached the desk, and she saw Rosin's lifeless body still in the chair. Brainerd stopped in front of the desk, made a note on the clipboard, and then moved around to the body. Danica stood back slightly, taking in the entire scene, steeling herself against the metallic smell of blood.

Brainerd spoke first. "You can see it's a close-range headshot," she said, using her pen as a pointer. "Powder burns all along the left side of the head. Well, what's left of it anyway, and gunpowder residue on the hand. The fatal wound is obviously self-inflicted."

"So it is a suicide," Danica concluded.

"Not so fast," she said. "We've got a hundred and eighty dollar dinner receipt from Jonathon's on the desk from tonight. And there's this," Brainerd said as she pointed across the office to a large over-stuffed wingback chair set against the floor-to-ceiling windows. The dark Dallas skyline loomed outside just behind the glass. "Why would a suicidal man pay almost two hundred dollars for dinner then pick up his dry cleaning just a few hours before blowing his brains out?" she asked. "Take a look."

Danica followed her towards the chair. Several expensive dress shirts—cleaned, pressed, and wrapped in light dry cleaner's plastic—hung over the chair, ready for a work week that would never come. "Check the receipt. He picked this up at 6:45 this evening."

Danica looked down at the receipt stapled to the plastic and confirmed what the CSI had just stated. The investigator had already walked away, leaving Danica alone by the chair.

"And over here we've got this."

Danica saw the CSI pointing to a small crystal ashtray on a side table beside a light brown overstuffed chair. She walked over and looked at the contents. Burnt remains of plastic, the size of a dime, were the only thing visible, a tiny melted lump in the crystal.

"Any idea what that is?" she asked.

"It's all that's left of the SIM card from his cell phone. The actual phone, or should I say, what's left of it, was in the trash can under the desk."

"Can we get anything off either this or the phone?" Danica asked, leaning in closer.

"I doubt it. There are just pieces of phone left. The SIM card holds all the information and memory. We can subpoena phone records, but data transmissions or the contents of any text messages are gone. I'd say he was trying to hide something."

Danica released the air inside her lungs slowly as she looked around the office. "Anything else I should know?"

"Yes, there's this." Brainerd pulled a large clear evidence bag from behind the clipboard. Inside was a clean sheet of paper. One short paragraph in twelve-point Times New Roman type was evident. "We found this back there in the printer."

Danica reached for the bag and focused her eyes on the printed contents.

I'm so sorry for what I've done. I cannot live with the pain I have caused any longer.

James Rosin.

Tetelestai

She studied the letter again, pushing the clear plastic of the evidence bag tightly against the white paper so the letters would become clearer. "It's a suicide note," she said. "But what's this word under his name?" she asked, handing the evidence bag back to Brainerd.

"No idea," Brainerd said but refused to hold the bag. "But look closer. What's missing?"

Danica pulled the bag back and looked again. She read the letter twice but couldn't understand where Brainerd was trying to go.

"Sorry, I don't see anything," she stated, puzzled.

"Exactly. We found that note in the printer behind his desk. Here's what is not adding up. There's blood spatter all over the bookcase, the books, and the printer. But that page is completely clean; nothing on it at all, not a spot. And there's no signature. I bet once I get it in the lab, his fingerprints won't be found on it either."

"So what's your conclusion?" Danica asked, the realization dawning on her.

"Detective, that note was printed after his death."

Chapter 4

"**W**here have you been? The Captain's looking for you." Danica certainly knew that, and she didn't need Detective Chris Leininger to tell her. She was all too familiar with the drill; it was standard operating procedure, etched in stone and burnt into her routine. Captain Daniel Cooper always called his detectives in for a debrief immediately after their attendance at a major crime scene. He wanted the blood fresh, the impressions raw, and the details unvarnished before the paperwork had a chance to sanitize the horror.

But Detective Chris Leininger needed some way of justifying his presence on the fourth floor of Dallas Police Plaza. Over the years, he had devolved from a functional officer into something more akin to an annoying mascot than an actual detective—a relic of a bygone era who refused to leave the building. She had heard the rumors that he was good at one time—a sharp investigator early in his career who could crack a case just by looking at a suspect—but those days were long buried under layers of apathy, carbohydrates, and endless bureaucracy. Now, the aging, overweight detective just lived at his desk, a permanent fixture of the furniture like an old, lumpy sofa, patiently waiting out the days until his pension kicked in. To pass the time, he paid special attention to everyone else's business, making it his goal in life to know everything that went on in the department before the official reports were even typed. Leininger was generally well-liked for his jovial nature, usually good for a laugh or a piece of gossip, but he could easily become suffocating. And to Danica Harris, exhausted and on edge, this was one of those suffocating times where his voice felt like sandpaper on her last nerve.

"I'm sure he is waiting, Chris," she said, walking past the man's desk as quickly as possible, holding her breath to avoid the sensory assault. His area always seemed to carry the lingering, pungent odor of bad Mexican food—onions, cumin, and stale grease that clung to the fabric of his cubicle walls like a second skin.

"What kind of mood is he in?" she asked over her shoulder, needing to be prepared for the ambush. She was tired, bone-weary from not having slept at all again. She had managed to cut away from the scene at Rosin's office shortly after six that morning to clean up, but the adrenaline was fading fast, leaving a hollow ache behind her eyes. She had spent hours watching the crime techs gather, tag, and bag every-thing in sight, turning a man's life into inventory. Fingerprints were pulled from every surface possible, and the metallic smell of their dusting powders and harsh chemicals still seemed to linger on her clothes and skin, a phantom scent of death and sterile procedure she couldn't scrub away no matter how hard she tried.

She had made the quick stop back at her loft, stealing just enough time to take a long, scalding shower, change into fresh clothes, and get back on the case. She had almost left without feeding the cat, which was nowhere in sight, but her mother's voice—a nagging echo in her head reminding her of responsibilities she didn't want—made her go back and tend to the ungrateful animal.

"All I know is that the Chief was in there earlier," Leininger offered, leaning back in his creaking chair which groaned under the strain. "He left a while ago, and Coop's door has been closed ever since. Not a peep. The blinds are drawn tight, too."

She let out a deep sigh in frustration and took another mouthful of coffee from the cup that always seemed to be grafted to her hand. It had become her trademark, a shield against fatigue and a prop to keep her hands busy. She walked across the squad room to the message board, her eyes scanning the thumbtacked notes without really reading them—missing person flyers, inter-departmental memos curling at the edges. She realized how aggravating the constant buzz in the area had become; the cacophony of detectives on the phone barking ques-tions, the frantic clacking of keyboards, the hushed conversations about the latest Cowboys scores or a kid's birthday party. It was the sound of life going on, mundane and trivial, while she was stuck wading through the aftermath of death. She made her way back to her desk and drank the last of the lukewarm coffee, slowly savoring the caffeine sludge as if it were fine wine.

The thought of sitting down for a moment of respite passed quickly when the blinds in the corner office shifted. The Captain raised his head from the pile of papers on his desk, and their eyes met through the glass. It was a look devoid of warmth. He didn't smile. He simply waved her in with a sharp jerk of his hand.

"Sit down," he said without even looking up as she entered, not bothering to acknowledge her presence beyond the command. He continued to scrawl a signature on a form, the pen scratching loudly in the quiet room. "What have you got on this Rosin thing?"

Captain Daniel Cooper was a long-time veteran of the department, a man carved out of granite and old-school policing. His face was a roadmap of tough cases and late nights. His management style consisted of equal parts intimidation and sarcasm, a brutal combination that kept his subordinates on their toes, but to his credit, it worked. Cooper's department held the highest clearance percentage in the entire precinct, a statistic he wore like a badge of honor and used as a bludgeon against the brass.

"We believe it's been made to look like a suicide. There are a few things that don't fit the narrative," she reported, sitting on the edge of the stiff wooden chair, refusing to get comfortable. "I'm going to see Brainerd as soon as I'm done here for the preliminary forensics."

"Talk to me. What doesn't fit?"

"The circumstances don't make sense. The psychology is all wrong," Danica said, counting the points off on her fingers. "The suicide note was printed after he shot himself—physically impossible unless he's a ghost. His dry cleaning was picked up just a few hours before the time of death. There was a dinner receipt on his desk for a substantial amount. It's hard to believe someone would go through all that normal, everyday routine—errands, dinner, future planning—with the specific intention of taking his own life that same night. People who are checking out don't usually worry about starch in their shirts."

Cooper closed the file he was reading with a heavy thud, dust motes dancing in the sudden displacement of air, and passed it across the desk to Harris. "You can add this to the investigation now as well. Take a look. I think you'll find it interesting."

"What is it?" she asked, taking the folder. It felt heavy, burdened with more than just paper.

"Tarrant County detectives sent this through an hour ago. It came down directly through the Commissioner. Does the name Cole Simpson ring a bell?"

"No, should it?"

"Big oil and gas man from several years ago. Made himself a huge fortune quite fast in the late eighties and early nineties, then retired to a two-hundred-acre estate south of Fort Worth to play cowboy. His wife found him five days ago. He hung himself from the rafters inside his barn."

Danica looked confused, her brow furrowing. "So why is this related to Rosin, and why is a Tarrant County file now part of my case? Suicide isn't exactly a contagious disease, and jurisdictionally, this is a nightmare."

Cooper leaned back in his chair, the leather groaning under his weight. "The suicide note is inside. Take a look."

Danica opened the file and flipped through the glossy crime scene photographs quickly—images of a wealthy life ended in a dusty barn, the juxtaposition of expensive boots dangling above a dirt floor. Sealed in plastic behind the autopsy report was Simpson's suicide note. She held it up to the light, squinting at the text.

I'm so sorry for what I've done. I cannot live with the pain I have caused any longer.

Cole Simpson

Tetelestai

She read the note twice, her heart rate picking up a tempo. She looked up at Cooper. Neither spoke a word for a long moment. They didn't have to. The Captain had already seen it and made his own assumptions. The wording was identical. The font was identical. The message was identical.

"Tell me what you make of that?" he asked, steepling his fingers and peering over them.

"I'm going to have to go through the file and let it soak in," she admitted, her mind racing to connect the dots, spinning webs of conspiracy. "What I thought was a questionable suicide in Rosin's case... well, this changes everything. We're looking at a pattern. A signature."

"There's been a request," he said, his voice dropping an octave, losing its usual bluster. "You're going to have some help on this."

"From?" Danica asked, instantly defensive. Her hackles raised. She didn't need a babysitter.

"Both Simpson and Rosin were not only prominent figures in this state, but they were also well connected politically. And this request comes from inside the capital, Austin. High places, Harris. The kind of places that can end careers with a phone call."

"Captain, what's going on? I'm not having some state flunky watching over my shoulder on this. You know I work better alone. If this is some Texas Ranger power trip or some political favor being called in..."

"Harris, stop. It's an order coming from way above my head and both our pay grades combined."

"Who?"

22

"I don't know who filed the request. I didn't ask, and honestly, I don't want to know. Plausible deniability is my friend right now. This order came directly from the Chief, and I'm going to follow orders on this one just like you will," he stopped and gave her a steely look that immediately told her he wasn't taking this order lightly. "If not, then I'll pull this case from you entirely. I know you don't play well with others, but swallow your damn pride, Harris, and dump that huge chip you've got on your shoulder before it crushes you."

She let out another deep, frustrated breath and opened the file again, not really intending to read anything in particular. She just wanted to avoid eye contact with her superior while she processed the loss of control.

Cooper leaned forward. The squeaking mechanics of his chair were starting to grate on her frayed nerves like fingernails on a chalkboard. "They want us to pull someone in to help you on this. A consultant."

"Who's that?"

Before she could even finish her question, Cooper opened the top drawer of his desk and retrieved another file, this one thinner, worn at the edges, looking like it had been handled often but rarely opened. He placed it on his desk and flipped open the cover.

"His name's Delgado. Nicholai Jayden Delgado. He's retired FBI."

Another sigh was forced from her lungs, and Cooper became aware of her escalating frustration. He slammed the file shut with a sharp crack to gain her full attention.

"Just listen, Harris. Delgado was one of their top profilers and an expert in high-tech crime. A hunter. He hung it up four years ago after his last case went bad."

"So you want me to bring in some old guy who screwed up his last assignment? This is just great. A washed-up Fed with baggage. And tell me, how is this supposed to help my investigation? I need fresh eyes, not tired ones."

"Let's get something straight!" Cooper rose to his feet and yelled, his face flushing red. He walked around his desk towards the doorway of the office. With force, he slammed the door shut, rattling the glass pane. Outside, Leininger's head popped up from his desk like a meerkat sensing a predator, trying to see what all the commotion was.

"I'm not pulling the strings on this, and neither are you," Cooper hissed, lowering his voice but keeping the intensity burning in his eyes. "Harris, this is coming from somewhere above all of us. I don't know who, but we have got to play along. And that's an order."

He made his way back to the side of his desk but remained standing, looming over her. He hovered over the female detective, casting a shadow across the files. "This so-called 'screw up' you've referenced...

he lost his wife and only daughter in that case. He didn't just lose the case, Harris. He lost his life."

Danica stopped her train of thought and felt her heart suddenly sink. The anger evaporated, replaced by a cold knot in her stomach.

"What do you mean? What happened?"

"Delgado spent eighteen months tracking a serial killer all through the South. His name was Jeremy Quinlin. He targeted those big-box retailers—department stores, malls. His victims all had the same physical traits: female, under thirty years of age, short blonde hair, slightly overweight. Delgado tracked him from the Florida coast, up into South Carolina, then Alabama, and Mississippi. He thought they had him nailed in Shreveport once, but then the trail went cold. It seemed Quinlin went underground for almost two months."

Danica was speechless and embarrassed by her earlier outburst. She stayed silent, letting the Captain continue.

"But then it got personal, and the whole game turned quickly. The hunter became the hunted. Quinlin came after Delgado with several online threats and then through the media. A journalist was the go-between. Quinlin sent him letters; weird, cryptic messages mostly, taunting Delgado, telling him he was getting closer. The reporter would pass the information on to Delgado and his team. But two months into that, the reporter was found slaughtered in a fleabag hotel room in Baton Rouge. Cut into pieces. After a few days there trying to salvage the lead, Delgado flew back here to Dallas, went home, and found his wife and daughter…" Cooper trailed off, gesturing to the folder. "It's all in here. The whole thing wasn't pretty. It was a massacre. He walked into his own nightmare."

"I don't remember hearing about this."

"That's because Quinlin disappeared again. They assumed he went underground or fled the country after all that. And as of now, Jeremy Quinlin hasn't been found. He just disappeared off the face of the earth like smoke."

"And now?" she asked softly.

"The file is still active, but the Feds have kept it quiet to avoid a panic. The case is sealed tighter than a frog's butt, and nobody seems to want to touch it. From what I know, the whole mess almost destroyed Delgado. He was one of the best they had, and he just pulled out. Total psychological collapse. He didn't just retire; he vanished."

"Where is he? What's he doing now?"

"He's still in Dallas, or at least somewhere in the area. After he left the Bureau, he cut off all ties. Everyone thought he would just disappear, and he's tried. But he enrolled in a seminary somewhere south of the Metroplex. Who knows why? Maybe he figured he could find answers if he got closer to God. But the word on the street is he spends a lot of time on some boat at Lake Ray Hubbard out near Rockwall. I guess he's become a bit of a recluse now. Can't say I blame him." Cooper stayed quiet and looked at Danica, his expression softening slightly. "But someone from the capital wants him on this."

Cooper tossed Delgado's file across the desk. It slid over the polished wood and stopped at her fingertips. She cautiously picked it up, treating it like an unexploded bomb. Without opening it, she looked hard into the Captain's eyes. "What am I supposed to do with this?"

"Go find your new partner. It's an order."

Danica rose from the chair, clutching the files, and turned towards the door.

"Harris," he said.

She kept her hand on the doorknob and turned back to face him.

"Keep this in mind," Cooper warned, his voice grave. "Delgado has gone to a lot of trouble to disappear. He's not going to like the fact that you've found him."

Chapter 5

It was too late in a much-too-long day to get anything accomplished or even started. The sun had long since surrendered to the neon glow of the city, painting the streets in artificial hues of red and blue. Danica needed her diversion: The West End Tavern off Greenville Avenue. It was a dark hole-in-the-wall, the kind of place where the floor was permanently sticky with spilled lager and the air smelled of stale beer, cigarette smoke, and regret. It was a place for people who didn't want to be found, which suited her perfectly.

She nursed her second Jack and Diet Coke alone, wrapped quietly in her thoughts at the far end of the bar. She preferred to sit at the far end, back against the wall, in the shadows. It was her dark corner, a sanctuary away from anyone else. Plus, the vantage point allowed her to scan the room, watching the other patrons as they came and left or mingled with the regulars like they were one big happy family. She was always amazed at how a little bit of alcohol seemed to make complete strangers care just a little bit more for each other—or at least pretend to. The laughter sounded genuine enough, but she knew it was just the liquor talking.

She was enough of a regular that her usual drink was brought to her spot without a word. But still, she wasn't enough of a regular for the bartender to know that Danica Harris didn't care for the slice of lime he always placed inside the glass. She grinned cynically when he placed

27

the third drink in front of her, complete with another slice of lime floating amongst the melting ice cubes like a shipwreck.

The bartender always checked with her just before the last sip of the third drink. She rarely ordered a fourth, but he knew to always check. And tonight, with images of blood-spattered bookcases and suicide notes burning in her mind, she needed that fourth drink. She needed the numbness it promised.

Danica already had an uneasy feeling about the case. It settled in her gut, heavier than the whiskey. High-profile victims always brought a completely different set of rules to the game. The media was more determined and aggressive, vultures circling for a headline, and the upper brass was more intense and demanding. She couldn't decide which group was more annoying: the media with their blinding cameras and invasive questions, or management with their politics and need for quick, neat closures.

And suicides... they were always something she never quite understood. They made her uncomfortable in a way homicide didn't. Murder was theft; suicide was surrender. What kind of person would take their own life? What possessed someone to believe that death was the only way out of a situation? Were they that desperate? Was life so bad for a wealthy man like Rosin that he had to end his life like that? Or did he?

The note. Tetelestai. And now Simpson.

The whole concept of death was something she thought about a lot. She was intrigued and afraid at the same time. She never wanted to know the how anymore—she saw the how every day at work in graphic detail. She just wanted to know why. Why did the light go out? Where did the energy go?

She had been taught in Sunday school, years ago before life hardened her into the skeptic she was now, that suicide meant a sure trip to hell. Did she even believe there was a hell? Or even a Heaven for that matter? Knowing and understanding were two very different things, and she couldn't grasp the latter. She had been to church when she was young; she sat in the pews, smoothing her dress, listening to stories of fire and brimstone. They learned about the two places, but they never seemed quite real to her; just some fantasy places grown-ups made up and used to scare others into behaving. Or tools that the polished Sunday morning televangelists yelled about on their slick broadcasts in a desperate effort to raise much-needed funds to complete their next multi-million dollar project. She often wondered just how much it cost to guarantee that trip to Heaven and to avoid hell. Of course, they never put the exact price on either destination, but they certainly took checks.

She tipped the glass to her mouth, the ice clicking against her teeth, and slowly drank the last of the fourth drink. The burn was welcome, trailing fire down her throat.

"Can I buy you another one of those?"

The voice from behind should have startled her, but it didn't. Her reflexes were dulled by the alcohol and the fatigue. She turned and stood face-to-face with a stranger. Her mind quickly scanned the man who appeared at least twenty years her senior. His unpressed suit matched the wrinkled shirt and stained tie—a businessman who had clearly had a rough day, or perhaps a rough decade. He swayed back and forth slightly, finding his own personal equilibrium, but the bottle in his hand stayed remarkably steady.

"Yes, you could," she replied with a tight, artificial smile. It was a reflex, a polite lie to diffuse the awkwardness.

He returned her smile with a sloppy wink of his own, thinking he had found an opening, a connection in the dark. But his face quickly turned flat as Danica eased her body away from him, grabbing her purse. His expression remained flat, a mask of rejected loneliness, as he watched the young detective walk out the door and into the humid night. He was just another ghost haunting the West End, looking for someone to validate his existence, and she had nothing left to give him.

Chapter 6

Rockwall was less than an hour's drive east from downtown Dallas, but it felt like a different world. The drive was all city, concrete and congestion, with no breaks the entire way along the interstate. But as soon as Danica crossed the long bridge over the lake, the entire atmosphere changed. The tension of the metroplex seemed to dissolve into the water. It was relaxed and serene. She opened the car window a few inches, letting the air rush in. It smelled of algae and wet earth, a distinct change from the exhaust fumes of the highway. The four-lane interstate bridge crossed the lake at two different points, and the sun's glare off the water was blinding, making her eyes squint behind her sunglasses each time. From inside the hot car, she spotted the odd sailboat off on the horizon, a white triangle against the blue, and for a fleeting moment, it looked inviting—a symbol of escape she knew she couldn't afford.

It was a stark difference from the typical North Dallas neighborhood she had just left. Danica had easily found Nicholai Delgado's home address in the file but failed to find the man. His address had never changed, even if his life had shattered.

From outside the house on Windsor Lane, she could tell it had been well cared for; the lawn looked manicured to perfection, the grass a vibrant green, and the hedges were trimmed with geometric precision. Twenty-one Windsor Lane looked like any other home on any other street in any other nice neighborhood of Dallas. It was the picture of suburban bliss. But she was confused. She expected ruin. She expected a house that reflected the tragedy that occurred inside— overgrown weeds, peeling paint, a physical manifestation of grief. Instead, she found a facade of normalcy that felt unsettlingly deceptive.

She sat quietly in the car for quite a while, the engine ticking as it cooled, trying to gather her thoughts and rehearsing what she wanted to say to the man before making her way up the walkway. When she finally felt ready, Danica walked to the door. She knocked quietly at first, respectful of the ghosts she knew lingered there, and then waited for a response. When none came, she rang the doorbell twice. The chime echoed hollowly inside, a cheerful sound ringing in an empty tomb. The curtains were drawn tight, blocking any view inside, but she could tell. It was obvious no one was home. The house felt asleep, or perhaps in a coma, preserved in time.

"Can I help you?" a voice from the sidewalk startled her.

She spun around, hand instinctively moving toward her hip before she caught herself. "I'm looking for Mr. Delgado. Have you seen him?"

"Can I ask why you're looking for him?" the man asked, stepping onto the lawn. He was middle-aged, wearing gardening gloves and holding a trowel, looking like the quintessential neighbor.

Danica showed her ID. "I'm with the Dallas Police. I just wanted to ask him a few questions. Who are you?"

"My name's Chad Deteau. I live just up the block," he told her, gesturing with the trowel. "You here about what happened?"

"Sorry? What happened?" she asked, playing dumb. She didn't want to get specific with any details, not with a neighbor who might gossip.

"That incident years ago... with his wife and the girl?" Chad's tone dropped to a whisper, as if saying it aloud would conjure the violence back into existence. She could tell the man had been affected more than he was letting on; the neighborhood still carried the scar, a hidden trauma beneath the manicured lawns.

"No, Mr. Deteau. It's concerning a different matter. I'm sorry, but I can't go into details."

"That's alright, I understand," he said, looking at the closed door of Delgado's house with a mix of pity and fear. "I've only seen his car a few times lately. He comes and goes pretty fast. Other than that, he never comes around here much anymore. We all feel bad for him. I guess it's just hard for him to ever come home again," Deteau said, shaking his head. "Too many memories in those walls. I don't know how he steps foot in there."

"Why doesn't he sell the house and move on?" the detective asked. It seemed the logical thing to do. Why keep a mausoleum?

"No clue. He doesn't like to talk about that night," he said, looking down the street to his own safe, happy home. "There's a lot that's changed in this neighborhood now. Just not the same anymore. People lock their doors earlier. We watch the street a little closer." He paused. "You sure you're not here to help him?"

"No, I'm not, sorry. It's just police business. Do you have any idea where he might be?"

Chad looked down the other side of the street, squinting against the sun. He was thinking. "Did you try the lake? He spends all his time on the water now."

After their conversation was complete and the concerned Mr. Deteau had moved on back to his garden, Danica sat quietly in the car again. She recalled the brutal details of Delgado's file. She had forced herself to study the crime scene photographs and the detailed accounts of the scene before leaving the station. The reports indicated both mother and daughter had been tortured before being murdered. Just three days shy of her seventeenth birthday, lying on the living room floor, Sara Delgado was discovered, tied and gagged with multiple cuts and bruises. Twenty-one Windsor Lane was the only home she had ever known. Thirty-seven-year-old Jessica Delgado was discovered in the master bedroom in almost the identical condition as her daughter, but she had several defensive wounds on both hands and arms. The medical examiner's final report summarized that the mother had fought hard, fought viciously, to save both her daughter and herself.

"Doesn't fit," Danica said aloud as she closed the file and looked back at the pristine home. It was hard to believe that in such a serene setting, this peaceful neighborhood could carry the weight of such a horrible tragedy. She had attended plenty of crime scenes throughout her relatively short career, but this one seemed different. She could feel it down in the pit of her stomach, a heavy dread she seemed to have trouble shaking. The whole scenario kept her mind completely occupied almost all the way to the marina.

"Good afternoon. Can I help you?" a tanned, weathered man asked from the back room behind the counter in the marina office.

The space seemed more like a quaint country store rather than a business establishment. Danica stepped inside, the air conditioning a welcome relief from the Texas heat, and studied the room with a quick eye. The walls were painted a faded nautical blue, peeling in spots to reveal older layers of paint. Coolers filled with sweating bottles of soda lined one long wall, while the wrap-around windows covered the other three. The industrial metal shelves were fully stocked with outboard motor oil, fishing tackle, bright lures, accessories, and candy bars. It smelled of gasoline, floor wax, and bait—a masculine, functional scent.

Everything one would ever need to enjoy their day on the lake—or hide from the world—was under one roof. For a moment, breathing in the air, she felt like she had actually been able to step away from the city.

The layout of the office and the windows allowed a full view of the lake and the covered docks. Just outside, Danica watched a large cruiser pull away from the dock slowly and clear the breakwater. Bikini-clad girls covered the deck of the boat, laughing and drinking, while a tanned, shirtless man stood behind the controls and throttled the twin engines. A wake of frothy white water churned behind them, slowly disappearing inside itself across the lake. It was a scene of carefree indulgence that felt alien to her current mission.

"I'm looking for someone," she said, turning back to the man. "A man by the name of Nicholai Delgado. I understand he has a boat somewhere around here."

"My name's Joel. I'm the manager here," he stated with a sudden sense of authority, leaning his elbows on the counter. "Can I ask why you're looking for him?"

Danica reached behind her back and pulled the badge and identification from the back pocket of her jeans. Joel watched her closely from behind the counter. At the level he was standing, he hadn't noticed the holstered gun at her side. When he did, his eyes widened slightly, and he studied it for a moment before moving his gaze back to her face. The innocence she projected with her ponytail and sweatshirt didn't match the cold grey steel of the sidearm she carried. The confusion in his mind made him want to answer her question without paying attention to the police identification she held up.

But she didn't give him a chance. Danica spoke first. "It's just police business, nothing official yet. I need to ask him a few questions."

Joel smirked, a defensive glint in his eye. "Come on, you can't tell me the Pastor is in any kind of trouble?"

"No, it's nothing like that," Danica responded quickly. She wasn't the least bit interested in making friends with the man or explaining herself. She just wanted her information. "I have a few questions for him regarding a case."

Danica wasn't going to ask at first. She tried to let it go, but curiosity got the better of her. "You called him 'Pastor'? Why?"

"Because he is," Joel stated flatly. "At least to us, that's what he is. He listens. He helps the folks around here when they're hurting. It's more than just a title."

Neither of them spoke for a moment, the hum of the refrigerator filling the silence.

Finally, Joel gave in, realizing she wasn't going away. "He's on down H dock. Turn to your left as you walk out and head straight down the walk," he told her, pointing a calloused finger. "He's in slip number twenty-seven. It's the thirty-two-foot Catalina named the Sara Rose. Beautiful boat. You can't miss it."

Sara Rose, Danica thought. His wife and daughter. The realization hit her with the force of a physical blow. He was living inside a memorial.

"Thank you," she said before turning towards the door.

"You'll need the code," she heard Joel say from behind the counter.

"Excuse me?" She paused, hand on the doorframe.

"The gate code. It's 316."

She could tell he wanted to say more, so she waited.

"Go easy on him," he said quietly, almost embarrassed by his own protectiveness. Danica noticed a sad change in the man's eyes and his demeanor. It wasn't what she expected to see or hear, and she stopped short of leaving.

"We're all quite protective of the Pastor. That man has been through some tough times." Joel looked directly at her, his expression earnest. "But he has become a good friend to a lot of us here. Just... show some respect. He's earned it."

Chapter 7

She tried making as much noise as possible while making her way down the wooden dock towards slip number twenty-seven. The calm and peace of the area made her uncomfortable; the silence felt heavy, almost judgmental compared to the chaotic noise of the city she had left behind. It wasn't an environment she was used to, and her defenses were already up.

As she walked along the dock, her eyes checked the faded numbers stenciled on the sun-bleached wood that identified each slip space. The further down she went, the more she could feel the afternoon air cooling, the humidity dropping as the water absorbed the heat. A slight, refreshing breeze had picked up from across the lake, smelling of algae and wet rope. The loose halyard lines swung in the breeze on the moored sailboats, tapping rhythmically against the hollow aluminum masts. Clink, clink, clink. The sound was relentless, almost reminding her of church bells ringing in the distance—or a timer counting down.

Slip twenty-seven was halfway down the dock but approached a little too quickly for her liking. Now that she was here, amidst the gentle lapping of water against fiberglass hulls, there was a certain peace that she found surprisingly comforting, and she didn't want to disturb it.

Danica saw him first. She noticed his form silhouetted against the glare of the water. His back was turned, but she could tell he was obviously in shape for his age; the muscles in his shoulders moved with fluid precision as he worked. His short salt-and-pepper hair stood out against his deeply tanned skin, a testament to days spent under the Texas sun. He was shirtless, and she noticed beads of sweat rolling down his back, tracing the line of his spine. His stained, faded khaki cargo shorts looked worn but comfortable, utilitarian clothing for a man who had stopped caring about appearances.

"Not interested," he said abruptly without so much as even glancing in her general direction. His voice was low, gravelly, and carried a tone of finality. The response was quick, rude, and took her completely by surprise.

"Excuse me?" she asked, stopping in her tracks. She tried to make it sound authoritative, but the confusion bled through. "How did you know I was here to see you? I haven't said a word."

Nicholai Delgado rose to his feet on the deck of the Catalina sailboat and turned to face her. He steadied himself by holding one of the rigging lines he had been adjusting, his grip loose but confident. He pushed, then tugged on the thin metal line, checking the tension and pull, treating the boat with the care of a surgeon. But all the while, his deep blue eyes stayed focused on her, dissecting her presence.

"The shoes," he said, gesturing vaguely toward her feet. "The only people who come down here are sailors or visitors. And I haven't met many sailors who wear three-inch heels on a floating dock. I could hear those things clicking against the wood as soon as the gate closed." He grinned, a flash of white teeth in a weathered face, and waited for her response.

"Well, you didn't have to be so rude," she replied, crossing her arms.

"It wasn't meant to be rude. Efficient, maybe. All I said was, I'm not interested," he stated flatly. "And I'm not."

"I'm... I'm not selling anything," she tried to explain, her voice rising slightly. He had thrown her off balance. Danica had rehearsed her request over and over again in the car, planning to appeal to his sense of duty, but she was frustrated that she had allowed him to control the conversation before it had even begun.

Delgado teased, leaning against the boom, "That's your first mistake, young lady. We're all selling something. Salvation, insurance, justice... everyone has a pitch."

"I hate to burst your bubble, but you're wrong. I'm not here to pitch anything. I'm here because—"

He turned his back and moved away from her, walking along the top deck of the boat with an enviable balance, and then he stopped and faced her. "Come on. Get on board."

"Mr. Delgado, I didn't come here to play games or spend the day enjoying the view. I have work to do, and I came here to ask for your help regarding a sensitive matter."

Delgado turned again and continued walking away from her toward the cockpit as if she hadn't spoken. He ignored her protest and continued checking the rigging, his hands moving with practiced familiarity. Danica was becoming even more frustrated with his dismissal and remained standing obstinately by the bow of the boat.

"I know why you're here," he yelled back from the stern, his voice carrying easily over the wind. "You want me to look at that police file tucked under your arm."

He caught her off guard again. Instead of looking at him, she looked down at the file she was clutching against her chest like a shield.

"I'm asking you to get on board," he continued, his tone softening slightly. "You'll be much more comfortable over here rather than standing over there in this heat. The reflection off the water will burn you in ten minutes."

Now slightly embarrassed and frustrated, the detective made her way along the slip to the stern of the boat. Delgado unclipped the lifeline, opening the gate, and reached his hand out in an effort to help. She ignored his assistance, determined to maintain her independence, and attempted to raise her leg to step aboard. The boat shifted slightly under the weight transfer.

"Shoes," he said sharply. "Those aren't exactly appropriate for boarding a boat. You'll break a heel or an ankle, and I don't have the insurance for either."

"They're fine," she insisted, balancing precariously. "Like I said, I didn't come here to enjoy a day on the water."

"First of all, it's a lake, not a sidewalk. Now come on, take them off. They're gorgeous—I love them—but they're certainly not safe. The deck is slippery."

She looked up and into his eyes, searching for mockery, but found only practical concern. Slowly, she reached down to remove her heels. The wood of the dock felt warm against her stockinged feet. Without saying a word, she handed them over to him, and he placed them gently on the cockpit bench.

"Now that," he said, motioning to the file under her arm. Without waiting for her response, he reached for the file and took it. "Never board a boat with your hands full. One hand for the boat, one hand for yourself. It's the first rule."

She looked up and noticed his eyes again. They were a deep, piercing blue, and their depth made her take a quick breath. They were eyes that had seen too much, yet somehow remained clear.

He placed the file haphazardly on the seat, almost ignoring it as if it were a piece of junk mail, and turned to help the detective on board. Nicholai reached out and gently grabbed her hand, placing it inside his large, calloused palm. She could feel the strength in his arms and the roughness of his skin. With ease, he pulled her up towards him and inside the cockpit of the Sara Rose.

"Have a seat," he said, pointing to the cushioned bench along the starboard side of the cockpit.

Once he saw she was seated and comfortable, Nicholai slid the top hatch towards the bow and disappeared below deck. A slight breeze came off the lake, stronger now, and Danica's shoulder-length hair moved lightly across her face, sticking to her lip gloss. She moved it away with her hand and tried holding it back. Without making it obvious, she leaned down and tried to see what he was doing. The bright sun affected her eyes, and she had trouble focusing down inside the dark cabin. She heard the sound of a cupboard door closing and the clink of glass.

Nicholai reappeared from down below, climbing the stairs from inside the cabin holding two bottles of water. He handed one to Danica. He reached down for her shoes and tossed them below, securing them, then made his way towards the back of the cockpit. Danica watched in silence as he sat down behind the large stainless steel wheel and looked off towards the lake, scanning the horizon like a captain on the high seas. She brushed the hair away from her face again.

"How much time do you have?" he asked. His eyes were focused out on the water, checking the wind direction.

"I... I don't really know," she replied with a tone of confusion. "Why?"

He turned and watched as she brushed the hair away from her face again, struggling with the wind. He stood up and made his way around the wheel towards the open cabin again. Delgado bent over and reached inside a small drawer.

"Here," he said, handing her a black elastic hair band. "This should help. My daughter... she used to leave them everywhere."

"Thanks," she said quietly, avoiding eye contact at the mention of his daughter. She placed the water bottle on the seat beside her, reached behind her head, and pulled her hair into a tight ponytail. It felt like putting on her work uniform.

"I'm sorry," he said, his voice shifting to a more formal tone. "But you already know who I am." He stuck his hand out. Danica, a bit uneasy, reached out and lightly shook his hand.

"Detective Danica Harris," she replied.

Delgado made his way back to the wheel and looked out towards the lake again. He sat down behind the wheel and bent over slightly, checking the instrument panel. From her position, she couldn't see what his hands were doing, but she heard the rhythmic thrum-thrum-thrum of the diesel engine coming to life beneath her feet. The vibration resonated through the hull.

He stood up and gracefully stepped onto the upper deck, making his way towards the bow with the confidence of a mountain goat. She watched him bend over to uncleat the lines, then rise and with ease, he made his way back along the upper deck towards the stern, stepping down inside the cockpit. He quickly released the line on the port side, throwing it off towards the slip, and then did the same next to Danica on the starboard side. His arm lightly brushed against her, but they both ignored the effect of the touch.

Nicholai turned his back to her, faced the lake, and lowered his head. He stood motionless and quiet for a moment, his hand resting lightly on the wheel.

When he returned to the helm, he looked directly at her. "Well, Ms. Harris, ever been out on this lake? Or should I call you Inspector Harris?"

"No, I haven't, and Danica is fine. What did you just do?"

"When?" he asked, checking the throttle.

"Just now. When you were standing there with your head down?"

"Oh, that. I prayed," he stated simply. "I always pray before heading out. The water is big, and the boat is small."

"Mr. Delgado, I really want to talk to you about—"

"You're not the first," he said abruptly as he shifted the diesel engine into reverse. Danica felt the boat jerk slightly, then slowly back away from the slip space. The water churned white at the stern. "And you certainly won't be the last."

Nicholai smoothly eased the Sara Rose away from the slip, judging the distance perfectly. He turned his head back and forth, from the stern to the bow, calculating the drift. When he was confident the bow had cleared the dock, he shifted the transmission to forward, and the boat lurched ahead. Danica watched as they slowly made their way past several other sailboats tucked neatly away in their slips, floating past like sleeping giants. She felt the boat turn, clearing the end of the dock. After a few feet, Delgado turned the wheel starboard, and the boat headed towards the channel leading to the open lake.

Danica immediately felt nervous. She had been on a boat before and was comfortable on the water, but this was different. She had never been on a sailboat, especially with a complete stranger at the wheel who seemed more interested in God than the police. She felt he was in control—she even marveled at the ease with which he handled the vessel—but his unpredictable actions didn't help to completely ease her concerns.

Just twenty feet outside the breakwater, she heard the ratcheting sound of a winch coming from the cockpit. A blue and white jib sail started to unwind from the forestay, snapping loudly as it caught the wind hard off the port side. The boat leaned—heeled—suddenly. Delgado moved to the starboard side and pulled the jib sheet tight with his hands, his biceps straining, then secured it tight with the winch.

She felt the boat being pulled along the water, the engine noise fading as the wind took over. Her speed slowly increased, slicing through the small chop. She closed her eyes for a moment and felt the cool breeze move lightly across her face. She was glad her hair was tied back now. The vibration that once was at her feet had disappeared, and she realized that it was just the wind moving them along the water. The quiet was almost haunting, broken only by the rush of water against the hull, and it took her a few minutes to settle into it.

"You know what you're doing with all this," she said, gripping the bench. "Have you been sailing long?"

"A few years," he said, looking up at the wind direction arrow on top of the mast. "This is like my home. It makes sense to me. Wind, physics, action, reaction."

"You live out here?" she asked.

"For the most part, yes," he said. "Look at all this. I can't imagine anything more peaceful than spending time out here. Well, other than Heaven. Some people believe it's a way of shutting out the world, but for me, it's the opposite," he said as he stared along the horizon where the water met the sky.

"What do you mean by the opposite? Aren't you actually running away by hanging out down here? Hiding from reality?"

"No, not at all," Delgado said, correcting her gently. "I have to spend time here, in all this. Out here, I get to admire the glory of God and all He's blessed me with. It's my way of coming back to who I really want to become because the selfishness and futility of man almost destroyed me. In the city, everything is noise and lies. Here, the wind doesn't lie. If you mess up, the lake lets you know immediately."

They both sat quietly for a few moments until Nicholai spoke. "I still have a house in the city, but it's not a home anymore. It's just a building full of ghosts. I don't go there much at all." He looked over at Danica as she took a drink from the water bottle. "I know you've seen it. You went there first."

"How did you know that?" she asked, a bit surprised, lowering the bottle.

"I can tell. Besides, how else would have known where to find me? My neighbors talk, but they're protective. Someone pointed you here."

Danica looked away. She was impressed with his insight but kept that feeling to herself.

"Can I get you something else?" he asked, changing the subject. "I do have beer and wine down below if you like. Or something stronger if the sailing is making you queasy."

"Water's fine."

"I've been doing this for almost three years," he explained, adjusting the wheel slightly to catch a gust. "It's peaceful and exhilarating at the same time. It's just me, alone with God. I know He's the only one who can make this wind, but I've learned to harness it." She noticed his face getting a little brighter, the stoicism cracking just a fraction. "And when He takes the wind away, He's taught me to enjoy the peace and tranquility that comes with all that stillness."

It was the first time she thought back to his background since actually seeing him. The horror and heartbreak the man had experienced didn't quite add up to the calm, spiritual man sitting across from her. Danica was amazed at the confidence and control he showed maneuvering the Sara Rose. He wasn't broken; he was re-forged.

"Come over here," he said softly but still with a sense of authority.

She stood up slowly, balancing against the tilt of the deck, not knowing what to expect. Danica was surprised at the trust he had already earned with her in such a short time. He gently reached for her hand and pulled her close beside him behind the wheel. Nicholai placed her hand on the stainless steel rim and moved aside.

"She's all yours," he said.

"But..." she protested, pulling back slightly. "I don't know how to drive this."

"Just feel the wind on your face and watch the bow. Don't fight the wheel; guide it. As long as that sail stays full, we're fine."

She placed her other hand on the wheel and gripped it tightly, her knuckles turning white. Nicholai stepped aside and disappeared below deck.

"Would you like some music?" he yelled from inside the dark cabin.

She didn't get a chance to answer before hearing the familiar sound of Brooks and Dunn singing Neon Moon. The melancholy steel guitar drifted up from the cabin, mixing with the wind.

When the sun goes down On my side of town That lonesome feeling Comes to my door The whole world turns blue.

He reappeared with a plate of cheese and crackers and placed it on a small teak table that he unfolded in front of the wheel stand. He walked around and moved behind her, placing both hands on top of hers. She immediately felt his warmth and control, and for some reason, her grip on the wheel tightened. He adjusted her course by a fraction of an inch.

"I can take it now. Please help yourself to anything you want," he said, pointing to the plate. She ignored it and instead returned to her spot on the bench, feeling the adrenaline ebb away.

If you lose your one and only There's always room here for the lonely To watch your broken dreams Dance in and out of the beams Of a neon moon.

"Is this music okay?" he asked.

"Fine," she said. She was amazed at how the words of the song made her feel at that moment. It was actually one of her favorite songs—a guilty pleasure—but she wasn't going to admit that personal detail to him. It felt too intimate.

"Okay, now tell me about it," he said, never taking his eyes off the bow of the Sara Rose.

"I brought the file for you to look through."

"I don't want to see it; no interest in even looking through it. I want to hear it from you."

Danica reached for the file and opened it. She flipped the cover page over, the paper fluttering in the wind.

"Inspector, please," he said, holding up a hand. "Sorry, I meant Danica. I said I don't want to see that. I want to hear it. Hear it from you. How does it smell? How does it feel?" His head turned towards the port side. She turned and saw the marina disappearing behind them in the distance, a cluster of white shapes against the shoreline.

Nicholai continued, "I've been around long enough and attended to more crime scenes than any man should have to endure to know the difference. That file contains reports, words, stats, and more than enough glossy pictures. The real details are in your mind, inside your thoughts, observations, and opinions. That's what's crucial. Your gut feeling is going to solve this. Not all that paper."

She sighed and closed the file. He was right. "Where should I start?" she asked.

"The call," he said. "The one you got in the middle of the night when you couldn't sleep."

"How did you know that?"

"Not important. Just keep going. Tell me about the room."

She looked at him, puzzled, but started filling him in on the details of Rosin's crime scene. She spent the next twenty minutes detailing the scene as best as she could remember. She described the smell of the gunpowder mixed with the expensive leather, the surreal glow of the monitor, the neatness of the dry cleaning. She recalled the autopsy report and Pam Brainerd's notes and comments. Then she told him what she knew about the Simpson case in Tarrant County—the barn, the wealth, the hanging. The entire time she spoke to him, his eyes were focused on the bow of the boat, analyzing the wind, but she could tell he was listening to every inflection in her voice.

"We're still waiting for the toxicology reports on both cases. They should be complete and available tomorrow or the next day at the latest. I've requested a rush on them," she said, finishing her summary.

"I'd be surprised if there was anything in those," he said dismissively. "I wouldn't wait on them."

"Why?"

"Rosin was an intelligent, driven, successful man. Probably graduated top of his class from Harvard, Columbia, somewhere like that. Simpson was a ruthless businessman worth millions who pried and manipulated his way to a nice fortune, but he was still unsatisfied with his life. They both were. Something's going on that caused them to do this. It was presented or perceived as their only way out of a situation."

"What do you think?"

"Obviously, both men met their match. Whoever it is, they are someone far more intelligent and conniving than either of them. Detective, these are not everyday suicides. Control freaks don't just decide to check out on a Tuesday after picking up their laundry. These men were forced into taking that step. They were cornered."

Danica looked off at the horizon. The sun had now almost completely disappeared, dipping below the water line, but an orange and violet glow illuminated the sky. She saw the faint image of a half-moon rising high in the darkening canvas.

"How can you be so sure?"

"I may live on a boat and spend most of my time trying to save the few lost souls I meet, but I still keep up with what's happening. Rosin was a powerful man. I met him a few times years ago at charity galas. He was well connected and floated in just the right circles." Delgado stopped and looked off across the lake. "A man like that, with that kind of prominence and stature, has control—complete control—of his life. He has every part in line with such strict discipline that nothing ever slips by him. He didn't have money problems, and you won't find a drug habit either. I never met Simpson, but I've heard enough about the man and his business antics to know the type. They don't surrender. They negotiate."

Nicholai moved his focus to the boat's performance. He leaned forward and pulled the jib sheet tighter. The sail grabbed the wind and stopped luffing, pulling the boat faster. Danica gripped the side rail tighter as the boat heeled a few more degrees on the port side, the water rushing closer to the rail.

"Now, what makes you believe these two cases are related?" he asked. "Beyond the wealth."

"The suicide notes are identical; same wording, typestyle, and format. And there is a strange word or code at the end of both of them."

"Code? What is it?"

"It's a word I've never heard of. It was typed right under the signature. Tetelestai."

His face dropped, and the brightness disappeared instantly, as if a cloud had passed over the sun. His head jerked hard to face Danica.

"Tetelestai?"

"Yes. What is it? Do you know what that means?"

Delgado stared at the young detective for a moment, his eyes searching hers. His look made her suddenly uncomfortable, and she squirmed slightly on the seat. The silence stretched, heavy and thick.

"It's Greek," he said quickly, his voice tight. "It's an accounting term, originally. It means 'paid in full.' But historically… it's what Jesus said on the cross before he died. It means 'It is finished.'"

Delgado turned his head away, looking back at the wake. She couldn't seem to take her eyes off him, and he felt her stare. She felt there was something else, a deeper resonance to the word for him, but she also knew he wasn't going to say anything more about the subject.

She was the one who decided to move the conversation on. "Where should we start?"

"With them. Study both men and their lives carefully. Look under every rock, and when you're done, look again. Find a common denominator; there has to be one. Find a weakness, a secret, and you'll find what happened."

"You make it sound easy."

He laughed, a dry, humorless sound. "Easy? Don't ever take that attitude when you're dealing with something like this. There is someone behind this. And like I said earlier, whoever it is, is far more intelligent than they were." Nicholai paused, his expression darkening. "And there is a certain evil involved in this as well. Calculated, patient evil."

Danica suddenly felt a chill that had nothing to do with the wind. She crossed her arms tightly across her chest.

"And when that's evident, there's usually no rhyme or reason to any of it. Just destruction."

"So you'll help? You'll get involved?"

"No," he said quickly, shaking his head. "I walked away from all that years ago. I'm done."

"But I can set it up. I'll get you reinstated as a special consultant. The Captain is already—"

"I can't, Detective. No."

"Please, call me Danica."

"Okay, Danica. The answer is still no. I won't help. I can't."

She sat forward, desperation creeping into her voice. "I didn't want to pull this card, but someone from the state has requested your involvement. It came from the top."

"Is that supposed to intimidate me or make me feel honored? Which one?" he grinned, but it didn't reach his eyes. "I might consider it if God or the President called. But I highly doubt that would ever happen."

Danica sat uncomfortably still. She couldn't look at him now, but she wanted to. Finally, after several silent moments, she said, "I know what happened. I read the file, and I'm sorry. It must have been horrible. I can't imagine what you went through, but..."

"You read the file and you can't imagine?" he laughed, a sharp sound that cut the air. "Remember my comment about your file over there? Paper, reports, and pictures. Well, that's all you looked at. That's what you saw. But you have no idea what I have seen and what I now have to live with." He stopped and looked off into the dark Texas sky. "I said no. I can't."

His sudden response frightened her. It was a reaction that didn't fit the calm man she had spent the past hour with. The pain was raw, just beneath the surface.

"I'm sorry. I didn't mean to bring the past back to you. I just need your help. They say you were the most talented profiler and technical investigator in FBI history. I thought I could…"

"Why would they think someone like you could bring me back in? I get requests like this all the time," he said, his voice weary. "And like I said earlier, you're not the first. Or is it because you're a woman? Did they send the attractive one to entice me? Sorry, I don't work that way."

"Listen, this wasn't my idea. I told you someone at the state level has made the request through the Chief. I had nothing to do with this. I'm just the messenger."

"Well, Ms. Messenger, you can now take my answer back."

"I will," she said, standing up as best she could on the moving deck. "And I'll close this case on my own soon."

He looked at her with a sudden concern, the profiler in him reawakening for a split second. "Who's on this with you?"

"Unassigned right now. My former partner retired six weeks ago. But I'm fine. I can handle this," she said. Her confidence was starting to come back through, and she almost believed what she had just said.

Delgado looked hard at the detective. At just the right moment, their eyes met and stayed on each other briefly. He saw the fear she was hiding; she saw the grief he was wearing.

"Be careful." He wanted to say more but didn't.

"I told you, I'll be fine," she said, turning away from his blue eyes.

Her head turned towards a winding sound coming from the bow of the Sara Rose again. The jib sail slowly wrapped around the forestay and quickly disappeared inside itself as Delgado engaged the furling line. Nicholai leaned over and turned the ignition key, and Danica felt the vibration of the diesel engine fire up below her feet. She turned sideways and tucked her left leg under her body and watched as the Sara Rose cleared the breakwater and entered the marina.

The glare of the half-moon now beamed off the calm water inside the marina. It was quiet. She imagined the area being a hub of activity on any given Saturday night. But during the week, on that particular evening, it was silent.

Delgado calmly moved the Sara Rose along the water and turned towards H dock. He eased off the throttle and made a hard right turn, aiming the bow toward the slip space. Silently, the boat eased its way securely inside the space. Before coming to a complete stop, Delgado gracefully leaped onto the dock with a line in his left hand. She watched as his figure disappeared on the far side of the bow, and she felt the boat stop against the bumpers.

Danica stood up, regained her balance and composure, and then reached for the untouched police file. She felt his hand on her shoulder, and it startled her. He noticed but wasn't going to comment or apologize.

"Let me take that," he said, reaching for the file. She handed him the folder, and Nicholai extended his free hand for assistance. Reluctantly,

Danica placed her hand inside his. He gently helped her off the boat and safely onto the dock.

"I did enjoy the company," he said quietly.

"Yeah, fun," she said quickly and with a bite of sarcasm. "Can I have my shoes, please?"

"Certainly can't forget those, can we?" He turned and stepped inside the cabin and returned, handing her the heels. She slipped them on, instantly growing three inches taller and returning to her official stature.

"Another time?" he asked.

She didn't answer. Instead, the detective reached out in an effort to take the file that he still held. But he pulled it back out of her reach.

"Can I say one last thing?" he asked. She knew it really wasn't a question.

"God blessed me with a gift," he said quietly as he lowered his eyes for a moment. When he raised his head back up and looked directly at her, she noticed his bright blue eyes were moist, but they still had a slight glow despite the darkness of the warm Texas evening. "But that gift has now become my curse. It's something I have to live with for the rest of my life. Unlike you, my nightmares don't stop when I wake up. I see things… patterns… motives… that others miss. And once I see them, I can't unsee them."

"Take this any way you want," he continued. "Philosophy, belief, doesn't matter. But mostly it's my warning. It's very difficult entering inside the mind of evil because deep down we all have it in us," he said, his voice dropping to a whisper. "But finding your way back out can be a fearsome journey. I know because I'm still trying to get out."

Nicholai looked up into the black Texas sky, searching for stars that were hidden by the city lights, then back down at Danica. "I've almost made it, but it was only with His help, guidance, and prayer that I've been able to come this far."

Finally, he handed Danica the unopened police file, and their hands touched. Neither of them felt the need to pull away too quickly. She felt comfort in his touch, a strange anchor in the storm she was about to enter, and they both held on to it as long as the moment lasted.

He looked at the detective, his face grave, before finally saying, "Detective, if you do decide to go into that darkness, I beg you, please don't go alone."

Chapter 8

The Sara Rose was already tied down and secured for the night, the dock lines pulled taut against the cleats. Delgado was tired—a deep, marrow-level exhaustion—but the restlessness was already itching beneath his skin. He struggled with the urge to cast off again, debating whether he should untie the lines he had just secured.

He wanted to; he almost felt like he had to. The last few hours and the intense conversation with Inspector Harris had dredged up the silt from the bottom of his soul, bringing back the images and memories he fought daily to suppress. The file she offered was just paper, but the look in her eyes—the determination, the confusion—reminded him of the life he had left behind. Those memories always exhausted him emotionally and drained him physically, leaving him feeling like a hollow shell.

Leaving the marina, the lights, the people, and the noise had become his escape mechanism. It was his own private secret, a way to outrun the ghosts that couldn't swim. He never went out far, maybe a mile or so, but it was always far enough. It was far enough away to leave the city's electric hum behind and spend time on the water in the comfort of the Lord. He usually sailed the Sara Rose south around Heath Point and anchored her in a hidden cove protected by a line of trees. It was quiet, peaceful, and truly isolated—away from anyone asking him anything, away from the expectations of the living. It's what he did when he wanted to be alone with his grief. There was something about being floating on the lake, anchored in the black water, that intensified the peace and solitude. God had certainly shown Nicholai Delgado how to cherish the silence, teaching him that peace wasn't the absence of trouble, but the presence of God within it.

But something told him to stay in the marina on this night. A check in his spirit, heavy and undeniable, anchored him to the dock more securely than any rope. He didn't know what it was, but the more he contemplated his choices, the more he felt the invisible hand pressing him to remain in the slip space. The hunt had come to him; running from it tonight felt futile.

He went below deck, sliding the hatch shut behind him, and turned on the inside cabin lights. The warm yellow glow illuminated the teak interior, casting long shadows. The temperature outside was starting to cool as the Texas heat finally broke, but it was always warmer down below. He slid the port window open and immediately felt the coolness of the night air drift across his face, carrying the scent of water and distant exhaust. He closed his eyes momentarily, leaning his head back, and tried to gather his scattered thoughts.

When he opened his eyes, he looked up at the ceiling of the cabin. "What do I do?" he asked quietly, his voice rough in the silence. "Why are you doing this now? I told You I was done."

Nicholai turned and placed both hands on the small galley counter, leaning his forty-five-year-old frame forward until his knuckles turned white. Some of the weight seemed to leave his body as he pressed down hard, transferring the burden to the fiberglass and wood. Finally, when he straightened up, he felt the gentle, rhythmic motion of the water beneath his feet—a heartbeat he understood.

He reached inside the bottom cabinet and removed the half-empty bottle of Seagram's VO. The amber liquid caught the light. He poured just over an inch into the first heavy glass he saw. Nicholai bent down, opened the small refrigerator, and removed a full bottle of ginger ale. The contents fizzed sharply as the cap was twisted off, the sound loud in the small space. He filled the glass with the soda, diluting the dark color of the expensive rye whiskey into a pale gold.

He lifted the glass. With one long pull, the glass was half empty. He savored the smooth, burning taste of the liquor in his mouth before slowly swallowing, letting the warmth spread through his chest. He thought of finishing the drink completely, of pouring another and drowning the night, but instead, he placed the glass back on the small counter space with a clink. He needed his mind clear, even if clarity hurt.

His weathered, tanned hands moved towards his face, and he rubbed his tired eyes, trying to massage away the headache forming behind his temples. His mind moved in several directions at once—Rosin, Simpson, Tetelestai, Danica—and he eventually took a deep, shuddering breath to center himself.

He turned and looked around the small cabin space. It was tight and close, filled with the essentials of survival and little else, but there was comfort in the small monastery he had created.

He looked down and saw it lying on the small dining table. He always kept it there, within reach for reference and comfort; mostly comfort, but sometimes for answers that seemed to hide between the lines. Delgado reached across the table and picked up the leather-bound Bible. The weathered cover was soft to the touch, and the worn edges showed its age and the desperation of its use over the years. He opened the cover and looked at the handwritten inscription on the first page. His fingers gently traced the fading blue letters, feeling the indentation of the pen.

"Happy Anniversary. Love always, Nic."

It had been a gift; one that was given with purpose and meaning back when their life was full of hope. Nicholai had always given gifts to her with those thoughts in mind. They meant more to her and to him than jewelry or clothes. He had given Jessica the Bible on their eighteenth wedding anniversary, two years before the world ended. It was one of the few memories he had brought from the house to the Sara Rose. There were a few other items scattered around the boat—a framed photo, a small cross—but this was the one he cherished most because her hands had held it every day.

The inside pages of her Bible were well-read, the paper crinkled from turning, and the yellow highlighted sections always stood out like beacons. He often wondered what she was thinking when she highlighted certain passages. Was she looking for strength? Was she thankful? Or did she, in some maternal intuition, know she would need these verses for a darkness she couldn't yet see?

Nicholai closed the Bible but held it tight in his hand, feeling its weight. With his free hand, he grabbed his glass, swirled the remaining ginger ale and whiskey, and took another drink. He looked up through the companionway to the square of stars visible above, then took the stairs topside.

The cool breeze coming in off the lake felt refreshing against his warm skin, drying the sweat from his earlier exertion. The lights from the interstate flickered off in the distance, a river of white and red twisting through the darkness. The sounds of the traffic were hidden by the rhythmic clanging of halyards against the masts of the other sailboats in the marina—a chaotic wind chime. He recalled a while back when he found the sound annoying, a constant interruption, but he had learned to enjoy it and appreciate the invisible breeze that created it all. It was proof that things moved even when you couldn't see them.

He took a seat on the cockpit bench where the young inspector had sat only an hour before. He could almost smell her perfume lingering in the air, a stark contrast to the smell of diesel and lake water. Nicholai leaned against the fiberglass side of the Sara Rose. The Bible lay in his lap while he held the drink loosely in his hand.

Out of the three important women he cherished most in his life—Jessica, his daughter Sara, and this vessel—the Sara Rose was all that was left now. She was the only one he could still protect, the only one who went where he steered her.

He looked off into the darkness of the lake for a few moments, watching the reflection of the moon dance on the black water. He closed his eyes, listening to the wind.

"Is it time?" he asked quietly to no one in particular, but to the One who always listened. He feared the answer, because deep down, he knew the peace he had found on the water was just a pause, not an ending. The hunt was calling him back.

Chapter 9

"You've got a visitor," Detective Chris Leininger said, his mouth full of egg and chorizo.

He had been working on his third breakfast burrito when Harris walked into the squad room, and the smell of onions, cumin, and grease hung heavy in his cubicle like a fog. It was a visceral assault on the senses so early in the morning. He swallowed hard, the lump traveling visibly down his throat, before telling her anymore. Withholding information was the last remaining morsel of authority Leininger had left in his stalling career, and he savored every moment of it just as much as his breakfast. He wiped a smear of bright red salsa from his chin with the back of his hand, enjoying making her wait, watching her patience fray at the edges.

"Who?" Danica asked, already dreading the answer. She dropped her purse onto her desk, the thud echoing her frustration. She didn't have time for Leininger's games today; she was running on caffeine and nerves.

"Some guy with a nice tan. Last name is Delgado, I think. He had an official pass from the Chief's office, so I let him in." He grabbed a stained Styrofoam cup, the rim chewed and misshapen, and took a long, slurping drink of lukewarm coffee. He made a show of refreshing his memory, playing the gatekeeper. "He said he was helping you with

53

the Rosin investigation. Didn't know you needed a babysitter, Harris. Thought you were the department's golden girl."

"Where is he?" Danica asked, her annoyance spiking at the lackluster attitude of the aging detective. She ignored the jab about needing a babysitter, though it stung more than she let on. She scanned the room, looking for the intruder, her eyes narrowing.

"He walked right in, took the case files off your desk like he owned the place, and went into interrogation room four. He's been there for a few hours. He closed the door, and I haven't heard a sound from him since. Probably rearranging the furniture."

Danica wanted to say something biting, something that would wipe the smirk off Leininger's face, but she didn't have the energy to waste on him. She turned and walked to her desk and confirmed that the Rosin and Simpson files were indeed missing. The empty space on her desk felt like a personal violation; those files were her responsibility, her burden, and someone had just walked in and claimed them. Her sanctuary had been violated. She looked down the hall and saw the heavy steel door to room four closed tight. A sliver of fluorescent light appeared under the door, cutting through the hallway shadows like a laser. She walked over, her heels clicking aggressively on the linoleum—a warning rhythm to anyone listening—and grabbed the door handle. The cold metal bit into her palm. She paused for a split second, let out a deep, centering sigh to compose her face into a mask of indifference, and entered.

Delgado had both files open, and papers were scattered across the long, scarred metal table in what looked like chaos but was likely a specific, calculated order. He wore wire-rimmed reading glasses, which she hadn't seen the day before on the boat. The frames softened his face, making him look like a distinguished college professor grading theses rather than a retired FBI hunter searching for patterns in blood. His navy blue button-down shirt was crisp, pressed, and definitely not standard police issue; it spoke of a man who still maintained discipline even in retirement.

"Good morning," he said without looking up from the autopsy report he had been studying. He underlined something with a pencil, the scratch of graphite loud in the silence.

She didn't respond. She just stood by the door, hand still on the knob, refusing to fully enter his domain. She watched him work, analyzing him just as he was analyzing the files.

"You look surprised," he said, finally removing his glasses and looking up at the detective. His blue eyes were clear, sharp, and devoid of the melancholy she had seen on the lake. They were the eyes of a predator now, not a mourner.

"I am," she said, walking to the opposite side of the table, putting the metal barrier between them. "After yesterday, I didn't ever expect to see you again. You were pretty adamant about staying retired. You practically threw me off your boat."

"Things change," he replied, putting his glasses back on and refocusing on the report in his hand. "Perspectives shift when you let them."

"What happened? Did the President call you?"

"For now, can we just drop that?"

"No, we can't. Why are you here?" she asked, leaning her hands on the table, encroaching on his space. "Yesterday you were preaching about the peace of the lake. Today you're in a police station, sitting in a room that smells like desperation."

"Because it's the right thing to do."

"Oh, and you always do the right thing, correct?" Her sarcasm was biting, a defense mechanism springing up to protect her territory. "Must be nice to be so righteous, to just float in and out of people's jobs whenever your conscience pricks you."

"Remember, you came looking for me. Do you want my help or not?"

"Me?" she snapped back quickly. "No, I don't. But this wasn't my choice. It still isn't. It was an order, and I'm just following orders." Danica shut the door hard, the sound reverberating in the small room like a gunshot, and looked down on Delgado. "I guess you can say I'm just doing the 'right thing' too."

"And you always follow orders, correct? Is that how you see yourself? A good soldier?"

"Whatever." She couldn't find the right comeback; he was too calm, too centered. Instead, she decided to take control because that was when Danica Harris felt the most comfortable. He had beaten her emotionally the day before on the water, exposing her vulnerability, and she wasn't going to allow that to happen again on her turf.

"Fine by me," she said, pulling a metal chair across the floor. It scraped loudly, a harsh sound in the quiet room designed to grate on the nerves. She sat across from him, crossing her arms. "But we need to set some ground rules first."

Nicholai placed the report down on the table, removed his glasses, and folded them deliberately. He stared across at the detective, then put both hands on the table and clasped them together tight.

It was the first time she noticed the gold wedding ring on his finger. She hadn't noticed it the day before on the Sara Rose, perhaps because he had been moving so much, or perhaps because she hadn't wanted to look. The sight of it—a symbol of a bond that no longer existed, a promise kept to a ghost—almost threw her off again. But she pushed past it, hardening her resolve.

"First and foremost, I am the lead on this," she stated firmly, locking eyes with him. "You have the position of a special consultant, which means you consult. You consult with me. You don't override me, and you don't go rogue. Second," she continued, ticking the point off on her finger, "I need to know everything you know and everything you're doing. No secrets, no mysterious disappearances." She watched for a reaction, but his face was a mask. "I want to know what you think and what you're doing even before you do it."

Nicholai looked away and stared at the nondescript cinder block wall of the interrogation room, painted that depressing institutional grey that was meant to suppress hope. He seemed to be weighing her words against his own internal code.

"So tell me, what you've found out so far?" she asked, tapping the table impatiently.

"Fine." Delgado smiled, a small, enigmatic shifting of his lips that didn't quite reach his eyes. "Not much on the case yet," he said. "But regarding the investigation environment... let's see."

He placed the report neatly back inside the file and closed the cover, smoothing the manila folder. He placed both hands back on top of the file and clasped his hands together again, leaning forward slightly, invading her personal space with nothing but his gaze.

"So far, I've discovered that I've been asked to help someone who doesn't really want my help. She is an independent, intelligent, capable, driven, attractive woman who has developed a deep-seated mistrust for men that borders on disgust. You stand with your weight on your back foot, ready to retreat or attack, never just to exist. You checked the exit twice before you sat down."

Danica stiffened, her spine locking against the chair.

"Could be some unresolved daddy issues lurking below the surface," he continued, his voice smooth and clinical. "High achiever, seeking validation from authority figures but resenting them at the same time. You hated Leininger not just because he's gross, but because he represents the stagnation you fear. I believe she's quite stubborn, too. I'm guessing maybe a failed marriage had a lot to do with it as well?" Nicholai stared hard at Danica, watching her pupils dilate. "No, wait... no ring tan line, but the defensive posture suggests deep hurt. You guard your left hand. It didn't even get that far. He broke her heart—or perhaps her trust—before they could take that big step."

Danica hid her thoughts behind a stony expression, but her heart hammered against her ribs. His comments were invasive, accurate, and completely violated the professional barrier she tried to maintain. It felt less like an observation and more like a vivisection.

Delgado continued, relentless. "She has a strained relationship with her father—you mentioned doing the 'right thing' with a tone of resentment that suggests obligation rather than love. And her mother passed away not too long ago; I see the grief in the way you pause when you talk about the past, a momentary breathless gap in your speech. Unexpected, I assume. She has trouble sleeping—the dark circles under the makeup give that away, no matter how much concealer you use—drinks far too much coffee to compensate for the nightmares, and doesn't like anyone to get close." Nicholai stared across the table, his blue eyes piercing through her defenses. "How am I doing so far?"

"You're not," she lied, her voice flat, though her knuckles were white where she gripped the table edge. "I was referring to the case, not my personal life. And for the record, that parlor trick is exactly why people find profilers annoying. It's arrogant."

"Oh, really? Well, I don't know anything more about these cases than you do right now. All I've been doing is getting up to speed with what everyone else knows. That's all that's in here," he said, patting the file dismissively. "Reports are static. They tell you what happened, not why. The leads and answers are out there, in the world, not in this room."

"Well, where do we start?" she asked, eager to shift the focus off herself before he dug any deeper.

"We start by adjusting some of those guidelines which you seem to have put in place already. Now let's get something straight, Inspector Harris. You have a job to do, but this is not my job anymore. I don't need the pension, and I don't need the glory. You asked me to help. I'm here, and I have my own reasons for getting involved."

"And what are those reasons?" she asked, genuinely curious now.

"That's something I will keep to myself for now. It's my business, and don't worry, it will not interfere with the investigation. But I work by instinct, not just procedure. If you want my help, you have to give me the leash to run. I chase the scent, not the paperwork."

"Fair enough, for now," she conceded, realizing she didn't have much choice if she wanted the case solved. "Where do we start?"

"We start by getting out of here. This room smells like fear and stale smoke. It stifles creativity. Plus," he checked his watch, "it's been what... fifteen, twenty minutes since your last coffee? You're starting to fidget, tapping your foot. Let's go."

Chapter 10

The ride was quiet; the silence inside the unmarked Ford Taurus was thick enough to choke on. Neither spoke for the longest time, the only sound the hum of the tires on the hot asphalt and the rhythmic thump-thump of expansion joints on the highway. Even the usual small talk standing in line at Starbucks had been strained—forced comments about the humidity and the Dallas Cowboys' upcoming season while they waited for their order, surrounded by the chaotic noise of espresso machines and chatter. Danica had ordered her usual grande drip, black, needing the bitterness, and Nicholai waited for an extra hot latte. They both kept their distance from each other, physically standing on opposite sides of the pickup counter, neither wanting to let the other in yet.

Back in the car, the air conditioning blasted against the Texas heat, creating a cold, artificial bubble that separated them from the world outside. Delgado was the first to break the standoff while Harris seemed preoccupied with maneuvering the car through the aggressive interstate traffic, using the driving as an excuse to avoid conversation.

"I hope I didn't offend you earlier," he asked, looking out the passenger window at the passing strip malls and glass towers, trying to avoid any possible chance of direct eye contact with her. He seemed fascinated by the blur of commerce passing by.

"When?" she asked, feigning ignorance as she merged lanes, cutting off a pickup truck with practiced aggression.

"Back in the interrogation room. You asked what I had found, and I went into that rude little rampage about you. Profiling the partner is... bad form. It's a defense mechanism of my own. I apologize."

"Not really, no," she said, gripping the steering wheel a little tighter. "I've had worse said to my face by perps. But how did you know all that? It wasn't just lucky guessing."

"Was I correct in my assumptions?"

"From what I remember... yeah, pretty close. Scary close," she admitted, glancing at him for a fraction of a second. "It makes me wonder what else you see."

"Good. I sometimes wonder if I've lost it," he smiled, a genuine, self-deprecating expression, and she noticed the tension in his shoulders drop slightly. "It's a muscle. If you don't use it, it atrophies. I haven't flexed it in a long time."

"Why did you feel the need to do that anyway? Show off? Prove you're the alpha in the room?" she asked, her tone softening just a degree.

"Partly," he admitted. "But mostly, I figured if we're going to work together on these cases—life and death cases—it's only fitting I know as much about you as you know about me. We need to know where the cracks are. If pressure is applied, I need to know where you'll break."

"How do you know what I know?"

"I saw the file in your desk drawer this morning. The one on my family," he said, looking away again, but this time he wasn't smiling. His voice was low, heavy with the memory. "You didn't hide it very well. Or maybe you wanted me to see it."

"I did look through some of it," she said, slightly embarrassed at being caught. "I needed to know who I was dealing with. It wasn't morbid curiosity; it was due diligence. Listen, I'm very sorry about what happened. Like I said the other day, I can't imagine what you went through."

"That file doesn't... can't begin to tell the whole story. It lists the facts, the times, the causes of death. It doesn't list the silence that comes after. It doesn't mention the birthdays missed or the clothes still hanging in the closet."

There was an awkward silence for several moments as the car idled at a red light. The engine hummed, filling the space between them.

"It's taken me some time to try and separate the job from the personal," Delgado finally said, watching a pedestrian cross the street, a young woman with blonde hair that made him flinch slightly. "I still can't do it completely. It's a struggle that I have to deal with daily. Every case looks like that case. Every victim looks like them."

"How does someone even begin to do that?"

"If I had that answer… I'd be a different man. All I know is that the line is blurred. Sometimes it disappears entirely."

"What line?"

"The line between the investigation and the tragedy. I couldn't focus on a case without crossing over it. I started seeing the killer in everyone I interrogated. I started seeing Jessica and Sara in every victim. It made the investigation impossible because I wasn't seeking justice anymore; I was seeking revenge. And revenge makes you sloppy."

"Is that why you left the Bureau?"

"That's part of the reason, yeah. I was a liability. A loose cannon with a badge."

"What's the other part?"

"I needed answers," he said, looking in her direction, but she was too busy watching the traffic flow to meet his gaze.

"What answers? Who killed them?"

"No. Bigger answers. Why me? Why them?" Delgado stated, his voice intensifying, filling the small cabin of the car. "How do I now live, go on with the choices I've made? If there is a God, how could He let this happen? I spent my life fighting evil, standing in the gap, and evil walked right into my living room while I was looking the other way."

"Have you found them? The answers?" Danica didn't know if she really wanted to know. The rawness of his pain was terrifying, a glimpse into an abyss she hoped never to fall into.

Nicholai looked away for a moment, watching the city pass by, the reflection of the buildings sliding over the glass. "No, not everything. Some things remain a mystery, locked away until the end. But I know now that God is the only One who has the capacity to hold that much pain. Only He knows the reasons, and in order for me to survive every single day—to literally get out of bed without putting a gun in my mouth—I have to look to Him for everything. I have to."

He took a sip of his latte, the cup trembling slightly in his hand. "Every morning before my foot hits the floor, I ask the Holy Spirit to direct my every thought and movement. It's the only thing that keeps me going. It's not piety, Danica. It's survival. It's the only oxygen I have left."

He stopped and looked away again. Danica tried to look at him, really look at him, and she struggled to find the right words. The silence wasn't awkward anymore; it was reverent.

"I don't want the past to be my identity anymore," he said quietly. But she heard his comment loud and clear.

"I refuse to live out the remainder of my life where I am now," he said, his voice gaining strength, shifting from grief to determination. "I feel I am stagnating at this point. Locked in that marina, safe but useless. And I'm convinced there's more."

Nicholai looked at her again, but she seemed focused on the road, though her grip on the wheel betrayed her attention. "There's more of the Holy Spirit and more of God than I am currently experiencing. I want to go there, not just intellectually, but in life, with everything that I am. I want to find a way to bring justice without losing my soul again. I want to finish the race, not just drop out."

Chapter 11

The twelve-foot-high solid wood arched door was meant to send a specific message to anyone standing on the porch: private, protected, and better than you. It was a fortress masquerading as a home. Inspector Harris took the lead, smoothing her blazer before she pushed the brass intercom button to the right of the door. She waited, listening to the silence of the exclusive Highland Park neighborhood. It was a quiet that money bought—no traffic, no sirens, just the manicured rustle of leaves.

She turned towards Delgado, who was busy staring up at the security camera tucked away in the corner of the portico. He wasn't just looking at it; he was analyzing its blind spots. Danica looked up, following his gaze, but the sharp click of the door latch releasing from inside brought her eyes and thoughts back down to earth.

A mid-thirties brunette opened the door slightly, peering out through the crack. "Can I help you?" she asked quietly, her voice brittle.

Danica immediately noticed the sheer amount of makeup on the woman. It was a thick, frantic application of foundation and mascara, a porcelain mask attempting to hide the devastation underneath. It was obvious she had been crying for hours; the redness around her eyes defied the concealer, and her lips were pale and trembling.

"Good morning," Danica said, keeping her voice soft but authoritative. She flashed her police ID in front of the woman. "I'm Inspector Harris and this is Mr. Delgado. We're here to see Ms. Rosin."

"Yes," the woman said, looking down, almost ashamed to be seen in the light of day.

"Ms. Rosin?" she asked to confirm. "Ashley Rosin?"

Danica didn't wait for a response; the body language confirmed it. "We're sorry for your loss, and I know this is a difficult time, but we have a few questions regarding your husband's death. May we come in?"

The grieving widow turned to look behind her into the shadows of the house, as if checking for permission or perhaps fearing someone was there. Ashley Rosin seemed nervous, her fingers picking at the hem of her silk robe, as she turned back to face Harris and Delgado. Nicholai remained silent, his presence looming in the periphery.

"Questions? Why are the police investigating a suicide? I thought... I thought it was closed."

"It's all just standard procedure, ma'am. We have to dot the i's and cross the t's," Harris replied professionally, stepping slightly closer to the threshold.

"Can't this wait? It's really not a good time... I haven't even called the funeral home yet."

"Ms. Rosin, I promise we'll be brief. We just have a few questions, then we'll be gone. It's better to get this out of the way now so you can focus on... other arrangements."

Frustrated, Rosin exhaled a sharp breath, opened the heavy door, and backed away. Danica entered first, the cool air of the house hitting her instantly. Delgado followed close behind. He still hadn't said a word, but his eyes were already working, scanning the foyer of the large home like a camera lens, recording every detail.

"Is there somewhere we can sit and talk?" Danica asked.

Quietly and with an obvious lack of energy, Ashley Rosin replied, "This way."

Delgado and Harris followed the widow through a massive great room filled with an Old World flair that felt more like a museum than a living space. It smelled of lemon polish and emptiness. An open second-floor balcony ran the entire width of the home, exposing the upper landing like a gallery. A massive, freestanding curved staircase joined the first floor to the second, acting as the architectural focal point. Weathered, hand-scraped wood floors brought a rustic elegance to the home, but they echoed their footsteps loudly, emphasizing how few people actually walked there.

They followed closely behind Rosin through a large opening behind the staircase into a bright, casual den that overlooked the pool. A massive stone fireplace along the back wall dominated the room, cold and clean. Two oversized burgundy sofas and a matching chair were angled to create a comfortable sitting area in the center of the large room, though the cushions looked stiff and unused.

Ashley Rosin sat down gently on the sofa, released a loud, shuddering sigh, and motioned for Danica and Delgado to sit on the adjoining sofa. Danica sat, pulling out her notepad, while Delgado remained off to the side, standing. He eyed the room, taking in the spacing, the art, the lack of personal photos. He moved silently towards the fireplace and looked at the unique setting on the mantle. There was a collection of expensive candles that had never been lit, intricate hand-carved wooden boxes, and a few other small items placed with geometric precision.

"I don't understand all this," the widow stated from across the room, wrapping her arms around herself. "Why are you really here?"

"This is interesting," Delgado said, ignoring her question as he picked up a small hand-carved wooden mask from the mantle. It was a grotesque face, mouth sewn shut. "Did you get it locally?"

"No," Ashley replied, distracted by his intrusion. "James picked it up on one of his trips to South America. Brazil, I think. I really don't remember. He collected things. What is this all about?"

Danica looked over at Delgado. She was starting to become embarrassed by his casual and seemingly crude demeanor in a house of mourning. She quickly turned her attention back towards Ashley Rosin to salvage the interview.

The Inspector noticed a boutique tissue box and a half-empty glass of red wine on the large coffee table. It was barely 10:00 AM. Crumbled, used tissues lay on the floor like fallen petals. Ashley reached back and pulled a cashmere comforter off the back of the sofa, then wrapped it tightly around her shoulders as if she were freezing. The heavy makeup couldn't hide the fact she had spent hours crying; she appeared pale, and her eyes were sunk deep in her face, dark circles bruising the skin. Despite her present appearance, Danica could tell the widow was once a very attractive and vibrant woman, the kind of trophy that men like James Rosin acquired to complete their collection.

"We're just trying to be as thorough as we possibly can, Ms. Rosin. Your husband was a very prominent man in North Texas," Harris stated, keeping her tone neutral. There wasn't much compassion evident in her voice; she needed answers, not tears. "And I promised we'd be brief."

"Do you mind if I..." Delgado's voice quietly interrupted the detective again.

Rosin's wife looked up, startled, and Harris turned to look at Nicholai with a warning glare. He had moved away from the fireplace and stood closer to the doorway leading to the back of the house.

"I'd like to look around your husband's office to get a better idea of who he was, if you don't mind. The living room tells me about the house, but the office tells me about the man."

"What?" Ashley asked, a bit perturbed by his wandering. "Yeah, sure, whatever you need. It's down that hall, the last door on the left. Just... don't make a mess."

Nicholai didn't wait. He disappeared from the room before she had even finished her sentence, moving with the silent grace of a cat.

Danica cleared her throat, drawing Ashley's attention back. "Ms. Rosin, had your husband been acting any different lately?" she started, diving right into her direct questions. "Had you noticed any changes in your husband's behavior or personality at all? Mood swings? Paranoia?"

"No," she replied, reaching for the wine glass and then stopping herself. "Everything seemed the same. Business was always a priority for James. His mind was almost always focused on that. He lived in that bank."

"Did you ever feel neglected?"

"Neglected? Now that's funny," she said, a bitter, dry laugh escaping her throat. "Excuse me? I don't remember your name."

"Inspector Danica Harris."

"Well, Inspector, when you marry into all this," she said, waving a hand around the expansive room, "you are never a priority and never will be. You are an asset. That's part of the whole image you learn to accept. Yes, there's neglect, but the money, the prestige, and everything that comes with that can take the edge off just enough to make one's life bearable. It's a transaction, Inspector. I provided the arm candy; he provided the Amex."

Harris suddenly felt uncomfortable with the naked honesty of the statement. "So, had money ever become an issue between the two of you?"

"Don't know. I have no idea what we have... or I should say had. I've always been able to spend what I want, when I wanted. James never questioned that. I guess it was his way of making up for what I really lacked. Guilt is a powerful currency."

"Ms. Rosin, do you have any idea why your husband would take his life? Was there a specific trigger?"

"No, I don't. I haven't got a clue. We were supposed to go to Cabo next week."

Danica thought for a moment before asking the next question. "Had he been out of town a lot lately or been coming home from the office later than usual?"

"No, just the usual business trips. He had his yearly hunting trip a few months ago. That was something he's done for years. I guess it was his male bonding time. He liked to pretend he was rugged."

"Was he spending time alone, or did he seem preoccupied?"

"I know the financial markets have been unstable and that always agitated him, but no, nothing out of the ordinary. He was James. Cold, distant, efficient."

"Who were his close friends? People he would associate with outside of work?"

"James only had one or two friends that he kept in touch with; his hunting buddies. He didn't seem to have the time or any interest in socializing unless it was a networking event. He didn't have friends, Inspector. He had associates."

"Ms. Rosin, my next question is standard procedure, so please don't take any offense. I have to ask it."

Ashley turned away, pulling the blanket tighter. She knew what was coming.

"Do you, or had you ever, suspected another woman?"

She laughed again, but it wasn't from joy. It was a sharp, jagged sound. She reached for another tissue from the box and then put her head down for a moment. When she did raise her head, she found it impossible to look directly at Danica.

"Of course," she finally replied, her voice barely a whisper. "That's part of the lifestyle I bought into. I'm an educated woman, Inspector, and certainly not naïve. Men like James need constant validation."

"How did you know?" Harris asked gently.

"He lost interest in me years ago. A woman can always tell when that is going on. You don't need to look for lipstick on a collar or check credit card statements. You just feel it in your stomach. The silence changes."

"Do you know who?"

"Of course not!" she said quickly and with bite. Danica could tell she was getting agitated with the line of questioning. But the grieving widow continued, defending her ignorance. "Money buys privacy, and prestige ensures security. At first, I wanted to know, but then after a while, I realized I couldn't spend all my hours wondering and searching. It tears you up inside as it is. Why add fuel to the fire? Ignorance is expensive, but it's peaceful."

"Ms. Rosin, is there anything you can think of that could help us figure all this out? Names, places, anything?"

"Listen, I'm trying to figure out my next move. I can't... no, I won't spend my time trying to figure out why James did this. He was always a selfish, self-centered man. He died the way he lived—thinking only of himself. Don't get me wrong. I knew what I was doing when I got into this marriage, but I never expected it would end like this."

"What do you mean your next move?"

"His life insurance doesn't pay off when the cause of death is suicide. I was informed of that this morning by the lawyers," she spat the words out, the anger finally breaking through the grief. "I don't know what I have to deal with as of yet. The accounts are frozen. My future is the priority now. It has to be. He left me with a mortgage on a mausoleum and no liquidity."

"One last question, ma'am, then we'll be going. Does the word 'Tetelestai' mean anything to you?"

Ashley Rosin looked perplexed while she thought, her brow furrowing beneath the heavy foundation. "No. Is that Italian? Never heard of it."

Danica stared at her for a moment, looking for a flicker of recognition, but saw only genuine confusion and exhaustion. She didn't know what more to ask. She hadn't learned anything new, and the trip now seemed to be a waste of time. There wasn't much to go on, and she could now tell Rosin's widow was more consumed with financial anger than tragic grief. She felt the whole afternoon was a dead end.

Just as she was about to close the interview, Delgado reappeared in the room behind her. He moved so quietly that Ashley jumped slightly.

"Ms. Rosin?" he asked quietly, holding up a slim silver laptop. "I found this on his desk. I wonder if we might borrow your husband's laptop for a while. It may give us some clue as to why this all happened and what his state of mind was before all this happened. The office was... sterile. This seems to be the only thing personal in there."

"Take it," she said, waving a hand dismissively. "He had that thing so locked up and protected, I never could use it; password after password. He took it everywhere. Good luck with it. Keep it for all I care. Maybe it has the name of his whore on it."

"Thank you again, and we're sorry for your loss. We'll see ourselves out," Harris said, standing to her feet. "I'll leave my card if you think of anything that might help. Anything at all." She placed her card on the coffee table next to the half-empty tissue box. Ashley Rosin started to weep again, the anger fading back into despair, and reached for another tissue.

Nicholai had the laptop under his arm, and with his free hand, he tugged on Harris' sleeve. Nothing was spoken, but the urgency was clear. They quietly exited the room, leaving the widow alone in her cavernous den, and made their way to the front door.

Danica opened the heavy arched door, walked outside into the blinding Texas heat, and waited while Delgado took one final look around the foyer. He closed the door behind them, the heavy thud sealing the cold, hollow echo inside the elaborate home.

"Let's go," Delgado said, walking briskly toward the car. "Before she changes her mind."

Chapter 12

“It's about power,” he finally said, breaking the heavy silence that had settled over the car.

Neither had spoken for the first few minutes after pulling away from Rosin's home. They drove slowly through the exclusive subdivision, passing manicured lawns that looked like green velvet and wrought iron gates that cost more than most people's yearly salaries. It was a pristine, sterile world where imported vehicles sat in driveways like sculptures, and the ugliness of life was hidden behind twelve-foot mahogany doors.

Danica noticed Nicholai was consumed in his own thoughts, his eyes tracking the passing mansions with a look of disdain mixed with pity. She couldn't tell where his mind was heading or what specific detail he was dissecting, so she decided to remain quiet, keeping her hands at ten and two on the wheel, waiting for him to speak first.

“What is?” she finally questioned, glancing at him. “The suicide?”

“The motive. All of it,” he replied, shifting in his seat. “He's doing this to gain a sense of power. Not just over himself, but over the people he leaves behind.”

“What about money?” Danica countered. “In a neighborhood like this, it's usually about the money.”

"Well, that could be part of it too. It could be he believes money buys power, happiness, status," Delgado said, rubbing his chin. "But men like Rosin… they don't kill themselves because they're broke. They kill themselves because they've lost control. And in his final act, he tried to regain it."

"I didn't let on to her that we suspect more than a suicide," Danica said, checking her rearview mirror as the gates of the community closed behind them. "She has no idea that anything else was going on. She thinks he just checked out."

"Did she know about the infidelity?" Nicholai asked abruptly.

Danica nearly hit the brakes. "How did you know?"

"It was just a feeling at first. The way she talked about him—cold, transactional. But I was able to check out the master bedroom and bathroom while you were downstairs asking the standard questions."

Danica looked over at Delgado, who was staring at nothing in particular through the passenger window, watching the city landscape shift from mansions to strip malls. "And what did you find? Did you find a note? A number?"

"No, nothing that obvious. I found the psychology of a desperate man," he said. "When a man of Rosin's age and tenure gets himself involved in a new relationship, he starts to care more about his appearance. He stops looking at the bank ledger and starts looking in the mirror. I found high-end anti-aging cream—the kind that costs three hundred dollars an ounce—hidden in the back of the vanity. I found newer underwear in his drawer, silk boxers instead of the cotton briefs he's probably worn for twenty years. And a few new shirts in the closet, tags removed but clearly unworn. They were a completely different brand and style than the older ones—more European, more fitted. More expensive."

"Okay?" It wasn't a question, but a prompt. She replied with some skepticism. "Maybe he was just going through a mid-life crisis."

"Don't act surprised. It's a tale as old as time. Women do the same thing," he said, finally looking at her with a knowing grin. "I'm sure even you have that special outfit wrapped in tissue and hidden away in the back of your top drawer, waiting for the right occasion or the right person."

She did—a black silk dress she hadn't worn in three years—but there was no chance of her taking their discussion in that direction. She wasn't about to discuss her lingerie drawer with a consultant she met yesterday.

"Here's what I don't understand," Danica said, steering the conversation back to safe ground. "That saying, the Greek word for 'it is finished.' If it's finished, then why is he still doing it? If Simpson was the first, then why keep going with this? Why make Rosin type it out too?"

70

Delgado didn't answer immediately. The question hung in the air, mixing with the hum of the air conditioner.

Danica felt the need to fill the silence. "If you want my opinion, I think it's a revenge thing. Payback for something these two did. Maybe a deal gone wrong, or a partnership that dissolved."

"It very well could be. Revenge can give one a certain sense of power as well, a feeling of divine retribution," Delgado mused. "But that feeling doesn't last. It burns hot and fast, like magnesium. This feels... colder. More calculated."

"Do you think we'll find anything on that?" Danica asked, motioning to the silver laptop resting on Delgado's knees.

"I don't know, but it's a common denominator in both incidents. Both men were possessive of their digital lives."

"What are you thinking?" she asked, turning off the freeway onto the access road.

Nicholai thought for a moment, longer than usual, and the wait made Danica uncomfortable. He ran his hand over the smooth metal surface of the computer.

"Every man has his secrets," he finally said. "The burnt SIM cards from the cell phones mean both of them were trying to hide something specific, likely communication. Rosin's computer in his office is networked directly into the bank's mainframe—it's monitored, backed up, watched by IT security. He was an intelligent man. I don't think he'd be dumb enough to store anything incriminating on there," Delgado said, tapping the laptop lid. "And Ms. Rosin certainly doesn't seem like the financial genius type who would crack his encryption. Why would he have to secure this laptop so tight? Why all the passwords? Because this is where the real James Rosin lived."

"We'll drop it off at Forensic IT and see what they can pull off of it," Danica suggested.

"No," Delgado said sharply. "If we send it to the lab, it gets logged. It gets put in a queue. We lose days, maybe weeks. I have a better idea. Did the Fort Worth police take Simpson's computer?"

"Yes, they did. I saw it logged in the evidence file from what I recall. It should still be in the evidence locker in Fort Worth."

"Turn around," he said quickly, his voice carrying the authority of his former rank. "I haven't been to Fort Worth in quite a while. We need to compare them side-by-side. If there's a pattern, it's hidden in the binary code."

Chapter 13

"Tetelestai," he said, thinking aloud. The word was supposed to slip out quietly, a private muttering to himself, but the interior of the car was quiet enough that Danica heard it. Or so she thought. Or maybe it was just on her mind as well, echoing in the silence.

"Yes, I know," she finally said so he could hear, keeping her eyes on the road. "You said that meant 'it is finished.' You mentioned it on the boat."

Delgado took a deep breath before answering, shifting the laptop on his knees. The air in the car felt suddenly thin. "There's more," he said without looking at her, staring straight ahead at the heat shimmering off the asphalt. "A lot more. It's not just a definition; it's a declaration."

Danica continued to drive, but without even being aware, her foot eased off the gas pedal, and the car slowed down. She waited for him to continue, sensing that he was accessing a part of his brain—and his history—that he usually kept locked away. He sat in silence for a long moment, watching the telephone poles whip past. She started getting annoyed at his silence, but she wasn't sure if it was at him or the tension filling the vehicle.

Finally, she spoke. "Well, are you going to fill me in? Or do I need to enroll in seminary?"

"John 19, somewhere around verse twenty-eight," he finally said, his voice taking on a rhythmic, reciting quality. "Jesus was on the cross. He had been beaten, mocked, and crucified. In his final moments, knowing that all things had been accomplished, He claimed to be thirsty. The guards that had been assigned to watch over Him soaked a sponge in wine vinegar and put it on a stalk of hyssop and lifted it to His lips. The vinegar acted like a mild painkiller to ease His misery. After He took some, Jesus said, 'Tetelestai.' Loosely translated, it means 'it is finished.' Then He bowed His head and gave up His spirit."

"Okay, but I still don't get the connection," Danica claimed, frowning. "Why would a suicidal banker and a retired oil tycoon use the last words of Christ? Are they claiming to be martyrs?"

"In Greek, it's the perfect passive tense of the word telos," Delgado explained, ignoring her question for the moment to lay the foundation. "That means to end; to bring something to completion; to accomplish; to fulfill. Or as in this case, to finish. Anything that has reached telos has arrived at completion, maturity, or perfection."

Nicholai again sat quietly for several moments before continuing. A chill seemed to move through the car, despite the Texas sun blazing outside. Danica reached out and turned the air conditioner down slightly, but the cold seemed to be coming from the passenger seat.

"There are several nuances to that word as well," he said, turning to look at her profile. "Some of them have great significance. First, this was Jesus' statement that He had finished the work God had sent Him to do. The work having been fully completed, He died. Some scholars say it meant 'I have done exactly what you requested.' In that moment when Jesus cried out, He was telling the entire world—and the heavens—that He had faithfully fulfilled the Father's will and that the mission was now accomplished. He had been faithful to His assignment even in the face of unfathomable challenges."

"I'm still not getting the connection to all this," she said, confused with what Nicholai was trying to explain. It sounded like a Sunday sermon, not a criminal profile. "It wasn't making sense. These men weren't completing a holy mission. They were running away."

Nicholai continued, his voice dropping lower. "The word tetelestai was also the equivalent of the Hebrew word spoken by the high priests when they presented a perfect sacrificial lamb—one that was without spot or blemish. The animal was perfect in every way. Every year, the high priest would pour the blood of that spotless lamb on the Ark of the Covenant. The moment the blood touched the Ark, atonement was made for everyone's sins for another year."

He paused, letting the image sink in. "But when Jesus hung on the Cross, He was both the lamb and the priest. In that Holy moment as our high priest, Jesus offered His own blood for the permanent removal of sin. He offered up the perfect sacrifice. This was a sacrifice so complete that God never again required the blood of a sacrifice for forgiveness."

"But there is another meaning," Delgado said, shifting gears. "In a secular sense, the word tetelestai was used in the business world to signify the full payment of a debt back in biblical times. Tax receipts on papyrus have been found with tetelestai written across them. When a debt had been paid off, the parchment on which it had been recorded was stamped with that word, which meant 'paid in full.'"

"Paid in full," Danica repeated, the words tasting like copper in her mouth.

"Exactly. So from a Christian definition, that means that once a person accepts the sacrifice, no debt of sin exists any longer. The debt is wiped out because the price was paid."

"And in classical Greek times," he added, "the word depicted a turning point when one period ended and a new period began. When Jesus said, 'It is finished,' it was indeed a turning point in the entire history of mankind. The Cross is the Great Divide in human history."

Danica was overwhelmed and impressed at the same time. She didn't know where to take the information or even how to process it all. She searched for the words to desperately find a comment on what Nicholai had just explained. It was too much to absorb all at once, and she needed time to think.

But the silence between the two was even more uncomfortable. She needed to speak. She needed to bridge the gap between theology and homicide. "So what do you make of it? How does all that relate to this case? Are we looking for a religious fanatic?"

"Like I said earlier, the motive in all this is power," Delgado said, his eyes narrowing. "Or some sense of achieving that power through the settling of accounts. People think revenge is a single incident. But this... using that word... implies a debt. Someone believes these men owed a debt. And someone forced them to pay it in full. Not with money, but with their lives."

"You think they were forced?"

"I think they were convinced that death was the only way to balance the ledger."

"What are your thoughts? Where do we go?"

"It's finished for Simpson and Rosin. They're done. Their debt is paid," Delgado said. He turned his head and glared out the passenger window. The car moved quickly along the interstate, past vacant buildings with their "For Lease" signs blazing in bright red letters, symbols of failed ventures and unpaid debts.

Nicholai turned to Danica at the same time she took her eyes off the road to check her mirror. Their eyes met. She looked deep into his blue eyes—deeper than before—and she saw a flicker of genuine fear she hadn't seen before.

"What's wrong?" the young detective asked, her hands tightening on the wheel.

"I'm afraid it's not finished at all," he whispered. "I feel it's all just starting."

Chapter 14

The drive back to Dallas took an hour, a very quiet, heavy hour. The tension from the conversation about debts and sacrifices still lingered in the air conditioning of the Taurus, thicker than the humidity outside. Danica followed Nicholai's directions implicitly after they left the Fort Worth Police Department evidence locker, the second laptop now resting securely in the trunk like contraband.

He directed her off the freeway once they cleared the corporate financial towers and glass monoliths that marked the downtown Dallas skyline. The sun reflected off the green glass of the Bank of America Plaza, an image that always reminded her of the Emerald City in The Wizard of Oz. It was a towering beacon of prosperity, visible for miles across the flat plains. But like the movie, Danica knew that behind the curtain of shimmering lights and oil money, there was usually just a small man pulling levers he shouldn't be touching, manipulating the smoke and mirrors to keep the illusion alive. The city looked clean from a distance, but up close, the cracks in the pavement were filled with secrets.

She took the first exit off the interstate as directed, leaving the polished city behind for the gritty reality of the industrial outskirts. She drove several blocks past numerous auto-body repair shops where sparks flew from welding torches in dark bays, and "Buy Here, Pay Here" used car lots offering beat-up sedans to anyone with a pulse and a down payment. She had lost count of the numerous tattoo parlors and 24-hour taco stands too quickly. The deeper they went, the more the city seemed to crumble around them. Finally, Delgado quietly pointed her down a narrow side street, the asphalt cracked and neglected, sprouting weeds through the fissures, then instructed her to turn into an alley off Greenville Avenue.

"This is the place?" she asked in stunned disbelief, checking the rearview mirror to ensure they weren't being followed. The alley was a dead end of urban decay, a place where stolen cars went to be stripped.

He sat quietly, staring out the window at the graffiti-stained brick, and smiled. "Looks can be deceiving. Isn't that the first rule of undercover work? You hide the crown jewels in a shoebox, not a safe."

"You're sure about this?" she asked again, putting the car in park but keeping the engine running, her foot hovering over the brake.

Stepping out of the car, the heat hit her instantly, carrying a complex bouquet of scents: rotting garbage, ozone, stale grease, and the metallic tang of old rust. It reminded her unpleasantly of Detective Leininger's desk, magnified by a hundred degrees. On their right, a vacant lot had been closed off using eight feet of chain-link fencing topped with razor wire that glistened menacingly in the sun. She couldn't figure out if the piles of trash scattered amongst the weeds and unkempt brush had been put there before or after the fence had been erected, but it looked like a graveyard for the city's refuse—broken furniture, rusted appliances, and the skeletons of bicycles. She fought the urge to spend valuable time and energy analyzing the blight; she needed to focus on the threat assessment.

Delgado had both laptops tucked firmly under his arm as he exited the passenger side of the car. Harris stood by the driver's door, looking up one side of the alley and down the other, her hand resting instinctively near her holster. The shadows were long, stretching out from the buildings like grasping fingers, and the sight lines were poor. She made another quick check of their surroundings—a stray cat darting behind a dumpster, a flickering streetlight buzzing overhead—before following closely behind the pastor.

Nicholai stopped at a solid steel door just a few yards from the car. The outside façade was brick, stained with decades of soot and layers of graffiti tags that had been painted over and re-tagged in a never-ending war of territory. The rusted door would easily pass for the entrance to any other anonymous, abandoned warehouse in the five-block area. But as Danica looked closer, trained to spot anomalies, she noticed the frame was reinforced with heavy-gauge steel, and the hinges were interior-mounted. Nicholai reached out with his free hand and pushed a nondescript button to the left of the door, hidden beneath a layer of grime that looked suspiciously applied.

After a few seconds of silence, a voice from high above their heads crackled through the warm air. "Yes."

They both looked up in the direction of the sound. Danica stared at a small, rusted speaker box mounted ten feet up. Next to it, looking jarringly out of place, was a modern, high-definition security camera with a motorized lens that swiveled silently to lock onto them. The glass eye zoomed in with a faint mechanical whir. The male voice sounded distorted, similar to the static that emanates from a fast-food drive-through speaker, but the tone was sharp, intelligent, and wary.

Delgado took a step back, looked directly into the camera's lens, and waited, letting the operator verify his biometrics.

"Well, if it isn't the Pastor!" The voice echoed down the dirty, deserted alley, bouncing off the brick walls.

"Yeah, Griffin, it's me," Delgado said, speaking clearly in the direction of the camera. "I need your help."

"Well, get up here. Long time, no see. I thought you were saving souls, not slumming it with the heat."

Danica immediately noticed a sense of excitement in the voice, masked by sarcasm. A moment later, the heavy sound of magnetic locks disengaging—clack-clack-clack—came from inside the metal door, followed by the groan of heavy bolts retracting. Delgado pulled the heavy door open; it moved on well-oiled hinges despite the rust, gliding silently. He motioned for Harris to enter first.

Cautiously, she moved just inside the dark space, her senses on high alert. She was guarded, only stepping in far enough to clear the fatal funnel of the doorway, making sure Delgado was right behind her. The solid metal door slammed shut automatically, sealing with a hiss of air pressure that cut off the outside world completely. It took several seconds for her eyes to adjust to the sudden, suffocating darkness.

"Follow me," he said. Danica felt him move past her, his footsteps confident on the concrete. "Stay close to the wall. Don't trip on the pallets."

They quickly made their way through the dark, empty shell of the warehouse. It was obvious Nicholai knew his way around the maze of old pallets and structural support beams. The smell of mildew and damp concrete was strong, mixed with the faint scent of dust, and Harris could tell the main floor space had been vacant for some time. Water dripped from a pipe somewhere off in the darkness, the plink-plink-plink echoing through the vast space like a metronome counting down time. Danica kept one hand on Delgado's shoulder to guide herself, her other hand ready to draw her weapon.

He stopped at another solid metal door, this one looking like the entrance to a bank vault, polished and imposing. He knocked hard once with the side of his closed hand. A keypad beeped, followed by the mechanical thud of a deadbolt retracting and the whir of a retinal scanner. Nicholai pulled the door open. This time, he was the first to enter.

In a dramatic contrast to the dank, cavernous space they had just walked through, the room was blindingly well-lit and climate-controlled. The blast of cold, conditioned air stunned Danica for a brief second, chilling the sweat on her neck, and she took a deep breath, forcing the moldy air out of her lungs. The hum of high-powered cooling fans filled the room, a white noise that signaled serious processing power.

Her eyes, once adjusted, surveyed the room quickly. This wasn't just a computer room; it was a nerve center. A large server bank hummed along the far wall, blue lights blinking in rapid succession like a constellation. Overhead cables, bundled neatly in color-coded groups, snaked through the metal rafters and dropped down to feed a semi-circle of workstations. The concrete floor was polished to a shine, reflecting the lights from above. The whole space reminded her of a mad scientist's laboratory crossed with a NASA control room, hidden in the belly of a rotting beast.

"Over here, Pastor Nic," a voice yelled from behind a wall of monitors. Delgado motioned for Danica to follow. Her eyes and mind were still taking it all in, trying to reconcile the exterior with the interior.

The man who emerged from the digital fortress was no surprise to the stereotype, yet distinct in his energy. He was thin and pale, with the kind of translucent complexion that hadn't seen the sun in years. He wore thick glasses that magnified his eyes and oversized clothes that appeared well-worn and at least ten years out of date—a vintage grunge look that wasn't a fashion statement, but a lack of interest in anything analog.

"Good to see you. Who's your friend? You don't usually bring tourists," the man said, wiping grease from his hands onto his pants.

Nicholai walked over quickly, shook the computer tech's hand, and placed his arm around his shoulder with genuine affection before turning to face Danica. "Inspector Danica Harris, meet Ward Griffin, the world's greatest technical geek and digital locksmith."

He extended his hand first as Danica approached. "Nice to meet you, Inspector. And Pastor, as always, you're far too kind. Flattery will get you everywhere."

"Griffin," Nicholai said quickly. "Just call him Griffin."

"Griffin," she said politely, shaking a hand that felt fragile but vibrated with caffeine energy.

"Yeah. My friends just call me Griffin. My enemies call me... well, they can't find me to call me anything."

Nicholai patted Griffin on the back again. "Trust me," Nicholai smiled at Danica. "This guy is the best high-tech freelancer on either side of the law. If it has a chip, he can talk to it. If it has a firewall, he can walk through it."

Harris looked at both men who smiled at each other with a shared history she wasn't privy to. "Either side? Do I want to ask?"

"Nope," Delgado said quickly. "Let's just say he owes me a few favors from a previous life. A life where badges weren't always part of the equation."

"Crap, Pastor! Please. I think I'm paid up in the favor department," Griffin said with some seriousness, adjusting his glasses. "I'm still scrubbing my digital footprint from that mess in Shreveport."

"You think so? Let me see what we have here." Delgado turned and walked towards a long workbench that ran the entire length of the room. Monitors lined the back of the bench—Danica estimated at least a dozen, displaying everything from scrolling code to live traffic cam feeds from downtown Dallas.

Nicholai walked over, placed the two laptops down on an anti-static mat, and randomly found a dark monitor. He reached up and pushed the power button on the closest one. "Let's just take a look," he said.

The monitor slowly lit up and displayed a grainy, black-and-white scene from inside a high-rise office. Men in suits were walking around a boardroom, gesturing at charts. The timestamp in the corner was live.

He turned to the computer expert and raised an eyebrow. "Griffin? Do I want to know why you're watching the live feed of the New York Stock Exchange's boardroom?"

Griffin smiled sheepishly and tapped a key, switching the feed to a cartoon. "Market research? Judge Judy was a rerun today. Besides, you'd be amazed what people write on whiteboards when they think no one is looking."

Both men laughed, leaving Danica unaware of the inside joke and slightly uncomfortable with the casual display of illegal surveillance.

"Okay, Pastor Nic. You win. Just promise me I'll be in your prayers tonight."

"Griffin, it's a good thing salvation implies grace," Nicholai laughed. "Now, I need you to look at these."

He walked over to the bench, and Delgado spread the two laptops beside each other—Rosin's sleek, high-end ultra-book and Simpson's heavier, older model. Griffin plugged them in one at a time using a heavy-duty power strip secured against the concrete wall. He connected them to his own system via a series of cables, bypassing the standard ports. Danica walked over and stood close to Delgado, watching the screens come to life.

"What am I looking for?" Griffin asked, cracking his knuckles and settling into his ergonomic chair.

"Don't know for sure," Nicholai said. "Something hidden. Money transfers, emails, encrypted documents. We're looking for a common denominator on both; something that ties these two men together. We need any recent activity as well. Check the deleted caches, check the shadow files."

Griffin went to work on Simpson's laptop first. Danica watched as his fingers flew across his customized mechanical keyboard, the clicking sound rapid and rhythmic. He was fast; too fast for her eyes to track the commands he was entering. The screen went black, and she watched white lines of code scroll by quickly from the bottom of the screen to the top—a cascade of data representing a man's life. Suddenly, they stopped. Griffin focused on the last few lines on the monitor, his brow furrowing, and started typing again. The scrolling resumed for a brief moment, then hit a red wall of text.

"Okay," he said, rubbing the back of his shaved head before turning to Rosin's laptop. "Let's see if your brother is just as shy." She watched as the computer tech repeated the same exercise, bypassing the standard Windows login with a few keystrokes and diving straight into the BIOS.

"Grab something cold," Griffin said, pointing to the right with his chin. His eyes never left the screen. "Brain fuel. I run hot when I'm digging."

Delgado walked a few feet away, then stopped. "Would you like something?" he asked Harris.

"I'm fine," she said, her eyes glued to the monitors, mesmerized by the flow of information.

Danica watched as Nicholai made his way to a large stainless steel commercial refrigerator on the far wall. He opened the door and the light revealed rows of energy drinks and sodas arranged by color. Danica turned her attention back to Griffin, who had Rosin's screen reacting the same way Simpson's laptop had done. When the scrolling stopped, she saw Griffin looking back and forth between the two computers, comparing the code structures.

"Here." The sound of Nicholai's voice broke her concentration. He handed her a cold Dr Pepper, the can sweating in the cool air. She popped it open before even realizing she had initially declined his offer. She took a sip, the sugar hitting her system, and looked at the retired FBI man. He was watching Griffin intensely, reading the tech's body language.

"This is going to take some time," Griffin said without taking his eyes away from the two screens. "The architecture is... unique. It's elegant."

"What did you find?" Danica asked, leaning in.

Griffin turned and looked at her, magnifying his eyes through the thick lenses, then turned to Nicholai.

"Both hard drives have hidden partitions," he said. "Identical formatting, identical byte size on both. It's not standard manufacturer bloatware. This is custom."

"Which means?" Delgado asked.

"Did these two people work for the same company? Or use the same IT guy?" Griffin asked.

"No," Danica replied. "They were in completely different industries. One in banking, one in oil."

Griffin looked at Nicholai, his expression serious. "There is something in common then. The partitions have been set up and are password protected tight. I'm talking military-grade encryption. Like I said, they are identical in size and location on the hard drive. That's only common on a system that's been set up by an organization or group who are into the same specific network. They were running the same ghost software. It's like a handshake only they knew about."

"Can you break it? Tell us what's on there?" Delgado asked.

"I don't know. There's always a backdoor in any system if you knock hard enough. But this... this is designed to brick the drive if forced. It's going to take me a while to crack the handshake protocol without triggering a wipe."

"Just get whatever you can, please," Danica urged.

"Yes, ma'am," Griffin replied, typing furiously again, sweat beading on his forehead despite the cold room.

"Griff, this is important," Nicholai said, placing a hand on the desk, grounding him.

"For you, Pastor, I know. Are you going to tell me about this one?"

"Nope," Nicholai said quickly. "It's just important we get everything we can off those before the trail goes cold."

"Must be vital if whatever this is has brought you back into the field. Are you doing okay? You look... tired. Like you haven't slept since the last time I saw you."

Nicholai looked at Danica. She looked away, pretending to watch the scrolling data.

"It is, and I don't know yet, Griff. Just find the key."

"Well, I do know one thing for certain right now," Griffin said, his voice dropping to a whisper. He stopped typing and pulled his hands away from the keyboard as if it were hot. "But I don't know if this helps or not," he said, turning back to the laptops.

"Let us decide what's pertinent," Danica said.

Griffin looked at Nicholai, fear flickering behind his glasses, and then spoke to Danica.

"Both these were manipulated remotely before being shut down. The timestamps on the partition access don't match the user logs." Griffin leaned back in his chair slowly, his eyes darting to the ceiling camera in the corner of his own lab. "Someone out there has root access to these drives. And the moment I pinged the partition... it pinged back."

He looked at Delgado. "Whoever it is, they know we're here. They're monitoring us right now."

Chapter 15

She knew what men wanted. It wasn't complicated; it was biology wrapped in ego. If she dressed sexy, she knew they would think she wanted the same thing they did. They would mistake her calculated presentation for availability. But that was far from the truth; it was her dirty little secret, her weapon of choice. She had been forced to learn about life the hard way, clawing her way up from nothing, but finally, her big payoff would be coming soon. And no one deserved it more—or even as much—as she did. The scales were finally tipping in her favor.

Tonight she was blonde, a platinum shade that caught the light like spun glass, but that wouldn't last. It never did. She shed identities like snakeskins. When she was done with this assignment, she'd go back to her natural chestnut brown color again, slipping back into the shadows. She smiled at her reflection in the darkened window of the cab and contemplated maybe becoming a redhead when this was all complete. Fire seemed appropriate for what was coming.

She had done her research and knew exactly what would attract his attention. She knew his vices, his preferences, and the specific visual triggers that would bypass his logic and appeal directly to his lust. She was going to leave a lasting impression tonight—a ghost that would haunt him until she decided to become real.

She had become a master at the game of attraction and even more astute when it came to manipulation. She had been blessed with the looks and the body for the attraction part—genetics had been kind—

but she had learned the science of manipulation over time, refining it through trial and error. What she lacked at the beginning, she had easily bought and paid for. Her body had been sculpted by the best medical hands in the field, investments in her future, and her mind had been twisted by an intense sense of entitlement and a complete, liberating lack of guilt.

She liked the way the cab driver spent more time watching her in the rearview mirror than keeping his eyes on the road in front. He was dangerously distracted, risking a wreck just to catch a glimpse of her neckline. It gave her that sense of validation she needed, a warm-up for the main event. She was really on tonight. The voltage was high.

Just as she ordered, the driver stopped the cab at the front door of The Marble Club. She smiled with pity at all the wannabes who lined the front street behind the velvet ropes, shivering in their desperate, feeble attempts to get inside the exclusive nightspot. They sold their dignity for a chance to stand near money. But tonight, she didn't have to worry. She never had to stand in line for anything. Lines were for people who didn't matter.

She opened the door of the cab and seductively placed one foot on the pavement. She took her time, letting the moment breathe, knowing the girls in line would be admiring her Valentino Rosette peep-toe pumps while their boyfriends admired the perfect, toned legs they would never have access to, even in their wildest dreams.

She walked with an air of arrogance along the line and past the front door, ignoring the bouncers who straightened up as she approached. She could feel the eyes on her, a physical weight she carried with ease, as she made her way around the east side of The Marble Club. No, she didn't need to stand in line like cattle. Her backdoor pass—a favor called in from the owner—was all she needed to get access inside at any time of the night.

She made her way down the dark, narrow corridor, the concrete vibrating with the energy from inside. She pushed past the heavy steel doors marked "PRIVATE" and stepped into the main bar. The transition was instant. The bass of the music hit her like a physical wave, soaking its way through the thin black silk of her dress and settling nicely in her bones. The air was thick with the scent of expensive cologne, sweat, and adrenaline. It all felt good, and she knew she looked even better.

At the bar, she ordered her favorite drink, Hpnotiq on ice. The electric blue liquid glowed in the dim light, a beacon in her hand. That first drink would be the only one she would need to order on her own. If she had to order another one, then she knew she wasn't succeeding.

She stood at the bar, sipping the sweet, fruity liquor, spying the room through the mirror behind the bottles. She scanned the crowd, filtering out the noise, until she spotted him. Finally, there he was, off in the far VIP corner, holding court. He was with two other men—sycophants hanging on his every word—but he stood out like a wolf among sheep. His suit was custom cut, Italian wool that draped perfectly over his frame. His silk tie was loose around the collar of his crisp white shirt, signaling that the business day was over and the hunt had begun.

She watched and planned, waiting for just the right moment to make her move. She analyzed the gaps in his conversation, the way his eyes roamed the room looking for a distraction.

She desperately wanted more—to approach him, to finish it now—but she had become disciplined enough to know that patience only made the end of the game more intense. Anticipation was the hook; she just needed to bait it. She could wait. Tonight was just a taste for him. A teaser trailer for the ruin to come.

She swallowed the last of her drink, the ice clicking against her teeth, and placed the empty glass on the bar. She pulled a small compact from her clutch, applied a fresh coat of bright red lipstick, and checked her work. Perfect. Dangerous.

She took a deep breath, centering herself, before making her way around the crowded dance floor towards his table. She moved with the rhythm of the music, letting the crowd part for her. As she moved closer, her focus became laser-sharp. Her eyes never left him. Men knew when she looked their way; it was a primal sense, a warning and an invitation all at once. She slowed her pace until it was just right, a slow-motion glide.

Then he looked. He saw her. His eyes locked onto her, and she saw the recognition of desire flare in his pupils. But she looked away. She wanted to look in his direction, to hold his gaze, but she wouldn't. Not yet. That was all part of her plan. Deny, then deliver.

She slowly moved closer, encroaching on his territory, and could now feel his eyes burning into her skin. It took longer than she thought, but it was working, and she felt a surge of power. When she was right in front of his table, she stopped. She turned slowly and looked directly into his eyes, breaking down his defenses with a single glance.

She smiled first. She always did. It was a smile that promised everything and nothing.

The conversation he had been involved in stopped mid-sentence. His glass hovered halfway to his mouth. His entire focus had shifted to her, standing just a few feet away, bathed in the strobe lights. He was mesmerized, caught in the trap.

She looked closer, ensuring the image was burned into his retina, and smiled again—a smaller, more intimate smile—before turning on her heel and walking away. She didn't look back. She didn't need to. She knew he was watching her walk away, memorizing the sway of her hips.

She was finished for now. The seed was planted. Everything had worked perfectly. It always did.

Chapter 16

A smooth jazz piece played a little too loud through the overhead speakers, a frantic saxophone solo that grated on her nerves rather than relaxing them. Danica couldn't focus, and she was tired. Dead tired. Her thoughts were scattered all over the place, like glass shards on a highway. It had been another long night with not much rest. The cat slept—curled up in a mocking ball of contentment—but she didn't.

Danica sat alone at a small corner table, watching the young employees dressed in their standard-issue green aprons move with practiced efficiency behind the counter. In one hand she held the paper coffee cup, the heat seeping into her palm, while the other brushed a stray lock of auburn hair away from her face. She took a long sip of the lukewarm coffee; it tasted burnt, but she needed the caffeine more than the flavor.

He had been forty-five minutes late for their morning meet. To make matters worse, the moment he finally arrived, looking flushed and distracted, Nicholai had to take a call. He quickly excused himself and stepped outside the coffee shop, leaving her alone with the jazz. He had been out there for almost twenty minutes now.

Her curiosity kept pulling her attention away from the buzz of activity behind the counter to Nicholai pacing just outside the glass door. She could tell his conversation was passionate. His hand gestures were sharp, his pacing rhythmic. Every so often, he caught her looking through the glass and then would turn away, shielding his mouth with his hand, creating a barrier of privacy that annoyed her.

She pulled out her Blackberry to check for messages, emails, or any other communication that related to the case. There was nothing but a digital void. She deleted a few spam emails that had somehow bypassed the filter to her personal account, then looked up to see Nicholai still pacing outside. Then, suddenly, he stopped. He closed his eyes and leaned his forehead against the brick wall of the building. She couldn't read his lips, but his demeanor shifted from agitation to a sudden, stoic calm. He pulled the cell phone away, ended the call, and looked through the glass at her. Danica instinctively turned her eyes away, feigning interest in her coffee lid.

"Sorry about that," he said after returning to the table, sliding into the chair opposite her. He looked drained.

"Is everything alright?" she asked, studying his face. "That looked intense."

"It was. I don't know if everything will work out. I'll have to wait and see," he said, rubbing his temples. "That was a friend from the marina. He's struggling with a few things—addiction, family trouble—and he needed prayer. He needed to know he wasn't alone."

"Do you get that a lot?"

"Yeah, I do. I am a pastor, Danica. It's all part of the job. You don't clock out."

"So people just call you for prayers? Like ordering a pizza?"

"All the time. Sometimes it's the only lifeline they have left."

"Whatever." She grinned, but it didn't reach her eyes. "And that works, right? Sending good vibes into the ether fixes everything?" Danica's sarcasm bit through the air, sharp and defensive.

"Of course it does. Why are you saying it like that? Don't you pray? By the way, are you a believer?" he asked, firing the questions too quickly for her liking.

"A believer in what?" she asked, not expecting an answer, swirling the dregs of her coffee. "I believe there is good and evil. I see the evil part of life all the time. I see it in the morgue photos and the crime scenes."

"And the good?" Nicholai asked softly.

"Is there really any good left in this screwed-up world? I mean, look around. Look at what you've experienced," she said, playing the trump card of his own tragedy. "Believe me; I did my Sundays at church for a long time. I sat in the pew, sang the hymns. Didn't really do me any good. It didn't stop bad things from happening."

Nicholai didn't answer immediately. He waited for her comments to sink in, letting the silence stretch between them. He wanted Danica to hear the echo of her own hopelessness.

Finally, she was the one to break the uncomfortable silence and speak again. "I'm sorry. I didn't mean to bring that up again. I'm just... tired."

"It's okay, and you're right. There is evil all around us. It's aggressive and it's loud," he said, leaning back in the chair. "But look over there." He motioned for Danica to look through the tinted window.

A young couple sat close together under a green umbrella at a small wrought iron table outside the coffee shop. Just as Danica looked, the young man reached under the table and held his companion's hand. She smiled—a genuine, unguarded expression—and leaned in to kiss him on the cheek.

Danica watched but couldn't understand the purpose of the observation. "What am I supposed to see? PDA?"

"That! Right there. Danica, there is never a time when God is not present or speaking. And there isn't a place where He is not present. Look at those two out there. Despite the evil that surrounds us—despite the headlines and the murders—He brings that light. That connection."

She looked outside again at the couple. The woman slid her chair closer to the man, seeking his warmth.

"Sorry, but I don't get it," she said, looking back at Nicholai with a shake of her head.

"That's because you've never asked for it. You're looking for the fire, not the warmth."

"Asked for what?"

"For Him to come into your life and take control. To open your eyes to the subplot." Nicholai leaned in closer, his voice dropping. "There is never a place so dark that He doesn't speak. During those times of painful solitude and through the darkness of life, He is by our side. There is a passage that says, 'Never will I leave you: never will I forsake you.'"

She laughed, a dry, cynical sound. "Nicholai, you're a romantic. All I see are two people sitting outside a coffee shop. Probably on their first or second date, putting on their best faces. They'll probably get married in a few months, and after a couple of kids and unhappy years together, get divorced and move on to the next set of problems. I see the statistics. It's the same story; a few months of bliss followed by years of heartache, lawyers, and regret."

"Stop," he said quickly but with a calm presence that halted her tirade. "Stop projecting the past onto the future. Stop and look at the moment that is right in front of you. Look at that couple in this moment."

"I am."

He continued, "Here's your problem, Danica. And trust me; you're not alone in thinking like this. It's not explosions of lights or lightning

91

bolts that we should be looking for. It's a gentle glow that brings hope into darkness. It's the resilience of love in a world that tries to kill it."

Danica looked outside again, then back to him. Her eyes were drawn to his, and she noticed a change. They were soft but intense, holding a conviction she couldn't quite dismiss.

"Because we expect a loud shout or an explosion," he said. "We miss His sweet whisper. We have to learn to feel and appreciate the warm embrace of a friend or the touch of another's kindness. That's when He speaks the loudest."

Nicholai smiled and continued. "One of my favorite passages is 'When you doubt, look around. I am closer than you think.' Did you see that woman's reaction when he reached out for her hand? Did you see the look on her face? She beamed. For a second, the world wasn't heavy for her."

"Yeah, I did," she said quietly, turning away from him, feeling a crack in her armor she didn't want to acknowledge.

Their conversation was broken suddenly by the shrill ring of her Blackberry vibrating against the table. The spell was broken.

"Harris," she said professionally, her voice shifting instantly back to detective mode.

Nicholai could tell she was listening intently, her jaw tightening.

"Where?" she asked, grabbing a pen. "Text me the address. We're on our way."

She disconnected the call and looked out at the couple outside who seemed to have moved even closer together, oblivious to the call that had just come in. She turned away from them quickly and looked at Nicholai, the cynicism rushing back in to fill the void.

"What's wrong?" he asked.

"We've got another one."

Chapter 17

It didn't take them long to swing the unmarked DPD car through the open wrought-iron gates of Buffalo Creek Estates. Two uniformed officers stood at the entrance, looking bored, and waved Harris' car through the perimeter.

Buffalo Creek Estates was a new subdivision tucked in an exclusive, established area off Preston Road in North Dallas. It was "new money" trying to look old. The community had only been established the previous two years, and it had the eerie, suspended feel of a construction site paused in time. Several homes were occupied, manicured islands in a sea of red mud, while a few still remained under construction, their skeleton frames rising into the sky.

As Danica turned the car down the second street, Nicholai saw the location immediately. It was the only house on the block with activity. Four marked DPD cars were parked haphazardly along the street, their lights still flashing on top, painting the stucco walls in rhythm. The coroner's white unmarked van had been backed into the driveway, blocking the view of the garage. The back doors remained open, a gaping maw waiting for its cargo. Danica spotted Pam Brainerd's vehicle on the far side of the white van.

"What have we got?" Danica asked the officer positioned just outside the front door of the home, stepping out of the car into the heat.

"Victim's name is David Roberts. Fifty-eight-year-old white male," he said, reading the notes from the small pad in his hand. "He built this place. He's the developer."

The house was a Tuscan-style estate, a massive structure with arched windows, reclaimed brick, and a stone façade under a traditional Italian roofline. It was beautiful, but it felt hollow—a model home that no one had ever really lived in.

"Who discovered the body?" she asked. The standard questions were almost memorized and robotic, a script she followed to keep the horror at bay.

"Young couple, Tom and Sandra Fillion. They're waiting in the kitchen now. The wife is quite shaken up."

Danica looked through the open front door. She couldn't see any furnishings inside but noticed impressive terrazzo tile with hand-scraped plank flooring stretching out into an empty great room.

Danica turned to Nicholai, who was scanning the outside of the home, checking the landscaping, the windows, the lack of forced entry. He had already made mental notes of the setting—the isolation, the visibility from the road. She entered first, and Nicholai followed, his eyes moving constantly, taking it all in.

The foyer was as impressive as the outside of the home. The smell hit them first—not rot, but the chemical scent of new paint, sawdust, and floor wax. The home's centerpiece was obviously the elegant spiral staircase built with a combination of dark wood and decorative iron, winding up to a second-floor gallery. An impressive two-story library and office was situated on the right, shelves empty of books, with a large formal dining room to the left.

Danica spotted the couple in the kitchen and made her way towards them. They looked small in the cavernous, empty room.

"I'm Detective Harris," she said, extending her hand to Tom Fillion. Sandra had her arms folded tightly against her chest, and her head was down, staring at the granite island.

"When can we get out of here?" Tom Fillion asked immediately, his voice tight. "My wife is extremely upset with all this. I want to get her home. We shouldn't be here."

"I know this is difficult, but I have just a few quick questions," Danica replied, keeping her voice calm. "How did you find the body?"

Sandra Fillion gasped and placed her hand over her mouth, a sob escaping. She turned away. Her husband placed his hand on her shoulder in an effort to comfort his distraught wife.

"We were walking through the area and saw the open house sign. We're in the market for a new home and decided to take a look." Fillion looked at his wife then back to Danica. Nicholai stood silently behind the detective, watching their body language. They were terrified, but innocent.

Tom continued, "We walked through the front area into the den. I called out to see if anyone was here—the door was unlocked—but no one answered. We thought maybe the realtor was in the back. We found him in the master bathroom, in the tub."

"Did you touch the body or move him at all?"

"No! No, not at all. I could tell he was... gone. He was blue. We walked back out here, and I called 911 immediately from my cell. We didn't touch anything."

Danica looked at Nicholai. "Do you have any questions?"

"No," he said quietly and turned away, dismissing them from his mental suspect list.

Danica turned back to Tom Fillion. "Did you see anyone leaving or hanging around the neighborhood? Anything out of the ordinary? A car speeding away?"

"No, nothing," he said. "It was dead quiet. Can we please leave?"

Danica thought for a moment then replied. "Yes, sure. Just make sure the officer at the door has all your contact information in case we have any other questions. And again, I'm sorry you had to see this."

They watched the devastated couple make their way out the front door, eager to escape the smell of death. Once they were out of sight, Danica slowly made her way through the empty den. Without furnishings to absorb the sound, the room looked larger than it actually was. The bare white walls and the high ceiling made the room cold and unfriendly, a mausoleum for the living.

"Not bad," she commented, looking at the crown molding.

"Sorry, not my style," Delgado said while still scanning the floorboards. "It has no soul."

Danica moved towards the short hallway that led to the master suite area. Nicholai followed close behind. Their footsteps echoed off the wood floor, sounding louder than usual in the vacuum of the house.

The master bedroom area was unfurnished like the rest of the house, just a vast expanse of cappuccino-colored carpet. Nicholai paused at the threshold. He noticed footsteps in the deep pile of the new carpeting—faint depressions that hadn't sprung back yet. The majority of indentations led from the door directly to the bath area. He followed her closely, stepping carefully.

Pam Brainerd was leaning over Roberts' body inside the large garden tub. The water was still in the tub, tinged pink. She removed the body thermometer and checked the dial.

"What have you got?" Harris asked, stepping into the tiled bathroom.

Brainerd made a quick note on the clipboard then turned to Harris.

"Well, body temp indicates time of death about eighteen hours ago; sometime between six and nine o'clock last evening. I'm assuming we've got an overdose of sleeping pills and alcohol. The classic cocktail. Bottles are right there on the vanity," she said, pointing towards the right-hand side of the room.

Nicholai made his way to the ornate vanity area. An empty prescription bottle of Ambien was next to an empty bottle of Jack Daniels on the granite counter. He leaned in, not touching, but sniffing. The air smelled of whiskey and something else... something floral.

"The note?" Nicholai asked. "Where is it?"

"Right here," Brainerd said. She pulled a plastic bag from behind the clipboard and handed it to Danica. "It was taped to that mirror over there," she said, pointing to the glass. "Eye level."

"Anything else?" Danica asked before reading the note. She already knew what the message was. "Laptop?"

"No," Brainerd replied. "No computer. But we found this in the sink." She handed another bag, smaller than the first, to Harris. Danica examined the contents through the thick plastic before handing it to Nicholai. He studied the burnt remains of the SIM card, a melted lump of plastic that looked identical to the others.

Harris looked back at the plastic evidence bag that contained the note.

I'm so sorry for what I've done. I cannot live with the pain I have caused any longer.

David Roberts

Tetelestai

She felt a chill that hadn't been there before. She stared at the note, almost hoping the words would be different, but they weren't. The font was the same. The spacing was the same. She needed to change the subject before the creepiness settled in. "Any usable prints?" Danica finally asked.

"Not many," the CSI stated, shaking her head. "I'm surprised how clean it is. This place has been on the market for over six weeks and open every Saturday and Sunday. There have probably been more than two hundred people in and out of this place. I thought I'd have a lot more to work with. But the surfaces have been wiped down. It's sterile."

"I'm going to take a look around," Nicholai said abruptly. He walked quickly out of the master bath and disappeared down the hall, his movements purposeful.

"He's cute," Pam smiled, watching him go. "Intense, but cute."

"Whatever," Danica replied, rolling her eyes. "What else have you got? I'm running out of leads on this, Pam. There has to be something that connects them besides a word."

"Nothing more, sorry," she said. "Looks like he came here alone last night to end it. Took a few shots from that bottle of Jack over there and then downed the pills. He didn't struggle. He just went to sleep."

Harris let out a deep sigh. "Let me know if you find anything else." She left Brainerd to finish and walked down the hall back towards the den. The house was quiet except for the muffled voices of the officers coming from outside.

She stopped inside the empty kitchen and listened. She heard nothing for a few moments, then the sounds of footsteps overhead. To the left of the area, Danica noticed a second, smaller staircase off the far wall of the kitchen, likely for servants. She made her way towards the stairs. The footsteps above stopped, then started again. This time they were moving faster, pacing.

Once upstairs, she noticed Nicholai leaning against the doorframe of one of the guest rooms. His hands were behind his back, and he glared inside the empty bedroom.

"What are you doing?" she asked.

Delgado didn't answer. He had a cold, serious look on his face, and his blue eyes glared at the empty space as if seeing a ghost. He turned quickly and made his way to the next room. He stopped and stared inside, checking the view from the window.

"Excuse me?" Harris asked, confused by his behavior.

Delgado ignored her and moved down the open hallway to the main staircase. He took the steps two at a time, sliding his hand down the banister. Danica had trouble keeping up. He acted as if he was on a mission of his own. He quickly made his way back inside the kitchen.

Nicholai stopped in front of the massive granite island. He leaned down until his face was inches from the surface. He ran his finger across the polished stone, picking up a microscopic layer of dust, then stopped at a clean patch. He rubbed his fingers together, brought them to his nose, and smelled them.

Citrus. And a faint, lingering sweetness. Lavender?

He looked off towards the master suite with an intense stare, visualizing the path. Danica stood still and watched as Delgado quickly moved past her again. He headed down the short hall towards the master bedroom. By the time the detective caught up, Nicholai was standing in the center of the room facing the large windows. His head was down, looking at the plush cappuccino-colored carpet again.

"What's with you?" she finally asked in frustration. "You're running around like a bloodhound."

"It's a woman," he said quietly.

His head moved up, and he turned his body towards Danica, who remained in the doorway.

"A woman is doing this," he stated with absolute certainty. "The surfaces were wiped down, but not with industrial cleaner—with household lemon wipes. The footprints in the carpet... the stride is too short for a man of Roberts' size, and the weight distribution is wrong. And she watched him die. She stood right here," he pointed to a spot near the window, "and watched him fade away."

Chapter 18

"How do you know that? How did you come to that conclusion?"

Harris was taken aback after hearing Nicholai's statement. It wasn't just the words that stopped her; it was the absolute certainty in his voice. The look on his face told her he was just as shaken by the revelation as she was. The actual words didn't cause her to step back; it was the allegation that made her freeze. A female serial killer was rare—statistically an anomaly. They didn't operate like this. They used poison, they killed for profit, they killed those in their care. They didn't stage elaborate suicides of powerful men.

"The impressions in the carpet," he said, his voice tight, almost in a panic. His mind was off somewhere else, reconstructing a scene only he could see, and Danica saw the frightening intensity in his face.

"I don't understand," she said after an awkward moment of silence, trying to pull him back to the present. "Explain it to me."

"Roberts has had this place on the market for a few weeks. He's been building and selling luxury estates like this for almost twenty years. The guy knows what he's doing. He knows his demographic."

Danica listened, trying to figure out where he was going with all this. She wanted to ask questions, to interrupt with standard police procedure, but she knew he was on a particular train of thought—a profile— and needed to compile the data in his own way.

"Look at this," he said, pointing to the plush, untouched cappuccino carpet on the master bedroom floor. "Heels. High, narrow heels. Stilettos."

"So a woman was in here. It doesn't mean she's behind all this," she stated, playing devil's advocate. "It could have been a realtor, a buyer, a mistress."

"Of course not. It's not just that she was here. It's how she moved. Come over here. Don't step where I point."

Danica made her way carefully towards Delgado, who stood by the expansive window of the bedroom. When she got close, she looked at the floor at an angle to catch the light. She saw the faint, circular indentations of a woman's high heels pressed deep into the pile.

"I see the impressions, but there has to be more to your theory than just shoes."

"There is. It's all adding up. I just can't figure out why." As she moved closer to the spot where Delgado stood, he stepped back and sat on the wide window ledge, facing the room. He closed his eyes for a second, then opened them.

"Look at the position of where and how she stood. The impressions show that she walked in from here," he pointed to the doorway with a sweeping motion. "Now, think about real estate. If a woman is interested in buying a home like this, there are two places she looks at first; the kitchen and the master bath. Roberts knew that. That's evident by the way he built this; he was catering to the specific wants of a female buyer. Both rooms are oversized, opulent, designed to appease a female's taste. If she was interested in this house, she would have walked from that doorway, straight into the bathroom to check the tub, the vanity, the closet space."

Danica saw the line of impressions in the carpet again, and this time his theory was starting to make sense. The path was wrong.

Nicholai continued, his voice gaining speed. "She didn't do that. She walked in and stood here, facing the bathroom. She stood still. The impressions are deeper here—she shifted her weight, waiting. She didn't go inside there. She didn't even look at the view from this window, which is the selling point of the lot. Look at the other impressions. There's an obvious trail proving that point. She came in, she watched, and she left. She wasn't a participant; she was an observer. An audience of one."

"But how do you know it wasn't someone else? A realtor checking the lights?"

"It's Friday afternoon. Roberts knows that weekends are prime time to show these places off. He opens them Fridays and closes them down Sundays. Makes sense to clean these homes Thursday so they show immaculate for the weekend crowd."

"How did you know that?" she asked. Danica was starting to understand the logic, but she needed the physical evidence.

"The smell," he said, tapping his nose. "There's still residue on the kitchen counters from the cleaning solution—lemon oil and ammonia. And it's all over the bathroom counters as well. The air is still heavy with it. I checked the other carpeted rooms. No vacuum lines have been disturbed. No one's been through this house since the cleaners left."

"The Fillions were here. You saw them. Maybe the wife wore heels."

"No car. They walked here from down the street. Mrs. Fillion wore casual leather sandals—flat soles—and he had tennis shoes on. I checked their footwear while you were questioning them. Nice couple, terrified, but definitely not the killing type. They went into the kitchen first, then they came in here. Look close and you'll see their impressions over near the door—shuffling, uncertain. Mrs. Fillion's steps stop at the bathroom doorway; she peeked in. He went in to check the body, and then he took her into the kitchen to call 911. It happened just like they said."

He was extremely focused, vibrating with a dark energy. Danica could almost feel the intensity radiating off him. He was back in the zone, the place where he had lost himself years ago.

"Other than the cleaning staff yesterday, the only people that have been in this place are Roberts, the Fillions, and her. And she's the one we need to stop."

"Why?" Danica asked, looking at the deep indentations by the window. "Why did she just stand here?"

Delgado stood up and walked to the spot, placing his feet carefully beside the marks. He looked into the bathroom where the body lay.

"Because she wanted to make sure he took the pills," Delgado whispered. "She wasn't here to kill him. She was here to ensure he killed himself."

Chapter 19

Danica threw the newspaper onto Captain Cooper's desk with enough force to scatter his paperwork.

"Whose stupid idea was this?" she yelled, her voice echoing off the glass walls of his office.

"Relax, I've already seen it," he said without lifting his head, continuing to sign a requisition form. "I saw it this morning before my coffee. The Chief's office released it."

Danica glared at the bold headline staring up at her: RETIRED FBI PROFILER CALLED TO SAVE STALLED INVESTIGATION. Below it was a file photo of Nicholai from ten years ago, looking younger and less haunted, next to a photo of her walking out of the Rosin estate.

"I wondered why Brad Thompson from The Star kept calling. I've got fifteen voicemails and a stack of messages on my desk from that poor excuse of a reporter asking for a comment on my 'incompetence.'"

"Did you call him back?" Cooper asked, finally capping his pen.

"Of course not. I can't stand reporters. You know that. They're vultures."

"Inspector, maybe if you had called him back, you could have set the record straight. Controlled the narrative."

Danica was angry, her face flushing. "Set the record straight? Are you kidding? They're all bottom feeders just interested in their next big front-page headline. They don't care about the truth; they care about selling ad space."

She turned her back to the Captain and folded her arms, pacing the small length of the office. Cooper knew her well, and he knew she was far from finished venting. He also knew he wasn't going to be able to stop her rampage. She had to finish it on her own.

She spun around quickly, pointing a finger at the paper. "And that article implies that Delgado was called in because we couldn't handle this case on our own. It makes the department look weak, and it makes me look like an amateur who needs her hand held."

"That wasn't my call, Harris, and you know it," Captain Cooper tried to explain, his voice calm but firm. "The press release wasn't my idea either, so don't even try to pin this on me. The Chief is feeling the heat from the Mayor's office. Dead rich men make politicians nervous. They wanted to show we were pulling out all the stops."

"How am I supposed to explain this to him!" she yelled, grabbing the paper and shaking it. "He didn't want anything to do with this case at first. I practically had to drag him off his boat. But for some reason, he is part of it now. He's actually engaging. But it's by his choice, not someone's orders. He values his privacy more than anything. This article paints a target on his back."

"Harris, relax. He's been around this block long enough to know how the game works. He knows politics. Maybe you could even learn something from this guy about rolling with the punches."

"Learn something?" she replied, incredulous. "If he sees this—if he sees his face plastered next to the words 'Serial Suicide'—I doubt I'll ever hear from him again. He's fragile, Captain. He's hanging on by a thread."

Cooper laughed, a short, dry bark. "What do you mean?"

"This article alone will probably scare him back out again. It brings up his past, his family... everything he's running from. I wouldn't be surprised if he sails off into some stupid sunset, never to be heard from again. And honestly? I wouldn't blame him."

"I highly doubt that," Cooper said, looking past her shoulder.

She looked hard at her superior, confused by his sudden shift in demeanor. "How can you be so sure? You don't know him like I'm getting to know him."

"Because," Cooper said, nodding toward the door, "he's right behind you."

Chapter 20

"I'm here, and that's all you need to be concerned with," he said calmly, sitting at the metal table with his hands folded.

Danica had stormed out of Captain Cooper's office, grabbed Delgado by the arm, and pulled him into the nearest empty interrogation room. The air inside was stale, smelling of old sweat and nervous energy. After slamming the heavy door hard enough to rattle the one-way glass—and loud enough for the entire squad room to hear—she paced the small length of the room, trying her best to apologize for the article in the newspaper without losing her composure.

"But still, I want you to know I had nothing to do with that," she tried to explain again, her hands moving frantically. "I hate politics, and I hate leaks. It makes us look incompetent, and it puts you in the crosshairs. I would never expose a source like that."

"Please, Danica, stop apologizing," he said, his voice steady and low, cutting through her anxiety. He stopped and briefly looked away at the scarred wall. "It's done. The ink is dry. I'm here, and we've got work to do. Dwelling on it only gives the enemy an advantage."

Danica stopped pacing and leaned against the door, crossing her arms. "Are you staying? Really staying? Because if you walk out tomorrow, I'm the one left holding the bag."

"For now, yes."

"You never did completely explain why you changed your mind and decided to help," she pressed, needing to understand his motivation. "One minute you're throwing me off your boat, telling me to leave you alone with your ghosts, and the next you're profiling footprints in a dead man's bedroom. What changed?"

"That night after you left, something happened," he said quietly, his eyes finding hers. "I prayed about it. I wrestled with it, actually. I know that God puts situations and people in your life for a reason and purpose. We like to think we have control, that we can isolate ourselves on a boat and hide from the world, but we can't run from our assignment. Sometimes it's for His purpose, and we can't question that."

"We certainly differ on a lot of that," she said, skepticism dripping from her voice. "I deal in evidence, not divine intervention."

"Danica, sometimes that's what faith is all about; following without proof and not knowing what the outcome will be but trusting in Him. It's not blind; it's just... sighting beyond the horizon." He paused, shifting in the uncomfortable metal chair. "One of the passages of scripture I lean on is Romans 8:28. It kept me alive when I wanted to die."

He recited it from memory, his voice taking on a cadence that sounded more like a soldier than a preacher. "'And we know that in all things God works for the good of those who love him, who have been called according to his purpose.' I find great strength and peace in that passage. It tells me that even the wreckage—even the pain—is being used to build something."

"So you're telling me God has told you to do this," she said flatly. "The Almighty wants you to catch a killer?"

"I believe so, yes," he said. "I believe He gave me this specific skill set—the ability to see the darkness in others—for a reason. But that scares me too."

"Why does it scare you if you claim to have such strong faith?" she asked. " shouldn't that make you fearless?"

"Because of the nature of the enemy," he said. Nicholai pushed his chair away, the metal legs scraping loudly against the linoleum, and rose to his feet. He walked over to the small window covered in wire mesh and peered through the dirty glass at the busy station outside. He watched the officers moving about, oblivious to the war he felt brewing.

He turned back and looked down on her, his face shadowed. "Because whoever is behind all this... they believe that God is guiding them too. They believe their mission is just as holy as mine."

Danica felt a chill run down her spine.

"Unfortunately," Delgado whispered, "when this is all over, one of us is going to be wrong. And usually, the one who is wrong leaves a lot of bodies behind to prove their point."

106

Chapter 21

The cockroach stopped dead on the cracked linoleum. Its antennae twitched, tasting the thick, humid air. Then, as quickly as it stopped, it jerked to the left, scurried a few more inches, and stopped again. Finally, the two-inch filthy pest retreated silently to the right and disappeared inside a pile of soiled clothes next to the bare, stained mattress on the floor.

Jeremy Quinlin hadn't noticed the roach. It wouldn't have had an effect on him anyway, good or bad. The hundreds of other roaches that made his dark, musty apartment their home didn't make him flinch even in the slightest. They were just fellow occupants of the darkness. He wasn't even aware of the stench of black mold and rat urine that hung heavy in the air, thick enough to taste. Nothing physical ever bothered him. He was too focused on the voice.

The entire studio apartment on the third floor of the Heritage Arms Hotel off Ross Avenue was dark—hot, suffocatingly humid, and dark—just the way he preferred. It was a womb of filth. A thin sliver of sunlight struggled to make its way through the old, moth-eaten quilt he had nailed to the window frame to block out the world. The thin beam of light, dancing with dust motes, highlighted the tight muscle definition of his bare chest. He was lean, corded with sinew like a coiled spring, a physical contradiction to the squalor he lived in.

His hands were cupped behind his shaved head while his sunken black eyes glared at nothing in particular on the water-stained ceiling. Quinlin had chosen to remain in the same position for the past eight hours. Not because he was lazy, but because he was training.

Discipline. Restraint. Obedience.

Even the painful pressure of a full bladder wasn't enough discomfort for him to move out of that position. To move would be to surrender to the flesh, and Jeremy Quinlin was a master of the flesh. He was focused.

He knew it was time. His time. He was well-rested, his body honed, and now everything he was hearing was telling him to act again. The voice was getting louder by the day, by the hour, vibrating in his skull like a tuning fork. His orders were becoming clear and more precise, stripping away the noise of the outside world.

Quinlin took detailed notes, documenting the instructions whenever they came through the static of his mind. Sometimes they came too quickly, a rushing torrent of commands, but he always managed to write them out, terrified that if he missed a word, the mission would fail. He felt more would be coming through any time. He had to have his mind clear and ready to receive.

He eased over on his side, his muscles moving fluidly, and reached to turn on the lamp. The single bare twenty-five-watt bulb flickered to life, dimly lighting the room in a sickly yellow hue. The shadowy light barely exposed the minute handwritten letters that covered the dirty grey walls of the apartment.

It was a tapestry of madness. Almost every inch of wall space—from the baseboards to the ceiling—was already covered with his tight, precise penmanship detailing his instructions. There were no spaces between words, no capital letters, and definitely no punctuation. It was a continuous stream of consciousness, a scripture of violence. This was Jeremy Quinlin's bible, the instructions from the voice inside his head. An exact set of orders for his life that only he could decipher.

Along the far wall, an obvious blank area, no larger than four feet square, had been left clear for a reason. It was the final chapter.

He sat up, ignoring the stiffness in his joints, and glared at the open area before reaching down to the grimy floor. He grabbed the last fine-point Sharpie from the package. With his teeth, he pulled the black top off the pen, then spit it across the room with lethal accuracy. It hit the wall with a click. A startled roach scurried under the mattress.

Quinlin rolled himself off the mattress with precise, tight movements, ignoring the trash that crunched beneath his feet, then crawled on his hands and knees to the blank spot on the wall. With a smile that didn't reach his dead eyes, he started writing the new orders that were now flooding his mind. The ink flowed onto the plaster, black and permanent.

findhimfindhimfindhimtetelestai

His bladder was still full, and the pain was becoming almost unbearable, sending spasms through his abdomen. But that would have to wait, just like everything else. Pain was just information. There were more important and immediate items on the agenda now. It all needed to be done.

It was almost time. Time to finish what Jeremy Quinlin had started years ago. Time to finish what Nicholai Delgado had interfered with. The Pastor thought he had escaped, thought he had found peace on the water, but no debt is ever truly canceled until blood is spilled.

He pressed the marker harder against the wall, the tip squeaking. He was following the orders.

Discipline. Restraint. Obedience.

The hunt was back on.

Chapter 22

It was obvious she wasn't the first Mrs. Roberts. Alisha Roberts was less than half her now-deceased husband David's age, probably just a day or two older than his oldest daughter from a previous marriage. She sat on the edge of the expensive sofa, looking small and out of place in the cavernous living room. Danica had asked the same questions of the young widow as she had of the previous widows, expecting the same rehearsed indifference. The answers were factual and almost identical in content, but the delivery was worlds apart.

Alisha Roberts was far more upset than the others were. Her mascara was running, her hands trembled, and she wasn't worried about life insurance policies or bank accounts. It was probably due to the fact she had only been married to the high-end luxury homebuilder for less than a year. They had still been in the honeymoon stage of their marriage, living in a bubble of new wealth and affection.

"I don't understand it," she sobbed, clutching a wet tissue. "There was never any sign of this at all. He was happy. We were happy. He just bought tickets for a cruise next month."

After asking permission with a polite nod, Nicholai had wandered away from the tearful conversation between Danica and the grieving widow. He slipped out of the room like a shadow, leaving Danica to handle the emotional fallout. He spent several minutes in David Roberts' home office, a space that smelled of cedar and old paper. He scanned through blueprints rolled up in bins and sifted through client files, looking for irregularities. Nothing led him to any further leads; it was just the mundane paperwork of a man building empires for other people.

The laptop on Roberts' massive mahogany desk was turned off, sitting squarely on a leather blotter. Delgado powered the computer on, the hum of the fan breaking the silence, and waited to see the results. The password screen flashed, demanding authentication. He decided to leave the hacking to Griffin; guessing wasn't worth the lockout risk. He assumed Mrs. Roberts was probably not aware of the password, so there was no point in even asking. He also assumed the hard drive was partitioned just like Rosin and Simpson's computers—a digital safe room. He stared at the screen for a moment, his reflection staring back, before deciding to shut it down and close the lid. He was sure Mrs. Roberts wouldn't mind them taking it for a few days. Another trip to Griffin's warehouse was due, and soon.

Nicholai tucked the laptop under his arm and started to make his way down the hall. He stopped just outside the door, a nagging feeling pulling at him. He turned back and took one last look around Roberts' office, letting his eyes drift over the space one more time. He moved back inside and looked at a display unit tucked away off in the corner, shadowed by a heavy drape. Framed photographs, architectural awards, and travel souvenirs filled the shelves.

One item in particular caught his attention. A small, hand-carved wooden mask stood out among the glass awards. He picked it up, feeling the weight of the dense wood. He moved it delicately from one hand to the other, more lost in his own thoughts than analyzing the actual item. It was becoming clear. The mask was identical to the one found in the home of James Rosin—the same grotesque expression, the same sewn mouth. It wasn't a coincidence; it was a totem.

He took his eyes and mind off the mask just long enough to see the framed photograph that had been hidden behind it, tucked in the back of the shelf as if hidden on purpose. He looked at the photograph closer, his breath catching in his throat. The mask slipped from his hands and fell to the hardwood floor. He didn't hear the delicate piece shatter into splinters. His mind was completely focused on the two men in the photograph standing in front of a dense jungle.

Having heard the crash from down the hall, Danica and Alisha Roberts quickly made their way towards Roberts' office. When they entered, Nicholai was bent over, still looking at the photograph in his hand, wood pieces and slivers scattered around his shoes like shrapnel.

"What happened?" Danica asked, slightly embarrassed by her consultant's clumsiness.

"Do you know this man?" Delgado ignored Danica completely and thrust the photo toward the widow. "The man standing beside your husband in this picture."

Alisha wiped her eyes and squinted at the image. "James, I think his name is. He is... or was a friend of David's. I think they did business together years ago."

"Have you ever met him? When was this photo taken?" Nicholai fired the questions at the widow, his intensity spiking.

"No, I never met him. David kept his work friends separate. And I don't know when or where that was taken. Maybe one of his hunting trips to South America? I really don't know. I'm sorry, but I can't help. David had a life before me."

"What broke?" Danica asked, looking at the debris on the floor.

"A wooden mask," Nicholai said, placing the photo back on the shelf but keeping his hand on it. From the expression on his face, Danica knew something more was going on in his mind. He had found a link.

"Do you know when your husband last saw Mr. Rosin?" Delgado asked, turning back to Alisha.

"I really don't know. Maybe their last hunting trip a few months ago. David was quite private about those trips. I knew he loved the sport, so I never pried."

Danica stood back and let Nicholai lead the questions. She knew he was on a scent trail, and though she didn't know where he was going, she trusted the hunter's instinct he was displaying.

"Mrs. Roberts?" he asked, softening his tone. "There are a couple of things we need from you in order to clear all this up. I'd like to take this laptop with us if I could. It might hold the answers you're looking for."

"That's fine," she said, her voice trembling. "Take whatever you need. I just want to know why."

Danica could tell she was about to break down any minute.

"And his passport," Delgado added. "I'd like to take that with us as well. We need to see where he's been."

Chapter 23

He asked if they could make a stop at Delgado's home on Windsor Lane. Nicholai wanted to retrieve some old files for research—specifically files on the Quinlin case—before heading back to the marina for the night. His car was left at the downtown Police Plaza, and the stop was on their way.

The drive was heavy. The more he remained quiet, the more Danica wanted to get inside his mind. She wanted to know every thought and idea he had regarding the photo and the masks. What was he feeling? Silence had always bothered her; stillness made her uncomfortable. The discomfort was sometimes tolerable when she was alone, but when someone else was near, radiating tension like a heat wave, it was almost unbearable.

And now in the car, he was quiet, staring out the window at the passing suburbs. When she did ask him a question, the answer was forced out in monosyllables that made her even more uncomfortable. After several attempts, she finally just gave up and turned the car radio up louder, letting the traffic report fill the void.

When they got close to his house, he started giving her directions. She knew the way—she had been there just days before—but the sound of his voice eased her a bit, and she didn't want him to stop speaking.

The home was dark when she pulled the car into the driveway. It looked abandoned, a dark tooth in a smile of bright, well-lit homes. She opened the car door and stood looking at the structure. Nicholai remained in the car for a long moment. Through the windshield, she saw his eyes were closed, his head bowed. He was praying again, steeling himself to enter the mausoleum of his past.

Finally, he exited and made his way to the front door of his home. Danica followed behind, leaving a few feet of space between the two, sensing his need for room.

Danica was uneasy the moment they walked through the front door. The air inside was stale, recycled and hot. Nicholai turned the light on in the foyer, then the living room, and stood in the center of the room, motionless.

"Have a seat," he said, his voice echoing slightly. "I'll just be a minute. My office is in the back."

He disappeared down the hallway, leaving her alone in the living room. Even though the home was quiet, the area lacked any kind of peace. It was obvious that no one had lived inside for any period of time. There were no smells of cooking, no hum of electronics, no evidence of a family. Dust motes danced in the shafts of light from the streetlamps outside. It was just a space where time had stopped three years ago.

On the far wall, Danica noticed a collection of crosses hung randomly. They were all different in size, style, make, and construction—wood, iron, ceramic, glass. She counted twenty-seven in total. She contemplated each one, wondering if they each had a special meaning or significance, or if the entire wall was just a decorator's idea. It felt like a shrine.

"Would you like something to drink?" His voice from behind startled her.

"No, I'm fine," she said, turning around.

He turned and walked into a room she assumed was the kitchen. She heard water running, the pipes groaning from disuse, then a cabinet door close. He reappeared from the other side, walking through the dark formal dining room into the living room holding a glass of water. He made his way closer to where Danica stood.

Suddenly he stopped a few feet away from her. The glass in his hand tilted slightly, water sloshing over the rim.

"Someone's been here," he said. His voice was barely a whisper, but it carried the weight of a scream.

She turned quickly and faced him, her hand moving to her hip. "What?"

Danica hadn't seen or even expected the drastic change in Nicholai's face. She could tell immediately he was scared—not of a

116

physical threat, but of a violation. The blood had drained from his face, leaving him ashen, and his eyes were suddenly hollow, scanning the room with frantic intensity.

"How can you tell?" she asked, looking around the undisturbed room. "Nothing looks touched."

"I felt something the moment we walked in but didn't say anything. The air... it's displaced. The dust patterns are wrong."

"A feeling? That's it?"

"At first, yes. Now I notice something concrete. Look." He pointed a shaking finger at the wall Danica had just been admiring. "A cross is missing from over there."

Danica looked back at the collection. Now that he pointed it out, she saw it—a small, lighter patch on the paint where a cross had once shielded the wall from the sun. A gap in the pattern.

"Should I call it in?" she asked, reaching for her phone.

Nicholai didn't answer. He walked around the room several times in a highly agitated state, like a caged animal, then disappeared through the dining room and back into the kitchen. Danica remained standing in the same position for a moment, gun drawn now, then walked towards the wall where Delgado said the missing cross once hung.

"He sat right over there."

His voice startled her again and broke her focus from the blank spot on the wall. She turned to see he had entered the room from the far side, emerging from the shadows.

"Where?" she asked.

Nicholai walked over to the leather couch, the one covered in a thin layer of dust. "Here," he said, pointing to a disturbance on the armrest. A clear, clean patch where a hand had rested. "He leaned against the arm of the sofa and stared at the wall, taking a mental inventory of this entire room. He sat here and soaked in my grief. I know he thought long and hard about what to take. He didn't want valuables. He wanted a souvenir; something only I would notice. A message."

"Who? You're acting like you already know who was here."

Nicholai looked at her, and the fear in his eyes had hardened into a cold, deadly rage.

"It's Quinlin. He's back. I can feel him again."

Chapter 24

"I don't understand why you won't let me call this in," Danica argued, her hands tight on the steering wheel. "This is a B and E. It's a crime scene."

They had left the house on Windsor Lane in a hurry, tires spinning slightly on the pavement. Danica could tell Nicholai wanted to get away as quickly as possible, as if the house itself were contaminated. She saw the life drain from his face and his whole demeanor change in an instant, shifting from the confident profiler back to the haunted victim. The air in the car was thick with his fear and her frustration. She managed to drive a few blocks, putting distance between them and the empty rectangle on his wall, before feeling comfortable enough to speak to him.

"We should at least file a report, get some techs out to try and pull his prints," she insisted. "If he touched the wall, if he touched the couch... we could get him on a technicality."

"Why?" he asked, staring out the window at the passing houses. "They wouldn't find anything. You'd be wasting resources and time we don't have. The entire two years I was tracking him, he didn't leave us anything to go on other than what he wanted us to find. He didn't make mistakes, Danica. He wore surgical gloves and shaved his entire body—head, arms, legs, everything—so as not to leave a single hair follicle behind. He taped his cuffs so no skin cells would flake off. You have no idea how good he is at this. He's a ghost."

"So how do you know it was him? Really know?"

"Because he's not after valuables. He's after emotional currency. Jessica and I collected those crosses over the years from our travels. Each one represents a memory or occasion that was special only to us. That specific cross... we bought it in Santa Fe on our honeymoon. It was the first thing we ever bought for our home." His voice cracked slightly. "Taking it wasn't theft. It was a message. He's telling me he can reach into my past and take whatever he wants."

"Don't you want to get this guy once and for all? Letting him walk away from your house feels like surrender."

He slammed his fist into the dashboard, the sudden violence of the action making Danica jump. "You don't get it, do you? Of course, I want to get him. I want to tear him apart with my bare hands. But he wants to get to me more than I want to stop him. He feeds on the chase. If I call the police, if I bring the circus to my front lawn, he wins. He sees the lights, he sees the panic, and he gets off on it. And I'm not going to let that happen. I can't give him that satisfaction."

"What do you mean he wants you?"

"It became a game to him a long time ago. When he entered my space, my personal life, that was his effort to drag me into his reality. He doesn't just want to kill; he wants to break the hunter. He wants me to become like him—obsessed, lawless, desperate. And it worked once. I almost lost my soul trying to catch him."

"But if he's back out there," she said, trying to understand the twisted logic, "we've got to stop him. We can't just play by his rules."

"You're right, he has to be stopped," Nicholai said, his breathing slowing. He had calmed down and didn't seem quite as angry as he had been a moment before. The rage was replaced by a cold, hard resolve. "I managed to stop him once, but look at what it cost. He wants to start again, but in this game, there is only one way to win. Handcuffs won't end this. One of us is going to have to die. I died emotionally four years ago, and I'm desperately trying to come back. I won't let him kill what's left of me."

Chapter 25

It didn't take her long to find the house. She was resourceful, a predator in the information age. She used a combination of MapSearch on her laptop and the GPS system in her car to triangulate the general area. But the subdivision was new, a sprawling labyrinth of wealth, and the actual streets were still not fully listed on either system.

She found his actual address; that part was easy. Men with egos left digital footprints everywhere. Once she had located the exclusive Kingsbridge neighborhood, the rest was pretty straightforward.

Kingsbridge was slowly being developed as a high-end subdivision, a monument to excess, but the recent real estate meltdown had flattened the sales of luxury estates throughout the metroplex even more than the average three-bedroom ranch house stuck in the sub-urbs. It was a ghost town of mansions. Vacant, manicured two-acre building sites lined the empty streets like green cemeteries. There were some homes in various stages of completion—skeletons of timber and Tyvek—but only a handful were actually completed and occupied. It was perfect. Isolation was her ally.

His home was easy to find. She could tell the first time she drove by that it was exactly the type of home a man in his position would occupy—ostentatious, large, and shouting for attention. The online Collin County tax records had confirmed the address. She was able to pull up the information on the laptop sitting on the passenger seat.

Those same records listed the home at just over six thousand square feet. It was a one-story brick French colonial which seemed much larger as it stretched across the gated two-acre yard. A floor plan had been filed by the builder at the tax office prior to construction, and that gave her the basic layout of the rooms. She knew the house better than the guests did.

The second time she drove past his house, she was able to get a better look at the security cameras. The third and fourth times were more to build up her courage for what she had planned, checking the patterns of the neighbors.

His black Mercedes sedan was parked in the circular drive, gleaming under the streetlights. The white Cadillac Escalade could be inside the garage, but she wasn't certain. The front gate was open—a careless mistake born of a false sense of security. She thought there had been some movement in the house. His car was there, but where was his wife? Or had they gone out together?

On the fifth time around the block, she moved her car slowly, hugging the curb, and then stopped, almost blocking the driveway of the vacant lot next door. She studied the house before gently placing the transmission in reverse and pulling back a few feet into the shadows of a construction dumpster.

A white SUV appeared in her rearview mirror. She watched as the vehicle slowly drew closer. Her hands gripped the wheel tight, knuckles white, then eased off as the SUV passed alongside her and continued down the street. The vehicle stopped at one of the vacant homes down the street, and she watched a slender woman—a realtor, likely—exit the passenger side of the vehicle and remove a feature sheet from the plastic information box in front of the house. She glanced at the sheet, bored, then returned to the SUV. The brake lights went off, and the vehicle disappeared around the corner.

It was only then that she released the breath from her lungs and smiled. The stage was hers.

The ignition was shut off, and she listened to the silence of the neighborhood before quietly exiting her car. She walked up the driveway slowly, keeping her eyes focused on the house, moving through the blind spots of the exterior lights. She rounded the three-car garage, stopping only to place her hand on the hood of his Mercedes. The metal was still warm.

"I'd look good in this," she thought to herself, trailing a fingernail across the paint. "Better than she does."

The rush of the decorative waterfall in the backyard hid the sounds of her steps as she made her way along the pool deck. It was a perfect setting. The blue light from the pool illuminated the stone patio. It could have been the perfect shot for the cover of Better Homes and Gardens, and if she had her own way, someday it would be. She even imagined where she would stand for the photo shoot, wearing white, laughing at a joke no one else heard.

She could see clearly through the back windows of the home into the den. There was no movement inside. She checked the handle of the French door and found it unlocked. She eased it open and made her way inside, the air conditioning chilling her skin.

A large flat-screen television over the fireplace was on, but the sound was muted. Two nondescript college football teams were battling it out on a green field. A smiling cheerleader stared back from the screen, frozen in artificial joy, as the woman moved through the kitchen, running her hand along the granite countertops.

Muffled voices made their way from the far side of the kitchen, and she stopped before taking another step. She listened intently. Her movements were slow and tight like a cat stalking an unsuspecting bird. When she was certain it was safe, she made her way closer to the sounds, drawn to them like a moth to a flame. The voices were coming from behind the closed door at the end of the hall. She knew it was the master suite from the floor plan she had downloaded and memorized.

The sound was recognizable. It was the sound of intimacy.

She clenched her fists harder as she drew closer to the sounds of a husband and wife enjoying each other's pleasure. The rhythmic creaking, the soft moans, the laughter. She stood silent but tense outside the door, an intruder in their sanctuary. Every muscle in her body tightened with a mixture of arousal and rage. They were happy. They were safe. They had no idea how fragile it all was.

Won't last! The thought made her relax slightly, a cruel smile touching her lips. "Won't last."

She turned away, satisfied with her reconnaissance. She quietly slipped out of the home the same way she had entered, leaving no trace but the displacement of air. She took one long last look at the Mercedes, possessiveness burning in her eyes, before walking back to her car and speeding away into the night.

Chapter 26

Danica was surprised to find herself feeling more at ease this time out on the water. The tension that usually coiled around her spine like a steel cable had begun to slacken. Nicholai had maneuvered the Sara Rose easily from the slip, his hands moving with muscle memory, and guided them past the concrete arms of the marina breakwater.

She watched the jib sail unwind from the front stay, snapping loudly before catching the evening breeze with a satisfying thrum. The boat lurched forward, heeling slightly to the side, and she closed her eyes, feeling the warm air rush against her face. It smelled of water and distant cedar. She felt her muscles relax as the stale air of the city slowly eased from her lungs, replaced by something cleaner. She took a deep breath, opened her eyes, and looked at the man standing behind the stainless steel wheel.

Nicholai looked down at her just as she focused her eyes on his. He seemed part of the boat, balancing effortlessly against the roll of the waves.

"You ready to take the wheel for a minute?" he asked, his voice carrying easily over the wind.

She wasn't, but something made her stand and move in his direction. It was a challenge, and Danica Harris never backed down from a challenge. She navigated around the helm stand and stood beside him, leaving just enough space between them for her own comfort—a buffer zone she wasn't quite ready to surrender. Nicholai moved away after a moment, checking the lines, and then disappeared below inside the cabin.

She nervously gripped the wheel, her knuckles white, acting as if she was in control while the boat responded to the shifting wind. It felt alive in her hands, vibrating with energy.

"Here you go," he said, popping his head back up and handing her a cold can of Dr. Pepper.

"I didn't know you had this on board," she said, taking the can with one hand while keeping a death grip on the wheel with the other.

"I just bought them today. I noticed you drank a lot of those back at the precinct, and I wanted to make you feel as comfortable as possible out here. I bought a few other kinds as well, just in case you wanted something else. Ginger ale, Coke, water."

"Do you happen to have a Starbucks franchise down there?" she joked, taking a sip. The sugar hit her system, a familiar comfort.

He laughed, a deep, resonant sound, and Danica smiled. It had been a while since she saw his face light up like that, free from the shadows of the case.

"No, but I do have a French press and some coffee put away. If you get desperate and out of control, we'll manage," he said. "I know better than to keep a detective uncaffeinated."

"Whatever," she replied, rolling her eyes but appreciating the gesture more than she would admit.

Nicholai looked at her behind the wheel, checking her posture, then turned towards the bow of the boat. He looked back at Danica, satisfied, then took a seat along the side of the cockpit, stretching his legs out.

Danica looked a bit surprised. "Are you going to take this back?"

"No," he said, leaning his head back against the cushion. "You're doing fine."

"But... what if I hit something? What if the wind shifts?"

"Stop that," Nicholai grinned at her, keeping his eyes closed. "You've got control, and you're doing fine. Just keep the jib full and steer her straight. Don't fight the water; work with it. I really think she likes you."

"You like this, don't you," she said after a few moments of silence, watching the wake churn behind them. Delgado had his head back, his eyes were closed, and his face was soaking in the cool breeze like a man dying of thirst.

"I love it when He makes the wind. And yes, I do like this. It's usually just me out here," he said softly. "But when someone else can take the helm and let me relax for a while… that's a treat. It's rare that I trust anyone enough to close my eyes."

The comment hung in the air, heavier than the humidity. Danica tightened her grip on the wheel, feeling the weight of that trust.

"We haven't talked about the other day at the house," Danica brought up the topic, breaking the peace. She knew he wouldn't bring it up on his own.

"Not much to say," he replied without opening his eyes.

"Have you been back?" she asked.

"No."

"Why?" she asked, probing the wound. "Are you afraid?"

Nicholai thought for a moment, the lines on his forehead deepening. "I don't know. I've been praying about it, but haven't gotten an answer yet. Sometimes silence is an answer."

"Are you afraid of him? Quinlin?"

"Yes and no," he said quietly. He opened his eyes and looked at the horizon. "Physically? No. I can handle myself. I've taken down men twice his size."

Danica tried to keep her focus on the jib and the direction of the boat, but she was being drawn to Nicholai. The vulnerability in his voice was magnetic. "Then what do you mean?"

"It's what he has done emotionally to me that scares me most. It took me some time to fully understand the damage that man did to my moral fiber. He didn't just kill my family; he destroyed everything I valued and cherished in my life. He made me question everything I stood for." He felt her eyes on him but turned away, staring at the water. "I'm afraid of who I become when I hunt him. I'm afraid of the rage."

"I'm sorry," she said. It was inadequate, but it was all she had. The sun was starting to set, painting the sky in bruised purples and fiery oranges, and the line between the water and sky was starting to disappear.

"It's okay. Danica, you don't have to apologize." Nicholai turned back to her, and their eyes met across the cockpit. "I've learned that spirituality is an exercise of the mind. What you focus on is what you believe. When I was active with the Bureau, I was so consumed with the evil in this world because it was my job. I breathed it, I ate it, I slept with it. The only light I ever had was my family, and he took that from me. He stole it!"

Danica saw the change in him again. Visions of their visit to the house on Windsor Lane came back hard in her mind—the empty wall, the missing cross.

Nicholai sat forward, the relaxed sailor vanishing. "He ripped it all away just to get to me. And it worked. I let him. I became a different person. I didn't know who or what I was for a while. Everything I knew that was me, that was mine, he took." His voice wasn't loud, but there was a painful strength in the resonance, a vibration of barely contained fury.

Danica watched as Nicholai stood and faced the bow of the boat. His silhouette was dark against the setting sun. The light wind blew through his hair, and she saw the shape of his muscles through his shirt tighten as he gripped the railing. He stood silent against the bright light and lowered his head. Danica watched as his shoulders lowered slightly and he took a deep breath, exhaling slowly, forcing the tension out of his body. Nicholai placed both hands on the upper deck and leaned forward.

"Are you okay?" she asked quietly.

He took his time before turning towards her. The mask of peace was back in place. "I'm fine now," he said. "If you'd like, I can go below and make some coffee. It's getting cooler."

Before she could even answer, he made his way down the stairs and inside the cabin. She could see him looking through the lower cabinets, but she tried to stay focused on the sail and the direction the boat was headed. They had been on the water for almost two hours, and the lights from the marina behind them had disappeared, but the Dallas skyline appeared on the horizon, a distant galaxy of artificial light.

"Water's boiling," he said, making his way back up the stairs. "It'll be just a minute." Nicholai's demeanor had changed back to the gentle host, and Danica's grip eased off the wheel slightly. He stood in the center of the cockpit and scanned the darkening sky.

"Not bad for a rookie," he smiled at her. "We're at my favorite spot and almost just in time."

"I'm confused," she said, looking around at the open water. "What are you talking about? It's just water."

"You'll see," he said. "Let's drop anchor and sit. I want to show you something God is painting."

"I'll bring in the jib, and you can let the wheel go. There's a lock clip on the side. Slide it down when I tell you."

Danica didn't answer. She watched as he pulled the jib sheet from the lock and held the line tight. Nicholai reached below the wheel and turned the furling winch on. She watched as the jib sail wound itself around the main halyard and disappeared, the sound of the flapping canvas dying down. Nicholai eased himself onto the top deck and made his way to the bow. Night was coming slowly, but she could still see him reach for the anchor and slowly ease it into the water. He made his way back towards the stern but stopped at the mast and turned back to face the sky.

128

Danica saw something she hadn't seen in the man since her first visit. In less than a few minutes, Nicholai had gone from a frightened man, drowning in the depths of a broken life and shattered dreams, to a man who had reached out and grabbed the strength to embrace the wind and the elements to come to a place of calm and peace. She could tell this was where he belonged. She understood it, but it frightened her. She couldn't quite understand where he had found it or even where it had come from, but it all intrigued her, and she found herself wanting to know more.

The sun was now almost gone, dipping below the horizon, but he seemed brighter. His figure against the darkening sky looked strong and in control.

Nicholai turned and made his way back to the stern and stepped into the cockpit. It was then Danica realized she had been holding her breath. She didn't know how long, but she let the air release from her lungs and she took in more. The clean air felt good, crisp and untainted by the city.

"Dani, sit, relax for a bit," he stopped suddenly almost in mid-sentence. "Is it okay if I call you Dani?"

"Whatever," she said with the hint of a smile, stepping away from the wheel. "Just don't call me Inspector."

"I'll get the coffee and be right back."

From the cockpit bench, she could see him inside the cabin, bathed in the warm yellow glow of the interior lights. Nicholai had the glass French press on the small cabin counter and was filling it with dark coffee grounds.

"Music?" he asked without waiting for a response.

The sound of a light guitar chord eased from the cockpit speakers and surrounded the open night air. She watched as he slowly poured the boiling water into the glass container as the familiar lyrics from Lifehouse's "Broken" softened the mood.

"And I am here still waiting, Though I still have my doubts, I am damaged at best, Like you've already figured out,"

The coffee grounds rose to the top of the French press, turning the hot water black. She could smell the rich aroma from outside, mixing with the scent of the lake. He gently placed the press inside and eased the screen to the water line. Nicholai turned his head and saw she was watching him.

"It's cooling down. Would you like a blanket?" he asked from the cabin.

"I guess," she replied, hugging her arms. "It is a little chilly."

Nicholai walked towards the front berth and returned with a thick navy wool blanket. He leaned against the stairway and handed the cover to Danica through the companionway. She sat back and wrapped the navy flannel around her bare legs, tucking it in tight, and she closed her eyes, letting the music wash over her.

"I'm fallin' apart, I'm barely breathing, With a broken heart, That's still beating, In the pain is there healing? In your name, I find meaning,"

"Here you go." Nicholai stood over her holding two ceramic cups. She opened her eyes and saw the steam rising in the twilight. She grabbed the one from his left hand.

"How did you know that was yours?" he smiled.

"I didn't," she said. "I just took the one closest to me."

"It's okay. I knew you'd grab that one," he laughed, then motioned to the empty space on the bench next to Danica. "Do you mind?"

"No." That was all she was going to say, but she shifted the blanket slightly to make room.

Nicholai settled beside her. There was a space between them—maybe six inches—that neither noticed nor cared about at that exact moment.

"So what did you want to show me?" she asked, sipping the coffee. It was hot and strong, exactly how she needed it.

"Pardon?" His eyes were closed, savoring the coffee, but he opened them and looked directly into hers.

"You said earlier you wanted to show me something. Before we dropped anchor."

Delgado smiled, then pointed off the port side. "Look. God's masterpiece."

The sun settled halfway across the horizon. The sky was full with colors and tones Danica had never before seen. Blues, yellows, and bright oranges blended together, creating the most brilliant portrait of beauty far beyond anything she had ever seen in an art gallery. The water reflected the sky, doubling the majesty, turning the lake into a sheet of liquid fire. Words couldn't explain at that moment what Danica was seeing, but she knew there was nothing she could say that would do it justice. She sat back slowly, unaware the space between the two had disappeared.

"Is it always like that?" she finally asked quietly.

"Most evenings it is. We just forget to look up."

"So I'm holdin' on, I'm holdin' on I'm barely, holdin' on to you,"

"I see why you like it out here," she said before taking another sip of coffee. "Can I ask you what happened earlier? I know the house upset you. Are you okay now?"

"Remember I said spirituality was a matter of the mind? I have to break away sometimes. This world is broken," he said, staring at the fading light. "What we focus on, we strive for. We live for what we think. At those times when I go down, when the darkness tries to pull me under, I have to look back up to God. He will be there; He promised.

He's our Savior, and I go to Him. It's the only thing I have left to count on."

"It would be nice if I could go there most of the time," she admitted, her voice small. "I usually just go to the bottom of a glass."

"I'm hanging on for another day, Just to see what you'll throw my way,"

"You will, Dani," he said, his voice filled with certainty. "When the time comes, you will."

She leaned in closer, seeking warmth, and he felt her shoulder press against his arm. He didn't pull away.

"I can tell you from my experience," he said softly. "There are times when you feel life is never going to get any better. You've hit bottom and it all seems dark. You're trapped in the depths of despair, a darkness so thick you can taste it, and you fight desperately to find a way out of your own hopelessness."

"I'm hanging on to the words You say, You said that I will, will be okay,"

"Then suddenly your fear of it becomes the worst part. And then you open your eyes and see that," he said, pointing to the setting sun and brightly lit sky. "You see what God has given us. And just when you realize we don't deserve anything, you see He has given us everything. Dani, He has given us freedom, beauty, peace, and a love like you've never known."

"I still see your reflection, inside my eyes, That are looking for purpose, Instead of looking for life,"

Danica listened but said nothing. She heard the words of the song mixed with what Nicholai was saying, and for the first time in a long time, she didn't feel the need to fight it. She felt the warmth of his arm around her shoulders—she couldn't remember when he had done that, but it felt right. He breathed in, and Danica felt her emotional walls falling, crumbling into the lake, and she didn't want to stop them.

"I'm fallin' apart, I'm barely breathing, With a broken heart, That's still beating, In the pain there is healing, In your name, I find meaning,"

Danica looked out as the sun disappeared behind the horizon, leaving nothing but a fainting glow. She closed her eyes without any effort and let herself go. It was Danica Harris going somewhere new, to a place she had never been—a place of quiet surrender.

"So I'm holdin' on, I'm holdin', I'm barely, holdin' on to you."

Chapter 27

Danica opened her eyes, and the world was white. The brightness burned for a moment, piercing through her eyelashes and forcing her to squeeze her lids tight against the morning glare. It took her a few disoriented minutes to realize where she was; the gentle, rhythmic swaying was not the stillness of her loft. Even when the memory washed over her, she still couldn't quite believe it.

She lay quietly, wrapped in the heavy navy wool, trying to recall the entire evening's events. She remembered the song, the lyrics about brokenness still echoing in her mind like a residual haunt. She could still feel the visceral effects of the sunset she had witnessed—the colors bleeding into the water. It made her smile, a rare, unguarded expression, and she didn't want to move. The rocking of the boat soothed her body and mind, lulling her into a state of peace she hadn't felt in years. She closed her eyes again, inhaling the scent of teak oil and fresh water.

"Good morning," she said quietly, testing her voice. It sounded raspy, unused.

"Hey, sleepy," Nicholai's voice drifted down from the cockpit, warm and amused. "Didn't think you were ever going to wake up down there."

She sat up, rubbing her face, and looked up through the companionway. She saw him framed against the blue sky, sitting on the cockpit seat with a leather-bound book in his hand. He looked fresh, alert, as if he had been awake for hours.

"Coffee should still be warm," he said, gesturing to the small table. "It's in the French press. Grab a cup and join me up here. The view is better."

He was far too cheery for her. Danica was used to her own quiet solitude in the mornings; alone, quiet, dark, and usually accompanied by a headache. It's what she thought she liked—control. This was such an extreme contrast to her usual armored morning routine that she felt vulnerable. She thought about turning back around, pulling the blanket over her head, and crawling back into the berth to hide.

"Come on up. It's a beautiful morning. You don't want to miss it."

Danica sighed, defeated by his optimism. She poured herself a cup of coffee, the black liquid steaming in the cool air. She took a drink, then another, letting the caffeine jumpstart her system. She refilled her cup to the top, shook the sleep from her head, ran a hand through her tangled hair, and made her way up the stairs to the deck.

"Did you sleep okay?" he asked, closing the book.

"Actually, I did." She was slightly embarrassed by the admission. "I feel... rested. I can't recall falling asleep or even getting into the berth. I must have crashed hard." She looked down at herself; she still had her same clothes on—jeans and blouse, now wrinkled—and that made her feel slightly relieved, though she felt grime on her skin.

"It's bright out here," she said, squinting as she took a seat across from him. The water was a sheet of diamonds. She looked out at the expanse again before looking back at Nicholai. "How did I get down there?" she asked. "I remember sitting here, listening to the music, but after that..."

He grinned before answering, a boyish expression that took years off his face. "I carried you," he said simply. "You fell asleep up here, curled up like a cat. It started getting cold, and I didn't want to wake you, so I just carried you down there and tucked you in."

Danica felt a flush rise to her cheeks. "I'm heavy. You should have just woke me up."

"It's quite alright. You're lighter than you think. I could tell you were exhausted, Dani. You carry a lot of weight on your shoulders during the day. You combine that release with all this fresh air, and it can knock you out pretty hard. You needed it."

She waited before asking her next question, her detective's mind needing to categorize the night. She wanted to know, but then she didn't. "Where did you sleep?"

"There's a berth down below the cockpit, tucked in the back. I crawled in there and caught a few hours. I kept an anchor watch for a while."

She looked across the water again. There wasn't the slightest whisper of a breeze, and the lake was as smooth as glass, reflecting the white hull of the boat perfectly.

After a moment, she looked at him. "I didn't mean to stay out here all night. I have work. I'm sorry if I imposed."

He laughed softly and put down the book on the bench. She saw he had been reading the Bible, the pages worn and soft.

"Don't apologize, Dani. I told you, stop apologizing." He looked at her with a softness that unnerved her. "It's been quite a while since I've had a woman on board all night. It was nice to hear someone else breathing in the quiet."

"I noticed the name of the boat is Sara Rose. Where did you come up with that?" she asked, deflecting the intimacy.

"You're supposed to name a boat after a woman who has had an impact on your life," he said, his hand resting on the Bible. "Sara was my daughter's name. She was the light of my life. And roses... roses had always been my wife's favorite flower. Jessica loved them. We used to joke about having a granddaughter at some point and hoping her name would be Sara Rose. So, in a way, this boat is the family I have left."

Danica didn't know what to say to that kind of grief wrapped in love, so she stayed silent and took another sip of coffee, letting the liquid burn her throat.

Finally, Nicholai spoke, breaking the solemnity. "Would you like something for breakfast? I can fix something. Eggs, toast?"

"No," she said quietly, standing up. The bubble had to burst eventually. "I think I should get going. I have a captain who is probably wondering where his lead detective is."

"Okay, if you say so," he said, masking any disappointment he might have felt. Nicholai stood up and looked from the starboard side around to the port side, checking the clearance. "There's not much wind this morning. I can get you in faster if we motor in."

Nicholai rose up and moved around to the wheel. He reached down and started the diesel engine, the vibration humming through the deck plates. Letting it idle, he gracefully climbed onto the upper deck, making his way to the bow. He pulled up the anchor, securing it with a metallic clank, and came back, shifting the transmission into forward. He swung the Sara Rose around to starboard.

Within a few minutes, Danica saw the marina closing in, the rows of masts looking like a forest of dead trees. She felt it was too soon to go back to reality. It seemed the closer they got to the shore, the worse she felt—the tension returning to her neck, the headache pulsing behind her eyes. She truly didn't want to leave, but she couldn't grasp what she was experiencing or how to hold onto it. She watched Nicholai maneuver the boat inside the breakwater and close to the marina office with practiced ease.

"Are you not going to your slip?" she asked.

"No, it's closer for you if I drop you off at the gas dock up here. You can walk right to your car," he said. "I'm going to stay out for a while longer. If you don't mind, I'll meet up with you later. I need some time alone with Him before I face the city again."

"I understand," she said. And for the first time, she really was starting to understand the need for sanctuary.

Delgado eased the Sara Rose against the dock bumpers and then shut the motor down to a low idle. He grabbed a line and leaped onto the dock, tying her up tight to a cleat. He reached out and offered his hand in assistance. She gladly accepted, her palm sliding against his calloused skin. Once on the dock, she couldn't look him in the eye and tried her best to avoid his gaze, afraid of what she might reveal.

"I guess I'll see you later," she said, still holding his hand, lingering.

"You will," he said without letting go of hers. "Be safe, Dani."

Neither pulled away for a moment, the connection electric, but Danica reluctantly pulled away first, breaking the contact. She stood alone on the wooden dock as he reboarded the Sara Rose. She watched as he untied the line, pushed off, and engaged the engine. Her stomach was starting to hurt, a hollow ache, and her breathing was shallow.

It wasn't until he had cleared the breakwater and she saw the Sara Rose hit the open water that she took her first real breath. She saw the blue letters Sara Rose fade off in the distance, becoming a speck against the horizon. She didn't want him to leave. She wondered if he had looked back.

Finally, she turned and walked along the wooden walkway towards the parking lot, her heels clicking loudly. Her car was off to the side, covered in a thin layer of dew, but her mind was miles away.

"Morning, Inspector," Detective Leininger grinned as she walked by the open window of his car, which was parked two spots down from hers. He was likely sleeping off a shift or hiding from his wife. "Nice walk of shame. How was your evening?"

She didn't answer. She wasn't trying to be rude; he wasn't worth the energy. That wasn't the point at all. Danica Harris really didn't know how to explain her evening to anyone. Not even to herself.

Chapter 28

She read the same page over again for the fifth time. The words blurred together into a nonsensical gray smudge.

It was mid-morning, and from the moment Inspector Harris sat at her desk, she began looking through the same case file, trying to force a connection that wasn't there. Frustrated and angry because she hadn't discovered anything new on the Roberts case, she dug deeper for any new evidence or a breakthrough, fueled by caffeine and irritation. She was mentally blocked, but she felt she had to do something to keep her mind occupied—to keep it away from the lake and the sunrise.

The case was starting to wear on every aspect of her life. Her apartment was a mess. She hadn't seen the cat around the loft for the last few days. She could tell it was still there—the litter box was used, and the food bowl was always empty when she eventually did return home late at night—but the animal was avoiding her, sensing the stress radiating off her. Even the cat knew she was toxic right now.

Captain Cooper had the pressure on, and he was demanding some headway on the case before the press ate them alive. But every turn she made turned up blank. It had been two days since she had last seen Delgado. The image of the Sara Rose fading off into the distance still stuck with her, and it was hard to shake. She wondered if he ever thought about her, or if he was just out there praying for her soul.

"This was left at the front desk."

She looked up to see Leininger standing over her, blocking the fluorescent light. He handed her a letter-sized manila envelope. "Your name is on the front. Courier dropped it off, said it was urgent."

The detective dropped it on her desk and walked off to his own area without another word, trailing the scent of stale donuts. Danica stared at the envelope for a moment. It looked innocuous enough. She tried to decide if she should file it away for later or open it now.

The phone on her desk rang, shattering her concentration. It startled her, and she jumped. She checked the caller ID—unknown. She didn't need another distraction and ignored it, letting it go to voicemail.

Danica turned her attention back to the envelope. She turned it over and saw her name and address had been neatly printed by hand on a standard white mailing label. The handwriting was precise, block letters with no slant. The label was placed exactly in the center of the envelope, geometrically perfect. There wasn't a return address on either side.

The flap was sealed tight. She picked the corner away with her fingernail, tearing the paper. Gently, she lifted the flap and looked inside at the contents.

Danica looked away quickly, her breath catching, then forced herself to look back inside the envelope. She dropped the unopened envelope on her desk as if it were burning and scanned the room quickly. Was he here? Was someone watching her reaction? The squad room was busy, noisy, normal.

With the tips of her fingers pinching the corners, treating it like toxic waste, Danica lifted the envelope until the contents spilled out onto her desk blotter. She held her breath as she stared at the twelve photographs spread out on her desk.

At first, she felt nauseous, a physical sickness rolling in her gut. Then violated, her skin crawling. And finally, angry. All the emotions came and went within a few brief seconds, but the anger remained, cold and sharp.

She looked through the entire stack quickly at first, her brain trying to reject what she was seeing. Then, one photograph at a time, she studied them until all twelve had been analyzed and set in her mind.

They weren't just pictures. They were a timeline.

The first one was of her car parked at the marina. The second was of her walking down the dock. The third was taken with a high-powered telephoto lens. It showed her and Nicholai on the boat. The fourth was clearer. It was Nicholai handing her the Dr. Pepper. The fifth... the fifth made her blood run cold. It was taken from the water, from a different angle. It showed her asleep on the deck, covered in the navy blanket, defenseless. The red digital timestamp in the corner indicated it was taken at 3:00 AM. The last photo was of Nicholai carrying her down the companionway. The crosshairs of a lens were focused on his back.

That left her even more concerned and afraid. They hadn't just been watched; they had been hunted. The killer had been on the water with them, silent and unseen in the darkness.

Her thoughts shifted instantly to Nicholai. He was still out there. Alone.

She reached for her Blackberry to call him but quickly put it back down on her desk, her hands shaking. She pushed her chair away and walked over to the coffee pot on the far side of the room, needing to move, needing to pretend to be normal. But she stopped twice to look back at the pictures on her desk, ensuring they were real. It was a reassuring exercise in a twisted kind of way. It wasn't a dream or something she imagined; it was really happening. Someone was tracking them.

The coffee pot was empty, leaving only a burnt ring of sludge at the bottom. Usually, that made her angry, but not this time. The cold, empty pot didn't faze her. It felt appropriate.

Danica walked back to her desk, and this time she avoided looking down at the pictures, afraid they might change into something worse. She picked up her Blackberry and hit speed dial.

"Answer," she whispered. "Please, answer."

Chapter 29

"I don't need protection!" Delgado snapped, his voice louder than he intended. "I can handle this myself. I've done it before."

"Nicholai, listen to reason. We don't know for sure who took these, and until we do, I want someone on you. Just a shadow car," Danica said, keeping her voice low to avoid a scene.

"I know exactly who took them," Nicholai said, pacing frantically outside the coffee shop for almost thirty minutes now. "And you do too. It's Quinlin. He's marking his territory."

The photographs lay spread out on the small wrought-iron table like a gruesome tarot spread. Danica had called him, making up some flimsy excuse about a new lead to get him here quickly. She said it was urgent, and he was already there when she arrived, sitting inside, looking at the door. She grabbed her usual coffee and asked him to move outside. She knew he would be better off in the open air, and the corner table offered more privacy from prying ears, if not prying lenses.

Without saying a word or even warning him, she had handed him the envelope. He opened it, his hands steady, and pulled the photographs out, thumbing through them one at a time. His face had hardened with each image. The twelve pictures featured her and Nicholai, together and separately in different settings and locations. Someone had been tailing them for the last few days, ghosting them through the city. There was one of them leaving Griffin's warehouse, looking over their shoulders; another entering Police Plaza, heads bent in conversation; and one showing them leaving together in her car. Two photographs had been taken of her alone, outside her apartment complex, unaware she was in the crosshairs.

One photograph in particular bothered them both deeply. It was of Delgado standing on the bow of the Sara Rose, head bowed in prayer. They could tell the photograph had been taken from a distance based on the slight graininess of the picture, likely from the shore or another boat, but it was still too close for comfort. It was a violation of his sanctuary.

"Until we can get this guy off the street, I'd feel better if someone was assigned to you," she urged, her professional mask slipping. "Just for a few days." She was almost pleading for him to accept the offer of protection, knowing how vulnerable he really was.

"Listen, I'll be fine." He was starting to calm down, forcing his breathing to slow. "If I'm not with you, I'm on the boat out off the cove. I doubt Quinlin could swim five miles in that water to get to me there without being seen. Besides, you've already got that large, disheveled guy sitting in the parking lot at the marina watching over me. What's his name? Leininger?"

"You noticed Leininger?" she asked, surprised. "He's supposed to be discreet."

"Discreet? He eats burritos in his car with the windows down. I can smell him from the dock. Do you still have your gun? I checked with registration. Your federal carry license is still active."

"Yes, it's hidden on board. In a safe."

"Please carry it with you from now on. On your person. Not in a safe."

"I'm not comfortable with that anymore. I'm trying to be a man of peace," he said, finally taking his seat, his shoulders slumping. "Weapons invite violence."

"You'll be no good to anyone dead, Nicholai. Peace doesn't stop a bullet."

"I need to pray about all this," he said quietly, rubbing his face.

Danica let out a heavy sigh of frustration. She didn't know what else to say to convince him. She saw he was upset, fighting a war between his past instincts and his present faith. "Are you worried at all?" she asked. "Or is this just fatalism?"

Nicholai looked hard at her, his blue eyes piercing. "Of course I am. I'm terrified. But Danica, God loves you and me so much that He has brought us together for a reason. It's His purpose. And that purpose is to defeat this evil, not to hide from it." He stopped for a moment and watched a young man walk by and step inside the coffee shop, oblivious to the danger discussing life and death inches away.

"So yes, I'm worried," he continued. "But His love is the only comfort we need to succeed. And if He is with us—and I know He

142

is—no evil can stand against us. We just have to be willing to walk through the fire."

Danica felt her eyes well up, a sudden rush of emotion she couldn't control. She was afraid, but now she couldn't pinpoint the reason—was it fear for him, or fear of believing him? She started to feel a change in the atmosphere, a shifting of weight.

"I've got to get out of here," he said, rising abruptly from his chair. "I refuse to let Quinlin win by making me hide in a coffee shop. I have things to do."

"What do you want me to do with these?" she asked, pointing to the toxic photographs.

"I don't care. Burn them. Shred them. Just don't ever show them to me again. I know what he looks like."

She watched his white Porsche pull away and disappear into the traffic, a sleek ghost in the machine. She suddenly felt alone again and wondered if he felt the same isolation. She wondered just how strong he really was—emotionally, physically, and spiritually. Was he breaking, or was he hardening?

Danica stuffed the photographs back inside the envelope, sealed the flap with a sharp crease, and reached for her Blackberry. She held it in her hand for a brief moment, weighing her options, before dialing the number.

"Captain, we need to talk. Now."

Chapter 30

It was the perfect time: mid-week, mid-morning. The lull. All the kids would be at school, husbands were at the office gawking at their secretaries or focused on some meaningless deadline, trying to scam the bottom line. There was always an excuse for distraction.

Quinlin liked the store—not this one in particular, but the entire chain. They were all set up the same, a temple to consumerism. Same layout in different cities and different states, but they all looked the same inside and out—sterile, bright, and predictable. They were big and always crowded enough at this time of day to provide cover, but empty enough to spot a target. Perfect time, perfect location, perfect for everything one could want: hardware, sporting goods, clothing, electronics, and groceries all under one big blue and white roof.

He was especially drawn to the produce section, the fruit aisle to be exact. There was always something good to choose from if one was patient, and the selection of fruit was good as well. Nevertheless, that wasn't important. The fruit section was located close to the main entrance. It was the first place they always went, drawn by the bright colors. Their carts would still be empty. No one would notice an empty cart in the middle of the fruit aisle, but they may wonder about one that was left full and abandoned near the exit.

He spotted her coming through the automatic sliding doors. Actually, he first saw her through the glass even before the doors opened to welcome her. She grabbed her cart, wiped the handle with a sanitary wipe, and smiled at the elderly greeter. He liked her smile immediately. It was open, trusting. Quinlin liked her.

He stood off to the side behind the Granny Smith apple display, a shadow in the fluorescent light, and watched her. She made her way towards the berry section. She was perfect. Short, blonde, just shy of forty years old, wearing yoga pants and a light jacket. She looked like every other suburban mother. Perfect timing, perfect location, perfect victim. His heart pounded with excitement, a rhythmic thudding in his ears, and he was having a great deal of trouble controlling his excitement. It had been a while since the last time. The hunger was back.

He watched as she made her way along the wall display, inspecting the produce. He scanned the area to make sure no one was paying too much attention. A stock boy was bored, looking at his phone. A mother was wrestling a toddler. No threats. He eyed her again as she got closer.

She moved in front of the last display and reached down to grab a basket of strawberries on sale. She turned to put them in the cart, her back to the double doors, and that's when Jeremy Quinlin made his move.

He moved with the speed of a striking snake. Quinlin quickly placed his large, sweaty hand over her mouth and pulled her backward through the double doors marked "EMPLOYEES ONLY." The strength and force he used caught her by complete shock and surprise; she wasn't even aware her feet had completely left the ground until the doors swung shut behind them.

Once he cleared the doors with her, entering the cool, concrete back room, he quietly pulled the terrified woman behind a tall metal shelving unit stacked with boxes of paper towels.

Quinlin knew he had time. He had memorized the employees' break schedule over the past number of weeks, watching from the parking lot. He knew he had at least twenty minutes before anyone would be back there to restock. It had all worked before, and this time wasn't any different. Routine was their weakness and his strength.

The shock of her situation was starting to wear off, but the reality was setting in hard. She struggled, her heels scraping uselessly against the concrete, and tried to scream, but his grip was too strong for her to do either. His hand was a vice.

Like quicksand, the more she struggled, the tighter he held her. She was suffocating, panic rising in her throat like bile, and she could feel his hot breath on the back of her neck. His smell—sour sweat and old spice—made her want to vomit, but his hand was closed too tight around her mouth. She felt him pull her in closer again, pressing her against the shelving.

"I promise I won't hurt you if you shut up," he whispered in her ear, his voice a rasp. She felt his spit on the side of her cheek. His mouth touched her ear, and her whole body shuddered in fear.

"I need you to do me a favor," he hissed. "Yes or no? Nod your head if you agree. Don't make me squeeze harder."

His grip was tight, and she couldn't move her head, so he did it for her, forcing a nod.

"Good girl," he said, loosening his grip just a fraction.

"I'm really sorry to disappoint you, but you really are not my type anymore," he whispered, pulling her in even tighter, mocking intimacy. "At one time you would have been... perfect. But things change. Tastes mature. You know what I mean, don't you?" He moved her head in agreement again. She closed her eyes, tears squeezing out. "I really am a heartbreaker," he laughed softly.

"But," he whispered, his tone dropping to deadly serious. "You're really not worth the effort. You're just a message." He took a deep breath, smelling her terror. "Tell Delgado he's more my style now. Tell him I miss him."

She opened her eyes slowly, confusion warring with fear. She felt numb and wondered for a moment if she was still alive.

Suddenly, he released her. He shoved her forward and vanished through the rear loading dock door before she could turn around.

She realized she could finally breathe, gulping in air, but was deathly afraid to take that first breath, fearing he was still there. When she knew for certain he was gone, the adrenaline crashed. She let go of the shelf she had been clinging to, and her body fell to the floor silently, curling into a ball as she wept into the concrete.

Chapter 31

"I want security tapes of this entire store spanning over the last six hours," she ordered, her voice cutting through the murmurs of the gathering crowd. "Every angle, every entrance, every register. And I want them now!"

"Yes, Inspector," the uniformed officer replied, his face pale. He fumbled with his radio, clearly overwhelmed by the sudden escalation of a simple disturbance call into a major crimes scene.

"Where is she?" Danica asked before the officer could even turn away. She scanned the front of the store, where shoppers were being herded away from the produce section like cattle.

"She's back there in the manager's office. Paramedics are tending to her now. Do you want us to transport her downtown for a formal statement?"

"No. I need to talk to her now while it's all fresh in her mind. Before the shock sets in and the walls go up."

Danica made her way down the main aisle, ignoring the stares of customers clutching their milk and bread. She burst through the swinging door marked "PRIVATE" and entered the cramped administrative hallway. The air here smelled different—stale coffee, toner dust, and fear.

The manager's office was a small, windowless box cluttered with schedules and inventory sheets. The woman was lying on a cheap, vinyl corporate sofa, covered with a nondescript white blanket that looked too thin to offer any warmth. The letters EMT were emblazoned in blue on the back of the paramedic kneeling beside her. Her nose and mouth were covered by a clear oxygen mask, fogging with her rapid breaths, but her eyes were visible. They were red, swollen, and darting around the room, looking for a threat that had already vanished. One attendant was monitoring her pulse, his fingers light on her wrist, while the other stood by, marking vital signs on a clipboard with clinical detachment.

"How is she?" Danica asked as she approached the attendant holding the clipboard.

"She's shaken up pretty bad. Hyperventilating. We've just given her something to calm her down. It should hit her soon, but her heart rate is still through the roof."

"Can I still question her? It's critical."

The paramedic looked at his watch, then at the patient. "You've got a few minutes before the sedative kicks in. Keep it simple."

Danica moved slowly towards the sofa, broadcasting non-threatening body language. She bent down on one knee so she wasn't looming over the victim, bringing herself to eye level.

"Hi," she said softly. "I'm Inspector Harris. I'm going to help you. What's your name?"

The woman pulled the mask down, her hand trembling. "Tanya," she said quietly, her voice raspy. Her eyes were rimmed with red, and as she turned her head, Danica noticed the distinct, purple finger-shaped bruises blooming on her jawline and neck. He had held her hard enough to leave a map of his hand.

"I'm so sorry about all this, Tanya. You're safe now. Did you get a look at who did this?"

"No," she said, a fresh tear tracking through her ruined makeup. "It all happened so fast. He was behind me. He smelled like... like old sweat and metal."

"Tanya, it's okay," Danica put her hand gently on the blanket where Tanya's arm was, grounding her. "Is there anything you can tell me about the man at all? His voice? What he said?"

She shook her head no at first, her eyes squeezing shut as she relived the moment in the stockroom. Then, she opened them, and Danica saw a flicker of recognition.

"He... he had a message."

Danica leaned in closer. "What message?"

"He told me to tell someone something. He said... tell Delgado he's more his style now."

Danica froze. The name hung in the air like smoke.

"And you're sure he said the name Delgado?" she asked, needing absolute confirmation.

Tanya stared at the ceiling tiles, her breathing hitching. Danica watched as Tanya closed her eyes tight for a moment, processing the trauma, then opened them. Her eyes went from defeated to fierce in the moment it took to open them. The fear had hardened into something brittle and sharp.

"Yes, I'm sure. I'll never forget what he said or how he smelled. He enjoyed it. He liked my fear." Tanya tore off the oxygen mask completely and gagged, turning her head to the side as if to spit the taste of him out of her mouth.

"Thank you," Danica said, rising to her feet, her own anger flaring to match the victim's. "And again, I'm sorry."

"Inspector?" Tanya had pulled the mask away from her face again, gripping the blanket with white knuckles.

"Yes?"

"Get him," she whispered, her voice venomous. "Please. Kill him."

Chapter 32

"I haven't seen or heard from him in two days, Captain," she said over her Blackberry, pacing the hot asphalt of the store parking lot.

Danica had left Tanya in the store with the attendants, needing fresh air to clear the image of the bruises from her mind. She called Cooper on the way out to her car, shielding her eyes from the sun.

"I've had a twenty-four-hour watch on him just like you asked," Cooper said, the static of the line doing nothing to hide his frustration. "Leininger has been sitting in that parking lot eating tacos for forty-eight hours. He says the boat hasn't moved, but he hasn't seen Delgado on deck."

"He hasn't come back into the marina since he left the other day," Danica corrected him. "I know. I called Leininger on my way here, and he filled me in. He's watching an empty slip, Captain. Delgado never docked. He dropped me off and went back out."

"What do you mean he went back out? To where?"

"The open water. He anchors out there to think. But Delgado's not answering my calls, and now this... this message from Quinlin. It changes everything."

"How long can he stay out there?" Cooper asked. "Does he have supplies?"

"If I know him, he could be out on that lake for quite a while. He's self-sufficient. He has food, water, and enough fuel to circle the lake for a week."

"What do you want to do?" Cooper asked. "We can't send the marine unit out there without a warrant or a distress call. It'll look like harassment."

"I need him, Captain. The security tapes will be downtown in the next hour. If Quinlin is on them, even for a second, we need eyes on it. And I think Nicholai may be the only one who can positively identify Quinlin from a grainy video. He knows his walk, his posture. He knows him."

"Can you get out there and talk to him? You seem to be the only one he doesn't immediately shut down."

"He was really shook up even before this incident," Danica admitted, leaning against her car door. "Seeing the photos of us... it rattled him. Add this direct threat now—Quinlin using a civilian to send a love note—and he may just pack it in completely. Or worse, he might go hunting alone."

"You better find some charm and personality pretty damn fast, Harris," Cooper ordered, his voice dropping to a growl. "Get out there. Take a boat, swim, I don't care. But get him back. We're losing control of this, and I don't like it."

Chapter 33

It took her less than an hour to get to the marina, slicing through traffic with a disregard for speed limits that would have earned anyone else a ticket. Danica spotted Leininger's unmarked sedan off to the side of the gravel parking lot, parked under the only shade tree. She pulled up next to him, her tires crunching loudly, but he didn't flinch.

As she approached his car, she saw he was wearing large, noise-canceling headphones, eyes closed, head bobbing to a rhythm only he could hear. The window was open, letting in the humid lake air. She placed her hand firmly on his shoulder, shaking him.

Leininger jumped, ripping the headphones off. "Jesus, Harris! You trying to give me a heart attack?"

"Has he come in at all?" she asked, ignoring his complaint and skipping the small talk. Her voice was tight with adrenaline.

"No, he's still out there. Or at least, the boat is gone." Leininger rubbed his eyes, adjusting to the light. "From here, I can see his slip space and the marina office. I haven't seen a sign of him or that boat since I started this shift. It's been quiet. Boring."

"What time do you leave?" she asked, scanning the horizon.

"I'm off in forty-five minutes. Thompson's relieving me tonight. Why? What's happened?"

Danica put her hands on her hips and looked at the empty slip space where the Sara Rose belonged, and then across the vast, shimmering expanse of the lake. It looked too big to search. "I've got to go get him. He's in danger, and he doesn't know it."

Leininger tossed the headphones onto the passenger seat and eyed her as she stood next to the car, vibrating with nervous energy. "Did you bring a bathing suit? Because unless you can walk on water like your friend there, you're stuck."

"Nice try, Chris. Just stay here and keep your eyes open."

Danica walked off, heading towards the marina office, her boots thudding on the wooden stairs. She pushed through the door, the bell jingling aggressively. Joel was behind the counter, head down, working on his daily tally sheets. He looked up only when he heard the door slam close.

"Can I help you?" he asked quickly, the rote customer service phrase slipping out before his eyes moved off the paper. When Joel did look at her, his demeanor shifted instantly. He was back on guard. "You're that cop. The one with the gun. You were here a while ago looking for the Pastor."

"Yes, that's right," she said, leaning on the counter.

"Ever find him?"

"I did, actually. But now I need to find him again. It's urgent. He's out there," she pointed to the lake through the large window.

"Sorry, can't help you there. He likes his privacy. The DPD has a patrol boat across the lake over at the other marina. You can probably make a call and get them out here in an hour or two."

"I don't have time for bureaucracy, Joel. I need to get to him now. Is there a rental? A service boat? Anywhere I can get a ride?"

Joel thought for a moment, chewing on the end of his pen. "Sorry. My rental pontoon is out with a bachelor party, and the mechanic has the service barge apart."

Danica looked out across the lake, frustration radiating off her, then back at Joel. "Well, thanks anyway. I'll make that call."

She turned away and made her way to the door, her hand on the knob. Joel saw the genuine fear on her face—not the arrogance of a cop, but the worry of a friend.

"Wait," he said.

She stopped.

"Promise me he's not in any kind of trouble? He's a good man."

"I promise," she said quietly. "I'm trying to keep him out of trouble."

"Maybe there is a way."

"What?" she asked, turning back.

"Over there," Joel pointed through the window towards a row of covered docks. "AA dock, halfway down on your left. There's a retired

156

guy down there. He used to be a pilot, flies low and fast. He sits down there most afternoons tinkering. I saw his car in the lot earlier, so I think he's there. Ask him to take you out. His name's Don Vest. Tell him I sent you. Gate code is 245. His boat is called Jet Lag."

"Thanks," she said, a wave of relief hitting her. She left the office in a hurry.

Danica quickly made her way towards AA dock, punched in the gate code, and jogged down the walkway. She found Vest sitting on a faded white plastic chair on the finger pier beside a sleek, thirty-foot Ciera. The name Jet Lag was painted along the stern in bold, sweeping letters.

"Are you Mr. Vest?" she asked, breathless.

The man looked up from a fishing reel he was restringing. He had the squint of a man who had spent a lifetime scanning horizons. "Who's asking?"

Danica pulled out her police ID from the back pocket of her jeans. "Inspector Harris," she said.

"Police?" he asked, raising an eyebrow but not rising from his chair. "I paid my parking tickets."

"Yes, but this is personal. I need a favor. A fast one."

It didn't take long for Vest to get the Jet Lag ready. He moved with the precise efficiency of a pilot going through a pre-flight checklist. He secured the cabin, untied the dock lines, and made sure Danica was seated securely. The twin 454 engines fired up with a deep, throaty rumble that shook the dock. The moment the boat cleared the breakwater, Vest pushed the throttles forward.

The engines roared, and the bow lifted toward the sky.

"Where do you think your friend is anchored?" Vest yelled over the sound of the twin engines and the rushing wind. At fifty miles an hour, the hull slapping against the chop, the noise on the open water made it almost impossible to have a normal conversation. It was violent and loud, a stark contrast to the peace she had found on the Sara Rose.

"He told me he usually anchors off Heath Point," she yelled back, shielding her eyes from the spray.

"Let's try there," Vest said, banking the boat hard to starboard and pushing the throttle to the stops. As a former pilot, Danica could tell he wasn't afraid of speed; he treated the water like the sky.

After twenty minutes of pounding across the open water, Vest rounded the peninsula of Heath Point. The water calmed in the lee of the land, and Danica spotted the tall aluminum mast of a sailboat swaying gently in the distance.

"Over there," she yelled and pointed. "That's him. That's the Sara Rose."

She kept her eyes on the sailboat as the distance between them decreased. Vest slowed Jet Lag down as he got closer, the roar of the engines dropping to a burble to avoid waking the water. Danica spotted Nicholai coming up from the cabin, alerted by the noise. He shaded his eyes, watching as their boat approached. Vest masterfully eased Jet Lag along the port side of the Sara Rose, reversing the engines to hold position. Nicholai spotted Danica on the boat, his expression shifting from wariness to surprise. He reached for a line to pull the boats in tight together.

"What are you doing here?" Nicholai asked, securing the line to a cleat.

"First of all, I've been worried. You're not answering your phone," she said as quietly as she could, stepping onto the gunwale of Vest's boat. "And second, there's been an incident. A bad one. I need you to come back to view some security tapes."

Nicholai reached out and helped her bridge the gap, pulling her safely aboard the Sara Rose.

Vest looked at Nicholai, keeping the Ciera's engines running at idle. He looked at the two of them standing in the cockpit, sensing the tension.

"Will you be alright now?" he asked.

Danica turned and replied, "Yes, I'll be fine. Thank you for bringing me out, Mr. Vest. I owe you one."

Nicholai laughed softly. "I think he was asking me."

Vest smiled, a knowing glint in his eye. "Anything you need, Pastor. Just say the word."

"We're fine, Don. The engines sound great. You tuned them well."

"They do. I had that left-side impeller replaced last week, and she's running fine. I'll head back and leave you two to it." He looked at Danica and nodded respectfully. "Let me know if you need a lift back."

Vest climbed into the captain's seat as Nicholai untied the two boats. Once clear of the Sara Rose, Vest throttled Jet Lag hard, the stern digging in, and disappeared around the peninsula in a spray of white water.

"You know him?" she asked as the silence returned.

"Of course. He's a good friend. We attend a Bible study together on AA dock every Wednesday night. He's a good man to have in a storm. Now, tell me what's going on? Why the aquatic assault?"

"I told you I was worried. Why aren't you answering my calls? I thought he got to you."

"There's no signal out here. That's one of the reasons I like this spot. It's a dead zone."

She pulled her own phone out and saw the blank signal indicator. Panic flared again—she was cut off. "Well, I knew those pictures and the fact that Quinlin was in your house really upset you. I thought you may have walked away and removed yourself from the case. Or worse, gone hunting on your own."

"It did upset me. And I needed to come out here and get closer to God. This is my place where I can be alone with Him and get my head straight."

"Are you okay?" she asked, still slightly out of breath, searching his face for cracks.

"Sit down," he said gently, gesturing to the bench. "You're shaking."

"I need something cold to drink first. My mouth is dry."

"Help yourself," he pointed down below. "You know your way around."

Danica took the steps down below to the cabin. It was cooler there, smelling of old books and coffee. She saw the open Bible on the table next to a notebook filled with frantic scribbling. He had been taking notes, but she couldn't make out his handwriting; it looked like code. The pages of the Bible were open to the book of Ephesians, highlighting verses about spiritual warfare. She turned around and bent down to open the small refrigerator. She grabbed a cold Dr. Pepper, pressing the cold can against her forehead for a moment, and made her way back up to the cockpit.

"You didn't answer me. Are you okay now?" she asked, popping the tab.

"I'm getting closer to Him and getting better," he said, looking out at the water. "My faith gets strengthened by being alone with Him and spending time in the Word. It reminds me who is really in charge. So yes, I am doing fine. Better than fine."

He smiled at her, watching as she drank the cold soda. "In the end, He will be victorious. I just have to trust the timeline."

Danica looked off across the lake, watching a heron glide over the water. "Sometimes you amaze me. I wish I had that much faith in something I can't see. I trust what I can handcuff."

"In time," he said. "I've been in prayer for that too, Dani."

She hadn't heard him call her that in a while, and she still didn't know how to react to the intimacy of it. "I guess I still believe I can do it all myself."

"I know you do. Is that why you have your large friend babysitting me in the parking lot? To protect me, or to control the situation?"

"I'm sorry. I know you said you didn't need that, but I had to. I couldn't lose you."

"I really don't need it. But you did."

Danica looked at him, confused. "What do you mean, I did?"

"Tell me what you fear, Dani, and I'll tell you where your faith is. Don't answer that, just think about it. You fear losing control, so you place your faith in surveillance and procedure."

They both stayed silent for a moment. He liked that. He knew the silence would only cause her to think more. And the more time she had in her own thoughts, the more she would discover about herself.

She knew very well where her fears lay. Loneliness, failure, abandonment, and death were just a few of the demons she wrestled with nightly. But her faith? That was almost too much to contemplate. Faith required surrender, and surrender felt like dying.

When the silence in her own thoughts finally became too loud, Danica quickly broke the moment. "There's been another incident," she said, her voice hard, trying to gain control again.

"Another suicide?" he asked, his brow furrowing.

"No. An escalation. A woman was abducted in one of the big-box retail stores this morning. Taken right out of the produce section."

"Is she..."

"She's alive. Battered, terrified, but alive. He let her go. But he gave her a message."

"I'm not following you," he stated, though a shadow passed over his eyes.

"Nicholai, it was Quinlin. The message was for you."

Nicholai stood up quickly, the boat rocking with his sudden movement. "Did he hurt her?"

"No, she'll be fine physically. Emotionally, that may take some time. But Quinlin used her as a courier. He wanted you to know he's close. He wanted you to know he's watching." She continued on, filling him in on the entire situation—the taunt about tastes changing, the smell, the bruises.

"The store's security tapes are downtown. That's why I need you to come in and see if you can identify him. You know his gait, his posture."

"I will come in," he said, pacing the small cockpit. "But there's not much point in watching those tapes."

"Why?" she asked.

"Danica, I've never seen Quinlin. In two years of hunting him, I never saw his face. We've never been able to get a picture or even a composite sketch of him. He's a ghost. He avoids cameras, or he wears disguises. He'll be a blur on that tape."

"It's the only thing we have to work with right now, Nicholai. We have to try."

"I agree. But please, not tonight. Can't it wait until tomorrow morning? I really need another night out here to prepare myself. If I go back into that city tonight, with this rage... I might do something I regret."

Danica looked at him. He looked strong, but fraying at the edges. "I guess so. The tapes aren't going anywhere."

"I'll take you back into the marina when you're ready," he said, his shoulders slumping slightly.

Danica looked across the lake and felt the breeze on her face. It was peaceful here. Safe. She looked at the face of the Blackberry and checked the time. Daylight was fading, and the air was starting to cool, turning the sky a bruised purple. She didn't want to go back to her empty loft and the silent cat.

"Do you mind if…"

He didn't give her the chance to finish, sensing her need before she voiced it. "Of course not. You're more than welcome to stay. We have another hour or so before sunset. That will give me time to get dinner ready. I caught some fresh bass this morning."

"Thank you," she said, almost embarrassed by her relief. She was glad he knew what she wanted.

"I'll make the forward berth up for you again. I'm starting to get used to the couch. It's actually better for my back."

"I can take the couch," she offered weakly.

"No, wouldn't hear of it. Guests get the stateroom."

She smiled again, the tension finally leaving her neck. "Thank you."

"There's a change of clothes up front in the top drawer. A few t-shirts and some shorts. Go change. You'll be more comfortable out of that uniform."

"You keep women's clothes on board?" She was a bit surprised, raising an eyebrow.

"No," he laughed. "I bought them for you the other day when I got the sodas. I had a feeling you'd be back out here again. You have the look of someone who needs the water."

Danica was quiet and looked across the lake, overwhelmed by his thoughtfulness.

"Thanks, Nic."

She whispered it, hoping he hadn't heard her use the nickname. But he did, and he smiled as he turned towards the galley.

Chapter 34

She slammed her fist on the laminate table, the sound sharp in the quiet viewing room. "This is a waste of time!" she yelled, her voice cracking with exhaustion. "We're looking for a ghost in a snow-storm."

Danica was tired—bone-deep tired—and the frustration was leaking out of her in waves. They had been locked in the small, airless room at Police Plaza for the past four hours, staring at the same grainy footage until their eyes burned. The hum of the computer tower and the whine of the cooling fans were the only sounds filling the dead air between them.

They had viewed the security tapes from the store from every conceivable angle; every exit, every register, every aisle had been scrutinized until the shoppers became a blur of pixels.

"I'm sorry, but I really have no idea what or who I'm looking for," Nicholai said, rubbing his eyes under his glasses. "I told you earlier, we never did get a picture or even enough information to complete a composite of Quinlin. He changes his gait, his posture, his clothes. He could be any of these guys." He gestured helplessly at the screen. After a while, every man in a baseball cap looked like a killer.

"You've viewed every tape going back four hours before and four hours after the abduction. He's got to be in there somewhere," she insisted, refusing to give up. "He didn't just materialize in the produce section."

"I'll try again," he said, resigning himself to the task. Their focus was breaking apart, fraying under the strain of the hunt.

Danica pulled her chair closer, the metal legs scraping against the floor, and sat beside him in front of the console. She could smell the faint scent of the lake still clinging to him, a stark contrast to the sterile smell of the station.

"The incident took place at 10:14 AM," she said, her voice regaining its edge. "Back up to that point, and let's go through it frame by frame from then. We missed something."

"Which camera?" he asked, his hand hovering over the mouse. He decided he would go through the tapes one last time, but this effort wasn't really to find Quinlin—he was convinced the man was too smart for that. It was more to appease Danica, to show her he was still in the fight.

"There are four ways to get back into the store from the backroom area," he listed, ticking them off. "I've watched each one of those at least eight times and haven't seen anything suspicious. Just employees in their blue vests going in and out, stocking shelves. No one looks out of place."

Danica thought for a moment, chewing on her thumbnail. "From what you've told me, Quinlin is bold. He's arrogant. He likes living on the edge," she said. "He wouldn't sneak out the back if he could walk out the front and watch the chaos. Let's try looking at the main entrance right after the incident. Our victim said he held her for approximately ten minutes. That puts him exiting around 10:24."

Danica leaned in, pointing at the screen. "Go back to the main entrance camera at 10:24 AM."

Nicholai clicked the mouse, dragging the timeline bar back. The digital images reversed in a blur of motion until the timestamp at the bottom of the screen stopped at 10:24:00.

"How long are we going to sit through this?" he asked her softly. For a moment, his concentration broke when he realized how close she was sitting to him; her shoulder was almost touching his, and her intensity was magnetic.

"As long as it takes, Nic," she said, not looking away from the monitor. "He's got to be on here somewhere. I feel it in my gut."

They watched the screen, viewing dozens of people enter the store every minute. Shoppers walked in with empty carts and left with full ones, oblivious to the violence that had just occurred meters away. It was a parade of normalcy.

"There you are coming in," Nicholai said, pointing to the screen.

They both watched as the image of Danica entering the store flashed on the screen. She looked focused, moving with purpose, flashing her badge to the uniformed officer at the door.

"I was only on the scene for about forty-five minutes," she stated. "I can't imagine Quinlin hanging around the whole time we were investigating the incident. That's too risky, even for him."

"Nothing surprises me with him. He feeds on the reaction. He probably wanted to see if I showed up."

Danica started getting restless again. The images all seemed the same—families, elderly couples, teenagers. She started losing focus, the pixelated faces blending together, until Nicholai spoke up, his voice sharp.

"There you are coming out."

The overhead camera captured her walking out of the automatic doors, stepping into the harsh sunlight. She was holding her phone to her ear, her face tight with stress.

"Who are you talking to?" he asked.

"No one," she said, remembering the frustration of that moment. "I was trying to reach you. I left a voicemail. I didn't call Cooper until I was out of the store and at my car."

Nicholai lurched forward towards the screen, his posture rigid. "Wait!"

He slammed his finger on the spacebar, freezing the image just as Danica was leaving the right side of the frame.

"The guy behind you," Nicholai said, his voice dropping to a whisper. "That one."

He moved the mouse around the screen, drawing a digital box around the image of a man wearing a nondescript grey baseball cap and a windbreaker, walking directly behind Danica. The angle of his head was tilted down, hiding his face completely from the camera, but his body language was mocking. He was matching her stride.

Nicholai typed on the keyboard, executing the enhancement software. The image pixilated, then clarified as he zoomed in on the man's arm, which was raised to adjust his cap.

He stopped breathing. He took his hands away from the computer as if it had burned him and stared at the image.

"A tattoo?" Danica asked, squinting at the screen. "What is that? It looks like ink."

Nicholai slowly placed his hands back on the keyboard, his fingers trembling slightly. He zoomed in closer on the image, cropping out everything but the man's forearm. The man had what looked like a long, dark mark running along the outside of his forearm.

"I first saw it when he raised his arm up to pull the cap down over his face," Delgado said, his voice devoid of emotion. "It's not a tattoo," he said quietly.

He zoomed in one last time. The pixels sharpened into a distinct shape. The man had an arrow drawn on his forearm in black marker. The tip of the arrow pointed down to his wrist.

To a wristwatch.

"It's just a tattoo, Nic," Danica said, trying to make sense of it. "Maybe a gang sign?"

"No! Not the arrow. Look at what it's pointing to," he said, leaning back in his chair, his face draining of color. "Look at the watch."

It was a vintage silver timepiece with a distinctive blue face and a cracked leather strap.

"That's my watch," he whispered, the horror washing over him. "Jessica gave me that watch ten years ago for my birthday. He took it off my dresser the night he killed them."

Danica held her breath. The room suddenly felt very small and very cold. Not only had they found Quinlin, but he had been walking in her shadow, just five feet behind her, wearing a trophy from the man he was hunting.

Chapter 35

It was just after eleven o'clock in the evening when she left Delgado in the visitor's parking lot across the street from the office. The streetlights hummed overhead, casting long, lonely shadows. She thought about going back inside and rereading the files, burying herself in the work, but it had already been a long day, and her eyes were stinging.

She turned her car left out of the lot and saw Delgado's white Porsche turn right, disappearing into the city night like a phantom.

She was still curious about the man. She recalled his first impression—arrogant, broken, distant. Those few hours on the boat had left a mark, but now something was changing. The discovery of the watch had stripped away another layer of his defense. In the hours they had spent together in the dark viewing room, she could feel something inside her changing, too. A wall was coming down. She wanted to know more about him, the man behind the badge and the Bible, and not just the information a personnel file contained.

She made her way down the tollway, the rhythmic thump-thump of the tires lulling her into a trance. She took the usual exit towards her loft, driving on autopilot. She pulled into her assigned parking space in the underground garage and turned off the engine. The silence was instantaneous and heavy.

Danica sat quietly in the car for a moment, staring at the oil stains on the concrete wall, trying to shake off the thoughts of the day—the woman in the store, the watch on the killer's wrist, the way Nicholai looked when he saw it. It was going to be just another night alone. The usual microwave dinner, the usual television news shows playing to an empty room, and maybe a few minutes online before passing out. Her career was everything, but at the end of the workday, she realized with a pang of sadness that there was really nothing left.

She stepped out of the car, the echo of her door slamming sounding like a gunshot in the garage. She made sure it was locked—twice—and made her way towards the building's entrance.

The elevator door opened before she managed to push the button. A young couple, smiling and laughing at a private joke, exited the elevator. They were holding hands, their fingers intertwined, oblivious to the world. They walked past her, trailing the scent of expensive cologne and happiness, and walked off into the night together.

The elevator doors started to close, leaving her alone in the vestibule. She watched the floor lights flash on and off until the fourth floor stayed lit and the doors opened again, waiting for her.

Danica stood motionless inside the elevator, staring at the open doors of her floor. She knew the effort it was going to take to step out and walk down the hall towards her loft. It wasn't going to take much physical energy, but emotionally, she didn't have much left in the tank. The hallway seemed to stretch out for miles.

It was a short walk. She found her key, her hand heavy, and slipped it in the lock. She turned it, hearing the tumblers click—the sound of her isolation. The door opened, and the space inside was dark as usual. The air was stale.

She looked down at the floor and saw two small, bright red eyes staring back up at her from the shadows. Without a sound, the cat turned its back on her and slowly made its way to the kitchen, expecting to be fed, indifferent to her presence.

The loft on Lemmon Avenue was dark and quiet again. It was almost too quiet, a vacuum of sound, until the shrill ring of her Blackberry broke the silence, making her jump.

She pulled the phone from her pocket, the blue light illuminating her tired face. The display showed another address, followed by the now-familiar, dreadful code: 911.

She contemplated feeding the cat, just to do something normal, but didn't. She turned around and walked back out the door.

Chapter 36

"Inspector Harris, how are you?" Brainerd said, her voice clipped and professional, but her eyes moved past Danica and continued scanning the room, looking for contamination. "He's already here," she added, a hint of annoyance in her tone. "Back there in the bedroom. He walks soft for a big man."

"Sorry, Pam, I tried getting here before him." Danica had called Nicholai along the way, giving him the address, but she certainly didn't expect him to beat her to the scene. He moved through the city like smoke.

"Who is he, anyway? New partner?" Brainerd asked, snapping a fresh pair of latex gloves on. "You usually work alone since... well, lately."

"No," she stated quickly, cutting off the thought. "Retired FBI. The Captain brought him in as a special consultant on this case. He has... specific experience."

Just then, Danica saw Nicholai emerge from the hallway, his face unreadable. He looked at the floor, avoiding stepping on the evidence markers Brainerd's team had already placed.

"I'm sorry. I don't think I've officially met your new partner?" Brainerd said loudly enough for Nicholai to hear, clearly intending to embarrass Danica for the breach of protocol.

"Pam, this is Nicholai Delgado."

"Nice to meet you, Mr. Delgado. Pam Brainerd, Lead CSI." She extended a gloved hand, then retracted it, remembering the context.

"Same here," Nicholai said, nodding respectfully but barely making eye contact as he continued eyeing the room. He was vibrating with that same intensity she had seen at the Roberts estate.

Brainerd watched him wander off back towards the master bedroom and disappear around the corner. "He's intense," she muttered to Danica. "I like him."

"I assume the body is back there?" Danica asked, pulling out her notepad.

"It's all there. Davis Wright, forty-eight-year-old Caucasian male. Another self-inflicted gunshot to the head. Large caliber. It's messy. Time of death is sometime between three and five this afternoon based on livor mortis and body temp."

"Any sign of a computer or note?"

"There sure is. It's all in there," the CSI said, pointing across the living room to a dedicated office space enclosed in glass. Danica noticed a set of French doors off to the side of the living room. Both doors were open, revealing a pristine workspace.

"I left the suicide note in the printer. It was still in the output tray. Let me know when I can clear the scene; the ME is getting impatient."

"We probably won't be long. We know what we're looking for."

"My crew is on their way to pick him up and get him back to the lab for the full autopsy."

"I'll just be a minute. I'm sure you've got everything you need already."

"I'm done with the preliminary stuff. I'll start the autopsy in the morning and let you know what I find," Brainerd said, turning back to her kit. "But don't expect any surprises. It looks like a textbook suicide, just like the others. Almost too textbook."

Davis Wright lived high above the city of Dallas off Turtle Creek Drive. The Renaissance was exclusive, stylish, and the address sent a definite message of power and detachment. Davis Wright's unit was one of only two that occupied the twenty-second floor. The entire building had the same layout, only two units on each floor, ensuring privacy for the elite. One unit faced the green space of several parks, and the other—Wright's—looked out over the jagged Dallas skyline and the wealthy Preston Hollow area. It was a view to die for.

Danica walked down the hall towards the master bedroom area, her heels sinking into the thick carpet. She made a quick inventory of the framed photographs lining both sides of the hall like a gallery. There were the usual family portraits—smiling wife, kids in braces—

that looked staged. Then there were several golf foursomes at Pebble Beach and Augusta.

But as she got closer to the bedroom, the theme changed. The photographs became hunting conquests. Although Danica had never met or seen Davis Wright, she could easily pick him out in the pictures. They showed Davis on one knee, rifle in hand, leaning over an animal whose life he had just taken—lions, bears, elk. He smiled in every one of them, the master of his domain. Now, he was the trophy on the bed.

She walked away from the last picture, a disturbing image of a dead leopard, and turned into the bedroom.

The lifeless body of Davis Wright lay on the king-sized bed, sprawled awkwardly. The expensive white Egyptian cotton sheets were stained crimson. Blood spatter covered the white padded leather headboard and the wall behind it, a violent abstract painting. The gun, a heavy semi-automatic, was still loosely gripped in his right hand.

Off to the side, with his back pressed into the corner to get the widest view, Nicholai studied the scene. He wasn't looking at the body; he was looking at the room, the air, the lack of struggle. She saw the focus on his face and tried to figure out where his thoughts and mind were going.

"What have you found?" she asked.

Delgado didn't answer. The man didn't even acknowledge her question or even her presence. He was in the zone, reconstructing the final moments of Davis Wright's life.

"Nicholai?"

He moved his head slowly and looked over at her. She was still in the doorway, leaning against the frame, unwilling to step further into the slaughter.

"Sorry," he said, his voice distant. "The silence... it's heavy here."

"Have you found anything?"

He didn't answer her question; instead, he asked his own. "Have you seen the note?"

"Not yet, no."

Nicholai walked past her quickly, navigating the room without looking at the body again, and disappeared down the hall towards the office. Danica shook her head in frustration, turned, and tried to catch up to the former profiler. She found him in Wright's office, standing over the laser printer.

"Mergers and acquisitions," he said, looking at a diploma on the wall.

"What?" she asked. Danica was confused by the non-sequitur.

"Davis Wright was a mergers and acquisitions attorney," he said. "One of the best in his field. Highly respected by the Wall Street gang

171

and feared by everyone else. He swallowed companies whole. He was a predator in the boardroom and a predator in the wild."

"Did you know him?"

"No, just knew of him. Men like him leave a wake. Look," he said, pointing to the printer. "The note is identical."

"And the laptop? Anything there?"

"It's turned off, but it's been left open on the desk. We need to get it to Griffin," he said urgently. "If my theory holds, the hard drive is the key."

"Let me clear that with Brainerd first. I don't want any chain of evidence issues coming up later if this goes to trial," Danica said, though she knew a trial was unlikely. She stopped for a moment, dreading the confirmation. "Anything with the note?"

Delgado looked down at the printer then directly at her. "It's identical; same text, same font, same content. The printer log will show it was printed ten minutes after the time of death."

"Tetelestai?" she asked.

Nicholai didn't have to look at the printed page again. "Yes. And I found something else."

"What?"

Delgado reached up to one of the high bookshelves, pushing aside a legal reference book. He held up a hand-carved wooden mask. It was dark wood, polished smooth, but the face was twisted in anguish. The eyeholes had never been cut out, leaving it blind.

"This," he said, turning it over in his hands. "Rosin had the same mask. It was on the mantle above the fireplace. And Roberts had one too, hidden in his office. It's a marker."

"A marker for what?"

"I don't know yet. But three dead men, three identical

Chapter 37

They were both tired, hungry, and the adrenaline of the discovery was fading into a dull ache. It was late, the city lights blurring into streaks of neon as they sped down the highway.

"Are you in a hurry?" he asked as Danica drove down the interstate back towards Police Plaza.

"Not really," she replied, her eyes fixed on the road. "Just want to get this day over with. Why?"

"We haven't eaten since this morning, and I could use something before heading out. My stomach is protesting loudly."

"Heading out? Where are you going? Back to the lake?"

"Back to the marina, yes," he said. "It's safe there. Or at least, safer than anywhere else."

"Do you always stay there? I mean, do you ever stay at the house? You still own it."

"Not anymore," he said, his voice dropping. "I tried for a while, right after... everything. But it was too hard. Every room had a memory, every shadow looked like a threat. I haven't slept there in years. I just check on it to make sure it hasn't burned down."

"Why don't you sell it? Why are you holding on to it?" she asked. She took her eyes off the road long enough to see he wasn't looking away like he had in the past. He was staring straight ahead, facing the question.

"I'm not ready to let go yet, I guess."

"Let go of what?" She looked at Nicholai again, but this time his head turned, and he looked out the passenger window at the passing darkness. "I'm sorry. If I'm asking too much, just let me know. I push sometimes."

"No, it's okay," he said softly. "And if I'm uncomfortable, I'll tell you. I appreciate the honesty."

She waited, but he didn't elaborate. She looked over and saw him still looking out the side window, his arms folded across his chest in a defensive posture.

"So what are you holding on to?" Danica asked again, pressing gently. She thought he might have forgotten her question or chosen not to answer, but she needed to know.

"I don't know," he admitted. "I've let them go—Jessica and Sara—I know they're at peace. But I guess I'm holding on to something else. Maybe the hope that I can fix it. I'm not sure. I just know I'm not ready for that step yet. Selling the house feels like erasing the evidence that they existed."

From the corner of her eye, she saw him turn back and face the front again, shaking off the mood.

"Pancakes?" he asked suddenly.

"What?" He surprised her.

"There's an IHOP just off the next exit. The big sign is calling to me. Would you like to go there? It's open all night."

"I guess," she said, signaling the car and making a quick, aggressive lane change, taking the exit a little too fast. The tires squealed slightly.

"You must be hungry," he said, smiling and grabbing the dashboard.

It was the first time she heard her laugh that night, and he liked it. It was a rusty sound, but genuine.

"This was your idea," she reminded him.

"Hey, I just made the suggestion. You're the one driving like Mario Andretti."

She smiled and shook her head. "Delgado, for an old guy, you can sure be a real punk sometimes."

"Well, that's a first," he said, feigning shock. "No one's ever called me a punk. And what's this 'old guy' crap? I'm seasoned."

"Whatever," she laughed again. "Do I need to apologize for hurting your delicate feelings?"

"No need. But you're buying."

"Whatever," she laughed again. "I'm expensing this out. Cooper can cover this. It's part of the investigation—keeping the consultant alive."

Danica parked the car under the harsh fluorescent lights of the parking lot, and they made their way inside. The diner smelled of maple syrup, bacon grease, and stale coffee—a comforting, distinctly American scent. It was mostly empty, save for a few truckers and a table of college students studying late.

The young hostess, looking bored, seated them in a booth by the window along the far wall. She placed sticky laminate menus in front of them.

"Debbie will be your server. Can I get you anything now?" the hostess asked, popping her gum.

"She needs coffee, badly. IV drip if you have it," Nicholai said. "I'll just have water with lemon."

Danica looked at Nicholai, smiled, and shook her head. "Can you tell me where the restrooms are?"

"Over there and around the corner," the hostess pointed. "Debbie will be right over with your drinks and to take your orders."

Danica excused herself and walked towards the back of the restaurant to wash the grime of the day off her hands. Nicholai watched the interstate traffic speed by through the window, red taillights blurring into long lines.

"Hi, I'm Debbie." Nicholai turned and looked at the young, attractive waitress. She looked tired but put on a bright smile. She placed the coffee in front of him. He could tell she was overworked and probably coming to the end of a long shift.

"That's hers," he said, moving the coffee cup across the table. "I'm the water."

"I'm sorry," she said, correcting herself. "Would you like to order now or wait for your wife to get back?"

He smiled, amused. "She's not my wife, and we'll wait."

"That sounds great," Debbie smiled, lingering a second too long. "I'll be right back."

Danica returned, drying her hands on a paper towel, and saw Nicholai was smiling like the cat that ate the canary.

"What's with the grin?" she asked, sliding into the booth.

"Cute little Debbie assumed you were my wife."

"I hope you set her straight immediately."

"I did, and she seemed quite pleased about it."

Before Danica could respond with a retort, Debbie returned to take their order. She paid special attention to Nicholai, almost ignoring Danica entirely.

"I'll be right back with your order," she said, closing her notepad with a flourish. She looked at Nicholai and smiled, tucking a strand of hair behind her ear. "If there's anything else you need, just ask, Hun."

As soon as she was a safe distance away from their table, Danica looked across at Nicholai, raising an eyebrow. "You're not buying any of that crap, are you?"

He leaned back against the booth and smiled. "Do you really find it that hard to believe that an attractive woman just might be interested in a punk like me?"

"Whatever," was the only response that came to her mind at that moment. She took a sip of the coffee. It was hot and bitter, perfect.

"So what about you?" he asked, turning the tables. "Anyone special in your life? Besides the cat you mentioned?"

"Nope," she said quickly. "I thought you knew everything about me, Mr. Mindreader. Didn't you profile my dating history?"

"Not everything," he said. "I'm not a mindreader. I was only making calculated assumptions based on certain observations. And the absence of a ring doesn't mean the absence of a person."

"Well, your calculated assumptions were pretty darn close."

"So why no husband or boyfriend? You're... well, you're not hard to look at."

"I tried once, and that didn't work out," she said, looking down at her coffee. "I guess I'm one of those that's just destined to be single forever. Married to the job."

"Is that something you want? Solitude?" he asked.

"I don't know," she said, looking around the restaurant at the happy college kids. "I just know I'm tired of losing. Every time I open up, something gets taken away."

Nicholai looked at her across the table, his eyes softening. "So you cut them off before they get a chance to cut you out? Preemptive strike?"

Debbie returned before Danica could answer, and she was relieved for the interruption. The waitress placed their orders on the table—a stack of pancakes for him, an omelet for her—and looked at Nicholai. "Anything else, Hun? More water?"

He looked at Danica, who was trying to hide her smirk behind her cup. "No," he said. "I think we're good. Thank you, Debbie."

"Your dream girl is quite sweet," she laughed as the waitress walked away.

"Whatever," he said, imitating her earlier response. "Let me bless the food."

She felt a slight embarrassment as Nicholai closed his eyes right there in the booth and dropped his head. She watched him for a second, then lowered her own head out of respect.

"Father, bless this nourishment to our bodies. Keep us safe from harm's way and guide us in our days to come. Give us clarity for the task ahead. In Jesus' name, Amen."

When he looked up, he noticed her eyes were still open and she was still looking around the room, scanning the exits. He decided not to comment; survival instincts were hard to turn off. Instead, he wanted to continue their previous conversation.

"Debbie is sweet, but I wouldn't go so far as calling her my dream girl," he said, pouring syrup. "What about you? What are your dreams? What does Danica Harris want when she's not chasing bad guys?"

Danica swallowed slowly while trying to think of a response. "I've been through enough that I don't dream much of anything anymore. Survival is the goal. After everything you've been through, you must feel the same way."

"We all face hardships at some point in our lives," he said, cutting into his pancakes. "It may be something emotional that you struggle with, or it may be a dream that you feel you're missing out on. But whatever you're feeling, don't ever let it discourage you from believing in God's best."

"God's best?" she questioned, skepticism creeping in. "Is that what you'd call losing my mother to an aneurysm and having a fiancée walk out on me because I wouldn't quit my job?"

"I'm sorry," he said, pausing. "I didn't know the details."

"That's okay," she said, waving her fork. "It's not something I'm comfortable talking about. It's ancient history."

"But you think about it a lot, don't you? It still shapes your decisions."

She didn't answer. She took a bite of her omelet, chewing mechanically.

"Danica, the enemy knows you better than you know yourself," he said, leaning forward. "He knows your weaknesses, and he is going to use them against you. He wants to keep you focused on everything negative that's around you—the death, the loss, the fear. I know that from experience. I lived in that darkness." He took another mouthful and continued, "But don't let him steal the dream God has given you. The enemy knows that if he can deceive you into thinking things won't get any better, you're going to lose hope and give up. He wins by default."

Nicholai took another forkful and watched her. She was silent, but he knew she was thinking about what he was saying. He always marveled at the power of silence in a conversation; it forced people to listen to their own thoughts.

And he knew she wasn't going to respond immediately, so he kept going. "I know God has not brought you this far to say He is done with you yet. Refuse to give up on your dreams He has given you. God knows the challenges you face, and He has a way of turning things around for you. He turns ashes into beauty."

"Have you given up?" she asked, almost too quickly, turning the spotlight back on him.

"No," he replied firmly. "I'm still here."

"Then why are you holding on to a house you won't stay in, and why do you still wear that wedding ring?" She pointed with her fork. "You talk about moving forward, but you're anchored to the past."

"I told you, I'm not ready to take that step."

"Or is it fear?" she asked. "Fear that if you take it off, you'll forget her?"

"I can't answer that."

"Can't or won't?"

"I can't because I don't know," Nicholai said honestly. He took another mouthful, then put his fork down. He pushed the half-empty plate away and looked out the window at the dark highway. "Maybe a bit of both."

"I'm sorry," she said, softening. "Sometimes I push too hard. It's the job."

"It's quite alright. You haven't asked anything new that I haven't already asked myself a thousand times in the middle of the night."

"The other day on the boat, you said you spend your time trying to save others, saving souls," she said. "You help the people at the marina, you help the department."

"I do, yes. It gives me purpose."

"When will you save yourself?" she asked. The question hung in the air between them, heavy and real.

Debbie returned to the table before Nicholai could answer, breaking the tension. "How's everything? Can I get you a box?" she asked, looking at their unfinished plates.

"Fine," he said quickly, pulling out his wallet. "Can we have the check, please?"

The ride back to Police Plaza was quiet. Neither spoke the entire time. The radio was off. They both felt like their conversation may have gone too far too fast, peeling back layers they weren't ready to expose.

Danica turned into the parking garage, the concrete echoing around them as she dodged the pillars.

"I'm on the third level," he said.

She made a hard right turn, tires screeching on the smooth floor, and rounded the corner.

"It's right there," he said, pointing. "The white Porsche."

"I know," she said. "Nice car. A little flashy for a humble pastor."

"It's just an old 911, but it gets me around. It reminds me that life is meant to be driven, not parked."

She pulled alongside his car and waited for him to move, but he remained in the passenger seat for a moment.

"So what's our next move?" he asked.

"I guess we wait and see what Griffin finds on those hard drives. I'll call you if anything surfaces on my end," she said.

178

"And I'll do the same."

"Have a good night, Nic." She didn't want to look at him; instead, she kept her eyes looking out the windshield at the concrete wall.

"When I believe I'm worth it," he said quietly, opening the car door and stepping out.

"What?" she asked, turning to him.

He bent down and looked inside the car, directly into her eyes. "Your question at the restaurant. You asked when will I save myself?"

She didn't respond, but she was caught in the intensity of his gaze.

"I'll save myself when I believe I'm worth saving," he said. "And when I find something so special again that it takes all my focus away from the past."

He closed the car door with a solid thud. Danica watched as he walked to his car, his silhouette framed by the garage lights, and eased himself into the Porsche. She waited for him to start the engine, the deep rumble filling the space, and pull away and disappear around the corner before she put her own car in gear and made her way home to an empty apartment.

Chapter 38

"Thank you for meeting me," he said, smoothing his silk tie. "It took me some time to figure out who you were, but when you said The Marble Club, I knew right away. I must say, you made quite the impression in a very short time. Most people wait weeks for an audience."

"No, I'm the one who should be thankful," she flirted, leaning forward just enough to catch the candlelight. "I can only imagine how packed your schedule is, and I'm flattered you took the time to get together with me. How's the campaign going? The polls look promising."

Thomas Sanford took another sip of his expensive single-malt scotch, the ice clinking softly against the glass. He watched her hand as she held the half-empty crystal wine glass filled with Chardonnay. Her fingers gently caressed the thin, delicate stem, a subtle, rhythmic movement that he noticed immediately. It was calculated, hypnotic.

"It's a campaign," he sighed, feigning modesty. "Same as all the others I've worked on; never enough time or money, but we're dedicated to taking this seat and keeping Clements in the House. We're fighting the good fight."

She smiled just the right way—a mix of admiration and challenge—and looked across the table at the Senator's campaign manager. She knew exactly what he needed to hear: validation of his power.

"Well, I'm proud to be able to help. I just wish I could do more than write a check. I believe in what you're doing."

"The Senator and I both appreciate any assistance you can provide. We all have to keep going if we ever expect to get this country back on track. And William Clements is just the man to do that," Sanford said with confidence. He projected strength and determination with every word he spoke, a practiced speech he had given a thousand times. She liked that. The more she knew who the man was—the more she understood the scope of his ambition—the more determined she became to stick to her own agenda. He wasn't just a target; he was a stepping stone.

"And this is just one of the steps in many more to come for the Senator," he said, lowering his voice conspiratorially. "We have big plans."

"And what might that be?" she asked, her eyes widening in mock innocence.

"William Clements has his eye on the White House in four years. And I intend to put him there."

She liked that. It meant the stakes were higher. It meant the fall would be longer.

"Four years is a long time in politics, Thomas," she said softly. "A lot can happen. Scandals, secrets... accidents."

"We handle accidents," he said, finishing his drink. "That's why I'm good at my job."

"I bet you are," she purred. "I bet you can fix anything."

Chapter 39

Danica watched as he frantically paced the small interrogation room in silence. Over the past few days, the room had transformed from a cold holding cell into their chaotic, unofficial office. Reports and crime scene photographs were taped to the cinder block walls, creating a collage of death. A large whiteboard, positioned directly across from the door, was filled with their random thoughts, theories, and notes written in frantic scrawl. The air smelled of dry-erase markers and stale coffee.

"We're missing something," Nicholai said, stopping his pacing to stare at the board. He ran a hand through his hair, which was standing on end. He was frustrated again as he looked back at the timeline they had constructed. They had been at it for over three hours without a break, and they both were tired, their eyes burning under the fluorescent lights.

"We've got a connection between them all, but it really doesn't answer anything," she said, leaning back in her chair. She reached across the conference table and picked up the hand-carved wooden mask—the one Nicholai had taken from the Roberts estate. It felt heavy and cold in her hand.

"If there's one connection between these guys, then there has to be more. We're just not seeing it. We're looking at the surface tension, not the current underneath," he said.

"I've got the forensic accountant digging through their financials now. I'm hoping he can find something—a hidden account, a shell company. Maybe they were laundering money," Danica said while turning the mask over in her hands, tracing the smooth wood.

"There's more to that as well," Delgado said, pointing a finger at the mask. He looked at it hard, then turned his back on it. He walked to the corner, turned on his heel, then folded his arms across his chest and stared at the whiteboard.

"They all knew each other; they went on the same hunting excursion every year at the same time. Their passports confirm that—Brazil, Argentina, Peru. They were a brotherhood of sorts."

"I'm hoping our forensic accountant can find out the name of the outfitting company that booked these trips. If we find the guide, maybe we find out what really happened down there."

"There's more too," he said, tapping his temple.

"Like what?"

"A group of high-powered, influential men, with the same interest in hunting in South America who rarely socialize or communicate with each other before or after their trip. That doesn't fit the profile of a 'buddy trip.' Hunters brag. They show off their kills. They hang heads on walls. Other than that mask, I've found nothing more. No photos of the kill, no taxidermy in their offices. And even that mask is puzzling. Why are the eye spaces not cut out? It's blind."

He paced again. "And their trip is kept quiet; even their wives don't know any of the details. Ashley Rosin didn't know. Alisha Roberts didn't know. It wasn't a vacation; it was a secret."

"What were they hiding?" she asked aloud, voicing the question that hung in the room.

There was a long, awkward time of silence in the room, filled only by the hum of the ventilation system. Danica saw that Nicholai was off in thought, his eyes unfocused. The look on his face became even more intense and focused, as if he were seeing something invisible to her. She wanted to speak, to say something to bring him back, but she was afraid of breaking his train of thought. She knew better than to interrupt the process.

Then, without a word, Nicholai walked over to the whiteboard and reached for the eraser. He madly rubbed off the notes on the left side—the timelines, the financial theories—completely clearing the section until it was pristine white. He stood back, looking at the blank canvas.

He looked down at the tray holder that held the different colored markers. He bypassed the black and blue and quickly chose the red one. He pulled the cap off with his teeth and started to write. The marker squeaked loudly against the board.

Once finished, he stood back and stared at the word. Danica looked at the letters, then back at him. In bold, bright red ink, Delgado had written the word TETELESTAI.

"That's it," he said quietly.

"What?" she asked with a look of confusion. "We already know that means 'It is finished.' You gave me the theology lesson."

"You're right, but we've been so focused on that word and its meaning as an ending," he said, turning to her with a revelation burning in his eyes. "We've been so consumed with this being finished—a debt paid, a life ended—that we haven't even considered where it started. 'It is finished' implies a duration. A process. A beginning."

He tapped the board. "This isn't just a suicide note, Danica. It's a timestamp. It marks the end of something that started years ago. We need to stop looking at their deaths and start looking at their lives. Specifically, when they started using that word."

Chapter 40

Danica left Nicholai alone in the interrogation room, the door clicking shut on his revelation about "Tetelestai" being a beginning rather than an end. She made her way up two floors to the forensic accountant's office, her mind racing with the implications.

The office was a stark contrast to the chaos of the squad room—quiet, sterile, and smelling of ozone and coffee. After fifteen minutes with the accountant, a man named Miller who viewed numbers as a language more honest than English, she was vibrating with excitement.

Miller had spent two days pouring over bank statements, credit card statements, and the personal financial records of James Rosin, Cole Simpson, David Roberts, and now Davis Wright. He had looked past the obvious expenditures—the mortgages, the cars, the jewelry for wives—and found the ghost in the machine.

"It's a pass-through account," Miller had explained, pointing to a spreadsheet on his monitor. "Shell companies set up in the Caymans, but they all feed into one specific entity in Brazil. All four men were paying into it. Monthly. Like rent. Or blackmail."

She moved as quickly as she could with the new information, clutching the printout in her hand like a weapon. She was excited to fill Delgado in; this was the physical evidence that grounded his psychological theories.

She hit the hallway button for the elevator, but the digital display showed the car stuck on the first floor. It would be too slow. She couldn't wait. She had to get to him before the trail went cold again. She turned on her heel and raced toward the back stairway, hitting the crash bar with her shoulder.

Her footsteps echoed loudly in the concrete stairwell as she took the steps two at a time, using the handrail to swing herself around the landings. She burst out onto the fourth floor, slightly breathless, and quickened her pace. She flew past Leininger's desk, ignoring him completely as he lifted his head from a magazine, and pushed the heavy door to the interrogation room open.

"Nicholai, you were right, it's—"

She stopped dead. The words died in her throat.

He was gone.

The room was empty, save for the humming of the ventilation system. The chair he had been sitting in was pushed back, empty. But the whiteboard was screaming at her. The red letters of TETELESTAI stood out, blazing against the white background like a fresh wound.

She felt a sudden chill, a premonition of danger that made the hair on her arms stand up. She turned back and hurried out to the squad room, stopping in the center of the area, scanning the desks.

Danica looked around frantically, checking the coffee station, the exits, the captain's office, but still couldn't see any sign of Nicholai.

"He left," Leininger said from his desk, not looking up.

"When? Did he say where he was going?" she demanded, marching over to him.

"Nope, and I didn't ask. He moved fast. I thought he went to find you. He looked pretty upset. Distracted."

She reached into her pocket and pulled out her Blackberry, her fingers fumbling slightly. She highlighted her call list and found his number, quickly pressing send. She held the phone to her ear, pacing tight circles, praying he would pick up.

She turned around quickly when she heard a sound—not in her ear, but in the room behind her. The familiar, muffled ring of his cell phone was coming from the interrogation room she had just left.

Danica walked back inside, dread pooling in her stomach. She saw his phone sitting in the center of the conference room table, vibrating against the metal surface. He had left it behind. He had gone off the grid.

Chapter 41

She was surprised at how quickly Thomas Sanford took the bait. It was almost insulting how easy it was. It was all her idea—the clandestine meeting, the hotel—and he seemed to like that. She had learned early in her career that most powerful men, men who spent their days commanding armies of staff and moving millions of dollars, usually had an underlying secret attraction to aggressive women. They wanted to surrender control, if only for an hour. Especially to an attractive one like her.

Sanford was impressed that she had booked the suite and had everything in order. The room was under her name, paid for with cash, so there would be no records of him even being there. That anonymity eased his mind and his conscience enough to enjoy their private afternoon together without looking over his shoulder.

In the past, it was usually the fourth or fifth meeting before a man made the first move, but she knew Thomas Sanford was different. He was a campaign manager in the final stretch of a race; he was running on adrenaline and stress. He needed a release. He needed someone to take control so he didn't have to think. She put the unspoken offer out—a glance, a touch on the arm—and he bit right away; making his intentions appear as innocent as possible until the door closed.

It was probably the stress of the campaign, the thought of a few hours alone with a woman who asked for nothing, or maybe the dollar signs of her substantial donation to the Senator's war chest. Sanford grabbed the offer faster than she expected, and she was more than accommodating. Both of them had their own motives. His was pleasure. Hers was destruction.

And like the others, she had now worn him out.

She stood by the bedroom door of the luxury hotel suite, buttoning her blouse, and peered at Sanford asleep on the king-sized bed. He was sprawled out, mouth slightly open, vulnerable. She recalled how easy Roberts was; that was probably because of his age and health condition. Davis Wright took a little more time and energy to sedate, but Rosin and Simpson went just as she had planned. Men were remarkably predictable once the endorphins kicked in.

And like the others, Thomas Sanford would be asleep for an hour; forty-five minutes at the very least. The sedative she had slipped into his second glass of scotch was mild but effective, designed to mimic a deep, post-coital nap. That was more than enough time to get her things prepared.

She quietly closed the bedroom door of the suite, engaging the latch silently. She always booked a suite because it suited her purpose better. She needed the separate living space and the privacy to work.

She walked across the small living area to the desk where she had left her belongings. She retrieved her oversized designer purse and removed a small, high-powered notebook computer along with a black thumb drive. She didn't have to spend a lot of time on logistics; that had already been done days ago. She placed the notebook on the hotel desk by the window, overlooking the city he thought he owned, and powered it up.

He had left his leather briefcase by the door, careless in his haste. She studied its exact position—the angle of the strap, the distance from the wall—before touching it. She didn't want to give him any indication that anyone had been through it.

Gently, she unzipped the main section, retrieved Sanford's laptop, and placed it next to her notebook on the desk. She turned it on and waited. The fan whirred to life. When the password prompt appeared, she didn't hesitate. She inserted a bootable USB drive into the side port. The computer started cycling again, bypassing the Windows login completely.

Her fingers flew across the keys. Files from the thumb drive were copied and hidden deep within the system architecture of his laptop. It took only a few minutes for the hard drive to be partitioned and secured. She watched the progress bar crawl across the screen—green pixels sealing his fate.

The new section she created would act as a parasite. It would automatically mirror the main hard drive and wirelessly transfer every file, email, financial document, and keystroke to a remote server she controlled. It was a ghost partition, invisible to standard scans, waiting for the command to execute.

When the partitioning was complete, she removed the drive and rebooted his machine to ensure it looked normal. The login screen reappeared, innocent and waiting.

She focused her attention on her own notebook. She double-clicked on her settings and waited for the handshake. Sanford's laptop received the new request, and she confirmed it by clicking on the "Execute" button.

Connection Established.

The simple confirmation from her notebook now gave her complete control over his digital life. And in the modern world, that meant control over his finances, his communication, his reputation, and eventually, his death.

She wiped down his laptop with a microfiber cloth, removing her fingerprints, and placed it back in his bag exactly as she had found it.

She checked her reflection in the mirror, smoothing her hair. In a few days, she would have her money and her revenge. She was almost finished with Sanford, and he had no idea that in less than a week, his life would be over. And the beauty of it was, the world would believe it was by his own choice.

Chapter 42

"Go back to that last entry," he said, his finger stabbing at the air near the monitor.

Griffin hit the back command, and the page reloaded with a digital stutter. "Why can't you just get on the department's mainframe and get all this? They have access to databases I have to tunnel through backdoors to reach."

"Too narrow," Delgado said, pacing the length of the workbench. "The only information logged in by the police has been input by the police. It's filtered through their bias, their jurisdiction, and their error rate. I need more. I need the raw data, the stuff that falls through the cracks. This gives me a bigger picture." He stopped and looked at the tech. "Plus, you have a unique way of getting into places that most people can't even see, let alone enter."

"Flattery gets you everywhere, Pastor. And where's your partner? The intense one?"

"She's back doing her own thing. Chasing the money trail." Nicholai looked at the screen, scanning the lines of code and data fields, and he wasn't impressed. It was just noise. "There's nothing there. It's dead data."

"What else can I do?" Griffin asked, sensing the rising tide of Nicholai's anxiety. "I can pull credit reports, DMV records, library fines..."

"I'm missing something, and I can't put my finger on it. It's hovering right at the edge of my peripheral vision."

"Tell me where you want me to go. My fingers can go wherever you want," Griffin smiled, cracking his knuckles. "Just point the way."

"Go to the state's vital records," Nicholai asked, stopping his pacing. "Search out suicides for the last two years. Not just suspicious ones—all of them."

Griffin pulled up the state's web page, bypassed the login screen with a script he had written years ago, and accessed the Vital Statistics database. The hard drive hummed as it crunched the query.

"One hundred and sixty-seven," he said, looking at the total count. "That's a lot of misery."

"Narrow the parameters," Nicholai ordered. "Men only. Ages forty to sixty-five. Let's see what we come up with."

Nicholai walked away again, unable to stand still, while Griffin typed in the new search parameters. A list of names scrolled down the screen.

"There's your list," Griffin stated. "Thirty-seven recorded. Thirty-seven men in the prime of their lives who decided to check out early."

"There's still too many. I need it narrowed down more. There has to be a filter." Nicholai walked away again and paced back and forth along the length of the room, his footsteps echoing on the concrete. Griffin watched him, concerned. He walked over to the stainless steel refrigerator and popped open a soda. He took a long drink, the carbonation burning his throat, then reached inside for another can.

"You make me nervous when you get like this," he said, offering the can. "You're vibrating. Do you want one of these or something stronger to calm you down? I keep a bottle of Jack in the server rack for emergencies."

Delgado didn't answer. He paced, his eyes fixed on the floor but seeing patterns in his mind. His mind was off somewhere else, reconstructing the lives of dead men. Griffin knew how focused he could get; it was like watching a machine process variables. He placed the unopened can back in the refrigerator and moved back towards the computer.

"Income!" Delgado shouted, spinning around.

Griffin jumped in his chair, nearly knocking over his keyboard. Delgado's outburst caught him off guard, and before he could turn around, Nicholai was at his side, leaning over his shoulder.

"Can you access IRS records?"

"Are you asking as a friend or a member of law enforcement?" Griffin asked, his hand hovering over the mouse. "Because one is a favor, and the other is a federal felony."

Nicholai glared at Griffin. The look alone—intense, desperate, and commanding—made Griffin uncomfortable enough not to bother waiting for an answer. He turned back to the screen. Within minutes, his fingers flying across the mechanical keys, he had accessed the Internal Revenue Service's website, bypassed the firewall, and made his way into their confidential, employee-only database.

"We're in," he told Delgado, who was anxiously watching the screen as if reading tea leaves.

"Now cross-reference those thirty-seven names based on the last tax returns they filed. I want income referenced highest to lowest. Show me the money."

Griffin executed the cross-reference script. The list of names reshuffled, separating the haves from the have-nots. A new page appeared, significantly shorter.

"How many are over two-hundred thousand a year?"

Griffin stared at the screen, counting. "Six," he replied. "Six men who had everything going for them financially. What are you on to?"

Delgado ignored his question. His eyes became intense, tracking the names. Rosin. Simpson. Roberts. Wright. And two others.

"One last thing," Delgado said, his voice dropping. "Homeland Security. Can you get in their system? I need travel records."

Griffin laughed, a nervous, high-pitched sound. "That one is even easier than the IRS. Their firewall is a joke."

"Good," Nicholai responded. "Let's see how many of those six visited South America in the last eighteen months. Specifically Brazil, Argentina, or Peru."

It took Griffin less than fifteen minutes to hack into the Homeland Security database and retrieve the travel manifests Delgado requested. The printer in the corner whirred to life.

"There's your answer," Griffin said, pointing to the screen.

"Give me everything on those two remaining names," he ordered, grabbing the paper as it ejected. "Even their last known addresses. We have to get to them before he does."

"Coming right up. It will come off that printer over there," he said, pointing off to the side.

Nicholai scanned the document. Two names remained. One was already dead—Davis Wright. The other was Thomas Sanford.

He reached inside his pocket for his phone, needing to call Danica immediately, but it wasn't there. He patted his other pockets. Empty. He realized with a jolt of frustration that he had left it back in the interrogation room in his haste to leave.

"I need a phone," he barked. "Now."

Chapter 43

Unknown Caller appeared on the display of Danica's Blackberry.

She stood in the center of the squad room, the noise of the precinct fading into the background. She rarely answered unidentified calls—usually reporters or telemarketers—but something told her to answer this one. The intuition that kept her alive on the streets was screaming at her. She was worried about Nicholai. She was concerned about where he was and why he had left so quickly without a word.

She pressed the talk button. "Harris."

"It's me." Nicholai's familiar voice made her feel better immediately, though the tone was urgent.

"Where are you?" she asked, relief washing over her. "You left your phone here. I thought... I don't know what I thought."

"I just realized that," he said quickly, cutting off her concern. "I found something. A pattern. The Tetelestai connection goes deeper than we thought. I need you to meet me in Highland Park."

"Highland Park? Where? Where are you now?"

"I'm with Griffin at the warehouse," he said. "I've got names, Danica. Two more potential victims. One is likely dead, but the other... Thomas Sanford. The Senator's campaign manager. He fits the profile perfectly. High income, travel to South America, isolated social life."

"Pastor?" Griffin called out from his console of monitors, his voice trembling slightly.

"Take this address down," he told Danica over the phone, ignoring Griffin. "It's Sanford's residence. If we're lucky, we can intercept him."

"Nic?" Griffin called out again, louder this time. "You need to see this."

"Griffin, wait a minute," he snapped, waving a hand at the tech. Delgado turned his attention back to the conversation he was having with Danica. "I can be there in twenty minutes, and I'll explain it all there. Bring backup, but keep them silent. We don't want to spook him."

"Good," she said. "I've got something from the accountant as well. Financial records that link them all to a shell company in Brazil. It matches your theory."

"Go," Nicholai ordered. "I'll see you in twenty." He hung up the landline phone he had borrowed.

"Delgado! We have a visitor!" Griffin's voice was now panicked, cracking with fear.

Nicholai spun around and stared at Griffin, who was pointing a shaking finger at one of the monitors on the far left of the console.

"What is it?" Nicholai asked, moving quickly to the tech's side.

"The alley cam. Someone just disabled the audio, but the video is still live."

Nicholai moved closer to the screen. The image Griffin was watching was a high-definition live feed from the overhead security camera in the alley, positioned directly above the reinforced back door. The late afternoon sun cast long shadows against the brick, but the figure standing there was clear.

Nicholai clearly made out the image of a man standing by the door, perfectly still. He wasn't trying to hide. He wasn't trying to pick the lock. He was waiting.

His head was covered with a nondescript baseball cap, and his face was angled down, obscuring his features. He wore a windbreaker that looked too warm for the weather.

"Is that him?" Griffin whispered. "Is that the guy?"

As if hearing the question through the cable, the figure moved. Nicholai and Griffin watched in horror as the man slowly looked up, directly at the camera. He didn't squint against the sun. He glared right into the lens, his eyes dark pits on the grainy screen.

Then, slowly, deliberately, he smiled.

It wasn't a smile of joy. It was a baring of teeth. A predator acknowledging his prey. It was the first time Nicholai Delgado saw the pure, unfiltered evil in Jeremy Quinlin's eyes, and he realized with a sickening jolt that the warehouse wasn't a fortress. It was a trap.

Chapter 44

There was urgency in his voice—a sharp, command tone that Danica rarely heard from Nicholai. She gathered her things, her hands moving with trained efficiency despite the spike in her heart rate. She grabbed her own phone, her keys, and the scrap of notepaper with the Highland Park address he had barked at her.

Her pace quickened to a jog as she moved through the squad room, ignoring the curious looks from the other detectives. She reached the parking garage, the air heavy and humid. As she unlocked her car door, a sound stopped her cold.

It wasn't her phone ringing. It was his.

She looked down at the passenger seat where she had tossed her pile of belongings. Nicholai's cell phone, forgotten in the interrogation room and retrieved by her only moments ago, was vibrating against the leather.

Danica stared at it, unsure of whether to answer. The caller ID showed 'Unknown Caller.' She remembered his last call from Griffin's warehouse had displayed the same anonymous ID. Logic told her it was Nicholai calling from a landline to see why she hadn't left yet.

"I'm on my way," she said without hesitating, answering the phone and sliding into the driver's seat.

The silence on the other end was heavy, thick with static. It wasn't the empty silence of a dropped call; it was the presence of someone listening.

She pulled the phone away, checked the connection, and placed it back to her ear.

"Nic? Are you there?"

Again, there was no response. She focused, pressing the phone tighter against her ear, and heard a low, rhythmic sound. Breathing. Slow, deliberate breathing.

"Hello?" she asked, her voice hardening.

"If I'm not mistaken, this must be Inspector Harris," a raspy male voice whispered. It sounded like dry leaves scraping across concrete.

Danica froze, her hand hovering over the ignition key. "Yes, it is," she replied, her mind racing. "Can I help you?" She was confused as to why someone would be calling her on Delgado's private phone—a number only a handful of people possessed.

"What a pleasure to finally meet you, Inspector Harris. I feel like we have already become very close friends. I've been watching you work."

The air in the garage seemed to drop twenty degrees.

"Who is this?" she asked, though a sick feeling in her gut told her she already knew.

"I'm an old but very dear friend of Nicholai's. We go way back." The voice paused, savoring the moment. "Let me introduce myself. My name is Jeremy Quinlin."

Danica stopped breathing.

"Tell the Pastor I'll see him soon," he laughed—a cold, humorless sound. "And tell him I have his phone. He really should be more careful with his possessions."

The call went dead, leaving a cold chill rippling through Danica's entire body that no Texas heat could thaw.

Chapter 45

She had beaten him to the address by using the flashing lights and a heavy foot to maneuver through the mid-afternoon traffic. Danica hit speeds of over eighty miles per hour down Legacy Drive, weaving through the sedans and SUVs of oblivious suburbanites. She turned into the Twin Oaks neighborhood, tires screeching slightly, and waited for him.

Quinlin's call had shaken her to her core. With no way of contacting Nicholai—since she was holding his phone—she was left alone in her panic, imagining the worst. Had Quinlin intercepted him at the warehouse? Was she driving to a meeting, or a crime scene?

She found the address he had given her quickly, but there was no sign of the white Porsche. The house was a sprawling ranch-style, set back from the road, but it lacked the pristine grandeur of the Rosin or Roberts estates. Several cars were parked haphazardly along the street. Neon pink Garage Sale signs littered the front yard, and a realtor's For Sale sign rocked back and forth in the light breeze, the "Price Reduced" rider hanging crookedly.

Danica sat inside her car, gripping the steering wheel until her knuckles turned white, and watched the prospective bargain hunters come and go. It was a macabre parade. People walked out carrying lamps, bundles of clothes, and kitchen appliances—the remnants of a life being sold for pennies on the dollar. An older Hispanic man struggled to load a large dining table into his pickup truck, shouting instructions to a teenager.

Finally, from the rearview mirror, Danica spotted the white Porsche round the corner. It moved fast but controlled. She exited her car before his came to a full stop, running to the driver's side window.

"He called," she yelled out before the window was even fully down.

"Who?" Nicholai asked, looking at the phone in her hand.

"Quinlin! He called on your cell. I thought it was you, so I answered. He knew it was me."

Nicholai's face darkened. "What did he say?"

"He introduced himself. He said you were old friends. He said he's been watching us." Danica's voice trembled slightly. "The call was too short to put any kind of trace on it, not that it would matter with a burner."

Nicholai looked away, staring at the dashboard. He struggled with what to say. He couldn't decide if he should tell her Quinlin had been outside Griffin's warehouse, staring into the camera just moments ago.

"That's all he said?"

"Yes, that's all," she said. Danica was starting to calm down now that she saw Nicholai was physically safe. "I had no way of contacting you. I was starting to panic."

Her comment helped him make the decision to keep quiet about the encounter at the warehouse. She was already on edge; telling her the killer was physically close enough to touch the door would only compromise her focus.

"I'm okay," he said, opening the door and stepping out. "Have you been inside yet?" he asked quickly, shifting the subject.

"No, I have no idea why we're even here. You ran out of the station without telling me where you were going, and you neglected to tell me why we're at a garage sale in the suburbs."

"Sorry," he said. "I did some of my own research with Griffin. I tracked all the suicides over the last two years in the area. Then I cross-referenced them with a tight set of parameters—income, age, travel habits. I found two more suicides that seem to fit the same profile we've been dealing with. I'm trying to figure out where, when, and how this all started. If Tetelestai is the end, I need to find the beginning."

"And this is one of them?" she asked, looking at the house.

"Yes. Bryan Falco. Forty-eight-year-old white male. He owned a chain of popular Mexican restaurants throughout the state," Nicholai informed her. He didn't need notes; he had the data filed away in his mind. "Sixteen months ago, his wife found him in the garage. The garage door was closed, and his SUV was still running when she arrived home. The reports claim the engine had run for almost twenty-two hours until it ran out of gas."

"And her alibi?"

"New York shopping trip with her girlfriends. Ironclad."

"What makes you think it's related to the others?"

Nicholai looked at the house as a young couple, each carrying a box of books, laughed their way to their car. They were happy to get a deal on a dead man's library.

"Prominent, well-established businessman, traveled to South America, suicide by unconventional means for his personality type. The whole scenario and profile fit. But I still can't figure out the motive for the wife, if she's involved. Falco's finances were supposedly solid."

"What do you expect to find here?" Danica asked.

"I don't know. Scraps. Leftovers. If we don't find an answer here, I've got one more to question. But look at this," he gestured to the yard. "She's liquidating his life."

"How do you want to work this one?"

Nicholai thought for a moment. "Just use the standard line you've been doing. Be the compassionate detective tying up loose ends."

"And you? Are you going to wander off again?"

He smiled, a sad, fleeting expression. "Dani, you've got to understand something about me. Sometimes I wander off to keep myself from getting lost. I look for the things people forget to hide."

"What?"

"Someday you'll figure that one out. Let's go. Her name is Donna."

They walked towards the house and decided to go through the open garage, passing tables laden with power tools and fishing gear. Donna Falco was seated in a fold-out lawn chair off to the side of the garage, behind a card table with a cash box. She looked tired, worn down by the haggling strangers picking through her memories.

"Good afternoon," Danica said, approaching Donna Falco. "I'm Inspector Harris from the Dallas Police." She placed her ID on the table in front of the woman.

"I haven't done anything wrong, have I? I made sure all the signs were on my property line," she replied quickly, defensiveness spiking.

"No, Ms. Falco, everything is fine. We're here to ask you a few questions concerning your husband," Danica informed her gently.

"Bryan? He's been gone for over a year," she said, looking down at the concrete floor. "Why would you be interested in him now? The case is closed."

"We're just trying to wrap up a few loose ends. There's been some new evidence concerning some other cases that we think may be related to your husband's death."

Nicholai stood silently behind the detective, taking in the surroundings. He seemed more interested in the items for sale than the

conversation—a set of golf clubs, a humidor, a stack of travel magazines.

"Cases? I don't understand."

"Ms. Falco, we're just trying to get a grasp on what happened and
why. We believe there might be a pattern."

"Join the club," she said bitterly. "I've been trying to answer all that
as well."

"What do you mean?" Danica asked.

Donna looked around the garage with blank, hollow eyes. She didn't
notice the young woman taking an interest in the stack of picture
frames on the sale table, removing the photos of a smiling couple to
check the price of the wood.

"We had a great life," she said quietly. "Or so I thought. Everything
was good. He was expanding the business. Then I came home to... to
that." She gestured vaguely toward the closed door leading into the
house.

"I understand," Danica said quickly. She didn't want the widow
focusing on the incident or reliving the grief. "Were there any signs of
depression? Had anything changed in him or his personality?"

Ms. Falco thought for a moment. "He did get kind of reserved a few
days before; quiet, shut down. He spent a lot of time in his office. But
it wasn't really a concern to me. Business was going really well at that
time. I thought he was just working on a new menu."

"You weren't aware of any money issues?"

"No, we were fine. I mean, look at this place. Most people dream of
all this."

Danica looked around the garage, then at Nicholai, who still remained silent, running his hand over a fishing rod. "I noticed you're
selling a few things and your home. Do you mind if I ask why?"

"Plain and simple: money. Bryan's insurance policy wouldn't pay off
because he took his own life. Suicide clause." She spat the words out.
"Business is down at the restaurants because of the economy. My
husband had his finger in every aspect of the restaurants, but now that
he's gone, everything is just falling apart. We've had to close or sell off
almost half the locations, and the rest are struggling to keep their doors
open. I'm selling the furniture to pay the property tax."

"Do the names James Rosin, Davis Wright, Cole Simpson, or David
Roberts ring a bell?" she asked.

"David Roberts, yes. He built our home. He was a nice man. The
others... no, I've never heard of them," the widow stated. "Should I?"

"We're just asking, Ms. Falco," Danica responded. "Was your husband a hunter by chance?"

"Avid, yes. He would go out several times a year. He made a few trips overseas. And once a year to South America. Why is that important?"

"Just asking," Danica stated. She didn't want to alarm the widow. "Did your husband leave a suicide note?"

"Yes, he did," she replied, but looked away from Danica's eyes, staring at a box of old records.

"Do you still have it?" Danica asked. "Where did he leave it?"

"I found it in the printer tray in his office. And no, I don't have it. It's not something I wanted to keep. I burned it."

Danica looked at Nicholai. He was standing over one of the sale tables in the back corner, his back to them.

"I hate to bring it up, but do you recall what the note said?"

"Not really. I was in shock," she murmured. "Something about not being able to live with what he had done. The pain he caused. I never understood that part. I still don't. He hadn't done anything wrong."

"Does the word 'Tetelestai' mean anything to you?"

Donna looked up quickly, her eyes widening. "Yes. That was at the end of the note. Right under his name. How did you know that?"

"Just a guess, Ms. Falco. A pattern."

"I still don't know what that means. That word haunts me even today. I looked it up, but... it didn't make sense for Bryan."

Nicholai spoke for the first time, his voice low, but he didn't look at either woman. "Do you happen to still have his computer?"

"No," she said. "That was one of the first things I sold. A college kid bought it for fifty bucks."

Nicholai still hadn't looked away from the table. Something had grabbed his attention amidst the clutter of a dead man's hobbies. Danica watched as his hand slowly reached for one of the items, his fingers trembling slightly. From her viewpoint, she couldn't make out what it was.

"I'll give you twenty dollars for this," he finally said, turning around.

He held up a small, hand-carved wooden mask. It was identical to the others—grotesque, blind, and silent.

Chapter 46

"We just keep getting the same thing over and over," she said, her hands tightening on the steering wheel. They had left Nicholai's car parked in front of the Falco residence, opting to take her unmarked unit to preserve the low profile of his Porsche. "Another widow, another dead end, another tragedy wrapped in money."

"I know, but we have to keep digging," he said, staring out at the passing concrete of the Dallas North Tollway. "We're panning for gold in a river of mud. We'll eventually find the nugget we're looking for."

"Now where?" she asked, checking her blind spot.

"This next one seems to fit the same profile, but with a medical twist," Nicholai replied, pulling a folded printout from his pocket. "Dr. Jason Fawcett. He was a plastic surgeon from University Park. He was a partner in one of the most successful aesthetic practices in Dallas. Very well known, very in demand, and very dead."

"Any details on the death?"

"Overdose, almost two years ago. His nurse found him in his private office when she went in to open the practice the next morning. He had access to an entire pharmacy and apparently took advantage of all of it. A cocktail of propofol and opioids. He went to sleep and didn't wake up."

"Anything about a note?" Danica asked as she merged the car onto the exit ramp, the tires humming against the grooved pavement.

"Nothing mentioned in the official report, but back then, nobody knew exactly what to look for. It was just another doctor with a god complex and a drug problem. From what I caught off the online file, the entire investigation was quick, quiet, and easy. Closed in forty-eight hours."

"And the widow?" Danica asked. "What do we know about her?"

"From the records, Lynn Fawcett still lives in the same home on Stanford Avenue in University Park. Other than that, she was a dead end in the initial report. Just a grieving trophy wife. That's why I want to see for myself. Grief changes people, but guilt changes them more."

Danica turned the car onto Central Expressway and exited at Northwest Highway, heading toward the exclusive enclave. The Fawcett residence was halfway down the block of Stanford Lane, a street lined with massive oak trees that formed a canopy over the road. Located in the central area of Dallas, the neighborhood was a unique mixture of older, dignified 1950s-style ranch homes dwarfed among newer, teardown mini-estates and limestone mansions. There was money in the area—lots of it. And it was old, established money. Wealthy parents lived down the block from their even wealthier grown children, creating a generational fortress of affluence.

Danica and Nicholai found the Fawcett home easily. It screamed for attention. The three-story brick and stone façade stood out aggressively among the more understated ranch-style homes on either side. It was a monument to excess. Gas lanterns flickered wastefully on either side of the massive front door, burning fuel in the bright afternoon sun. Even from the street, one could tell the inside of the home would probably be as impressive—and as cold—as the outside.

A landscape crew was adding the final touches to the front yard, trimming hedges that were already geometrically perfect. Danica and Nicholai walked up the cobblestone walkway to the front door, the sound of leaf blowers drowning out the birds. Danica rang the bell while Nicholai took his now-usual position behind her, scanning the perimeter cameras.

"Can I help you?"

The woman answered the door immediately, as if she had been waiting for a delivery. She was striking—blonde, taut, and surgically enhanced to a point of uncanny perfection. But she ignored them at first, peering past the detective and Delgado with a look of absolute disgust.

"Excuse me for a moment," she said rudely, pushing past them without waiting for an introduction.

They both turned and watched her walk quickly towards a short, stocky, well-tanned Hispanic man who was pushing a lawnmower onto a trailer. She swung her arms wildly, her gold bracelets clanking, eventually pointing a manicured finger along the edge of the driveway. She was making it quite clear she was unhappy with the results.

"No! I told you, the lines have to be diagonal!" she screamed, her voice shrill and piercing. "Are you deaf or just stupid? Look at this mess!"

She berated the man for several minutes in front of his crew of two other men, humiliating him for a perceived infraction that neither Danica nor Nicholai could even see. The man stood with his head down, taking the abuse in silence, likely knowing that speaking back would cost him the contract.

Shaking her head in dramatic exasperation, she returned to the front door, smoothing her silk blouse. "You have to constantly be on those types of people," she said to Danica, expecting camaraderie. "If you don't ride them, they get lazy. Now, what can I do for you? I'm assuming you aren't selling cookies."

Danica stiffened, her dislike for the woman instant and visceral. "We're here to speak to Ms. Fawcett. Lynn Fawcett. I'm Inspector Harris from the Dallas Police Department, and this is Special Consultant Nicholai Delgado."

"I'm Lynn Fawcett. How can I help you?" She leaned against the doorframe, bored.

"We have a few questions about your husband."

"Jason?" she asked, a flicker of annoyance crossing her face. "You're a little too late. He died almost two years ago. What could you possibly want to know now? I answered all the questions back then. It was an accident. He worked too hard."

Danica looked past the woman and inside the house. The air conditioning rushing out was frigid. "We're trying to wrap up a few loose ends on some related files. Do you mind if we sit inside and talk for a few minutes? This won't take long."

"I guess," she said, checking her diamond watch. "But make it quick, please. I have a pilates appointment this afternoon, and my instructor charges if I'm late."

"Beautiful home," Nicholai said as they stepped inside the dark foyer.

The interior was a cavern of expensive taste. The walls were heavily textured and tea-stained to look aged. Dark, heavy wood trim gave the home a rustic but elegant feel, heavy on the Mediterranean influence. Oil-rubbed bronze fixtures and crystal chandeliers created a dim, moody atmosphere that felt more like a hotel lobby than a home.

"Thank you," she said proudly, her demeanor softening slightly at the flattery. "I've done this all myself. Decorated it all. Every sconce, every tile."

"Is this a David Roberts build?" Delgado asked casually, running his hand over a banister.

Lynn stopped, surprised. "Why, yes it is," she replied, looking at him with new interest. "I see you know good taste when you see it. Not many people recognize the architectural signature."

"I've always admired his style and architecture," Nicholai lied smoothly. "Very impressive flow," he said as they made their way towards the back of the home.

Danica listened, surprised and slightly taken aback by Nicholai's behavior. He had never initiated conversation this early or been so forthcoming with compliments during an interview in her presence before. He was playing a game.

"So you knew Mr. Roberts?" Danica asked, seizing the opening.

"He was a friend of my husband's, yes. They ran in the same circles."

"Were they close by chance?" the Inspector continued before Nicholai could get a word in.

"Not really," she said, waving a hand dismissively. "Acquaintances more than anything else. David built houses; Jason built faces. They understood the pursuit of perfection."

"Do you know how or when they met?" Danica asked.

"Can't help you there. Probably at the club or some charity gala. Jason knew everyone."

"Have you had any contact with him lately?" Danica asked, following her into the den.

"No, not at all," she said. "I really didn't know him that well personally. Just the builder."

"Do you mind if we take a seat?" Nicholai asked, gesturing to the furniture.

"I'm pressed for time," she said, slightly agitated again. "Can't we do this standing?"

"Mrs. Fawcett, did you know David Roberts died?" Nicholai asked, dropping the bomb without inflection.

She froze for a split second, then her face composed itself into a mask of polite concern. She finally gave in and motioned to Nicholai and Danica to take a seat on one of the two velvet sofas in the den.

"Yes, I think I heard something about that on the news. What a shame. He was a talented man at one time." Lynn Fawcett sat across from them, leaned back, and made herself comfortable, crossing her legs. "Now, what is this all about? Why are you connecting my husband to David?"

She avoided looking at Nicholai, focusing her gaze on Danica.

"We have a few questions about some recent events that we believe may be related to your husband's death as well," Danica replied professionally, opening her notebook.

"Well, I don't know how much help I can give you. That part of my life is closed."

"Prior to your husband's incident, did he seem overly stressed or depressed?" Danica asked.

Nicholai sat quietly beside her, leaning forward, invading Lynn's personal space with his eyes. He watched the micro-expressions, the twitch of a muscle in her jaw, the way her fingers tapped the armrest.

Fawcett thought for a moment. Her eyes met Delgado's intense stare, and she quickly turned her attention back to Danica. "Not that I can recall, no. Jason was always high-energy. That's what made him successful."

"Can you tell us about the circumstances; where was he found, who found him?"

Lynn sat back in the chair and crossed her right leg over her left. Her expensive strapless heel hung off her foot and bounced rhythmically as she moved her leg up and down—a pendulum of nervous energy.

"I don't know much other than his nurse found him in his office early that morning. He stayed late to finish charts. He... miscalculated a dose to help him sleep. That's all."

"Was there a suicide note there or here at home?" Danica asked.

"No. Nothing at all." She sat forward, her voice hardening. "The police took statements back then, ruled it accidental, so why are you asking the same questions again? Are you trying to reopen a closed case?"

Nicholai finally cut in, his voice sharp. "You seem to have adjusted well since your husband's death." He fired off the statement before Danica could ask another procedural question. It was an accusation wrapped in an observation.

Fawcett's eyes bore down on Nicholai, her pupils constricting. "Sir, I learned a long time ago not to depend on any man for my happiness or my survival. Jason's death was devastating, but I'm quite capable of making my own way through life, thank you very much. I've worked hard for all this, and I'm not ashamed to say that I deserve it all. I'm a survivor."

"So no money problems since your husband's death?" he asked, glancing around the opulent room. "This creates a lot of overhead."

"If there was, it was just a small blip in the whole scheme of things," she responded defensively. "Nothing I couldn't handle. I'm resourceful."

"Were you involved in his practice at all?" Danica asked.

"No, that was Jason's domain. I hate blood."

"So you're self-sufficient; good for you. Are you in the medical field as well?" Nicholai asked.

Fawcett laughed, a cold, tinkling sound. "No, not me. I have my own consulting firm, which does quite well." She stood up abruptly, glaring at both of them. "In fact, you must excuse me. I am late for a meeting now, so if you're finished with your history lesson, I must ask you to leave."

Danica stood up first, sensing they would get nothing more from her today. "Thank you, Ms. Fawcett. We're sorry for your loss and for the intrusion."

"I'm sure you can see yourselves out," she said, turning her back on them to adjust a flower arrangement.

Nicholai remained seated for a beat longer than necessary, watching her back, before standing up. He followed Danica to the doorway of the den, then stopped and turned back.

"Ms. Fawcett, if I may ask, what type of consulting are you involved in now?"

She turned slowly, her eyes narrowing. "Why is that any concern of yours?"

"Just curious," he stated, flashing a disarming grin that didn't reach his eyes. "I'm a consultant too, but I'm certainly not doing this well," he said, gesturing to the vaulted ceilings. "I must be in the wrong line of work."

"Computers," she said, placing her hands on her hips, challenged. "Data management. Mostly high-tech stuff. Security protocols. That's where the money is these days. Information is the new oil."

Nicholai nodded slowly, the pieces clicking into place behind his eyes. "Indeed it is."

He moved away quickly, passing Danica and exiting the home first. The heat outside hit them like a physical blow. He walked down the cobblestone path, stopped in the driveway, and turned to look back at the looming brick fortress.

Danica was closing the front door when she saw the look on his face. It was the same look he had when he saw the watch in the video—a mixture of horror and recognition.

"What's wrong with you?" she asked, drawing closer. "That was rude, even for you."

His eyes were still focused on the Fawcett house, dissecting it brick by brick. He didn't speak for a long moment.

"Something happened in there. Tell me," Danica finally demanded, grabbing his arm.

"Not yet," he said, his voice low. "But don't look up. She's watching us right now from the upstairs window. The master bedroom."

Danica fought the urge to look. "Okay," she said, trusting his instinct. "Where to now?"

Nicholai turned to her, his face grim.

"I think we've got to make a doctor's appointment. We need to find out exactly what kind of 'consulting' a plastic surgeon's wife does with high-tech security."

Chapter 47

Dr. Jason Fawcett's cosmetic surgery practice still carried his name, a ghost lingering on the payroll. The name FAWCETT-BURKE was displayed prominently in sixteen-inch brushed gold letters along the top of the two-story brick building located on Gleneagles Drive in Plano. It was a fortress of vanity. Fawcett-Burke was well established and in high demand among the elite of Dallas—the wives who lunched, the oil heiresses, and the aging socialites fighting gravity. Dr. Robin Burke, the remaining partner, felt no need to make a name change after his partner's demise; death, after all, had a certain cachet in their world.

Delgado and Harris had been asked to wait in the outer office, a space designed to intimidate as much as comfort. It smelled of lavender and money. Soft, ambient music played from hidden speakers, and a water wall trickled soothingly behind the reception desk. Nicholai flipped through the latest fashion magazines on the glass side table, noting the marked-up pages where potential clients had circled noses and chins they wanted to buy. Danica paced the room under the watchful, surgically altered eyes of the receptionist, a woman whose skin was pulled so tight she looked permanently surprised.

She had explained to them, with a condescending smile, that Dr. Burke was in a consult and would be finished within fifteen minutes.

The fifteen minutes extended to thirty, then forty. It was a power play, and they both knew it.

Finally, a young nurse in designer scrubs entered the waiting room. "The Doctor will see you now," she said softly, escorting Danica and Nicholai back into the inner sanctum.

They passed consultation rooms with closed doors and muffled voices before entering Burke's private office. It was expansive, with floor-to-ceiling windows overlooking a private garden.

"Sorry to keep you waiting," Burke said, not looking sorry at all. He stood up from behind a desk that cost more than Danica's car, smoothing his custom suit. He extended his hand to Nicholai, but his eyes remained fixed on Danica, dissecting her face with clinical precision. His glare made her feel slightly uncomfortable, like a specimen under a microscope.

"I understand you have some questions about Jason," he stated, sitting back down. "Please, have a seat. I can give you ten minutes before my rhinoplasty."

"Yes," Danica told him, taking the leather chair opposite him. "We are trying to clean up a few loose ends on the file."

Dr. Burke leaned forward, tenting his fingers. "Great cheekbones," he said suddenly, looking at Danica. "Natural high arch. Very rare. Have you ever thought of highlighting them with a little filler? Just a touch to catch the light?"

"Pardon?" she asked. His question caught her completely off guard. She instinctively touched her face. "No, I haven't. I'm here for a murder investigation, Doctor, not a consult."

She looked at Nicholai, who was smiling slightly, amused by the doctor's lack of filter. "He's got a point," Nicholai said. "Structure is everything."

"Punk," she muttered under her breath. "Whatever."

"Dr. Burke," Nicholai cut in, his voice sharpening. "What can you tell us about your former partner, Jason Fawcett? Beyond his skill with a scalpel."

"Well," Burke thought for a moment, shifting gears. "He was an extremely talented surgeon. An artist, really. He was always on top of every aspect of the field and quite often the first to try innovative procedures or new techniques. He kept this place busy, and his name still draws them in. Women trusted him to make them beautiful."

"Personally?" Delgado asked. "We're more interested in his personal life. Hobbies, his marriage, finances. The man behind the mask."

"I didn't know much about the marriage details. Jason was quite private about his home life, which usually means it wasn't good," Burke informed them. "Financially, we were doing fine. Better than fine. That's what I still can't figure out."

"What do you mean?" Danica asked.

"He had it all. Money was flowing in here faster than we could spend it. He bought a new car every six months. Then he does that. Checking out early. It still doesn't make sense to me. Why build an empire just to leave it?"

"Fill us in on the aftermath," Delgado asked. "Who benefited?"

"No one, really. Because he took his own life, the personal insurance policy he carried wasn't required to pay out anything. Suicide clause," he said with a shrug.

"Yes, we've heard that before," Danica replied, noting the pattern.

"And professionally, the partnership agreement we had drawn up was pretty solid. Ironclad, actually. If one partner dies, full ownership passes to the remaining partner," he said, tapping his desk. "It keeps the practice intact."

"Why was that set up like that?"

"That's standard practice now in a lot of specialized fields. An agreement like that keeps unqualified beneficiaries—like grieving spouses who think they know how to run a medical practice—out of an established enterprise. It protects the interests of the remaining partner and the business continuity."

Delgado looked at Burke, reading the man's satisfaction. "So in other words, Lynn Fawcett gained nothing from her husband's death. No insurance, no share of the business."

Burke laughed, a short, cruel bark. "To her absolute surprise, yes. Trust me, she tried fighting it in court. She hired the most expensive sharks in town, but she lost. Thank God Jason and I had that agreement. It was the smartest thing he ever did."

"You don't seem to be shy about communicating your opinion of her. Was there a problem?" Nicholai asked.

"Sir, she is the last person I'd want involved in this practice. She's poison."

"Can you elaborate?" Danica asked. She sat forward in the chair.

"That woman is a real prize," he said. The sarcasm was etched into the lines of his face. "The only thing she ever cared about was herself and her bank balance. She treated Jason like an ATM with a heartbeat. I haven't spoken to her in over a year, and I have no intentions of changing that."

"Narcissistic?" Delgado asked.

"Textbook case," the doctor replied without hesitation. "DSM-V definition. She sucked the life out of him. She needed constant adoration, constant validation. If the spotlight wasn't on her, she'd burn down the theater."

Danica looked confused but continued on with her line of questions. "How was their relationship at the time of his death?" Danica asked. "Did Dr. Fawcett ever discuss that with you?"

215

"He didn't say much, but at the end, I knew there wasn't a marriage left," Burke said. "She filed for a legal separation and threw him out two months before he took his life. Changed the locks, canceled his cards. The guy was a mess during that whole time. He was sleeping here in the office on the recovery cot. I still say that's why he did it. He was broken."

Danica looked over at Nicholai. "He was that devastated over a breakup?"

"No, and that's the other detail that never quite added up either," Burke interjected. "He wasn't sad about losing her. He was happy to be getting rid of her. He was making plans."

"Then why was he so distraught?" Delgado asked.

"I had a feeling she had something on him," Burke replied, his voice dropping lower. He leaned forward and placed his manicured hands on the desk, then clasped them together. "I don't know what it could have been—maybe a botched surgery he covered up, or something financial—but I can tell you, it was tearing him apart. She was squeezing him, and he couldn't see a way out."

Chapter 48

"**S**o she lied to us."

Nicholai didn't answer immediately. They were on their way back to the Falco residence to retrieve his car, driving through the heavy afternoon traffic. He had been quiet for too long, staring out the window, and Danica was desperately trying to make conversation to break the tension radiating off him. She knew he was thinking, processing, but she needed to know what he was focused on.

"She painted herself as the independent survivor," Danica continued, "but Burke made it sound like she was extorting him. But that's not enough to bring her in, is it? Being a bad wife isn't a crime."

She asked, looking in his direction, but he still didn't answer or even acknowledge that she had spoken. He glared out the passenger side window with his arms tightly folded across his chest, his body rigid.

"You and Burke said something about narcissistic back there," she finally said, trying a different angle to engage him. "Explain that to me. I deal with scumbags and liars, but this feels different."

"Narcissistic Personality Disorder," he said, his voice mechanical, reciting facts to calm his mind. "Not every person who has this disorder is affected the same way. Distinctions have to be made on an individual basis. But for someone who is pathologically narcissistic, like Lynn Fawcett appears to be, they can be controlling, blaming, self-absorbed, and intolerant of others' views."

He was silent again for a moment, watching the telephone poles whip by. "They are completely unaware of anyone else's needs and the effects of their behavior on others, and they are very insistent that others see them as they wish to be seen. They have a complete lack of empathy. They view people as objects, tools to be used. They often react with disdain, rage, or defiance if criticized. They have a grandiose view of themselves."

He turned to Danica, his eyes cold. "And they will not tolerate a setback. Losing control is their greatest fear. If they lose control of a person, they destroy them."

Nicholai closed up again, retreating into his mind.

"What's wrong?" Danica asked. She could tell there was more on his mind than just Lynn Fawcett's personality disorder. She reached out and touched his arm, feeling the tension in his muscles.

"Yeah, fine," he said quietly, flinching slightly. "Sorry, I'm just in thought. Connecting dots I should have seen earlier."

"About what?" Danica asked as she moved the car off the freeway and turned towards Falco's neighborhood. "Is it the consulting firm? The computers?"

"Who brought me in?"

"What do you mean?" she asked, confused by the pivot.

"When we first met, you said someone from the state requested my assistance on this case. Specifically me. Who was it?" he asked. His look was starting to frighten her; it was the look of a man realizing he was in a cage.

"I don't know," she replied honestly. "Captain Cooper was the one who gave me the order, but I didn't think to go any further. It came from the Chief, via Austin. Why are you asking now?"

Danica swung the car off Legacy Drive and down the first street of the subdivision. She spotted Delgado's white Porsche exactly where they had left it in front of the garage sale, gleaming like a beacon. She pulled in behind the car.

Nicholai looked straight ahead at nothing in particular, his knuckles white.

"Why, Nic? What's the problem? You think it matters?"

He opened the car door quickly and swung his legs out, placing his feet on the pavement as if grounding himself. He kept his hand on the door but turned back and looked at Danica with chilling clarity.

"A narcissist needs an audience, Danica. They need validation. They need a worthy opponent to prove their superiority."

"So?"

"I have something to do, but you need to find out who initiated that request. You need to find the name."

"You think she asked for you?" Danica whispered, the implication sinking in.

"I think," he said, stepping out, "that I didn't find this case. I think this case sent an invitation."

He closed the car door with a slam and walked off towards his Porsche without looking back. Danica sat in the idling car, watching as he sped off, realizing that the hunter might have been the prey all along.

Chapter 49

"I hope you've got something more, Griff. I'm running out of road here."

"I do, Pastor. I was able to break it. But you're not going to like what I found."

Nicholai checked his rearview mirror, seeing a semi-truck bearing down on him. "Hold on a minute," he said, his voice tight. "Let me get off the road. I can't drive and hear this at the same time."

He pulled the white Porsche off to the side of the interstate, tires crunching on the gravel shoulder. The car rocked slightly as the heavy truck roared past, displacing the air. He shifted the transmission into neutral and pulled the handbrake.

"Okay," Nicholai said, pressing the phone to his ear. "I'm stationary. Tell me."

"I got into the partitioned sections early this morning. It was like cracking a safe inside a bank vault," Griffin explained, his voice tinny over the line.

"How?"

"I used a BCN pathway to bypass the standard handshake protocol," Griffin explained, launching into the technicals to steady his own nerves. "Then I set up a false binary environment. Basically, I tricked the hard drives into thinking they were talking to their master server. Once the gate opened, I slipped in."

Nicholai understood the process abstractly, but he was fixated on the end result. "And what did you find? What were they hiding in there?"

"The partitioned section of the hard drive was mirroring the entire system on each of these laptops. It was a ghost drive. Every keystroke, every file saved, every picture downloaded was being copied in real-time to this hidden sector. Then, at preset internal intervals—usually 3:00 AM—the entire system was being uploaded automatically to a remote server."

"Can you track the server?"

"I tried, but it's routed through multiple relays, bouncing back and forth all over the place—Russia, the Caymans, a satellite uplink in the Pacific," Griffin continued, the frustration evident in his voice. "Whoever set this up built a digital maze. But because I tricked the drive, I have been able to see exactly what was sent by using a residual memory sector."

"What was sent?"

"Everything," Griffin whispered. "All their documents, private emails, financial transactions, and a whole lot more. It wasn't just a backup; it was a surveillance feed. Someone was watching every move these men made."

Nicholai watched as the interstate traffic raced past him, oblivious to the darkness being uncovered.

"Anything we can use as evidence?"

"Plenty. It explains the deaths."

"Like what?"

"The suicide notes," Griffin said. "They came from an offsite template. They were remotely sent to each system's print spooler. They were never typed on the actual machines themselves by the victims. They were sent as an encrypted attachment, embedded deep in the system architecture. Then, they were triggered to print by a remote offsite command. These men didn't write their last words, Nic. Someone else wrote them, hit 'print,' and watched them die."

"What else?" Delgado asked, his grip on the steering wheel tightening.

"After the suicide notes were printed—almost to the second—a wire transfer of five hundred thousand dollars was completed from each system. It was an automated liquidation. Some funds came from personal accounts; Rosin's was drained from an internal corporate account from the bank, and Roberts' funds came from a construction trust account. Whoever was receiving this information had root access to all their finances. They wiped them clean."

"Can you figure out where the funds went?"

"No. Like the data, there are too many internal and external relays set up. It's a sophisticated laundering cycle called 'layering.' By the time the money hits the final account, it looks clean."

"There has to be a way of tracking that kind of money. That's almost two million dollars vanishing into thin air," Nicholai's mind was in motion, calculating the logistics. He was frustrated at Griffin's suggestion that they could be at another dead-end. "There has to be more," he finally said. "Money leaves a trail."

"There is, Nic. But it's not the money that's the problem," Griffin stated, his voice dropping to a register Nicholai had never heard before. "You need to get over here."

"Why? Just tell me."

"No, sorry, I won't describe it over the phone. I can't. You need to see this for yourself."

"What is it, Griffin? Give me a hint."

"I told you," Griffin snapped, sounding sick. "You need to see this. Just get here. And hurry."

Chapter 50

S he didn't answer the first time. Nicholai's call went straight to her voicemail, her cheerful recorded greeting feeling jarring against the urgency of the moment. He didn't leave a message. He was sure she would see his missed call on her display and call him right back; she was usually glued to her phone.

He still had a few minutes. Nicholai was only a few blocks from Griffin's warehouse, navigating the potholed streets of the industrial district, but he wanted her there. He needed a witness, and he needed backup. He tried her number again with the same result, but this time he decided to leave a message. Whatever Griffin had uncovered was important enough—horrific enough—that he wanted her there to see it.

"I'm on my way to Griffin's. He has something to show us—the missing piece. Call me back as soon as you can. I think we found the motive."

By the time he finished leaving the message, he had already parked the car along the dark alley in front of Griffin's back door, tucking the Porsche into the shadows between two dumpsters. He checked the rearview mirror twice and scanned the area in front of the car, his eyes adjusting to the gloom. The thought of Quinlin being in the area again made him extremely uncomfortable; the memory of the missing cross burned in his mind.

He checked his phone again for a missed call. Nothing. Where was she?

Nicholai dialed Griffin's number from the safe comfort of the locked car. "I'm here," he said.

"I'll buzz you in. Come straight to the back."

Delgado quickly moved from the car to the warehouse door, checking his perimeter. From a few feet away he heard the heavy magnetic latch unclick, and he pulled the steel door open. Before moving through the dark space, he pulled the door shut hard behind him and double-checked it was locked.

He checked his cell phone again. Still nothing. The silence from Danica was becoming a loud alarm in his head.

He made his way quickly through the dark warehouse. The eerie feeling of someone behind him caused his pace to quicken even more, his footsteps echoing on the concrete. He kept one hand free, ready to defend himself.

Griffin's interior door was just a few feet in front of him, and he reached it with a purpose. He pounded hard with his fist until he heard the latch inside release. Nicholai yanked the door open and slipped inside the climate-controlled server room quickly. The door slammed hard behind him, sealing them in with the hum of the cooling fans.

"Over here, Pastor," Griffin called from his workstation. He didn't turn around.

Delgado moved towards Griffin and checked his phone one last time. Nothing. He tried placing another call to her, but to no avail. Her voicemail picked up again. He shoved the phone into his pocket, a knot forming in his stomach.

"What have you got?" he asked, turning his full attention to Griffin.

Griffin turned in his chair and faced him. He looked pale, his skin translucent under the fluorescent lights. There was a look in his eyes that Nicholai had never seen in the man before—a mixture of revulsion and profound sadness. Their years of working together had taught Nicholai a lot about the high-tech recluse; Griffin had seen the dark underbelly of the internet, but this look was something new.

"It's not pretty," Griffin said quietly, rubbing his mouth with the back of his hand. "And I'm not going through it all. I can't. I've been sick to my stomach since I decoded the first folder."

"Just show me," he ordered, steeling himself.

Griffin turned around and faced the main monitor. He slowly reached for the mouse, his hand trembling slightly, and moved the pointer across the screen. He double-clicked on a hidden folder in the center of his desktop labeled simply TRIP_LOGS. The computer cycled for a second, and the screen lit up with a high-resolution photo.

Nicholai held his breath. The air left the room.

"My God," he whispered.

It wasn't a picture of a hunting trip. There were no animals, no guns, no jungles.

The photo showed a luxurious bedroom, likely in a villa. James Rosin was sitting on the edge of a bed, smiling at the camera. Next to him was a young boy, no older than eight, looking terrified.

Another photo flashed on the screen, followed by another, then another. It was a slideshow of depravity. He recognized the men— Rosin, Simpson, Roberts, and Wright. They were laughing, drinking, celebrating. But the innocence in the young, tear-filled eyes of the children next to them tore him apart.

"Stop," he said, his voice cracking. "Stop it."

"There's more," Griffin said quietly, not stopping the slideshow. "You need to see the scale of it."

"How many more?"

"I found over twenty-eight hundred photographs like these hidden on all four computers. Videos, too. They documented everything. Every trip. Every child."

Nicholai walked away from the screens, pacing the small room, and placed his hands across his face, trying to scrub the images from his retinas. The nausea rose in his throat. The "power" he had suspected wasn't financial or political; it was the absolute domination of the weak.

"What now?" Griffin asked, closing the file quickly, the screen returning to a benign blue desktop.

"Pedophiles," Nicholai said quietly, the word tasting like ash. "They were all pedophiles. A ring of wealthy, powerful men who thought they could buy anything."

"It looks that way, Pastor. And someone found out. Someone used this to bleed them dry and then kill them."

Nicholai walked away and stood alone in the center of the ware- house, staring at the server lights blinking in the darkness. The pieces slammed together—the secrecy, the separate lives, the shame in the suicide notes.

After a moment, he turned and faced Griffin, his eyes cold and hard.

"And now I know the truth," he said. "There were no hunting trips. The only things they hunted were children."

Chapter 51

He left Griffin's warehouse feeling physically nauseous, bile rising in his throat. His stomach ached, a cramped knot of revulsion from the thought of what he had just witnessed on the high-definition monitors. The images—thousands of them—were burned into his retinas like a flashbulb afterimage. He couldn't shake what he had just seen; the innocence stolen, the power abused. It made the murders seem almost like acts of mercy compared to the lives being destroyed in those photos.

He didn't move the Porsche. He couldn't. His hands were shaking too badly to grip the wheel. He sat inside the climate-controlled cockpit, still parked in the dark alley behind Griffin's, the engine idling with a low rumble. He tried to pray, to find some scripture that could scrub his mind clean, but he couldn't figure out where to start. The darkness felt too thick for words. He prayed again, a silent plea for erasure, but the images remained.

His cell phone rang, the shrill electronic tone shattering the silence. It broke his dark thoughts, snapping him back inside the car. He looked at the center console. The phone's display was lit, glowing blue in the dim interior, showing Danica's number.

He snatched it up, desperate for a sane voice.

"Finally," he said, his voice cracking. "Where have you been? I've been trying to reach you. You need to know—"

"I'm fine," she whispered quietly. It sounded distant, tinny. "Nic, I..."

There was something strange in her voice. It lacked her usual cadence, her usual strength. It sounded wet, broken.

"Dani, what's wrong? Are you alright? You sound—"

There was nothing but dead silence on the line; no response at all from the other end, just the faint static of an open connection.

"Danica, are you there?" He checked the signal indicator on the phone—full bars. "Danica?"

"Don't worry, Agent Delgado," a voice cut in—smooth, raspy, and terrifyingly familiar. "Your little friend is doing quite well. For now."

Nicholai's heart sank, dropping into the pit of his stomach as the nausea suddenly roared into an intense, searing pain. The voice was a ghost he had spent years trying to exorcise.

"Quinlin!" Nicholai screamed, gripping the phone until his knuckles turned white. "What have you done?"

Chapter 52

"Nothing yet. I haven't even started. I just thought I'd get to know your new friend a little better. She has... spirit."

Quinlin looked across the empty, cavernous warehouse and smiled at his work.

"Nic, don't do what he says!" Danica screamed, her voice raw and tearing at her throat.

She was bound to a heavy wooden chair, her hands tied behind her back with zip ties that bit into her wrists, cutting off circulation. Her eyes were covered with a filthy, grease-stained rag that smelled of oil and decay. The stench was causing her to gag, triggering dry heaves that racked her bruised ribs.

Quinlin had struck her several times, methodically and with terrifying precision. He had hit her hard enough to break her nose, and she could still taste the metallic copper tang of blood filling her mouth. Her head pounded with a blinding rhythm from the initial blow Quinlin had inflicted on her from behind outside her loft, and she could tell one eye was now swollen completely shut. The blood on the side of her mouth had started to dry and cracked painfully every time she tried to yell. Her bare feet stuck to the cold, damp concrete floor, grounding her in the nightmare.

"Quinlin, if you touch her..." Delgado yelled into the phone, his voice echoing in the small car.

"Relax, Nicholai. Or maybe I should call you Pastor. That is your new costume, isn't it?" Quinlin taunted. "Your little partner here is fine for now. She's listening. But her future—her very short future—is really up to you."

Nicholai couldn't sit still. The car felt like a coffin. He opened the door and paced the dark alley, the gravel crunching under his shoes. Now he couldn't hear Danica in the background, only the hum of the city. His stomach burned with acid, and his hands started to tremble uncontrollably.

He took a deep breath, forcing air into his lungs, making every effort to gain some sort of tactical focus. "What do you want, Quinlin? You have me on the phone. Leave her out of this."

"You," Quinlin hissed quietly, the word slithering out. "It's that simple. I'm surprised an intelligent man like you even has to ask. You should know by now how this game is played. I take what you love, and you fall apart."

Nicholai wanted to say more; he wanted to unleash a torrent of rage. But as long as Danica was in harm's way, he had to keep his emotions under control. He had to be the negotiator, not the victim.

"Tell me what to do."

"Oh, trust me, I will. I have a very specific itinerary planned. But not just yet. Anticipation is part of the flavor."

"Let's just get this over with. She has nothing to do with this. This is about you and me. It always has been."

"We can certainly agree on that. This is about you and me. A biblical struggle. But from what I've been able to figure, watching you two on that little boat... she's become a pretty important part of you. You let her steer your ship, Nicholai. You never let anyone steer."

Nicholai thought fast. He had to devalue her as a target. "You're wrong. She's a colleague. She doesn't mean a thing to me."

Quinlin laughed, a low, menacing sound, and moved the phone away from his mouth. He stepped closer to Danica's trembling body. He moved close to her right ear, invading her space.

"Did you hear that?" he whispered, his breath hot against her skin. She jerked her head away as far as she could and pulled on the restraints, struggling to break the plastic, but it was useless. "Your man said you mean nothing to him. Just a colleague. Expendable."

The sound of his statement, even though she knew it was a tactic, made her stop struggling. It cut deeper than the knife.

"Delgado, you punk!" she screamed loud enough for the microphone to pick up. "Don't you dare write me off!"

Quinlin laughed at her outburst, delighted by the chaos. He leaned into Danica, and she felt the heat of his body pressing against hers. He licked the side of her cheek, tasting the blood and tears, and she tried to pull away, revolted.

"I like this one, Pastor," he said, bringing the phone back to his lips. "Much more fight in her than your last one. What was her name again? Aww, yes, Jessica. She begged quite a bit at the end. Cute daughter, too, I must admit. Or she was," he laughed.

The mention of his family hit Nicholai like a physical blow, dropping him to his knees in the alley. "Let her go, Quinlin. I said she doesn't mean anything to me! Stop this!"

"I highly doubt that, Nicholai. But we'll see just how much she means. For now, I think I'll let you both hang in the wind for a while. Let the imagination do the work."

He pulled the phone away and looked at Danica. With a casual, almost bored motion, he used his foot to push her chair over onto its side. Danica couldn't break her fall. Her head crashed against the concrete floor with a dull, sickening thud. The pain shot through her entire body, exploding behind her eyes, and she wanted to vomit. Dizziness set in like a heavy fog, and her eyes rolled back.

Quinlin's voice trailed off into a buzz, and everything went dark.

Chapter 53

"Let us handle it, Delgado," Cooper ordered over the phone, his voice tight with sleep and stress.

Nicholai had spent twenty valuable minutes tracking down Captain Cooper. The 911 call had been transferred to the desk sergeant, then to the duty officer, and eventually patched through to Cooper's private cell phone. The call had pulled him away from the comfort of his recliner and the basketball semi-finals, thrusting him back into the nightmare.

"I have no idea where he's got her," Nicholai explained, pacing back and forth in the alley, his shadow stretching long under the streetlights. "I'm blind here, Captain."

"Was the call placed from her cell phone? Or yours?"

"Hers. He has her phone," Nicholai explained. "But it wasn't long enough to trace. He knew exactly how long to stay on the line."

"But she's got a Blackberry with 3G. Even if she's not talking, if it's on, it's pinging. We should be able to triangulate the signal off the towers to get an idea of the general area."

"The techs are already on that, right?"

"They're running it now. We could have a radius in the next few minutes."

"Quinlin's smart," Nicholai said, rubbing his forehead. "He's too smart to let that go. He knows how the technology works. That phone won't be with her long, or he'll use it to lead us into a trap."

"Think! Any idea at all where he could be holding her? Does he have a safe house? A pattern?" Cooper asked.

"He's not from the Dallas area, so I don't know how familiar he is with the Metroplex," Nicholai said, racking his brain. "The whole time we were tracking him years ago, he kept on the move. He used abandoned buildings, foreclosures. I have no idea how long he's been in Texas or what resources he has."

"We're covering every lead we have for now. I've got every available unit on standby."

"I'll be downtown in ten minutes," he said, moving back to the Porsche.

"No," Cooper barked. "Just go home. Or go to your boat. You're too close to this. You're compromised."

"I'm not going home!" Nicholai insisted, slamming his hand on the roof of the car. "She's gone because of me. This is my fault."

"Delgado, listen to me. It's not your fault, or your responsibility. You're a private citizen brought in as a consultant to assist on a case. That's it," Cooper fired back. "If you want to argue responsibility, argue it with her when this is all over. Right now, I need you safe so he can't use you as leverage."

Arguing with Danica anytime soon was not something that had even crossed his mind. Nicholai was too consumed with the terrifying thought of never seeing her again—of seeing her only as a file photo on a coroner's report.

"I've got to do something. I'm not going to sit back and let Quinlin do this again. I can't survive it twice."

"You know this guy better than anyone," Cooper said, softening his tone slightly. "What is he capable of? What is his timeline?"

Those thoughts had filled Nicholai's mind the moment he heard the voice. They were toxic, choking him. He couldn't shake them. The images of his wife and daughter—broken, used, discarded—played over and over in his head like a loop of film he couldn't cut.

"Well?" Cooper was now demanding an answer, needing a profile.

"Captain, I really don't know," Nicholai said, his voice hollow. The panic was leaving his voice, replaced by a profound, crushing sadness. "He's capable of whatever he puts his sick, twisted mind to. And he enjoys it."

Chapter 54

Nicholai coasted the Porsche quietly into the gravel parking lot of the marina, killing the lights before he stopped. He turned off the ignition and sat still, the engine ticking as it cooled, staring at the lake through the windshield.

Night had fallen completely. It had always been a serene setting, a place of refuge, but tonight there was something very different in the air. Everything was too quiet, too dark. The water looked like ink.

Leininger's car was gone. It was not in its usual spot under the tree, and he assumed the detective had been pulled in to assist with the massive search grid for Danica. That made him feel even worse—abandoned. Nicholai hated being there even more, but he had no-where else to go. The house on Windsor Lane was a tomb; the police station was a cage. He felt helpless and disconnected from God and man.

He walked to the gate, his feet heavy. He punched in the first two numbers of the gate code on H dock and stopped. He looked back down the dark path he had just walked. He contemplated ignoring Cooper's orders and heading back to Police Plaza, forcing his way into the investigation. He knew deep down there was something he should be doing to help her, but his instincts were clouded by trauma. Finally, he punched in the last number, and the gate clicked open.

The walk down the weathered wooden dock was hollow, his foot-steps sounding loud in the silence. Nicholai noticed a few empty slip spaces as he made his way towards the boat. The other sailboats were all silent, their owners asleep or away, and there was an eerie stillness in the humid air.

Sara Rose was secured in her slip, waiting faithfully. She had always brought him great comfort, and for a brief moment, he felt a flicker of it as he stepped aboard. But that too disappeared quickly, extinguished by the memory of Danica sitting on the bench just days ago. He looked across the lake at nothing in particular. Everything seemed dark.

Nicholai stood in the cockpit but found he couldn't stay still for long. The energy in his body was frantic. He moved behind the wheel stand and gripped the stainless steel wheel hard, trying to ground himself, before moving to the spot on the starboard seat where she had slept. There was no peace in the slip tonight.

He turned around quickly, made a decision, and untied the rear dock lines, throwing them over onto the wood. Then he stepped up on the top deck and removed the front lines, throwing them over as well. Back behind the wheel stand, Nicholai fired up the small diesel engine. It coughed to life, breaking the silence. He pulled the Sara Rose away from the slip, slamming the transmission into forward. The bow of the sailboat nudged the edge of the dock, scraping the fiberglass, but he didn't care. The Sara Rose left the marina at double the posted speed limit, leaving a churning wake. She quickly cleared the breakwater and headed off into the dark, open water.

Once out, he looked out across the black water and sky. He couldn't be bothered with the sails; he knew the effort was futile without even the slightest hint of a breeze. The air was stagnant.

For two miles, the small diesel inboard pushed the Sara Rose through the dark water. There was no definition between the water line and the sky; it was a void. It was all the same—hot, humid, and deathly still.

He killed the engine and let her coast silently to a dead stop in the middle of the lake. Tonight he wanted to avoid Heath Cove because of the lack of any cell signal. He couldn't hide tonight. He didn't want to miss her call, or Quinlin's call. He couldn't. And he wanted to hear from her, not Cooper.

Nicholai slid the top hatch open and made his way down the stairs inside the cabin. The temperature below was high, stifling, but he didn't bother opening the window. There was no point tonight; the air outside was just as heavy.

He poured himself the last of the Seagram's VO, the bottle shaking in his hand, and this time he ignored the ginger ale. The first drink was the longest, and there was no savoring the taste. The liquid burned as it flowed down his throat and into his stomach, a chemical fire. He closed his eyes tight and shook his head, welcoming the burn.

He turned around, leaned against the counter, and took another long drink. He closed his eyes again as he swallowed hard to force the liquor down. When he opened his eyes, it was there. He saw the Bible closed on the table. He glared at it, feeling a surge of betrayal, before turning away and making his way back up the companionway.

The air was still and dank, and the silence seemed deafening. With the glass still in hand, he stepped up onto the top deck and made his way to the bow. The mast lights forced a soft green glow to spread across the white deck, but they had no effect on the dark water below.

Nicholai sat on the bow, pulled his knees in tight to his chest, and looked out into the dark night. His mind suddenly filled with an intensity that made him afraid, and his hands started to tremble again. The old images and memories refused to go away, no matter how hard he tried to push them down. For the past four years, he had searched for answers and comfort, and for a while, he felt it coming; or so he thought. But now, all he felt was the pain and grief vigorously pouring back, filling the cracks in his soul. He thought he had been on the right track, but it turned out Nicholai Delgado was wrong again. He was cursed.

On the starboard side, a dim light off inside the dark caught his attention. The light moved closer to the Sara Rose, and it wasn't long before he spotted another. He watched as the image of another sailboat became clearer. The sounds of laughter and music from the vessel moved easily through the still night, carried over the water. It became louder as the sailboat moved closer. It didn't take long before he could identify the boat.

The Juliet cut through the water with ease, motoring slowly. She belonged to a local couple who loved spending their evenings entertaining friends with their late cruises. The Juliet had long earned the reputation of being the party boat; the wine and cheese vessel of the lake.

The Juliet was similar to Nicholai's Sara Rose in make and condition. A few years older, she was a solid, well-kept vessel. The owner, Ken Gezella, aptly named her after his wife Julie, and the two spent long hours together aboard, living the life Nicholai was supposed to have.

But now the sights and sounds of The Juliet were haunting. They mocked him. It made Nicholai miss his Jessica even more. He had never imagined his life would become like it was now—a solitary man on a boat named after ghosts. Nicholai and Jessica Delgado had such hopes, dreams, and plans; that's what kept them going. They talked often about how Sara would graduate, marry the perfect man, and then raise their perfect grandchildren. There were supposed to be huge family gatherings at Thanksgiving and Christmas in the house on Windsor Lane. And there were supposed to be memories, wonderful memories.

But Jeremy Quinlin took that all away with a knife and a roll of duct tape.

Instead of walking his daughter down the aisle in a white dress, Quinlin made him walk down a long, cold hallway in the basement of Police Plaza to identify her body. His sweet, innocent daughter lay next to her mother on a cold stainless steel table covered with a white sheet. It wasn't fair; it was a heartbreaking exercise in pain that no father and husband should ever have to endure.

The mast lights from The Juliet faded off slowly into the night, taking the laughter with them. He could still faintly hear the music coming from her passengers, or so he thought. He took another drink, draining the glass, trying to numb the feelings, but it wasn't working. The alcohol just fueled the fire. He missed them more.

He couldn't decide what was worse, the grief or the guilt. But the combination of them had brought him such emotional pain that at times it seemed almost unbearable. Prayer used to help. Feeling close to the Lord used to bring him comfort. He knew Jessica and Sara were both with Him, and that helped ease the pain some.

The words of King David helped as well. "I know he will never come back to me, but I will go to him." Those words became part of David's comfort after his own son's death.

Nicholai often wondered how the biblical figure, David, could have dealt with the guilt of his sins that caused the death of his son. Nicholai could relate, but he couldn't understand the strength it took to keep living.

It was his fault that Jessica and Sara suffered the horrible acts at the hands of Jeremy Quinlin. He had brought the darkness home. Maybe if he had taken a different career path, they both would still be with him. Or maybe if he had been smarter and caught Quinlin sooner, their lives would have been spared. There were too many different scenarios flooding his mind, but it all seemed to come down to the fact that their deaths were the fault of Nicholai Delgado.

And now Inspector Danica Harris was possibly going to have to experience the same horrible acts at the hands of a man he should have stopped years ago. He tried not to imagine what Quinlin was doing to her at that moment, but his years of coming face to face with the pure evil in men kept his mind and imagination far too active. He saw the chair. He saw the tools.

God had again blessed him with someone special, brought light back into his life, but now he failed to protect her as well. It was the same pattern. He had failed Jessica and Sara, and now Danica.

He should have turned her away that first day on the dock. He never should have agreed to help. He shouldn't have taken her out that first meeting. Danica didn't deserve this, and she definitely didn't deserve him. She deserved life.

He had lied to Quinlin when he said she didn't mean anything, but it was the only thing he could think of saying at that moment to save her. He desperately wanted her to know it had been a lie, but now it was probably too late. Now her screams echoed among the others inside his head. There were still times, late at night, when he would wake in a cold sweat and panic from the screams of his wife and daughter. They consumed his nightmares during the night and the light of day. And now Danica's voice was added to the choir of the damned.

"Delgado, you punk!"

He wondered if she meant it. He heard her voice again, clear as a bell.

Nicholai Delgado didn't want this pain anymore. He didn't want the nightmares, and he was sick of the cold sweats. He wanted Quinlin's deadly game to come to an end now. Maybe Rosin, Simpson, and Roberts and the rest had the right idea after all, he thought. They found the exit. They didn't have to deal with their pain or disappointment anymore. There was no more guilt consuming them, eating their insides. And the fear would certainly disappear as well.

There was a way to end Quinlin's game now. A way to cheat the winner. Jeremy Quinlin would have no one to play the last half with if the opponent forfeited. Nicholai knew this was all about him. Quinlin wanted to destroy the life of Nicholai Delgado slowly. That was the ultimate prize he was after. This had nothing to do with Danica, Jessica, or Sara. They had been innocent pawns to Quinlin.

If Nicholai was gone, the game was over. Quinlin would have no reason to keep Danica.

He knew taking his own life would lead to certain considerations he wasn't ready to face. He studied that in seminary. He read about it in the Bible, the same Bible he had given Jessica. But at that moment in Nicholai Delgado's life, he was trapped in his own living hell, and theology felt distant.

He recalled the comment he had told Danica; that one of them would have to die. He had tried his best to stop the killer, but he failed again. He failed his wife and his daughter. And now someone special had come into his life, and she was about to die if he didn't end the game on his terms.

Nicholai drank the last of the liquor and threw the heavy glass overboard as far as he could into the darkness. He waited for the sound of the glass hitting the water, but it never came; it was swallowed by the silence.

He rose to his feet, swaying slightly, and steadied himself by gripping the front halyard. The wire bit into his hand. He stepped closer to the edge, his toes hanging over the gunwale, and looked down at the still, black water. It looked like peace.

A cool breeze suddenly whispered across his face—the first movement of air all night. He felt a tear roll down his cheek, hot against his cold skin. Another one followed and landed on his shirt, leaving a tiny stain. The breeze suddenly seemed to pick up, rustling the sail cover. He felt a chill run through him as he looked out across the now-rippling water.

He took another step towards the edge of the Sara Rose, shifted his weight forward, and closed his eyes.

Chapter 55

The pain in her head was almost unbearable, a rhythmic thudding that matched the slow beat of her heart. Every breath was
followed by a deep, searing pain in her ribs, suggesting they were
bruised or broken. Danica had no concept of time or space, or how
long she had been unconscious in the dark. The blood on her face had
now completely dried, caking tightly against her skin like a cracked
mask, pulling at the fine hairs whenever she twitched.

Her eyes were still covered by the foul-smelling rag, and for a long
time, she was afraid to move, terrified that any sound would bring the
blow that finally ended it. She wanted to know if Quinlin was still in the
room, watching her suffering. She listened intently for some kind of
indication—the scuff of a shoe, the rustle of clothing, the sound of
breathing.

"Hello," she finally said quietly, her voice a dry croak. It echoed
back to her from hard, empty walls. "Hello?"

The silence that answered was heavy and absolute.

She took a painful breath, tasting copper and dust, and tried to
figure out her next move. She still couldn't tell if he was in the room or
even in the area, but she couldn't wait to find out. Her wrists were tied
behind her to the vertical slats of the chair, and her fingers dug into the
rough wood of the armrests, seeking purchase. Her ankles were

bound tightly to the front legs of the chair, and she felt the cold, damp concrete on her bare feet.

She pulled on the rope around her wrists, testing the knot. It held fast, the coarse fibers digging into her skin, cutting off the blood flow. She tried moving her legs, and the chair squeaked loudly against the concrete floor—a scream in the silence. She froze, waiting for a reaction. When none came, Danica planted her feet firmly on the floor and pulled on the ropes around her ankles again. The chair moved a fraction of an inch. She tried pulling again, gritting her teeth against the headache. The chair moved even more.

She could tell the chair was old; the joints felt loose. She used the weight of her body to start rocking back and forth, building momentum. On her final attempt, she managed to lean forward far enough to leverage her center of gravity and stand. It was an awkward, agonizing posture. The chair was still bound to her back like a tortoise shell, heavy and cumbersome, but she was able to place her weight on her feet.

She shuffled to the right, inching blindly into the void for several feet until her shoulder bumped against a wall. She leaned into it, verifying it was solid brick. She listened again for Quinlin, straining her ears, but heard nothing but the dripping of water somewhere far off.

She turned around, scraping the chair legs against the floor, and shuffled backward until the wooden back of the chair came in direct contact with the wall. She moved forward a few feet, took a breath, and threw herself backward, forcing the wooden chair hard against the brick.

Crack.

She heard the wood splinter on impact. She moved ahead once more and repeated the same movement, this time with greater force, channeling every ounce of her rage. She felt the frame of the chair start to loosen and give way.

Danica gathered her strength for one final assault. She moved forward again, this time making sure the space between her and the wall was farther than the previous attempt. She took another deep breath, ignored the screaming protest of her muscles, and with all her effort, forced herself backward to crash against the wall.

The chair exploded.

Wood shattered, joints popped, and the restraints went slack. But at the exact same moment, an intense, white-hot pain shot through her left side, stealing the breath from her lungs.

She collapsed to her knees, then rolled onto the floor, biting her lip until it bled to keep from screaming. She desperately tried to hold it in, gasping for air.

Her arms were free from the frame, though the ropes still dangled from her wrists. The more she moved, the greater the pain in her side became, radiating outward like fire. Her shirt became wet against her skin, a warm, sticky sensation spreading rapidly down her flank. She shook off the loose ropes and splintered handrails from her wrists, her hands trembling, then reached up and pulled the rag off her eyes.

It took a moment for her vision to adjust to the gloom. She looked down and saw the cause of the pain.

The chair had splintered apart, but the thick wooden vertical support of the backrest had split away at a sharp angle. When she hit the wall, it had acted like a spear. The inch-thick jagged piece of wood had entered her back just below the ribcage and impaled her. She could see at least three inches of the blood-soaked wood protruding out from her left side, having passed cleanly through the soft tissue. Blood now covered the side of her shirt and started staining the denim of her jeans dark black in the dim light.

She tried easing the piece of wood out of her body, her fingers slick with her own blood, but the slightest movement caused a wave of nausea and agony so intense her vision grayed out. It was stuck.

She couldn't stay here. She gathered what strength she had left, fighting the dizziness, and staggered to her feet. The room was a large, abandoned storage area, shadows stretching into corners. She spotted a high window on the opposite side of the room—a square of gray light. It was her only exit.

She staggered slowly towards the window, keeping one hand hovering protectively over the piece of wood jutting from her side. Every step was a battle.

The left side of her jeans was now soaked through, and Danica knew she was bleeding out. Her foot squelched in her own blood inside her shoe. She didn't know how much time she had left—minutes, maybe—but she was not giving up yet. She made it to the window and looked through the dull, grimy glass. The sidewalk was just a few feet below the window ledge; it was a ground-level window.

With her fist wrapped in her sleeve, she slammed against the glass. It didn't break. She hit it again, harder, screaming with the effort. It immediately exploded outward, leaving jagged teeth of glass in the frame and tiny shards embedded in her hand and tangled in her hair. The rush of hot, humid air hit her face.

The space was big enough to get her through, and she knew this would be her last attempt. If she fell now, she wouldn't get up. Dizziness was sinking in fast, and despite the heat, she started to feel violently cold.

Danica leaned forward against the window frame and turned to her right side, trying to keep the wooden stake in her body free from any contact. She managed to pull her upper body halfway through the opening in the broken glass, the fresh air tasting sweet, but she lost her grip on the ledge.

Unable to hold her balance, she tumbled forward and crashed hard against the concrete sidewalk outside. The impact jarred the wood in her side, sending a shockwave of pain that eclipsed everything else.

She tried pulling herself up to her knees, scrabbling at the pavement, but there was nothing left in the tank. The adrenaline was gone, replaced by the cold creeping up her limbs. The pain was now taking over, washing over her in waves, and for a brief moment, she was glad. It meant it was almost over.

She closed her eyes and gently placed her cheek on the hard, rough surface of the sidewalk. She was getting colder by the minute, the Texas sun feeling distant and weak.

"Oh God," she whispered in her last breath, a plea to the same God Nicholai trusted. Danica Harris now had nothing left to give. She was finally ready to give in and let it all go.

Chapter 56

The faint, distorted image of Captain Daniel Cooper was the first thing Danica saw when her right eye slowly flickered open. The world was a blur of white and beige. She tried to open the other eye, but saw nothing through the left one. It felt heavy and tight—swollen shut. She reached up to feel her face, her movements sluggish, and felt the tug of an intravenous needle taped to the back of her hand.

"Stay still, Harris," a gruff voice ordered, soft but commanding.

Cooper stood over her hospital bed, his usual stern face etched with deep lines of worry she wasn't used to seeing. He looked like he hadn't slept in days.

"What happened?" she croaked. Her throat felt like it was filled with broken glass.

"You're going to be alright. You're pretty banged up—broken ribs, concussion, impalement—but the doctors say you'll make it. You're too stubborn to die."

She moved her arm again, ignoring his order, and gingerly felt the side of her face. Her left eye was indeed swollen shut, the skin tender to the touch. The room was starting to come into focus—the heart monitor, the drip bag, the window overlooking the city. She tried to sit up, needing to orient herself, but a sharp, tearing pain shot through her side and forced her back down against the pillows with a gasp.

"You just refuse to listen, don't you," Cooper joked weakly, pulling a chair closer.

"What happened?" she asked again, the memories fragmented.

"One of the patrol cars found you on the sidewalk off an access road. You've lost a lot of blood, Danica. You were knocking on death's door."

"How long have I been here?" she asked, looking at the light outside.

"You've been out for two days. We kept you sedated to let the body heal."

The events were starting to come back to her, rushing in like a flood. She remembered the chair exploding. She remembered the agony of the wood piercing her side. She recalled the horror of the dark room and the smell of Quinlin. And she still felt his presence, a shadow over her soul.

"Did you find him?" she asked, gripping Cooper's wrist. "Did you get Quinlin?"

Cooper shook his head slowly. "No. We had half the force combing that area for you and him. We turned that warehouse district upside down, but there was no sign of Quinlin. He vanished."

"How did you know which area to search?" she asked. "I didn't know where I was."

"Delgado called us," Cooper said, watching her closely. "He called dispatch. Somehow he knew you were by the interstate off exit thirty-six. He gave us a three-block radius."

She closed her good eye and smiled painfully. She knew exactly how Nicholai had figured out her location. She had given him a clue—a desperate, Hail Mary pass—when she called him a "punk" over the phone while Quinlin was listening. She had prayed he would understand the reference.

Even though Quinlin had her blindfolded in the car, she had recognized the specific rhythmic sounds of the tires on the road and the direction he had taken her. She knew the IHOP restaurant where she and Nicholai had eaten—where she had called him a punk for the first time—was just a few blocks away from that specific exit. He had remembered. He had listened.

"Where is he?" she asked, opening her eye and scanning the room, expecting to see him in the corner reading his Bible.

"I don't know," Cooper replied, looking down at his hands.

"What do you mean you don't know?" Danica tried sitting up again, ignoring the pain this time. Panic started to rise in her chest, faster than the heart monitor could track. "I thought we had him covered. I thought Leininger was watching him."

"We haven't heard from him since he called us with your possible location. He verified you were safe, and then the line went dead."

"He's gone?"

"Harris," Cooper said, his voice heavy with resignation. "He pulled himself off the case the night you disappeared. He cleared out his slip at the marina. He's not answering his phone, and his Porsche is gone."

"He didn't run," Danica whispered, staring at the ceiling tiles. "He didn't quit."

"Then what is he doing?"

"He went hunting," she said, a tear leaking from her good eye. "He realized the law couldn't stop Quinlin. So he went to do it himself."

Chapter 57

Three days in the hospital and now two days stuck in her loft was getting to be too much. The walls were closing in. She paced when she had the energy, dragging her injured leg, but that still wasn't very often. She felt shut off from the world, trapped in a bubble of pain medication and silence. The suicide case had gone cold, the leads drying up like blood on pavement, and Quinlin was still out there somewhere, laughing. There were too many loose ends left dangling, personal and professional, and they were strangling her.

She had tried several times to reach Nicholai, but he never answered. And he hadn't responded to any of her text messages either. She tried putting him out of her mind, telling herself he was a coward who had cut and run, but she couldn't make it stick. She thought of driving out to the marina, forcing a confrontation, but she didn't have the physical energy for that. And the possible disappointment of confirming Cooper's comments about Delgado abandoning her was almost too much to bear. She couldn't let it rest, but she may not have a choice.

She eased herself back onto the couch, wincing as her stitches pulled, and tried getting comfortable. The wound in her side was starting to heal slowly, the angry red fading to pink, and the pain was becoming bearable with the right medication. Her new Blackberry was lying on the coffee table, a black monolith of silence. She reached for it, her fingers trembling slightly. She dialed his number and waited. It rang four times, then went to voicemail.

"Where are you?" she whispered to the empty room.

She dialed another number, needing a connection to the case. Griffin answered after two rings.

"It's Inspector Harris," she told him, her voice rasping.

"I'm sorry to hear what happened. The news said it was a mugging gone wrong. Are you alright?" he asked, his voice laced with genuine concern.

"I'll make it. I'm harder to kill than I look," she said, trying for levity and failing. "Have you seen or heard from Nicholai lately? He's gone dark."

"Not since that night. He left here pretty upset after seeing the pictures I pulled off these laptops. He looked like he had seen the devil himself. And then that whole issue with you came up, and I haven't heard a peep from him since."

"What pictures?" she asked, sitting up straighter, ignoring the protest of her ribs.

"He didn't tell you what we found?"

"No, he didn't," she said, gripping the phone. "He ran out before he could brief me. What did you find, Griffin?"

"Those guys... the hunting club... they were pedophiles," he said, the disgust evident in his tone. "And there were never any legitimate hunting trips. It was a cover. It's all pretty sick if you ask me. Organized, expensive depravity."

"And Nicholai knew?"

"Yeah. He figured it out right here. I showed him the files."

"He didn't tell me," she said, feeling a wave of nausea that had nothing to do with her injury. "He protected me from it."

"So I'm assuming you haven't heard from him either," Griffin asked.

"Nothing for the past few days. Cooper thinks he quit."

"Danica, he didn't quit. He's scared. He saw all of this, and when Quinlin showed up here, it really spooked him. It made it real. Then that whole incident with you happening right after... I know the guy's a real mess right now. He blames himself."

"Wait a minute! Quinlin showed up there?" She was standing now, the pain forgotten. "When?"

"Two days before he grabbed you. He was watching the back door. He smiled at the camera, Danica. He wanted us to know he could get in."

Danica started to pace, her mind reeling. Nicholai had known Quinlin was close, and he hadn't told her. He had tried to handle it alone.

252

Griffin kept talking, filling the silence. "He's the strongest guy I've ever met, but everyone has their breaking point, Inspector. I know the two of you were getting close. Even I could see that. But he may have gone for good this time. Sometimes the abyss stares back too hard."

Danica drew silent. Griffin's statement was starting to hurt more than the physical wounds.

"Are you still there?" Griffin asked.

"Yes, sorry. Thanks, Griff. I'll be in touch." She ended the call.

Danica gently placed the phone down on the table and started to walk away. She paced the room again, the limp more pronounced. Where was he? What happened to him? Was he alive? On her third trip around the room, she checked her Blackberry again. Nothing.

The doorbell rang, a sharp, intrusive sound. She turned quickly, almost forgetting the pain in her side, but the reminder came quickly with a sharp stab. She wasn't expecting anyone and definitely wasn't in any frame of mind to see anyone. She checked the peephole.

She unlatched the deadbolt and pulled the door open.

Nicholai stood there. He looked like a ghost.

"How are you feeling?" he asked quietly.

Chapter 58

"I'm okay," she said once the shock started to wear off. She leaned against the doorframe for support. "Nic, where have you been?"

Nicholai didn't answer at first. He waited it out, looking at her face—the bruising, the bandage peeking out from her shirt. He remained quiet for a moment, absorbing the damage. "I've been around," he finally said, his voice rough.

"Were you out on the lake?"

"No," he said. "I haven't been out there for a few days. I couldn't go back."

"Nic, what's going on? You disappear, and now you just show up?"

"Can we talk?" he asked, shifting his weight. "Please?"

"Yes, please."

She backed away from the doorway, letting him in. He looked drained; tired and worn out, as if he hadn't slept in a week. She could see he hadn't shaved in a few days, the stubble gray and thick, and his eyes were extremely dull, lacking their usual spark. He held two white plastic grocery bags, one in each hand, like peace offerings.

"What's all that?" she asked, looking at the bags.

"I know you haven't eaten anything substantial for the last few days. Hospital food is poison. I wanted to make you something. It's the least I can do."

She was glad to see him, relieved beyond words, but more concerned with what he wanted to say.

"Let me help you with those," she said, reaching down for the bags.

Nicholai pulled back sharply. "Don't you dare," he said, his voice firm. "You're injured. Just point me to the kitchen."

"Over there," she said, backing away slightly. "Sorry, I must look awful."

He looked at her before answering, really looking at her. "You look fine," he said quietly, with a sincerity that made her blush. He turned away and headed in the direction of the kitchen island.

She followed him and watched as he unloaded the bags onto the counter—soup, bread, fruit. "You didn't answer me," she said.

"Sorry, what was your question?"

"Where have you been?" she asked again, leaning against the counter.

"Around," he said, unpacking a carton of eggs, not wanting to get into the details with her just yet.

"Not good enough," she ordered, her detective voice returning. "You need to talk. We need to talk. I just got off the phone with Griffin, and he told me what you found. The photos. And he filled me in on Quinlin's appearance at the warehouse." Now she was starting to get angry. "Why didn't you tell me? We were supposed to be working together. I walked into a trap because I didn't know the threat level."

"Please sit down," he said without looking at her, cracking eggs into a bowl.

She made her way to the couch, sitting off to the side, hoping he would sit beside her, but he didn't. Nicholai moved across the room with a glass of water and settled in a chair across from her, keeping a safe distance.

"Danica, I'm so sorry," he couldn't look at her. He stared at his hands.

"What are you apologizing for? The silence? The secret?"

"Everything. You almost died at the hands of a man I should have stopped years ago, and I just can't... I can't forgive myself for that."

"Nic, this wasn't your fault. You can't control the behavior of someone else. Especially a man like that. He's a monster."

He didn't respond. He just stared at the floor.

"Now tell me, where have you been?" she asked again, but this time she meant it. "I want an answer. Cooper said you quit. Griffin said you ran."

Nicholai looked around the loft, checking the windows, checking the exits. "Outside," he said.

"Outside where?"

"The parking lot. Downstairs."

"Why?" she asked, confused.

"I wanted to keep an eye on you. Make sure he didn't come back to finish the job. I've been parked across the street since you got out of the hospital."

"You mean to tell me you've been living in your car for the past few days? Acting as my personal security guard?"

"Not my car, no. I borrowed one—a nondescript sedan. I didn't want Quinlin to spot the Porsche here. He knows my car."

"Why haven't you been on the lake? That's your sanctuary."

"I was for a while, right after he took you, but..."

"But what?" she asked gently.

Nicholai took a deep breath and finally looked at her. He filled her in on the last night he spent on the Sara Rose. He spoke about the pain and the disappointment he had felt, the overwhelming guilt. He told her that it all had almost overtaken him. And then, voice trembling, he told her about his thoughts on the bow and what he had felt compelled to do to end the game.

Danica sat in silence, unable to fully comprehend all he said. She saw him wipe away a tear. She couldn't—or didn't want to—believe that he had stood on the edge of suicide just to save her.

He still couldn't look at her directly, but there was more he wanted to say. "I'm afraid of failing again. I don't want to disappoint anyone else the way I did before. When it's just me and God, I know where I stand. With Him, I can fail and disappoint Him with every moment of my life, but He will always remain with me. He doesn't leave. Just like He was that night."

"I didn't know," she finally said, her voice a whisper. "I had no idea you were that close to the edge."

"What changed your mind out there?" she asked. "What stopped you?"

"The wind."

"What?" she was confused. "A breeze?"

"The first time we met, I told you on the Sara Rose that only God can make the wind but that I've learned to harness it. That night, there was nothing at first. Dead calm. Then I felt it. Just as I was about to step off... I felt Him in the wind. It pushed me back. I felt Him beside me and all around me. I dropped to my knees and prayed. And when I stopped praying, I wept for hours."

Danica sat forward, wincing slightly. "What did you pray for?"

Nicholai continued, his voice stronger now. "There's a passage in the book of Matthew that talks about the disciples, alone in a boat on the sea of Galilee. A violent storm comes up, and they become frightened. Peter sees Jesus walking on the water. He calls out, 'Lord, if it's you, tell me to come to you.' Peter steps out but becomes afraid of the waves and starts to sink. Immediately, Jesus reached out and caught him. He said, 'You of little faith, why did you doubt?'"

Nicholai looked at Danica, his blue eyes clear for the first time in days, and answered her question. "I asked Him to catch me. I asked Him to open the eyes of my damaged, sinful soul so that when I can't see, when it becomes too dark, I can still believe that He is holding me."

"Do you still believe?" she asked.

"Yes, more than ever," he said. "But I'm still afraid, and it still hurts. Faith doesn't take away the fear, Danica. It just gives you the strength to walk through it."

Chapter 59

Nicholai stood up after a few moments of heavy silence between the two. She wanted him to come closer, to bridge the physical gap that felt miles wide, but he didn't. He respected the boundaries, perhaps too much.

"Why don't you make yourself comfortable," he said, his voice gentle, a stark contrast to the hard edge he used with Griffin. "And let me get started in the kitchen. You need fuel."

"You don't have to do that," she said, instinctively trying to rise and winced as her side protested. "I can manage. I've been feeding myself for a long time."

"Please," he said, holding up a hand to stop her. "I at least owe you dinner after dragging you into this mess. And I'm sorry, but the way you look—bruised, battered, and barely standing—I'm not taking you out in public. We'd scare the patrons." He smiled, a soft expression that reached his eyes, and she knew he was trying to lighten the mood.

"Fine," she said, surrendering to the exhaustion. "But let me at least get cleaned up. Do I really look that bad?"

Nicholai looked her over, taking in the swollen eye, the split lip, and the guarded posture. "Not too bad for a punk," he teased gently.

"Whatever," she replied, rolling her eyes but smiling despite the pain in her split lip. She walked away slowly, favoring her left side. She

259

shut the bedroom door and sat on the edge of her bed for a moment, listening. She could hear him in the kitchen—the clatter of pans, the running water—and for the first time in days, she felt safe. The silence of the loft wasn't empty anymore.

She slowly eased her way into the bathroom, gripping the counter for support. A shower was out of the question; the wound in her side was still too fresh, the stitches pulling tight with every movement. She stared at her reflection in the mirror. The woman staring back looked like a stranger—hollowed out but alive. She washed her face with a cloth, careful around the bruising. She tried pulling a brush through her hair, wincing as it tugged at her scalp, eventually giving up and pulling it into a tight, functional ponytail. From her closet, she grabbed an oversized grey sweatshirt and loose-fitting yoga pants, dressing herself with the slow, deliberate movements of the elderly.

"Is this better?" she asked him as she entered the kitchen, feeling small in the baggy clothes.

"Not really," he laughed, turning from the stove. He actually liked the way she looked—stripped of the badge and the armor. "Now take a seat, young lady," he said, motioning to the bar stool by the island. "Fresh coffee is coming. The real stuff, not the sludge from the precinct."

"Listen, punk, you don't look much better yourself. You need a shave and about a week of sleep. But I see you've made yourself at home," she said, looking at the condition of the counters. Nicholai had spread out a variety of items—vegetables, broth, herbs. It looked chaotic but smelled divine. "What are you making?"

"Chicken soup," he said, chopping carrots with rhythmic precision. "My grandmother's recipe. Best thing for when you're under the weather or recovering from a stab wound."

"Well, this is a little more than just a cold," she said, touching her side. "But it smells good. Like home."

She eased herself onto the stool, hooking her heels on the rung, and watched him. There was a domestic intimacy to it that felt foreign to her. Nicholai poured her coffee into her favorite mug and placed it in front of her.

"You need to fill me in," she said, wrapping her hands around the warm ceramic. "Griffin told me the basics of what you've uncovered, but I need the details."

They spent the next hour comparing notes on the suicide cases and the new leads they had both uncovered. The steam from the soup pot filled the kitchen as they dissected the lives of dead men. The topic of Jeremy Quinlin hung in the air like smoke, but neither brought it up. Not yet.

"The outfitting company these trips were booked through is a shell company," she informed him as he stirred more ingredients into the pot. "I traced the registration. It doesn't exist physically. Rosin was the lead contact."

"And the money was funneled through him to someone in South America who ran the place. A facilitator," Nicholai added.

"Yes, that's right," she said. "Miller, the forensic accountant, found the pass-through account. It's a digital laundry mat."

"The good doctor, Jason Fawcett, was the first to be discovered," Nicholai mused, staring into the broth. "I believe he actually did take his own life to avoid someone from discovering his secret. The shame was too much for a man whose entire career was built on appearances."

"And the others?" she asked.

"Someone else discovered what they had been doing. Someone got hold of the photos Griffin found and threatened to expose them," Nicholai said. "They turned the hunters into the prey."

"Blackmailing someone for money is one thing," Danica argued, "but forcing them to that point where they take their own life doesn't make sense financially. If you kill the golden goose, the eggs stop coming. What would they gain by ending it?"

Nicholai stopped stirring. He placed the spoon on the stove rest and walked away from the heat. Danica tried to turn her body while seated to follow him, but the pain in her side made her stop with a sharp intake of breath. She stood up slowly as Nicholai stopped at the large floor-to-ceiling window, looking out at the city lights. He was silent for a moment, watching the traffic, and then turned to face her.

"Not they," he said. "She."

"Do you know who?" Danica asked, though the answer was already forming in her mind.

"I have a better idea now, yes. The profile fits perfectly. The narcissism, the control, the technical access."

"Let's get her picked up then," Danica said, her detective instinct kicking in. "I'll call Cooper, and we can get a warrant. We can get backup there within the hour."

"Won't work," he told her, shaking his head.

"Why not? We have the connection. We have the motive."

"Because technically," Nicholai said, his voice grim, "she's not doing anything illegal. She hasn't pulled a trigger. She hasn't pushed a chair. She's selling them silence, and they are paying for it. And when they can't pay anymore, or when she gets bored... she suggests an alternative. Suicide is a choice, Danica. A coerced choice, but a choice. Proving she forced them is going to be impossible without her computer."

Chapter 60

Lynn Fawcett checked her diamond-encrusted watch. It was time.

She walked into her home office, a space that was as cold and sterile as an operating theater, located just across from the opulent living room. She sat in her ergonomic leather chair and typed in the appropriate biometric passwords. The screen flared to life, recognizing her. She watched as the new file icon appeared on the desktop, a digital package delivered right on schedule.

She moved the pointer over the icon and double-clicked. The file opened immediately, displaying a stream of data from Thomas Sanford's laptop. She smiled, a cold, tight expression that didn't reach her eyes. It was all coming in—emails, bank routing numbers, campaign strategies. There were still a few more details she needed to ensure the transfer of funds was untraceable, and then it would all be over.

Finished.

Tetelestai.

She had always liked that word. She had heard it in church as a child, but she had repurposed it. To her, it wasn't a cry of sacrifice; it was the stamp on a paid invoice. It seemed fitting for what she was doing. Closing the ledger. The end of one era of weak men and the start of another. A beautiful era where she held the pen. Her beautiful era was going to start very soon, funded by the sins of others.

She opened the email file and prepared a new message to Thomas Sanford. The subject line was innocuous: "Meeting Confirmation."

Thomas, I have some new ideas for the campaign. I think you'll find them... revolutionary. Same time, same suite. Don't be late.

They were meeting again in two days. She knew he'd be excited to see her again, thinking with his ego instead of his brain. He had no clue it would be their last meeting. He had no clue that by the time he left that hotel room, his life would effectively be over.

She hit send and leaned back, watching the progress bar.

Chapter 61

They decided to eat without discussing the case. The horrors of the day needed to be kept at bay for an hour. Nicholai made one brief call to Griffin, asking him to search a few more specific financial records related to Lynn Fawcett's consulting firm, but then he put the phone away.

They sat at the small table, eating the soup in a comfortable silence. It was hot, rich, and exactly what Danica needed.

"That was good," she said, scraping the bottom of the bowl. "Really good. I feel human again."

"Thank you," he replied, standing up and taking their dishes from the table to the kitchen sink. "My grandmother would be pleased."

"I'll clean it up later," she said, starting to rise. "You cooked; I clean. That's the rule."

"No, you won't. Your job is to heal. That's an order." He walked back over to her. "Your job is to get back over on that couch and rest. Come on," he said, extending his hand.

When Danica took his hand, she realized the last time they had touched like this was on the Sara Rose, moments before everything fell apart. His grip was warm and firm. He helped her up from the chair, taking her weight, and placed his arm gently around her waist to support her injured side. He moved her through the dining room, into the den, and slowly let her sink into the soft cushions of the couch.

"Would you like to lie down?" he asked, arranging a throw pillow behind her back.

She pulled her legs up tight, wincing slightly, and leaned against the arm of the couch. "No, I'm okay like this. Lying down makes the room spin."

He handed her the television remote. "Here," he said. "Entertain yourself while I clean up. Find something mindless."

Danica smiled, taking the remote. "Thank you, Nic."

He walked away, rolling up his sleeves. She flipped through the channels, the light from the screen flickering over her face, but she wasn't paying attention to anything in particular. She was more focused on the sounds coming from the kitchen—the running water, the clinking of china. It was a domestic rhythm she had denied herself for years. She closed her eyes for a moment, just listening.

"I'm done," he said softly.

She opened her eyes to see him standing over her, drying his hands on a towel.

"That was fast," she said, blinking.

"Not really. You've been asleep for almost an hour."

"I'm sorry," she apologized, sitting up straighter. "Not very good company, I guess. I'm fading."

"It's okay," he said. "You need the rest. But I'm going to head out now and let you sleep properly."

"Where?" she asked quickly, the anxiety returning.

He thought for a moment, looking at the door. "I don't really know. Maybe find a hotel. Or sleep in the car again."

"You're not staying in the car again. That's ridiculous. Stay here, Nic, please."

"I don't know if that's a good idea," he said, hesitating. "I don't want to intrude."

"You can take the couch," she said, gesturing to the ample space. "I'll take the bedroom. It's huge. You won't even know I'm here."

He didn't answer immediately. He looked at the window, checking the darkness outside.

"I'd feel safer," she added quietly. "Please? I don't want to be alone tonight."

He thought hard about her offer, weighing propriety against the threat of Quinlin. Finally, he nodded. "Okay. I'll stay."

She got up, relief washing over her, and slowly made her way to the bedroom.

"There's extra pillows and blankets in the hall closet," she said. "Help yourself to whatever you need."

"I'll be fine. Good night, Dani," he said.

She turned around and took a few steps toward the hallway. Then she stopped. She turned back and saw Nicholai was still standing by the couch, watching her to make sure she made it safely.

"Can I ask you something?" she asked, her hand on the doorframe.

"Sure," he said.

"On the phone that night... when Quinlin had the gun to me... you told him I didn't mean anything to you. You said I was just a colleague."

Nicholai put his head down, the memory clearly painful. He eased himself onto the edge of the couch, clasping his hands between his knees. He leaned forward and looked up at her. Their eyes met across the dim room, and she saw the brightness in his blue eyes was starting to return, fierce and protective.

"No," he said, his voice steady and absolute. "It's not true. It was the only lie I could tell to save you."

Nothing more needed to be spoken by either of them. The truth hung in the air between them, solid and real, as she quietly closed her bedroom door.

Chapter 62

"**W**ho are you?" she asked the moment she stepped out from her bedroom, her hand instinctively reaching for a holster that wasn't there.

Danica expected to see Nicholai—perhaps making coffee, perhaps reading his Bible—and not the strange, uniformed man sitting in her living room at ten o'clock in the morning. He looked too young to be holding a gun, sitting stiffly on the edge of her couch as if afraid to wrinkle the fabric.

The officer jumped to his feet, his posture snapping to attention. "Officer Kalen, ma'am," he said, his voice cracking slightly.

"Why are you here? Where's Nicholai?" Her eyes scanned the room, looking for signs of a struggle, but the loft was exactly as they had left it the night before.

"He called in at four this morning and asked to have an officer assigned to you immediately. He said he had to follow a lead and couldn't leave you unsecured. He left a note on the counter over there," the officer said, pointing toward the kitchen island.

Danica brushed the sleep from her eyes, wincing as the movement pulled at the stitches in her side. She walked to the counter, seeing the piece of paper anchored by her coffee mug.

Gone to Griffin's. Found the link. Will call later. Stay put. — Nic

She read the note again, frustration bubbling up in her chest. He had gone off the grid again. After everything they had said last night, after the shared vulnerability, he had slipped out in the darkness to protect her. It was noble, and it was infuriating.

She looked at the young officer, who was watching her with wide eyes. "You can go," she said, crumpling the note in her hand.

"I can't do that, ma'am. I'm supposed to stay until Mr. Delgado or the Captain relieves me," he said, standing his ground. "Strict orders."

"I outrank you, Officer Kalen. I'm an Inspector, and I'm ordering you to leave. I need to get dressed, and I need to work. I can't do either with a babysitter."

The officer hesitated, looking torn between two conflicting commands.

"Go," she said, pointing to the door. "Now."

The officer didn't need to be told again. He sensed the volatility in the room and decided retreat was the better part of valor. He picked up his hat and made his way to the door. Hand on the knob, he turned back.

"He told me you'd do this," he said with a sheepish grin.

"Who said what?" she asked, pausing.

"Mr. Delgado, ma'am. He said, 'She's going to kick you out within five minutes of waking up.' He also said he wished you'd follow orders as well as you give them."

Danica stared at the closing door, a reluctant smile touching her lips. "Punk," she whispered.

Chapter 63

She arrived at the suite a full day early. Lynn Fawcett wanted everything perfect for their next meeting. Control was the only currency that mattered now, and she intended to hoard it.

She moved through the luxurious rooms of the Hotel ZaZa, checking sightlines and lighting. She adjusted the angle of the hidden camera she had installed in the ventilation grate, ensuring it captured the desk and the bed perfectly. She laughed to herself, a cold, hollow sound that bounced off the marble floors.

If everything went as planned, Thomas Sanford would be gone soon—another tragedy for the morning papers—and she'd have all the money she had lost when Jason died. She had most of the information she needed from his hard drive already; the partition was mirroring his financial data beautifully. In a day, the transfer would be complete, and the trap would be sprung.

Sanford would be the last one. She was almost glad. It was exhausting playing the part of the seductress, pretending to care about their egos and their politics. But he deserved it. They all did. They thought they were gods because they had money and influence, but they were just weak men with dirty secrets.

Chapter 64

Tetelestai, she smiled, checking her reflection in the mirror. It is finished. She liked the finality of it. It wasn't a surrender; it was a foreclosure.

"I'll be there in thirty minutes," he said over the phone, the background noise suggesting he was already moving fast. "Are you sure you're okay to do this? You should be resting."

"I'm fine," Danica said, pulling her jacket on carefully to cover the bandage. "I've rested enough. I'll meet you downstairs."

"Not alone you won't. I had Cooper assign that officer for a good reason. You stay inside until I get there," Nicholai ordered. "Do not step foot on that sidewalk until you see my car."

"Fine," she lied. She was already in the elevator.

He arrived in twenty minutes instead of thirty, screeching to a halt in the loading zone. She was waiting by the curb.

"Where are we going?" she asked once she got into his car. He had the Porsche back, and it smelled of leather and urgency.

"Griffin broke through the partitions on all the hard drives," he said, merging into traffic. "But he wasn't able to nail down the originating location of the server. It's bouncing through too many proxies. So, I took a different route. Last night, I went back to the source. I had Griffin cross-reference names from the Homeland Security database with the victims."

"We already did that," Danica said. "We know they went to South America."

"Yes, but we looked at where they went. I wanted to know who they went with. I wanted to see who traveled on the same flights at the same time with those guys. Who was the common denominator on the manifest?"

"And what did you find?" she asked, gripping the door handle.

"One name appeared on every flight manifest," he replied. "Then Griffin hacked into the bank records based on Rosin's deposits, and we found payments to Rosin's shell company for a 'hunting excursion' to South America."

"So we've got the organizer. But how does that help us get her? And you still haven't told me who she is," Danica asked, frustration mounting.

"It's Lynn Fawcett," Nicholai informed her, his voice flat. "I believe she discovered her husband's so-called hunting trips were actually trips to a private compound in South America. But they weren't hunting jaguars, Danica."

"What were they doing?"

"The outfit specializes in child prostitution," he said, the disgust evident in his voice. "Wealthy men pay a premium to do whatever they want, far away from US laws."

"That's sick," she whispered, bringing a hand to her mouth.

"I know it is. I saw the photographs on the hard drives," he said, his knuckles white on the steering wheel. "It's rampant, and these guys—Rosin, Simpson, Roberts, Wright—they were all involved. They were monsters in tailored suits."

"How did you trace it back to Fawcett?" she asked.

Nicholai turned the Porsche left, tires gripping the asphalt as he made his way onto the tollway. "I had my suspicions about her almost immediately. The narcissism, the control. We've heard over and over again how a life insurance policy is void when the insured takes their own life. Dr. Fawcett's suicide was just that—a suicide. But why?"

He shifted gears, accelerating. "She found out what he was doing. She likely found the photos or the financial trail. She filed for divorce, expecting to get half the assets from his practice, plus alimony. But she hit a wall. She threatened to expose him if he didn't hand it all over and go away quietly. But his partnership agreement with Dr. Burke protected the practice. It was ironclad unless he changed it voluntarily."

"So she squeezed him," Danica realized.

"I called the corporate attorney for Fawcett-Burke this morning. I verified that two days before he died, Fawcett tried to change the partnership agreement to liquidate his share, but he couldn't do it without Burke's consent. Burke refused."

"You've been busy," she said, impressed.

"Yes, I have," he said. "When Lynn Fawcett heard that he couldn't pay her off, she escalated her threats. He knew his career—his life—would be over if the public ever found out he was a pedophile. He would go to prison, he would be ruined. So he took what he perceived was the only way out. He overdosed."

"And that left her with nothing."

"Nothing but anger and a stack of incriminating evidence," he said. "And to get revenge—and the money she felt she was owed—she decided to play God. She went after the rest of the hunting party. She's punishing them for her husband's failure to pay."

"But that's extortion," Danica said, her mind racing through the penal code. "We can nail her for that."

"No, we can't. Not yet. We can't verify the financial payments because she wire transfers the money electronically after their death, using their own passwords. Griffin can't trace the deposits past the offshore relays. And these guys... they have taken their lives by their own choice. Technically, that's not murder. It's coerced suicide."

"What can we do?" Danica was confused. "We can't just let her kill them."

"All we can do is stop her before she succeeds with the next guy. We have to catch her in the act of the coercion."

"And who is the next guy?" she asked.

"I asked you to find out who requested me being brought in, remember?"

"Yes, but Cooper didn't know at the time. He said it came from Austin."

"I spoke to him this morning and forced the issue. It was a request from Senator Clements' office."

"The Senator? He's involved in this as well?" she was shocked.

"No," Nicholai said, shaking his head. "But his campaign manager, Thomas Sanford, sat next to James Rosin and Davis Wright on Flight 615 to Brazil last year. He's in the photos, Danica."

Danica was speechless. The web of corruption went straight to the steps of the Capitol.

"We have to get to Sanford," Nicholai said, pushing the car faster. "Before she finishes him."

Chapter 65

"I'm sorry, but Mr. Sanford is tied up right now," the young, overworked campaign worker informed Nicholai and Danica, barely looking up from her clipboard. The outer office was a hive of activity—phones ringing, volunteers stuffing envelopes, the smell of stale pizza and ambition thick in the air.

"Tell him it's an urgent police matter regarding federal crimes," Danica told her, flashing her badge. "And tell him we aren't leaving."

The young blonde's eyes widened. She dropped her pen, turned on her heel, and hurried away from the waiting area of Senator Clement's campaign headquarters. She returned within minutes, looking flushed, and escorted them back to Sanford's corner office, away from the prying eyes of the volunteers.

"How can I help you?" Sanford said, greeting them at his office door with a practiced smile that didn't reach his eyes. He smoothed his tie, projecting confidence.

"Have a seat, Mr. Sanford. This may take some time," Danica said, closing the door behind them and locking it.

"Well, I don't have much time actually," he said, glancing at his watch. "That's the nature of this business when running an important campaign like this one. Every minute counts."

"You'll make the time after hearing what we have to say," Nicholai stated, his voice low and dangerous. He didn't sit; he paced the room, inspecting the photos on the wall.

277

"What's this concerning?" Sanford asked, his smile faltering. He moved behind his desk, putting a barrier between himself and the detectives. He was starting to get nervous, and it showed in the way his hands fidgeted with a paperweight.

"What was your relationship with Jason Fawcett, Cole Simpson, James Rosin, David Roberts, and Davis Wright?" Nicholai asked, listing the names like an indictment.

The color left the man's face instantly, draining away to leave him ashen. "They... they sound familiar. Business associates, perhaps. Where is this going?" he asked, his voice rising an octave. "Do I need to have my attorney present?"

"That's not necessary," Nicholai stated, stopping in front of the desk. "You're smart enough to know that what you did wasn't illegal in this country because the violations happened in South America. Your attorney can't help you with morality."

Sanford didn't answer. He stared at his hands.

"Immoral, sick, pathetic, you name it," Danica said, leaning over the desk. "But unfortunately, we can't bring criminal charges against you here in this country for what happened there. Jurisdiction is your only friend right now."

"What's going on?" he asked, sweat beading on his forehead. His nervousness had quickly moved to palpable fear.

"You know those men we mentioned are all dead?" Danica asked.

"I knew about Jason and David... tragic accidents. But I just heard about Davis this morning. Are you saying all of them are gone?"

"They are, sir. Every single one. And we believe you're next on the list."

"But they committed suicide. They took their own lives. I don't know about the others." His hands were shaking now, rattling the paperweight against the glass desktop.

"Mr. Sanford, we know you're the one who made the request to bring me in," Delgado said, leaning in close. "Now I need you to focus and listen to what I am about to tell you. Your life depends on it."

"Yes, I requested you, Mr. Delgado. I had heard how good you were, and after hearing about Jason and David... I got scared. I saw the pattern. But please, can we keep this quiet? I could be ruined, not to mention the Senator. The scandal would destroy everything we've built."

"Mr. Sanford, listen to me," Nicholai ordered.

"Okay, tell me. What do you know?"

Danica watched the man sweat behind his desk, a pathetic figure in an expensive suit. She wished there was some way to charge him and have him put away for life, but the law was a blunt instrument.

"All those men we mentioned were with you on your trips to South America, were they not? Flight 615 to Brazil?"

Sanford didn't answer immediately. He looked at both Nicholai and Danica, then looked away at a framed photo of him shaking hands with the President.

"If you want our help, Mr. Sanford, you'll start with the truth," Danica informed him. "We can't save a liar."

He looked at Nicholai, searching for judgment and finding it. "Yes. They were."

"The wooden masks, Mr. Sanford?" Nicholai asked, pulling the broken piece of wood from his pocket and placing it on the desk. "Tell me about them."

"They were used so we could never be identified," Sanford whispered, turning his chair away. He couldn't face them. "It was part of the... privacy."

Nicholai looked at Danica. She saw the disgust on his face, mirroring her own.

"Your friends, Mr. Sanford," she said, her voice hard. "They have all committed suicide because they were being blackmailed. Someone was threatening to expose them, to release the photos and videos you thought were private."

"Who?" he turned back quickly, desperation in his eyes. "I need to know."

"Several days ago, a series of programs was installed on your laptop. You're not aware of this, but everything on there—every email, every donor list, every photo—has been uploaded to someone who intends to use it the same way she used it against the others."

"She?" he asked. "Who? My laptop is never out of my sight. My life, everything is on there."

"Early this morning, Mr. Sanford, we remotely backtracked a module that came from your computer and relayed it back through a private BNS pathway," Nicholai explained. "We've been able to monitor everything since seven o'clock this morning. We watched the transfer."

"How does that help me!" he stood up and started pacing, his composure shattering.

"Mr. Sanford, the woman you are meeting this afternoon plans to expose you if you don't take your own life. She wants you dead."

"Jennifer? That can't be. She's... she's different."

"Mr. Sanford, her name is not Jennifer. It's Lynn Fawcett. She is Jason Fawcett's widow," Danica said, disgusted watching the man pace the room like a trapped rat. "She blames you all for his death."

"I'll just offer to pay her off and make this all go away. I have resources. Like you said, I've done nothing illegal in this country. I can handle this." He was scrambling for a way to get himself out of the predicament as easily as possible, defaulting to bribery.

"Oh, she's already getting the money," Nicholai said coldly. "There is an electronic transfer request of one million dollars from the

Senator's campaign account pending and set to finalize at noon tomorrow. You authorized it with your digital signature this morning."

"I didn't authorize anything!"

"She did it for you. Feel free to check for yourself."

"How do you know all this?" he asked, slumping back into his chair.

Nicholai pointed to the laptop sitting open on his desk. "She has every bit of information that you have. And as of this morning, we do as well. Griffin has mirrored your drive."

"What do I do? Can you help me? Please."

"We want to stop her, but that's your decision, Mr. Sanford. We can arrest her for the extortion and the theft, but only if you cooperate."

Thomas Sanford knew he didn't have a choice. He put his head in his hands, defeated.

"Whatever it takes," he finally said quietly. "But what's going to happen to me?" he asked, looking up with wet eyes.

Nicholai glared at the man behind the desk. "Mr. Sanford, even though what you've done makes me sick, it's not my place to judge you legally for crimes committed outside my jurisdiction. That's in the Lord's hands, not mine, and certainly not Lynn Fawcett's. But your time will come when you'll have to answer for all you've done. For now, all I can do is stop this woman from playing executioner and keep you both in prayer, though God knows why."

Sanford was speechless, shame finally coloring his face.

"But there is something I can do, Mr. Sanford," Danica cut in, stepping forward. She placed her hands flat on his desk. "When this is over, you will resign your position here immediately. Today. Make up whatever excuse you want—health, family, you seem well versed in the area of lies. Then you will sign an affidavit ensuring no contact with children at any time. You will also voluntarily register with the National Sex Offender database within forty-eight hours."

"But my career... my family? The Senator?"

Danica leaned closer, her eyes burning. "The photographs contained on that computer are illegal, Mr. Sanford. Possession of child pornography is a federal crime here. And even though your high-priced attorney could fight the fact that we obtained them unofficially through a hack, there's nothing stopping them from getting into the wrong hands. The press would have a field day. The Senator would be destroyed."

She paused, letting the threat hang in the air.

"Do we have a deal?"

Sanford looked at the laptop, then at the door, realizing his life as he knew it was over. He nodded slowly.

"Yes."

Chapter 66

"Come on in, sweetheart," she purred, opening the door wide. Lynn Fawcett was not a professionally trained actress, but over the years, she had become an expert liar. Survival required performance. "It's so good to see you. I don't know if I could have waited another minute."

She wrapped her arms around Thomas Sanford and kissed him passionately, pressing her body against his. He tried his best to play along, kissing her back, but his lips felt cold and unresponsive.

She pulled back slightly, studying his face. "What's wrong, baby? You feel tense."

"I'm just tired. I've had a lot on my mind today," he tried to explain, loosening his tie. "The campaign?"

"Yeah, it's taking its toll," Sanford replied, walking past her into the suite. He scanned the room, looking for cameras, looking for a way out.

"Well, I've got quite an evening planned for tonight," she said, locking the door behind him. The click of the deadbolt sounded like a gavel. "Hopefully we can put all that campaign stuff aside for a while, baby. Focus on us."

Sanford stood frozen in the middle of the living room. He didn't want to be there. Every instinct screamed at him to run, but he was trapped by his own sins. He wanted to confront her, to scream at her, but fear held his tongue.

"Let me take your jacket," she said, slipping it off his shoulders. "Grab a seat and relax, Hun. I'm almost ready. Pour yourself a drink."

Once she was out of the room, disappearing into the bathroom to freshen up, Sanford took a ragged breath and sat down on the edge of the sofa. He looked at the mini-bar but didn't move. He needed a clear head.

"I hope you're hungry," she yelled from the bathroom, her voice echoing off the tile.

"Yes, I am," he lied. "Can we go out?" He felt that this might be his chance to get out in public, away from her control. There was a certain safety in a crowded restaurant; witnesses were his only shield now. The discovery of their affair was secondary on his mind at that moment compared to his survival.

"I'm all set," she said, entering the room. She was wearing a backless black dress that cost more than most people made in a month. He looked her over but couldn't see any sign of her lethal intent. She looked beautiful, elegant, harmless. Maybe the police and the Special Agent were mistaken. Maybe he was paranoid. But they had too much proof. Thomas Sanford didn't know what to think. He just knew he was afraid.

"Let's go," she said, leading him out the door, her hand firm on his arm.

"Where are we going?" he asked as they walked down the hallway.

She noticed a hint of concern on his face and squeezed his arm. "Dinner," she said. "But don't worry, it's private. No one will see us together. I know you have a reputation to protect."

Fawcett led him to the elevator. The doors opened, and she pushed the top button—the roof access.

"Why are we going up there?" he asked, watching the numbers climb. "The dining room is downstairs."

"I know," she said, her eyes glittering. "I have a surprise set up. I told you I was going to take care of you tonight. A private table under the stars."

The elevator stopped on the forty-second floor, and the doors opened with a soft chime. He knew it was the top of the hotel, the mechanical level, but still didn't know what to expect.

"I hope you're hungry," she smiled, stepping out into a service corridor.

Fawcett led him down the hall and out through a heavy fire door. He stepped out into the warm Texas night, the wind immediately whipping at his clothes. She followed behind, the door slamming shut. A dining table had been set out on the flat roof, surrounded by a low parapet. The table was set for two with fine china and crystal, a surreal island of luxury amidst the HVAC units and vents.

"How's this?" she asked, spreading her arms. "The view is to die for."

"Lovely," he replied, his voice hollow. His palms were sweating, and he rubbed them against his pant legs. She poured him a glass of wine, the red liquid swirling in the glass, but he didn't move towards it.

She sat across from him, perfectly poised, and saw the look on his face. The terror.

"Thomas, what's wrong? You haven't touched your wine."

He looked around at the area. They were alone. Forty-two stories up. He tried holding it in, tried sticking to the script the detectives gave him, but he couldn't. The pressure was too great.

"I know what you're doing," he said, his voice shaking.

"I'm not following, sweetie," she replied, taking a sip of her wine. "I just wanted this to be a special night for us."

"The police came to see me this morning," he said, standing up from the table and walking away from her.

"And?" she asked, her demeanor cooling instantly. She followed him, stalking him as close as she could.

He turned towards her and leaned back against the low ledge of the roof. The city lights sprawled out below them, a grid of electricity. "They told me what you've been doing. Rosin, Simpson, all of them. They showed me the transfers."

"So they did," Fawcett stated, dropping the act. Her face changed, hardening into something unrecognizable. "They got what they deserved. They were weak."

"How could you?" he asked, horrified. "You killed them."

"Me? I just took care of a bunch of sex offenders. I cleaned up the trash. I got them off the street when the law wouldn't."

"Oh, really. That's how you justify it. What about the money? You drained their accounts."

"I deserve every dime of what I took!" she yelled, her voice carried away by the wind. "Jason's sick, secret hobby ruined me. He humiliated me! I deserve everything I've taken from him and the others as compensation for my suffering. And I'll get my share of you as well. Your punishment is coming, Thomas, and you'll pay dearly for what you've done to those children!"

"That's where you're wrong," Sanford said, finding a spine he didn't know he had. "You're sick, and I'm not paying you anything. The transfer is canceled."

She laughed, a sharp, incredulous sound. "Do you expect me to wait for you to pay me? I'm taking what I want whether you like it or not. The transfer is automated."

"No, you're not," he said, moving closer to the edge, looking down at the dizzying drop. "I'm not letting it happen. I'm stopping it."

"You don't get it, Thomas. The money transfer is set. Not even you can stop it," she stated, stepping closer. "And when the account comes up one million dollars short tomorrow, a simple accounting procedure will show it coming from your computer. You authorized it."

He turned around and faced her, silence stretching between them.

"So here's what you have to deal with," she hissed. "Pictures of you with young boys released to the press, and a million dollars missing from an account that you control. You'll go to prison as a pedophile thief. You won't last a week."

"And I told you, I'm not letting that happen."

She laughed again, only this time, harder. "You can't stop me! I own you!"

Sanford put his head down in shame, acknowledging the truth of her power. But then, he slowly raised his head and looked her in the eyes.

"You're evil," he said calmly. "And yes, I can."

Before she knew what was happening, Sanford reached up, grabbed both her arms in a vice grip, and pulled her in tight against his chest.

"What are you doing?" she shrieked, struggling.

"Paying the debt," he whispered.

He twisted his body, using his height and weight as the advantage against her small frame. He leaned back, over the center of gravity, over the ledge.

Her feet left the ground, and her eyes went wide with realization. She had no chance or time to fight back. Both bodies tipped over the parapet, falling forty-two stories in an eerie silence, locked in a final embrace, until they hit the empty street below.

Seconds later, the heavy fire door crashed open. Nicholai and Danica ran to the edge of the roof, weapons drawn, but there was no one to aim at.

Nicholai looked down first. Far below, amidst the parked cars, lay two broken forms.

"We were too late!" he yelled, slamming his hand against the concrete ledge.

"We had her on tape," Danica said, holstering her weapon, her face pale. "That's all we needed. We told him to just get her to admit to the money, and she did. We were recording everything. Why did he do that? He had a deal."

Nicholai looked back over the edge at the tragic tableau. He knew why. It wasn't just about escaping prison; it was about reclaiming the only thing Sanford had left—the manner of his exit.

"I guess we'll never know now," he said quietly. "Tetelestai."

Chapter 67

On the tenth floor of the Bates Building in downtown Dallas, in a corner office now dark and empty, a computer hummed to life. Behind a locked door, the screen illuminated the room with an evil, blue glow.

The hard drive whirred, processing a scheduled task that no one was alive to cancel. After cycling through its operating system and verifying the date, a command was sent to the network printer.

The print spooler started, the mechanical rollers feeding a single sheet of paper. The ink jet sprayed its message with precise, detached efficiency.

A lone piece of paper slid out of the tray and fluttered to the floor, landing face up in the silence.

I'm so sorry for what I've done. I cannot live with the pain I have caused any longer.

Thomas Sanford

Tetelestai

But in the shadows of the room, a small green light on a hidden webcam blinked once, then went dark. Someone else had been watching. And the game wasn't over.

Chapter 68

"I've cleared it with Brainerd," she said, closing her flip phone with a snap. "We can take them both to Griffin. She'll hold off logging them into evidence until morning."

"Good," Nicholai said, his eyes fixed on the road.

They needed to get Sanford and Fawcett's computers to Griffin immediately to stop the automated money transfer. The coroner had arrived at the hotel, and the rooftop scene was being processed, the flashes of cameras illuminating the night sky like lightning.

Captain Cooper had personally arrived at the scene, looking disheveled and grim. He questioned both Danica and Nicholai extensively. They explained why Griffin could stop the transaction faster than the DPD department techs without disclosing too much of the hacker's questionable methods. Cooper could tell they were hiding something—he was too good a cop not to—but he felt it best not to know the details. Plausible deniability was a currency he was willing to trade. When he was satisfied that everything was procedurally defensible, he left the scene, but not before Danica had assured him the official reports would be on his desk within twenty-four hours.

Danica was still feeling the effects of her injuries. The adrenaline that had fueled her through the confrontation was fading, leaving a dull, throbbing ache in her side. She was tired—soul-deep tired—and looked forward to heading home to a quiet room. She thought she might even sleep without nightmares, but she had mixed feelings. The case was closed, or would be once she filed all the paperwork. Did that mean the end of her working arrangement with Nicholai? Was he going to sail off somewhere into the sunset? She didn't want to think about the silence that would follow.

"Are you ready?" he asked, pulling her back to the present.

"I am," she said quietly.

They rode in silence in Delgado's Porsche the entire way to the industrial district. The city lights blurred past, streaks of red and white. Both wanted to say something—to acknowledge what they had just witnessed on the roof—but neither did. They were both afraid that speaking would shatter the fragile peace they had found.

"Are we going to be here long?" she asked as they turned down the familiar, potholed street.

"No," he said. "We'll just drop them off. Griffin will know what to do with the encryption. He can kill the transfer script remotely." Nicholai looked over at her, his face illuminated by the dashboard lights. "Are you okay? You're holding your side."

"I'm tired," she admitted. "And I'm sore. But I'm alive."

"We'll finish up, and I'll get you home," he said softly. His idea sounded great until she wondered where he was going to go. The boat? The empty house? She stopped thinking and opened the car door as they pulled into the alley.

The alley was pitch black, the streetlight at the end having been shot out or burned out. Nicholai reached behind the seat and grabbed the two evidence bags containing the laptops. Danica made her way to the heavy steel door and waited, her hand hovering over the buzzer. She waited for Nicholai to get closer before pushing the call button.

"Stop," Nicholai whispered, his voice cutting through the darkness.

The sound of his voice, urgent and low, made her jump. "What?" she asked, freezing in place.

"The door," he said, nodding toward the jamb. "It's unlatched."

Danica looked closer. A sliver of darkness was visible between the door and the frame. Griffin's back door wasn't completely closed; the mag-lock wasn't engaged.

"Would Griffin have left it like this?" she asked, her hand moving to her hip.

"Not a chance," he said, placing the laptops gently on the ground. "He's a paranoid little geek. He triple-checks the perimeter every night. Someone's inside."

She reached behind her back and pulled out her service weapon, the weight of it familiar and comforting. "Where's yours?" she asked.

Nicholai looked at the car, debating. He walked back over, reached under the driver's seat, and pulled out his Sig Sauer. He checked the magazine, slid it back in, and racked the slide.

He didn't like the feel of it in his hand anymore. It felt heavy, cold, a tool of his past life. He moved it from one hand to the other, eventually putting it behind his back, tucked inside the waistband of his jeans.

"Stay behind me," he signaled.

Nicholai entered first, pushing the heavy door open with his foot. It swung silently on greased hinges. Danica had her gun drawn and stayed close behind him, clearing the corners. She pulled the door closed behind them quietly to cut off the backlight.

The warehouse was a cavern of shadows. They slowly made their way through the maze of pallets to the second interior door and found it open like the first. The keypad was dark—disabled. Nicholai turned to her and put his finger to his mouth. She knew the drill. He motioned to her that he would go alone at first to draw fire if necessary.

Nicholai eased the door open and quietly stepped inside the server room. The blast of cold air hit him. Griffin was not at his workstation. The monitors were dark, in sleep mode. The room was quiet except for the usual hum of the ventilation system coming from above.

"Griff?" he said quietly.

He waited for an answer. The silence stretched. He turned around and saw Danica still hadn't come inside the room; she was guarding the rear. He made his way to the main workstation and placed the laptops on the bench.

That's when he saw it. A spray of red across the keyboard.

He noticed the blood immediately and stepped back, his heart hammering.

"Griffin!" he yelled louder, abandoning stealth.

"He's kind of tied up at the moment."

Nicholai spun around, dropping into a defensive crouch, and came face to face with Quinlin for the first time in years. Through the dark, he could see the evil projecting from his eyes—eyes that were dead and full of life at the same time.

"What have you done with him?" Nicholai asked, his voice a low growl.

"Relax, Nic. He's napping over in the corner. You've really worked this guy too hard. I just figured he could use a rest." Quinlin gestured with his head to the far corner of the room, where Griffin lay slumped against a server rack, unconscious and bleeding from a head wound, duct tape over his mouth.

Jeremy Quinlin stepped out from the shadows, a large caliber handgun aimed steadily at Nicholai's chest. He looked exactly as Nicholai remembered—unremarkable, blending in, deadly.

"Is this how it ends, Jeremy? An ambush in a basement?"

Quinlin laughed, a dry sound like paper tearing. "After everything we've been through together, it is kind of anti-climactic, isn't it? I expected a chase. But you made it easy."

Nicholai didn't answer. He calculated the distance. Fifteen feet. Too far to rush him.

"What's wrong, Pastor? Nothing to say? No sermon?"

Nicholai still refused to respond, his eyes locked on the gun.

"After everything I've done to you, everything I've put you through, and you just stand there?" Quinlin asked, stepping closer, encroaching on the safe zone. "Come on, Pastor, there must be something you want to say? Scream at me. Curse me. I really didn't expect you to be this much of a coward. I wanted the FBI agent, not the priest."

"No," Nicholai said, his voice calm, infuriatingly steady. "I just feel sorry for you."

"Sorry for me?" Quinlin laughed, the sound echoing off the concrete walls. "I'm as free as a bird. I do what I want, when I want. You're the one who's stuck in some fantasy world living by rules and restrictions and a God who let your family die. I've got my instructions, and that's all I have to worry about. I am pure."

"What do mean my fantasy world?"

"Let's see... first there was that perfect little family. The white picket fence. Where did that get you? A plot in the cemetery. Then that stupid boat. That floating shrine."

"What about her?" Nicholai tried to remain calm, but his blood ran cold. He felt the gun in his waistband digging into his spine.

Quinlin reached onto the table next to him. "Here," he said. "I grabbed this before she went down. A souvenir." He tossed an item at Nicholai.

Nicholai snatched it out of the air. It was leather-bound, water-stained. He looked at the Bible he had given Jessica.

"I'm sorry," Quinlin said, mocking sympathy. "That's the only thing I had a chance to grab before she went under. She took on water fast."

"You sunk her?" Nicholai clenched his fingers around the Bible, the leather creaking.

"Oh yeah. Scuttled her. It was easier than I thought," Quinlin sneered. "There's four plugs inside the cabin below the waterline. Pull them all out, and bye-bye Sara Rose in less than thirty minutes. She's sitting at the bottom of the lake right now, with all your memories."

"Why?" he asked, the grief hitting him like a physical blow.

"Why not? I needed to clear the deck. Strip you bare." He paused, tilting his head. "By the way, where's your new little friend? The feisty one?"

"No idea," he said quickly. "She went home."

"You answered that too quickly. You know exactly where she is." Quinlin moved closer, closing the gap. The gun was still aimed at Nicholai's head. "I kind of like her," he said, licking his lips. "She breaks well. Once I'm done with you, it'll be her turn. I think I'll take my time with her."

He took a step closer. "Get on your knees," he yelled, his composure snapping. "Now!"

Nicholai slowly crouched down, keeping his eyes on Quinlin. He placed the Bible on the floor in front of him, treating it with reverence.

Quinlin laughed and kicked it aside, sending it skittering across the floor. "Do you really think that stuff works? Do you think that book is going to save you?"

"Yes, I do," Nicholai replied, looking up. "Love always wins. Even in death."

"Such crap!" Quinlin yelled, his face twisting in rage. "Put your hands behind your back slowly," he ordered. "I want to see the light go out of your eyes."

Nicholai slowly moved his hands behind him. His fingers brushed the grip of the gun in his waistband. He gripped it, thumbing the safety off, waiting for his move. He breathed in.

Quinlin lowered his gun, pushing the cold steel barrel hard against Nicholai's forehead. The contact was electric. The fingers on Quinlin's right hand tightened around the trigger.

"Let's see if your love can win now," he laughed. He cocked the trigger back, the metallic click loud in the silence, and pushed down hard against Nicholai's forehead, forcing his head back. "Say your prayers now, Pastor."

The gunshot echoed through the entire warehouse, a thunderclap that signaled the end.

Chapter 69

The gunshot was deafening in the enclosed concrete space, a thunderclap that shattered the tension and left a high-pitched ringing in its wake.

"What... what did you do?" Nicholai stuttered, his voice sounding distant to his own ears. He tried to find the right words, but his brain was scrambling to catch up with reality.

He stood frozen, his hands still behind his back, the ghost of the gun barrel still pressing against his forehead. The acrid smoke from the barrel of Danica's gun drifted through the air, stinging his eyes and momentarily blocking his view of her face. She stood in the doorway, her stance wide, her arms locked in a shooter's grip. Her gun remained aimed unwaveringly at the space where Quinlin had stood just a second before.

Delgado's eyes moved quickly from her statue-like position to the sound of a wet, guttural moan coming from the floor, then back to her. She didn't blink. She lowered her gun slowly, her hands trembling only after the weapon was pointed at the ground.

"Why? Why did you shoot him?" He whispered the question, but he didn't wait for her answer. He knew she didn't have one yet; she was operating on pure instinct.

Instead, he pulled his own weapon from the waistband of his jeans, clicked the safety on, and placed it on the floor. He didn't need it anymore. Without thinking, he rushed over to Quinlin and knelt beside him in the expanding pool of blood.

Quinlin was alive, but the light was fading fast. His eyes were open, staring up at the industrial ceiling, cold and rapidly losing focus. The bullet had taken him in the chest, a center-mass shot that destroyed the heart's ability to pump but left the brain alive for a few agonizing seconds. Blood foamed pink around his mouth, and his breathing was labored, a wet, rattling rasp.

"I guess you win, Pastor," he spit out, the words bubbling through the blood. He tried to smile, a grotesque baring of red teeth. "You brought... backup."

"There's no winning here, Quinlin. Stay with me. We'll get you help." Nicholai turned his head, shouting over his shoulder. "Dani, call it in! Get an ambulance! Now!"

Before Nicholai's last words were finished, the wail of sirens could be heard rising from outside the warehouse, a chorus of approaching judgment.

"Nah," Quinlin coughed, his body convulsing. "It's too late for me. I see... I see it."

"Nic, please." Danica had quietly moved closer, holstering her weapon. She stood over the two men, her face pale, her eyes wide. She placed her hand on Delgado's shoulder, grounding him, but he didn't look up. He looked at the killer as the life was draining from him, seeing not a monster, but a wasted soul.

"It's not too late, Jeremy," Nicholai said, his voice urgent, leaning close to the dying man's ear. "It is never too late. I can pray for you. Please, just ask. Accept the peace."

Danica took one step back in silence, giving them space. She stared at the two men—the hunter and the prey, the priest and the sinner. Her eyes opened wide as she watched Nicholai reach for Quinlin's blood-slicked hand, gripping it tight.

He closed his eyes, ignoring the blood soaking into his jeans, and placed his free hand on Quinlin's forehead. There was a silence in the room that was heavier than the gunshot. She watched Quinlin's face tighten, a look of terror passing over his features as the darkness closed in. His eyes bulged, seeing something beyond the room.

Then, slowly, the muscles relaxed along his cheekbones. The fight left him. His chest stopped heaving, and one last evil breath was forced out of his lungs—a rattle that signaled the end.

Nicholai remained kneeling beside the now lifeless body of Jeremy Quinlin. He didn't pull away. He opened his own eyes, filled with tears, and moved his hand slowly down Quinlin's forehead, closing the killer's eyelids for the final time. He gently placed the dead man's hands across his chest, granting him a dignity he had never shown his victims.

He closed his eyes again and bowed his head, his voice cracking.

"Dear God, please let this be a reminder to me and everyone I come in contact with that nobody ever has to go to hell, but that they can all be saved if they choose. Because we never know when we are going to take our last breath on this earth. Have mercy on his soul, Lord, for he knew not what he did. In Jesus' name, Amen."

The silence stretched for a long moment. Nicholai slowly rose to his feet, his joints popping, but he hadn't yet taken his eyes off the body. He looked exhausted, as if he had aged ten years in ten minutes.

"Why?" he asked again, turning to Danica. "Why did you shoot him? You had a choice."

"Nic, I had to," she replied, her voice shaking now that the adrenaline was dumping. "I couldn't take that chance. He had the gun against your head. He was squeezing the trigger."

"But I could have done it. I had my gun. I was ready."

"That was his intention all along," she said, stepping closer to him.

He looked at her, really looked at her. Something was different in her eyes. The hardness was gone, replaced by a fierce, protective clarity. "What do you mean?"

Before she could answer, the side door burst open. The EMTs crashed through, gear bags heavy on their shoulders, followed by uniformed officers with weapons drawn. Two paramedics knelt beside Quinlin, one on each side of the body, going through the motions. The older one checked for a pulse by placing his two fingers on the dead man's neck, waited three seconds, and shook his head. There was no life. He eased himself back and looked at his younger partner.

"Time of death, 23:42."

Danica reached out and touched Nicholai's arm, pulling his attention away from the corpse. "Nic, let's go outside. You don't need to see the rest."

He followed her silently, stepping over the yellow tape the officers were already stringing up. They walked out into the alley, the humid Texas night air hitting them like a physical wall. The flashing red and blue lights bounced off the brick walls, creating a disorienting strobe effect.

Nicholai turned to take one last look at the metal door, the tomb of the man who had caused such pain and anguish in his life; his wife and daughter's murderer. The chapter was closed.

"He wanted you to take his life," she said again, leaning against the brick wall, her arms crossed to hold herself together.

"But I could have done it. You didn't have to carry that weight."

"You don't get it, do you?" she asked softly.

He leaned against the wall next to her and ran his fingers through his hair, wiping away sweat and grime.

"His game wasn't to kill you, Nic. It was to destroy you. He knew the guilt and pain you've carried all these years because of what he did to Jessica and Sara," she said, turning to face him. "And now, you're trying to be a man of God, a man of peace. You've fought so hard to get there. If you had taken the life of another person—even someone as evil as him, execution style—you probably wouldn't be able to go on. It would have broken your spirit. No, Nic, he didn't want to kill you. Quinlin wanted you to live in unbearable pain and torment, just like he did. He wanted you to be a murderer."

Nicholai let himself slide down the wall until he sat on the sidewalk, pulling his knees in tight. He rested his head on his arms. She was right. Quinlin wanted to damn him.

Danica moved closer and sat down beside him on the dirty pavement, ignoring the chaos of the police scene around them. She looked into his eyes.

"But now you have to live with what you've done," he said to her, his voice full of regret. "You took that burden for me. You killed him to save my soul."

"I know," she said, reaching out to take his hand. "But eventually I'll be okay. I'm a cop. It's part of the job. But more than that... I did it for the right reason."

"What reason?" he asked, searching her face. "How can you justify taking a life so easily?"

"You said you'd save yourself when you felt you were worth it, and when you found something special to focus on," she said, her voice unwavering. "I shot him because I believe you're worth it. I believe you're worth saving."

"And that you're something special to focus on?" he asked, a flicker of hope lighting his eyes.

She smiled, a tired but genuine smile. She squeezed his hand, her fingers interlocking with his. She leaned in and kissed him on the cheek, lingering there for a moment, breathing him in. She pulled back and repeated the words he had once prayed over her on the boat.

"Open the eyes of my sinful, tortured soul so that when I cannot see through the dark, I can still believe."

Nicholai looked at her, stunned. She had heard him. She had understood.

"It's finished, Dani," he whispered. The debt was paid.

"I know," she said quietly, holding his hand tighter as the paramedics wheeled the body bag past them. "That part is finished, Nic. The past is done. And now, something new is going to start, if that's okay with you."

"I don't know," he said honestly, looking at the stars above the alley. "I have a lot to work through. I'm still broken."

Danica looked at him, seeing the scars but also the strength. "It's okay, and I understand. I'm broken too. I want to know who you are now, not who you were. I want to know where you are, not where you've been. But most of all, Nic, I want to know where you want to go so we can make our way there, to that place, together."

Nicholai squeezed her hand back. For the first time in four years, the future didn't look like a threat.

"Let's go home," he said.

Chapter 70

"Would you hand me a towel?" she asked as the soothing sound of the water inside the glass shower hissed to a stop. "Sorry, I forgot again."

Nicholai still had shaving cream covering the entire left side of his face, a stark white contrast against his tan skin. The razor was poised in his hand when he turned his head toward the direction of the corner shower, steam billowing over the top of the glass.

"No, I don't think so," he said, turning back to the mirror. "One of these days you'll learn to check the rack before you get in there. It's called situational awareness, Inspector."

He wasn't trying to be mean. This was just a game they played—a dance of domesticity that had started the day they became husband and wife. All newlyweds played games, but for most, the fun dies off quickly once the day-to-day routine of real life sinks in and steals the spark. But Nicholai and Danica were different. They had walked through the fire to get here. For them, the mundane was the miracle. It was still fun every day, every moment, every time he looked her way or she looked his.

Through the fogged shower door, he could see her place her hands on her hips. She was trying to act disgusted, angry, but even though he couldn't make out her face through the condensation, he knew she was smiling. She always did.

He had to admit, it was a lovely silhouette. He knew she enjoyed this part of their morning almost as much as he did—the safety of it.

"Are you going to make me get out and walk all the way over there to get a towel while wet?" Danica asked from behind the fogged glass, feigning indignation. "That's cruel and unusual punishment."

"No, not at all. Stay in there until you dry off," Nicholai responded, fighting a grin as he rinsed his blade. "Air drying is very healthy."

Like every other time, the glass door swung open, and she stepped out wet onto the deep blue bathmat. She wrapped her arms tightly around herself to take a bit of the chill off, water droplets clinging to her skin.

Through the corner of his eye, pretending to focus on his jawline, he watched her. He gazed in reverence at the beauty that was now his bride. He was amazed by her physical form, but even more in awe of the fact that someone like her—someone so strong, so independent—was in love with a broken man like him.

Then he saw it. The scar.

It was jagged, a raised line of pink tissue on her left side just below the ribs where the wood had impaled her. It was still evident, a permanent mark of the night she saved his life. He never mentioned it directly; he didn't want to remind her of the pain. But he thought about it often. To Nicholai, it wasn't a disfigurement; it was a symbol. It was a reminder of where they both had been and how far they had come. He never mentioned the scar on her back, and she never mentioned the scars he carried inside his soul. They were both healing together. What she didn't know was that every so often, when she was in a deep sleep and the nightmares were far away, he would lean over and lightly kiss that spot on her back, a silent prayer of thanksgiving that she was still here.

He didn't know why he tried to hide his staring. She knew. He could tell by the grin as she walked behind him, her bare feet silent on the tile, and reached for the towel on the shelf. Their eyes met in the mirror—blue locking with brown—and then they both looked away quickly, grinning like teenagers.

"Pay attention to what you're doing," Danica said, drying herself off vigorously. "That razor is sharp, and I don't have time this morning to clean up a mess of blood because you sliced something off. I'm off duty."

After watching her for another moment, he followed her orders. She wrapped the oversized towel around herself, tucking it securely above her chest, and moved to her side of the dual vanity. She reached for the cup of coffee he had left there for her—black, just how she liked it—and took a sip, then leaned over to smell the lone red rose in the crystal vase.

He was always the first one awake in the morning. It was quiet, and he did his best spiritual work at that time of the day. He could sit in the backyard for hours, praying and spending time in the Word while the city woke up. He had plenty to be thankful for. He loved the mornings; always had. But the one thing he adored the most now was walking quietly back into their bedroom and watching her sleep. She brought a certain peace to the room, to his life, and he felt it when her head rested on the pillow and her eyes were closed, the tension of her job finally gone. He often felt it was a shame to wake her, but then when she slowly opened her eyes, it reminded him of the sunsets they had shared on the Sara Rose.

The home on Windsor Lane had sold two days after her loft. They had both wanted a fresh start, a place with no ghosts. Together they purchased a modest four-bedroom home in North Dallas with a big yard. They had planted rose bushes in the backyard—Jessica's favorites—and each added their own touch to the home. And every morning since their wedding, Danica had a fresh rose on her vanity.

"Where's the cat?" she asked, looking around, breaking his train of thought.

"Last time I checked, she was eating. Again," Nicholai said, wiping his face with a warm towel. "By the way, are you ever going to name that poor thing? 'Cat' seems a little impersonal for a family member."

"Whatever," she replied, tapping her mug. "She answers to it. Are you going to name the new boat? It's been sitting in the slip for two weeks with no identity."

Nicholai laughed. "Perfect name for that cat—Whatever. And as a matter of fact, yes, I am going to name the new boat. I've already got a couple of possibilities in mind."

"Is it a secret, or can I get in on this?" she joked, leaning against the counter.

"Your breakfast is in the kitchen," he said quickly, changing the subject. "Omelet, peppers, no onions."

"You didn't have to do that," Danica said, softening.

"I know, but I like doing it," he said, kissing her forehead. "It's the least I can do."

"I know you do, and it's just one of the many reasons why I love you."

He looked over as she leaned in closer to the mirror to check her skin. The towel rose up slightly behind her, exposing the curve of her leg.

He smiled. "And that right there is the only reason why I love you."

She looked over towards him and laughed, swatting his arm. "Be quiet, punk. Just finish getting ready. I want to get out there. The wind is supposed to be perfect." They had planned a day alone on their new sailboat, a day to disconnect from the world.

"And listen," she ordered, her face turning serious. "Do you have any idea what today is?"

Nicholai froze. He rubbed his chin. "Trash day," he stated confidently. "And I already took care of that. Bins are at the curb."

"No! That's not what I meant." He loved it when she tried to pretend to be mad. She was a lousy actress; her eyes always gave her away.

"Okay, then what? Wednesday? I know it's Wednesday."

"You are the biggest punk ever! It's our first anniversary!"

He scratched his head, trying to play dumb. "Oh... sorry. It must have slipped my mind with the boat prep and all."

She let out a deep sigh of exasperation, but she couldn't hide her smile. The importance of the day hadn't slipped his mind for a second. When a man is blessed with a beautiful woman like the one he now shared his life with—after losing everything—that particular day becomes more important than Christmas.

He reached down and opened the top drawer of his vanity, pushing aside the toothpaste, and pulled out the small velvet box he had hidden earlier in the week.

"What's this?" she asked, her voice dropping.

"Happy Anniversary, Dani," he said, leaning in and kissing her on the cheek.

She opened the box, and her eyes lit up wide. He loved seeing the sparkle that illuminated from her brown eyes—life, pure and simple. She gently pulled out the diamond stud earrings, holding them up against her ears and turning to the mirror.

"They're beautiful," she said quietly. "Nic, you shouldn't have."

She turned back and wrapped her arms around him, burying her face in his chest. The towel fell to the floor, forgotten. The warmth of her body felt good against his and always made him feel at ease, grounding him in the present. Danica lifted her head, looked into his blue eyes, and whispered, "I love you."

"I love you too," Nicholai said, holding her tight.

Danica closed her eyes and gave him another kiss on the lips. Her mouth was soft, always inviting. He loved her kisses—anytime, anywhere. It was the seal on their covenant.

"I'll take that kiss as my gift," he said, trying to catch his breath from her intensity. "Best I've had all year."

"I have something else in mind," Danica said, pulling back slightly, a mischievous glint in her eye.

"Just take whatever it is back," he teased. "I already have everything I need right here."

She moved her eyes down to the floor, shifting her weight, but he didn't break his hold on her. Slowly, she looked back up and gazed into his eyes again, searching for the profiler inside the husband.

"You really think so?" she asked.

"Yeah, I do. Why? What did you get?"

"You're going to have to wait for this one anyway," she said, smiling a smile he hadn't seen before—secretive and radiant.

"Wait for what? Is it backordered?"

"I had a doctor's appointment yesterday," she said casually. "Your gift will be here in seven months."

Nicholai stopped. The room went silent. He looked at her, processing the data, reading the micro-expressions, the glow, the way she had been subconsciously touching her stomach all morning.

"What are talking about, Dani?" he asked, his voice trembling.

"Happy Anniversary, Nic," she said quietly, tears forming in her eyes. "We're going to need a bigger house."

He laughed, a sound of pure, unadulterated joy that washed away the last remnants of his grief.

"What's so funny?" she asked, wiping a tear.

"I knew already," he told her, pulling her close.

"How did you know?" she asked, stepping back and placing her hands on her hips. "I just found out."

"Calculated assumptions," he said, tapping his temple. "Plus, you have to admit, I am a better investigator than you. I noticed the decaf coffee. I noticed the nausea last week." He teased her, but his eyes were wet. "That's why I didn't call the new boat the Sara Rose II. I'd like to use that name somewhere else," he said, gently patting her bare stomach.

Danica looked up into his eyes and smiled, understanding immediately. She loved the idea of a daughter named Sara Rose. It wasn't a replacement; it was a legacy. A life for a life.

She stepped in close, smiled, and then wrapped her arms around Nicholai, pressing herself against him.

"Kiss me now, punk," Danica ordered.

And Nicholai always followed her orders, because he knew it was exactly the right thing to do.

Tetelestai. It was finished. And it had just begun.

www.ingramcontent.com/pod-product-compliance
Lightning Source LLC
Chambersburg PA
CBHW052023240626
47153CB00006B/1934